ALSO BY EDITH SCHEFFER

The Janie Chronicles

Saving Janie

Janie a Broad

Janie on Board

Janie vs. The Big Apple

* * *

Fallen Gracefully

* * *

Winged

THE JANIE CHRONICLES

EDITH SCHEFFER

JANIE A BROAD

The Janie Chronicles, Book 2

ISBN 978-1-954174-03-0

Edited by Louise Zanotto

Cover Art Design © 2020 by Croco Designs

GIVING THANKS

Editing and Soundboarding by: Louise Zanotto (Zia) and Keri Morales. I can't thank you two ladies enough for all the help, energy, work, support and love.

In my first book, *Saving Janie*, I thanked the women in my life for all the love and support. In this book, I want to take a chance to thank the men who have influenced me.

First and foremost, to my father, Gene Scheffer: I was blessed to have someone like you in my life. You were my healer, of both of body and mind. Your humor lives on in me. Thank you for all the love, direction, peace, making me feel like I was special and sharing your birthday with me.

Bill Tweed: I love you Uncle Bill. Thank you for teaching me how to fish and spending time with me.

Ernie Ollivares: You are my brother and I love the hell outta you.

Dave Pickett: (Big Dave) My lifelong friend, through thick and thin. I always knew you had my back, and I had yours. And always will. What can I say? Thank you. I will always cherish you.

Duncan Wible: Almost thirty years of friendship that I have

been blessed by. Your humor, intelligence and heart have been most appreciated in my life.

Gary Downum: You have been there for me and my family, more than I could have ever hoped, or would have ever asked for. These acts have made you family. Poor SOB. LOL.

Eric Durfee: Teddy. Always Teddy. A lifetime of friendship, I have been blessed with. I thank you.

The following may not be in my daily life, but they helped shape who I am, and I am grateful for them.

Rob Tweed, Dan Nelson, Perry Tompkins, William Clanagan, Frank Zanotto, (Zio) Roger Lagrange, Dana Hu, Jason Wade, Ronzo Bauman, Rush Alexander, Joe James, Mark Ames, Chris McKracken, Rob Pontius, Bruce Miller, Joe Miller, Steve Wible, Garrett Frantz, Dave Edmonds, Joe Mallack, Richard and Herbie Yue, Don Cheeseman, Gary Krause, Chris Votino, Ziggy, Emmett Royston, Phillip Haywood, James Isborne, Michael Hill, Jack (JP) Hedrick, Byron Cantu, Dave Morton, Randy Jones.

If you've read my books and have any comments or feedback you'd like to share, please find me on fb (fb.com/AuthorEdithScheffer).

1

AWAY WE GO

"Oh, my God, I'm late, I'm late!" I yelled, springing from my bed like the White Rabbit.

I was more than startled when Fitz sat up from the opposite side of the bed. "What are ya late for, Janie?" she asked calmly, while holding her hung over temple. Her Irish accent more pronounced with drink or in her case, with residual drink.

I let out a sigh, "I was dreaming that I was late for work."

"No Janie, yer not late. In five hours we fly to Ireland. Now get back in bed," she patted my empty space.

I curled back up in my spot. "Wow that was such a realistic dream. I was late and Dante didn't have keys, and the customers were lined up out front...all waiting for me."

"Yes, yes," soothed Fitz, "It all sounds horrible. Now just ya lie back down...and shut the hell up."

I lay back down trying to calm myself but a million thoughts were running wild in my head. I didn't fly well and was trying to avoid thinking about it. I instead tried to mentally focus on my packing skills.

"Fitz?" I said in a whisper.

"Huh?"

"Are you packed?"

"Aye."

"Did you pack razors?"

"Cream hair remover."

"Did you pack tampons?"

"Uh hum."

"Did you pack period underwear?"

"Why for the love of God, are ya so concerned with my hooha? Seriously Janie, I've kept her in check without anyone else's help for quite some time," Fitz said.

"It's just, I feel like I'm forgetting something. I keep going over everything I packed, but what if I forgot something?"

"But why are ya making ME go over everything I packed?" she questioned.

"Hints," I finally said.

Irritated, Fitz sat up, "I'm not going to play the 'Janie is neurotic', game. Be assured, they have stores in Ireland."

"What if I forgot something I can't get in Ireland?"

"Okay Janie, so this is the game we play instead of going over every damn thing in your bag." She looked me straight in the eyes and I could actually see the hangover on her face and recoiled a little. "What can ya not replace in Ireland?" she asked.

When she put it that way, the list was shorter. I thought for a moment and sprung from the bed again, "The Rune Diane gave me!"

As I headed to search my living room for the Rune, I heard Fitz say, "Wonderful," before she pulled the covers over her head.

I had met Diane, (a woman old enough to be my mother but certainly nothing like her) at a rebirthing ceremony thrown in my honor or horror. I still wasn't sure which. Turns out, I am the dating impaired. Fitz, (my best friend since before school had number grades) her mother, Mum, as we called her, and her batshit-crazy, tantra-sex-teaching, coke-bottle glasses wearing Aunt Marble, had brought the 'Ladies of the Moon' a coven of sorts, to the Pub so they could put me in a child's hard plastic kiddie pool and rebirth me with oil, flowers, salt, and who knows what else. But that weird incident, along with a "Getting to Know Myself," chat with Diane had pushed me to follow my dreams. I finally asked to display my paintings at the coffee house where I have worked since 10th grade. (Don't judge. I love that place) Which in turn led to a gallery owner seeing my work and having me fill a last minute opening in his auction. That in turn led to Fitz's boyfriend's dad, Martin, hiring me to do two paintings: One of his Castle and the other of Callaghan's distillery, in Ireland. The Rune, a small stone with the symbol of a lightning bolt, had been part of a mojo bag Diane had given me. Crazy, huh? Oddly enough, this tiny stone had found its way into my pocket on several occasions. I started to think of it as a good luck charm and didn't want it to have to cross an ocean to find me. Although, some part of me, the 1% that believed in magic, thought somehow... it would.

I took off as fast as my own slight hangover would allow and ran straight into Cecil, his exceptional build knocking me backwards. Catching me around the waist, he pulled me back towards him.

"Whoa there," he said, putting me right on my feet. "Where's the fire, Janie?" I was surrounded by Irish accents, (between Fitz's family and her boyfriend's) and they always made my knees a little weak.

His sandy hair a mess, he was shirtless and rippled in all the right places, wearing a pair of 501 jeans and a huge white smile. "Sorry," I said, trying not to stare at his well chiseled chest. I took a step back, and asked, "What are you doing here?"

"Ya don't remember?"

A wave of fear washed over me then I saw Scotty, Fitz's

boyfriend, and Cecil's big brother, asleep on the couch. "Not really."

Cecil wasn't exactly a stranger to my home. After we first met, I had taken a very short, but not-so-sweet beating from my ex-boyfriend, John. (To be honest, John was trying to win me back, after having dumped me in an airport terminal and taking a woman he had been having an affair with for six months to Hawaii, in my place. Yeah, that was seriously screwed up.) I was unconscious from hitting my head on the side of the pool at Mum's house, when Cecil gave him a whipping. Afterward, Cecil stayed at my house for a week, to babysit me, feed me, and make sure that I took my pain pills, instead of succumbing to my favorite form of numb, Irish whiskey. The second week, he stayed with me because he had grown fond of my bed and preferred it to his hotel room. Don't get too excited though, I slept on the couch.

2

THE FLASHBACK

It was coming back now...well, parts of it. I thought it was to be a Bon Voyage Party since Fitz, and I were headed to Ireland for an extended working vacation. I was to do the paintings, and Fitz with her flowing red mane, emerald green eyes and porcelain skin, would be the perfect spokesmodel for the Callaghan distillery and brewery. What it turned out to be was actually a combo Bon Voyage/26th Birthday for me. I showed up at the pub as requested, after a torturous birthday dinner with my parents. My mind yelled to me, "Start there!" so I did.

It was the usual painful hour or so, out of my every week since I had moved out on my own. My mother was...hard to describe. She had a dream-crushing way about her that extended to my life as a whole. My hair was cut and styled incorrectly, long and straight, usually in a ponytail. My make-up was always too much, or too little. "Whore of Babylon," or "Did you even bother to look like this?" I didn't dress girly enough, 501's being my favorite go to style. All of this could be fixed to suit her, but I was also too tall. She criticized everything I did, said and wore.

Even my thoughts, at times were invaded and judged. I loved her none-the less. None-the-more for damn sure, but none-the-less either. My father was my saving grace and the polar opposite of mom. I loved and adored him, more-the-more. There was talk of a fix-up, as there would always be, with a mother who had once tried to set me up with my cousin. Yep! You read that right. She only noticed the error of her ways, when said cousin, was fired from the lab he worked at, for stealing fecal specimens. I repeat, STEALING. FECAL. SPECIMENS!

Mom had started in again, as she passed the potatoes. “I just don't like you being a whole ocean away. Especially, with that Fitz, I mean, that girl just invites poor decisions right through the door.”

I had heard this from my mother since kindergarten. I let out a sigh.

“What?” my mother asked, doing a palms up, like she had no idea how old hearing these things had become.

“Just stop, mom!” I said, shaking my head.

“I've said it before,” she started.

I cut her off, “Yes, you have. And I'm tired of it.”

“Well, you know, all the bad decisions you've ever made, have been...”

“Have been mine!” I interrupted. “Stop! Just stop blaming Fitz for my life! I made the decision to not go to college! I made the decision to continue working at the same job I've had since high school! I made the decision to move out and live on my own! Me! Not her! Stop trying to blame all the things I've done, that make me a failure in your eyes, on Fitz! Not only is it old, mom, it's inaccurate.”

“Well, she...”

“No mom, it's time for you to realize, I'm grown. 26 today. You've done your job. Now you need to get a life that isn't about trying to control mine!”

My father, who had never seen me really talk back to my mother, stared at his plate awkwardly.

"Well, if you don't need me in your life..." she started.

"I do need you in my life, mom, just not trying to control it!"

It was the most uncomfortable birthday dinner, I had ever had. That included my seventh birthday, where Fitz started a cake fight that left my mother's bleach cleaned walls covered in chocolate. I felt horrible for fighting with her, but, I was trying to take control of my life. And that meant I'd have to wrestle it out of her hands.

3

TO THE PUB I GO!

As I walked into the pub, heads turned and applause began. It took a moment of me looking around, to know that this was for me. Quickly, I started to recognize the faces in the crowd as old friends. I smiled as they began to sing 'Happy Birthday'. Fitz came and wrapped an arm around my neck, kissing me hard on the cheek. Muahhh!

"Happy Birthday, Janie girl," she yelled over the crowd.

I hugged her, and smiled from ear to ear. I wasn't fond of crowds, but these were all friends and their mates, making this crowd a reunion. As I walked the bar, I stopped at damn near every stool and table to say hellos, give hugs and do a quick catch up. From somewhere in the crowd appeared a Black & Tan and a shot of Bushmills.

"Down it," I heard my old friend Ashley, yell.

I held the shot over my head, cheering to my old friends, and took it down in one gulp. One hand removed the empty glass as another handed me a full one. As I pounded the second shot, I reminded myself that I was flying to Ireland the next day and needed to take it easy. Mum appeared with a giant chocolate sheet cake ablaze with what I am sure was at least fifty candles. I made a wish and blew out every last one of them with one long breath. It took about an hour to make the rounds, but slowly people began to let their focus wander back to others. I could relax and enjoy my party without being the center of attention, which I was never really comfortable with. I had gone to Catholic school with most of these folks, and where you have a bunch of Catholics cutting loose you have yourself quite a party.

I was sitting at the end of the bar taking a breather and sipping my Black & Tan when I caught sight of Barry walking toward me.

Oh sweet God, I thought to myself. Barry was Fitz's youngest brother, which still made him three years older than us. Six feet tall, brown hair, green eyes and a body I tried not to think about. He had been my secret crush since we were kids. I had almost been brave enough to kiss him just a few weeks ago. But then, right before I could find and summon the balls needed to go all in, his psycho ex-girlfriend tried to assault me. During the altercation he told her the words that still hurt my heart, "She's a friend of my little sister's. I'm just being a good person to someone who's had a really bad week." He had tried to apologize. Whether it was for what he had said, or the ex, I still wasn't sure. But by then I was having a date related issue of my own, now known as the "Henry Incident." My sixty-ish year old Southern Belle landlord, Betty, had sent Henry my way as a set up of sorts. It didn't go well. Henry, although a gorgeous well built god who spoke fluent Italian, was also a jealous, somewhat delusional whack-job. Barry and I didn't get to clear the air before he left for Ireland for his best friend's wedding. He returned early so he could wish his little sister Bon Voyage. This was the first time I had seen him since he arrived home and my knees were knocking under the bar.

"Happy Birthday, Janie," he said. "May I sit?" His Irish accent made my knees knock harder.

"Of course," I extended my hand to the empty stool next to me. "How was Ireland?" I asked, smiling.

"Ireland is so beautiful, Janie. I never remember how much I miss it, till I go home. You'll love it. How long do ya think you'll be gone?"

"Not sure. However long it takes me to do the paintings."

He nodded and looked at his beer before saying, "About Ireland, Janie, I understand Mum shared the news with the ladies about me finding my soul mate."

I nodded, feeling either my heart dropping, or was it the whiskey rising? Mum had indeed told us that my biggest crush since I was five, had found the love of his life within twelve hours of being in Ireland.

"Well, I didn't know that you and Fitzy had become part of the group. I guess I should have assumed that at some point, you girls would be invited. But I didn't know that it had already happened."

He was speaking of The Ladies of the Moon. He knew about them? My mind began to twist. Did that mean he also knew about my embarrassing rebirthing ritual? Done as I stood dressed in frog boxers (with a caption that read, "Sometimes you have to kiss a lot of frogs" on the crotch) and a bra, in a little plastic kiddy pool? (Not one of my finer moments) The ritual that was held because I hadn't just been horribly dumped once again, I had been the dumpee in every relationship I ever had! I couldn't stand the thought of him feeling sorry for me and my pathetic inability to successfully date.

"I had no idea you knew about the group," was all I could say while trying not to blush.

"Sure," he said. "Mum's always been a little..." he searched for a word, different!" he smiled. "But, that's what makes her so incredible."

I nodded again, "I hear you found an incredible woman of your own, Calle right?" I said, forcing a smile. I had the mental image of some perfect Irish lass, hair blowing in the wind as she stood on a lush green bluff. Eyes all shiny and when she smiled, her teeth emitted a sparkle like diamonds in the sun.

"That's what I wanted to talk to ya about," he said.

I didn't want to be a bitch, had no reason to be either, other than of course, pure jealousy. But the thought of listening to him gush about her made me... yeah, bitchy was the word. I smiled as best I could and let him continue.

"Ya see Janie, Calle isn't exactly..."

Mum came out of nowhere and cut him off before he could finish his thought. Being the only unmarried son, Mum had been working overtime to get him to the altar. I even had my suspicions that she had tried to "Potion" him, like she had tried to do with me. Apparently, 'potion-ing' and 'drugging' are NOT the same thing, according to Mum.

"Oh, are ya tellin' Janie of yer girl in Ireland? Seriously son, when am I to meet this woman who has stolen my baby's heart?"

"Ummm," Barry stammered eyes darting from me to Mum.

"Yer not gettin' any younger, son!" she shook her head. Ya may want to be thinkin' of weddin' bells. Ya know, before I'm dead," Mum added. "In fact, I have some ideas I'd like to run by ya."

"Uh, well yeah Mum, I'd love to hear 'em, but..."

Barry was cut off again, "To be sure, you'll want to be gettin' married in Ireland," Mum's eyebrows raised.

"Well, yeah," said Barry. "I always assumed I'd marry back home, but..."

"Well, you can't put it off too long. Planning a weddin' in

Ireland will be more difficult from the States," Mum broke in again. "Ya can't be expectin' her to do it all on her own, and I have lots of ideas to run past ya," she beamed.

"I think I should go find Fitz," I said standing. "You two have a lot to talk about."

"Alright Janie girl," said Mum, pulling me down to her height so she could kiss my cheek. "Don't ya leave though without findin' me for yer blessin'."

Barry said, "I, ugh, I..." he looked back at his mother, "I guess I'll talk to ya a little later then, Janie."

I nodded, "Yep, sounds good."

I was grateful for the volume of the band, as I walked away. It was drowning out Barry and Mum's convo, as well as my own thoughts. Further down the pub close to the bandstand, Fitz sat at a table with Scotty, Cecil, and Mona of all people. Mona was Fitz's third brother Paul's wife. She hated me, but was kind enough to wrap her dislike in condescension and backhanded compliments. Fitz and I had come to the conclusion that maybe she and Paul had stayed drunk before their wedding and once upon a time, she wasn't a raging bitch. Since we had never seen her drunk, or nice, this was all theoretical.

As I approached the table, Mona said, with a drunken slur, "Well, Janie, there you are! You must be enjoying all the trouble MY family went through to throw you this shindig. You being an attention seeker and all," she snorted a laugh.

Fitz narrowed her eyes as I shook my head ever so slightly to her. Fitz was, for all practical purposes, not just my best friend, but my sister. And she didn't take kindly to someone talking ill of her family. Even by family forced on her by marriage.

"Unfortunately, you just blend into the crowd, don't you?" Mona asked. "Well you would," she laughed, "If you weren't man sized. But plain as you are I could still see you coming from across the bar," she did a drunken snort.

Finally, after years, our theory had been disproved. She was just a bitch, I thought. Five ten! I'm an inch and a half taller than Fitz, and this woman tries to torture me with it. Honestly, I had always wished my stature was a little less statuesque, but I wasn't about to back down from her. I had had just enough whiskey, and was in just enough of a mood, "Not all of us can be hobbit sized," I said, smiling.

"You know what they say," she retorted, "Good things come in small packages." She held out her hand to expose her 3 carat diamond wedding ring. "Like this," she slurred, "It came in a Tiffany's box. Look at it hard, Janie. It may the closest you ever get to one."

"I guess you haven't heard what else they say, then?" I replied, "GREAT things come in even bigger packages," I motioned to my boobs. In fact, I had three things she was jealous of: 1. A real spot in the Fitzpatrick family. The other two were my aforementioned C's.

She had her hand on Cecil's knee, and he looked uncomfortable with her over aggressiveness. Especially since Mona was married to Fitz's brother, Pauly.

"I hope you don't mind," she said, "I was keeping your boyfriend warm for you."

Cecil looked up at me widening his eyes. Cecil had introduced himself to Mona as my boyfriend when they met last week. Basically just so she would stop torturing me about being dumped by John. So I knew what her game was. But the look on his face was riddled with a 'Please Save Me' expression.

"Well, thank you Mona," I said. "But your assistance is no longer required," then I turned my back to her and plopped down in Cecil's lap, pinning her hand underneath my ass as I did so.

She pulled it free and huffed before grabbing her drink and teetering off.

Cecil smiled and put his arms around my waist, "My savior," he grinned and hugged me.

"Yes, you're safe now," I said, moving forward towards a seat of my own.

"Where ya goin'?" he asked, tightening his arms around me. "I like ya right where ya are."

"Not sure this chair is meant for two people, especially when one of them is a gargantuan woman."

"Never ya mind Mona's comments. She's a snake. And yer light as a feather."

I put a kiss on his cheek and moved to my own chair. "You know, eventually, she's gonna find out that you're not really my boyfriend. It may even make her back off of you."

Cecil asked, "Why do you put up with her?"

Fitz and I replied in unison, "Pauly!"

"Surely he knows she's a bitch?" he stated, matter-of-factly.

"I'm sure he does," I said. "But having us attack her would hurt him, so we hold our tongues."

"I hold my fists," Fitz uncurled her hands to show nail indents in her palms. "But, speaking of holding our tongues," Fitz said, and motioned to one of the cocktail waitresses hired to work the party. Fitz held up four fingers, the girl nodded and headed to the bar.

I laughed, "The cocktail waitress has been pre-programmed I take it?"

"Definitely! I wrote her a list of what we wanted, in which order, and told her I would display a finger count of how many we needed."

Next thing I knew four Redheaded Slut shots, four Bushmills shots, and four Black & Tans arrived. "Holding my tongue I can do all alone, but, you may be holding my hair later," I said to Fitz. "I think I better stick to beer from here on out."

"Nonsense," Fitz responded. "This is to yer Birthday and our Bon Voyage. Down the gullet," she yelled, raising her glass. We raised our glasses back at her, and shot down the Redheaded Sluts...followed closely by the Bushmills.

"Whoo," said Scotty, breathing sweet fire after the Redheaded Sluts. "I'm not used to things that sweet."

"I beg yer pardon," said Fitz, feigning offense.

"No," said Scotty, pulling Fitz on to his lap, "I am used to hot, sexy, 200 proof you!"

Cecil and I sat awkwardly, as their kiss turned into a moaning, hair pulling, just short of mauling moment. Just a few short weeks ago, Scotty could barely get up the nerve to speak to Fitz. Now he couldn't keep his hands off of her. And Fitz, not the dating kind, was smitten. I give the credit to Mum and Aunt Marble's potion. They had actually planned to set me up with Scotty. But their plan went to hell, when they reluctantly had to give the potion to Fitz's dad, (Da, as we all called him) instead of me. Turns out, Scotty had had the biggest crush on Fitz for quite some time. The "Push," (a potion of sorts) he had been given, had enabled him to finally voice his feelings to her dad. Thanks be given to St. Peter, Da had been potion-ed also, or Scotty's awkward declaration of love could have gone badly.

"Ya know," Cecil said to me, "We should make out too, and make them uncomfortable."

"It wouldn't make me uncomfortable in the slightest, little brother," said Scotty.

"Hush, big brother. I'm trying to convince Janie to lock her lips onto mine." He smiled at me, "No?" he asked.

I shook my head and smiled back, "No."

"Alright...but yer missin' out. I've heard from hundreds of women that I am great kisser."

I smiled again, but didn't have the heart to tell him that the hundreds of women was the problem for me. Cecil openly admitted that during his years spent on hiatus in South America he had “Had” several women. It was one thing to know your guy had exes. It was entirely another to know that he bedded half of a country. In all honesty, Cecil was someone I enjoyed. He had a great personality, was gorgeous, funny, smart, gentle, a great cook, quick witted, loved Meg Ryan movies, thought Drew Barrymore was the epitome of sexy, and let’s not forget, beat the crap out my ex, when he knocked me unconscious. But he had admitted to being a 'Letch in Recovery.' And with my horrible dating stats, I didn't think I should be his first encounter after giving up on sluthood. Plus, I wasn't a “Fling” kind of woman.

I was starting to feel the effects of the booze kicking in and told Fitz it was time for me to slow down. To that, she raised eight fingers in the air and grinned. This is where it all went downhill for me.

4

FLASHBACK, CONCLUDED

Back in the present, I told Cecil that I remembered everything, until our third round of Redheaded Sluts.

"That would have been around midnight," he said. "Most of the people were leavin' about then. Ya stood at the door and said yer goodbyes."

"God, I kind of remember that."

"You were fine, a little wobbly but good. By the way, those last shots you remember were doubles.

I winced.

And they weren't the last shots, either."

"Oh...My...God!"

"The only people left were the Fitzpatrick brood, although, there are a bunch of them," he laughed. "Yer friend Ashley and her husband stuck around till about one or so, dancing. Aunt Marble and her boyfriend were still grinding on the dance floor when we headed home."

My face squished up at the thought. Crazy Aunt Marble, sixty-ish, in a muumuu with piles of brown hair on top of her head and coke bottle glasses, grinding a skinny, bald Jewish man in short pants with black sox and white Velcro sneakers. A moment passed before I asked, "Was I okay?"

"Ya really don't remember, do ya Janie?"

I made a face and shook my head.

"Yeah, Fitz was determined to get ya blotto. She just kept calling for shots. I guess I could tell ya anything and you'd believe it, huh?"

I let out a sigh. "Come on, Cecil."

"Alright, calm down. You were fine. A little wobbly, like I said. And a little slurry," he flashed his winning smile, "but completely adorable."

I grinned, "So, no issues?"

"Not with you directly."

"What do you mean?"

"There was a small misunderstandin' when we were leaving."

"With who?" I asked, concerned.

"Fitz's brother, Barry," he said.

"Barry and who?"

"Barry and me," he said, like this was no big deal.

"What happened?" I couldn't even imagine why Barry would have any issues with Cecil.

"It wasn't a big deal. Turns out, his little sister isn't the only girl he's protective of."

"Again, what happened?"

"I picked ya up to carry ya out to the cab, but Barry stopped me and told me to put ya down. You had fallen asleep waitin' for the cab to arrive."

I rolled my eyes, "Of course I did," I said, feeling embarrassed and wondering if I was snoring.

"Well, I told Barry I was takin' ya home, and he repeated, "Put her down." I let him know that I would put ya down...in the cab. Then I asked him to move. He refused and said he didn't know who I was, and because of that, I wasn't takin' ya anywhere. Finally, Fitz and Scotty walked up and explained that all four of us were headin' back to yer house. He still seemed put-off by the idea, but allowed me passage, sayin', "Take care of her, Fitz!"

"Hmmm," I said, biting my lower lip.

"He was much nicer when he came round this morn to pick up his jacket."

"Barry was here this morning?" I asked. My stomach churned.

"Yeah, Fitz wore his jacket home last night and he wanted to get it back before you two left for Ireland."

"You weren't dressed like that when he showed up, were you?"

"Of course not."

I let out a sigh of relief.

"His knockin' woke me, so I just had on my boxers when I answered the door," he said.

I winced again.

"What's the big deal? Surely he's seen a man in his boxers before."

"I just don't want him to get the wrong impression."

Frowning, Cecil asked the question I should have been asking myself, "Why do ya care what he thinks?"

He was eyeing me, like he was seeing something he hadn't before. I tried to change the subject. "Oh God," I rubbed my temples. "I should feel way more hungover than this."

"Especially considerin' ya opened two more bottles of wine when we got home," Cecil added.

"What?"

"Yeah, then you did a striptease on yer coffee table."

I gave him my best 'Bullshit' look.

"I went too far," he smiled, trying to break our newfound tension. "But the rest of it is true."

"Seriously, I don't know how I feel this well, considering."

"I do," he said. "I made ya my famous pre-hangover drink."

"Really?"

Cecil nodded.

"What the hell's in it?"

His face squished up a little, "I think it may be better that ya don't remember."

I stared at him for a moment, before nodding, "You're probably right," I mentally went over what I had in my refrigerator. Yeah, none of that would be good, I thought.

I searched the table, no Rune. Then I went through the papers on my desk, no Rune. The entertainment center, nothing. Where the hell could it have gone? I grabbed my purse and searched, "Damn it," I said. Finally, I went back to my bedroom, and there, on the floor next to the jeans I had worn the night before, was the tiny good luck stone. It started up at me. "There you are," I said.

I woke Fitz with a quad mocha before I jumped in the shower. I figured by the time I got out, she'd be awake enough to function. Out of the shower and dressed, I pulled my long blonde hair into a ponytail. The Rune I put into the front pocket of my 501's. I patted it and felt relieved that it would be making its way to Ireland with me. I wanted to go through my suitcase one last time, so I wouldn't forget anything else. Fitz walked up beside me.

"Are ya packin' a friend to take with ya to Ireland?" she asked.

"A friend?" I asked, confused.

"Ya know," she nodded slowly. Wide eyed, "A friend," she repeated.

"Are you asking if....?"

"We're going to be in Ireland for some time, ya know. And

not to be rude, but ya become quite bitchy without the company of a friend. Unless ya plan on..." she grinned.

"I don't "Plan On," I assured her, "Plus I don't even own a friend, Fitz."

She stared at me the way someone would, when they've had a great epiphany. "Well, that explains everything. I wonder if we have time to go shoppin'?"

5

OFF WE GO

Martin, Scotty and Cecil's dad, (Fitz's and my new employer) sent a limo to fetch us. Before we headed to the airport, we had to stop by Fitz's to get her suitcases, and have Mum say an Irish blessing over us. Apparently, I was too unconscious the night before to receive my blessing. I wasn't at all surprised to see Aunt Marble sitting at the table sipping coffee. I was however, a little taken aback when Marble's boyfriend, Benny, came out of the bathroom holding the morning paper under his arm.

"Top of the mornin' to ya!" said Benny. "Or however you Irish folk say it," he smiled.

Mum giggled, "How do ya Jewish folk say it?"

"Get up, you lazy bums," Benny replied, grinning. "Or at least that's how my mom said it."

Mum offered us coffee, but I had had my fill and Fitz was looking a little green. Guess she didn't drink Cecil's concoction.

"Boy, Barry was sure in a mood this morn," Mum said.

"Really?" asked Fitz. "Doesn't sound like him. What's the matter?"

"He wouldn't say, just kept mumbling under his breath about Scotty's brother, Cecil. I know they had a misunderstandin' last night, but they worked it all out just fine. Then this morn, he was foul about him again. It's not like Barry to hold a grudge," Mum said, looking bewildered.

"Indeed not," said Marble. "Did he say anything to you girls?"

"I didn't see him," said Fitz.

"What about you, Janie?" Mum asked.

"I didn't see him either," I said. "I guess Cecil gave him back his jacket when he came over this morning."

"What could have happened to stir him up again?" asked Mum.

Fitz and I both did a shoulder shrug, but I was wondering if Cecil's half-nakedness had anything to do with his mood.

"Maybe it's his man-time," Aunt Marble suggested.

"What the hell is man-time?" Benny wanted to know.

"It's like a period for men," she answered.

"Such a thing exists?" Benny questioned, putting his palms up.

"Sure. They're studying that very thing right now at one of those rich kid colleges," Aunt Marble said. "I can't remember which one. Harvard? Or was it Oxford? Anyway, they're saying men have cycles as well. But theirs are every 33 days instead of 28, or something like that."

"Well, I don't want one of them mood swing thingies," said Benny.

All four of us women just stared at him.

"What?" he asked after a moment, raising his shoulders. "Those things look brutal. I mean, you can actually get away with murder during your, uh...cycle. As a man, it's frightening. It's like being placed in a cage with a wild animal...that hasn't eaten in a week...and has a thorn in her paw."

Again, the four of us just stared.

Benny stood and grabbed his coffee, "I am also to understand you women all do that cycle thing at the same time. So I'm gonna go find Da before I become a victim of a tag team murder."

He hobbled out of the room on his knobby knees before Aunt Marble said, "Don't ya worry ladies. I'll break him in right."

Fitz said, "Auntie, you've gone through the change. You don't have mood swings anymore."

"The oil may be low, tis true, but that only makes the car run rougher," answered Marble.

"Wait! We still have actual mood swings after menopause?" I asked.

"Sure," said Mum.

"Great," I said, already defeated by my distant future. "How come you always seem so...calm?"

Mum reached for a pint of whiskey, and smiled as she poured a healthy shot into her coffee, I add a little 'I don't give a shite'," to my morn. Tis good to be Irish," she raised her cup.

"He'll need a better sense of womanhood if he's to play with my engine," said Marble, well after the conversation had ended.

I looked sidelong at her and tried to hide a shudder. Aunt Marble was a muumuu wearing spiritualist, with horn rimmed glasses so thick that her eyes appeared three times their normal size. She taught Chakra Aligning, Moon Magic, Astral Projection and scariest of all, Tantric Sex. I loved her as my very own aunt. But that didn't mean I didn't think she was batshit crazy. "We should round up the guys and get goin'. It's that time," Fitz said.

Mum and Marble stood, as Fitz and I knelt. This was tradition in the Fitzpatrick family and always made me feel like I belonged. Standing over us, one hand on the crown of each of our heads, Mum said a prayer in Gaelic for protection and blessings.

After Fitz's five bags were loaded, Fitz, Scotty, Cecil and I, piled into the limo and headed for a private airstrip in the Valley. The closer we got to the airport the more I began to fidget, wringing my hands. I didn't enjoy flying on a large airplane, much less a smaller jet.

Cecil saw my overactive nerves and put his hand on mine. "Calm yerself, Janie girl." He looked deep into my eyes, "I won't let anything harm ya."

"This is kinda out of your control, isn't it?" I asked.

He held my gaze before saying, "No. It's not." Bringing my hand to his lips for a quick kiss, he repeated again, "I won't let anything harm ya."

I wasn't sure why, but I blushed. He really had gone above and beyond to make sure I was taken care of. From fighting John off of me, to becoming my caretaker during my recovery from the concussion John had gifted me. I didn't want to be attracted to him, but I knew I was and it bothered me. I smiled at him and nodded, letting him hold my hand.

We pulled up to the tarmac and I was amazed. It wasn't such a small plane after all. It comfortably held twelve, or in our case, five people, a pilot, co-pilot and Fitz's luggage. When we boarded, to the rear of the plane was a private office and restroom. Toward the nose was an open space with six plush, swiveling reclining chairs, three on each side. Two small couches with tables were further forward, leaving a walkway between them that led to the cockpit. A wet bar and small kitchenette was further forward on the right, and a giant T.V. was on the left. This was nicer than my house. I knew the boys, Scotty and Cecil, had been born into an affluent Irish family, but they weren't just rich. They were 'Richie Rich' rich. Fitz didn't seem fazed, and why would she? Her family was rich. She worked with the rich, famous and beautiful as a model. Me? I was scared to death. I began to fidget for a totally different reason, now. Rich people never had any impact on me or how I treated them. But the things they bought with their money could be broken, and I was the clumsiest person I knew.

There were two gentlemen, dressed in white from head to toe, loading our baggage. When they had finished, they came to offer me a mimosa or other beverage. I took the mimosa thinking alcohol may make the flight more bearable. I didn't want to seem like a lush and ask for a double whiskey on the rocks at 2pm. But Cecil ordered that exact thing, one for him and one for me. I smiled, grateful for how well he knew me.

When the whiskey came, I took a sip and let out a, "Mmmm, this is wonderful!"

"It's ours," Cecil said, enjoying my reaction.

"It's amazing. I wish they carried this in the states," I replied.

"Well, they probably wouldn't carry this one in particular," Cecil answered.

"Why?" I took another sip, "It's so smooth."

"It better be," he grinned, "It's fifty years old."

I looked at my glass, "Wow! It's almost twice my age."

"And just think," he said, "You'll be even better than this at fifty.

A voice overhead welcomed and informed us of our cruising altitude, and what time we would be arriving in New York. I don't know why I hadn't assumed that we would have to stop along the way.

Martin finally arrived. Apparently, he had a business meeting that ran longer than anticipated. "Hello, lovely ladies," he said, hugging Fitz and me. Then he turned to hug both of his boys. I loved how affectionate their family was. Calmed me right down. I guess the whiskey was helping too.

"Please forgive me ladies as I adjourn to my office for a spell.

I still have some proposals to look over and people to contact. Please help yerself to anything ya need or want," he smiled. "Adam and Andrew," he pointed to the attendants, "are at yer service," he smiled at them.

The two gentlemen smiled and nodded to their boss.

As we ascended into the blue sky, I felt my stomach drop, and the whiskey threatening to rise. I took a deep breath and willed them both to calm.

"Ya okay, Janie girl?" Cecil asked.

I nodded.

"Would you like a Dramamine?"

"I don't think they mix well with whiskey, do they?"

"Yer probably right. We should play a game instead. Ya know, to keep yer mind off the flight."

"Like what?" I said, trying to breathe normally, while wringing my hands.

"Truth or Dare," he said, after a moment.

"Seriously, how many dares can we pull off in the air?"

He grinned, "I'm willin' to find out."

Just then we noticed Scotty and Fitz whispering to each other before heading off to the bathroom together. I assumed the 'Mile High Club', was about to accept two more members.

Cecil and I eyed each other and giggled. His smile widened and he said, "We could do that."

I laughed, but the way he was staring made me fidget again. I mentally went over how long it had been for me. If I was adding it up correctly, I was looking at more than six months without. I had always believed that I had to be in a relationship to make sex legal, so to speak, to keep from thinking of myself as a slut. Yet Fitz, up until now, had always partaken without the need for a relationship. I had never thought of her as wallowing in sluthood. Even though I knew my mind didn't work like hers, my body was starting to show signs of craving. Strange dreams had crept in. And now daydreams were starting to invade my 'awake' time. I had even found myself staring a little too long at the male underwear models in Calvin Kline ads. I had even started reading a cheap romance novel (which was code for girl porn) that was now tucked beneath my underwear in my suitcase, like a dirty secret. Maybe Fitz was right. Maybe I needed a "Friend" to get me through my strong hormonal pull, without making a huge mistake.

"Janie?" Cecil's voice brought me back from my own never-never land.

"Yep," I said quickly, hoping he wouldn't see my inner dialog.

"You okay? Ya kind of went somewhere deep inside there."

His choice of wording caught me off guard, "No I didn't," I said defensively, trying to hide a blush.

"Okay," he said, slowly. "Maybe ya want to get some sleep? When ya wake, we'll be landing."

I nodded and moved to one of the couches. Shoes off, I stretched out. Cecil came and put a blanket over me and kissed my cheek. "Sweet dreams, Janie."

I fell fast asleep, could have been the whiskey, or altitude. The next thing I knew, the plane began to shake. I let out gasp and sat up, wide eyed. No one was in the cabin. I was alone, on a plane going down! Panic rose in my chest, and I was frantically trying to stand. Just then, Cecil appeared from nowhere. Wearing just a pair of 501's, his tanned and chiseled chest dripping with sweat, he grabbed me in his arms. "If we're goin' to die, I'm not leavin' this world without havin' ya." His lips found mine, in a warm and passionate meeting, making my breast heave with anticipation. My arms went around his neck, as he pulled off my Carmen Miranda Tropicana dress to reveal my perfectly matched bra and panty set, and six pack abs. The monkey in the background, wearing the fruit headdress, went to fly the plane. Cecil pushed me to the couch and unbuttoned his jeans. A gust of wind blew his hair back, and he struck a pose, before forcing open my knees. "Cecil. Cecil," I moaned...then I woke up with a start, and cried out Cecil's name. Breathing hard, I looked around the cabin. Cecil sat staring with a strange look on his face, somewhere between amazed and amused. He said nothing, but grinned from ear to ear. I'm sure I looked guilty, but in what sense? We held the stare for a moment before I said, "I was dreaming."

Cecil kept grinning, "I know," he said, nodding his head. "I like the way ya dream. Especially that part where ya kept callin' out my name."

"I had a dream that the plane was going down," I said defensively.

"Oh, so that was a scary dream, huh?" his grin becoming devilish.

I was so embarrassed I could barely look him in the eye. He knew. I knew I had called his name out loud, at least once. But what else had he heard...or seen me do? I blushed at the thought. Just then, Scotty and Fitz re-entered the room from their own encounter.

"Janie, are ya okay? You look a mess. Oh, are ya havin' trouble flyin'?" Fitz asked.

"Uh," was the only sound I could emit.

"Poor thing, had a dream the plane was going in," Cecil winked at me. "I mean...down," he said slowly.

"Don't make fun, Cecil!" Fitz scolded him. "She's afraid of flyin'. Look at you!" she said, coming to my side. "Yer all flushed and breathin' hard. I shoulda stayed by yer side," she soothed.

"It's okay Fitz," said Cecil, "I didn't mind watchin' her. Not at all," he added.

I finally looked at him, his burning stare and that sly grin, boring into me. I let out the breath I had been holding. There was no way out of this one. I decided to curl back up, with my head buried in the couch. I could still feel him staring, waiting for me to fall back asleep, and reveal needs I didn't want to have.

I never did fall back asleep, and was reluctant to meet Cecil's eyes, when we landed in New York. Martin had come out of his office and explained that we would be staying in New York for a couple of days, while he worked out a distribution deal.

"I hadn't planned on doing this till next month, but unfortunately, I prefer to kill two birds with one stone. No offense ladies, but once I am home, I won't want to go abroad again for months. The joy of an old man is his hearth. I already reserved yer rooms at the Park Ritz, and please charge whatever ya need. Maybe a massage would help, Janie?" Martin said. "You look stressed. Was the flight okay for ya, luv?"

"Fine, thank you," I said, forcing a smile.

"Yeah," said Cecil. If we could only find a way to get you relaxed, that would be great. You may want to take yer seat, Janie."

I turned to look at him questioningly.

"The plane has to be pulled into the hanger...before ya can get off," he added.

I wondered how long he would be torturing me with this whole 'dream thing'. It's not like I had any control over them. Yes, that was plural. But I had only been caught once...I think.

6

NEW YORK, NEW YORK

It was dark when we disembarked the plane, and were immediately placed into a limo and driven to the Park Ritz. Walking into the enormous lobby, lined with wood and chandeliers, all I could think of was my bed. I was exhausted and craving a place to sleep without the worry of dreams. Three adjoining suites were reserved. Realizing that Fitz was sharing one with Scotty, and Martin had one for him, meant that I would be sharing a suite with Cecil. At least I would have my own room, I hoped.

When Cecil was given the key to our suite, he held it up and said, "It's like a dream come true, isn't it Janie?"

I let my head drop and shook it, "Not gonna let this go, are ya?"

We stepped onto the elevator and took opposite sides. "The button pusher," as I called him, or young elevator operator, greeted us with a smile. "The Park Suite, please," said Cecil, then turned to me and asked in a whisper, "Why are ya making such a big deal out of this?"

"I'm making a big deal?" I crossed over to him, looking at

Fitz, Scotty and Martin, who were engaged in their own conversation. "You're the one torturing me with them!"

"Them?" Cecil's smile came back. "I thought it was just the one dream?"

I glared at him, "Oh, shut up!"

"My curiosity is piqued. I just want to know what I'm doin' in these dreams. I assume I have a starrin' role?"

The poor elevator operator had been the only one to hear us. He stood rigid as a board until he announced our floor.

The suite was beautiful, but I was sure I would enjoy it more tomorrow. Fitz and Scotty had disappeared for the evening to 'sleep', she said with a hug and a wink. Not exactly code, I thought.

Cecil asked if I was hungry and wanted anything from the room service menu. I asked for a bacon cheeseburger and made happy yummy noises as I sank my teeth into it. Cecil was grinning, again.

"I like watching ya eat," he said. "Ya don't eat like a girl."

I furrowed my brow, with a mouthful of burger.

"Not like that," he said. "Some women won't eat in front of a man. They order a salad and pick at it to show how dainty their appetites are. At the end of the night, I'm payin' twenty bucks for a half eaten salad, while she's probably piggin' out on old pizza from the night before."

"I didn't think her finding her way to her own bed, much less fridge, was the way your dates usually ended," I said, after I swallowed.

"What exactly do ya think of me?" he chuckled.

I had hoped this question would never arise. Truth was, I wasn't sure. "Well, when we first met, you kind of made it sound like you were possibly man-whoring your way through South America."

He raised an eyebrow at me, and nodded. "And what do ya think of that?"

"Not my place to judge," I said, hoping it would put an end to the conversation. "I need to go to bed."

"Great," Cecil said, rising and pretending to follow me to my room.

"To sleep," I said, backing him away with a hand to his chest.

Cecil smiled, "Tell me in the mornin', if that brings ya any relief."

I looked back at him, and there was a moment of silence before I said, "You know it was just a dream, right? I wouldn't read too much into it."

"More than one, if I'm not mistakin'," he said raising his beer to me.

"You know, I can breathe underwater in my dreams too. But I don't plan on trying that anytime soon."

"It's always best not to plan it," he winked.

With that, I found my bed and passed out as soon as my head hit the pillow.

On a tiny couch in a room lined with books, I lay. Cecil sat on a chair to the head of my resting body, writing in a file with my name on the cover. "How does that make you feel?" he asked. Slowly, I began to unbutton my blouse. He never lifted his head, but waited for a verbal response. "I'm not sure doctor," I said, kicking off my heels. I stood and moved over to his chair. When he looked up, I ripped the file from his hands. "How can YOU make ME feel, is the question," I said. I pulled my long hair from a clip, and let it fall down my back. I took his face in one hand and lifted my skirt with the other. Straddling him, he said, "You can't do this. We're not dating." I put a finger to his lips, arched my back, head skyward, I let out a moan as I grinded my body against his. Suddenly, a bell rang, "I'm sorry, your hour is up," he said. I woke to the phone next to my bed ringing. What the hell, I thought, while reaching to answer it.

Fitz's voice rang loud and clear, "Hey, can ya wake Cecil? Scotty has been tryin' to get a hold of him. They have a meetin' at nine-thirty, and Martin wants him there, too."

I bit my lip again. "Okay."

"You sound weird, ya okay? Did ya sleep well?"

"Yep," I said, mentally going over my dream. What the hell was the matter with me?

"Ya wanna explore the city today? I know you've never been here before, and I know my way around a little. As soon as the limo drops off Martin and the guys, it's at our disposal."

"Sounds great," I said, still trying to shake the dream from my mind.

"Okay, get Cecil up!"

"Okay." I rang off.

I walked to Cecil's door and knocked. "Cecil, time to wake up," I said, louder than I had anticipated. No response. I knocked harder, nothing. Finally I opened the door a smidge and yelled again, "Time to wake up Cecil!" I stepped into the room, still wary of my dream, "Cecil," I said louder, but not a sound was returned. "Crap," I whispered, as I moved closer to his outstretched body. "Cecil," I put out a hand to nudge his shoulder. I yelped as he grabbed my arm, and pulled me down on the bed next to him. He wrapped his arms around me and nuzzled in my hair.

"Very funny, but you have to get up," I said.

"I am up," he said, tightening his grip.

Was this innuendo, I wondered? "You have a meeting soon," I reminded him.

"I'm so comfortable though," he snuggled me.

I was anything but comfortable. My heart was racing and my palms began to sweat. "Come on," I peeled my body from his. "Time to get up! Or do I have to pull you out of bed?" I asked.

"Depends," he said grinning.

"Depends on what?"

"Depends on just how much of me, ya want to see."

I stared at him. "Are you naked?"

"I have on shorts."

"So?" I did a palms-up. "What's the problem?"

"No problem...per say, he just wakes up before me," Cecil said moving his eyes downward.

I shook my head, and started out of the room.

"So no help, then?" he called after me.

I went and ordered us both breakfast from room service, while Cecil showered. When it arrived, I sat his dome covered plate on the table, and happily dug into my own Eggs Benedict.

When Cecil entered the room, I was awestruck. He was in a grey pinstriped suit complete with loafers. Honestly, I was a jeans and T-shirt girl, but from time to time seeing a man in a suit was sexy as hell. And sexy as hell, is exactly how I would have described him. I wondered what kind of dream I'd have now, with this new vision of him.

"You look..." I searched for a word, "Really good," is all I could come up with.

"Yeah? Is this look workin' for ya?"

I couldn't help but grin as he spun in a circle, so I could take him all in. "Very good," I updated my previous comment.

"Just one problem," he raised his brows, holding out his tie. "Do you know how to tie one of these things?"

"Didn't you have to wear a tie at school?" I questioned, remembering the boys Catholic School Uniforms.

"A clip on," he admitted.

I walked over to him and put his collar up. "Around the neck," I said. "One side longer...long side, over short side...then around, and back up, through the top...then down." Straightening it and smoothing it in place, I asked, "Did you get that."

Our eyes met, he shook his head. His joking manner had disappeared, "Not one word of it."

Seriously the bluest eyes I had ever seen, were staring back at me. I cleared my throat to enable breathing, "I got you Eggs Benedict," I said, stepping away from him.

Back in neutral corners, I felt safer. I pulled the morning paper up, to block my face from his view. Shortly thereafter, he stood and said, "Wish me luck." He brushed a quick kiss on my cheek and headed for the door.

"Good luck," I said, and dropped the paper that I hadn't read one word of. Fitz entered as he was leaving. Quick pleasantries were exchanged as he breezed out the door.

"What's up with Cecil? No smart ass comment? Is he mad at me?" she giggled.

"I'm really not sure," I said, honestly.

"And what the hell is the matter with you?" she asked. "Ya look funny, too."

I shook my head, "I honestly don't know."

Fitz raised an eyebrow, "Did you two, bang boots?"

"What? No!" I responded. "Why would you think that?"

"I'm graspin' at straws here," she ate a piece of ham from my plate.

A moment passed before I said, "I have a question."

"Shoot," she said, taking a seat.

"What do you do, when you're...ya know?"

"What? Hungry?"

I shook my head.

"Bloated?"

"No why? Do I look bloated?"

"I do hate these games we play. You've been my best friend

since before I knew my ABC's, and still due to yer moments of neurosis, I have to guess what the hell yer talkin' about. And no, ya don't look bloated."

"Horny," I said. "And why were you five when you learned your ABC's?"

"Oh," she said. "I get ya. Personally, I get on top of someone. I had older brothers who thought it was funny to teach me the wrong way."

I furrowed my brows, "What?"

"The end of that was about the ABC's," she explained.

"Ah," I said, grateful for the clarification.

"So yer horny, huh?"

"God I hate that word, and yes," I admitted. "It's been almost half a year, Fitz. I thought I'd be fine, ya know, going 'without', till I found myself."

She nodded. "Right. Wait! You and dopey didn't have sex?"

"Not for the last five months of our relationship."

"What the hell? Why did you stay with him so long? I mean, it's pretty obvious there were some real problems in the relationship, if ya weren't gettin' laid. Why didn't ya tell me?"

"Because you would have told me to leave him," I answered honestly.

"And oddly enough, I would have been right. I may have even been able to spare ya that airport break-up," she grinned.

"Ha ha," I said, sarcastically. "Can we get back to horny?"

"Okay," she said, putting on her sex therapist hat. "What kind of horny, are we talkin' about?"

"Are there different kinds of horny?" I asked, dumbfounded. "What are the levels?"

"Well, ya have Period horny."

I nodded, knowing full well how real Period horny was.

"Next ya have Ovulation horny."

I nodded again. That was biological. You couldn't argue with nature.

“Then ya have Revenge horny, Sad horny, and Angry horny,” she began counting on her fingers.” Then ya have I Just Got a Wax, horny.

I furrowed my brow, never having heard of this horny before.

Break Up horny, I look too good to not get laid horny. Lonely horny. He looks too good not to give him some horny, Forbidden horny.”

I raised my eyebrows, “Huh?”

“Ya know, like when he's yer college professor or an on duty cop in his patrol car. Then there's Night Club horny, or Dance Induced horny, Bored horny, Long drive horny, Camping or Hotel horny.

“Plane horny,” I added for her benefit.

“She smiled and nodded, “Definitely!”

She had long been out of fingers, and my head was spinning. “Okay,” I said, stopping her. “What about Dream horny?” I asked. “Is that a thing?”

“Oh, that's the best, and worst, kind,” she said.

I made a face.

“Well, think about it? If you have a great dream, and you have a significant other next to ya...potential for mind blowing, ‘life altering’ sex. Great horny! But if yer alone...‘worst kind of horny ever’! Are ya dream horny, then?”

I let out an exhausted sigh, and nodded, “Yep.”

“Does it suck horribly? Is it as bad as I imagine?” she asked empathetically.

I nodded, “Yes. Yes it is.”

“Wait a minute, who are ya dream horny about?” she raised a brow.

I bit my lip, and looked towards the door Cecil had walked out of.

"No! Really?" she asked, looking towards the door herself. "Does he know?"

I nodded.

"How?" she asked.

Now for the embarrassing part: I explained the whole thing, from the first dream, to the one on the plane, and Cecil's reaction to the one I had last night.

Fitz was laughing her ass off. I hoped it was about the monkey and not my six pack abs. Truth was, I didn't want to know which part was making her laugh so hard.

"It's not that funny, Fitz," I said. "This is torture for me," I wallowed, covering my face with a throw pillow.

"Okay, Janie. Calm yerself. Maybe ya just need to roll in the hay with him."

I pulled the pillow from my face, "Any other piece of advice, would have been well received, 'Do the monkey,' would have been more 'well' received."

"I don't understand ya," said Fitz. "He's handsome, successful...well he will be when all his ducks are in a row, smart and funny, obviously protective of ya...

"A total man whore," I added.

"Ah, now I get why yer fighting this so hard. But, ya are aware of the fact that he hasn't so much as looked at another woman, since he met ya? I still say, he smitten with ya, Janie."

I let out a sigh. "But look at his past."

Fitz let her mind wander and began to nod her head.

"Now look at mine!" I said.

Once again, she looked off in the distance, then winced.

"You see the problem, right? And we work for his dad. A horrible break up, would burn bridges neither of us wants burnt."

She nodded, "But ya have to admit, some part of ya still craves him."

I nodded, "So what do I do?"

"I think we need to do some shoppin'. Finally find you a friend."

I made the 'ewww' face. "That just seems undignified. The fact that I have to take care of myself..."

"But ya don't!" Fitz practically yelled at me. "Look, ya have options, right? And by doin this, yer not sayin' oh, woe is me, I have to take care of myself. Yer sayin', I CAN take care of myself. There's a power of its own there, Janie. Now, put away yer ugh face, strap on yer I am a powerful and independent woman face, and lets go get ya a friend!"

"First, don't say "Strap on" to me, when I'm going to buy myself a "Friend," I used air quotations. "Next, when the hell did you become the Norma Ray of vibrators?"

"Since you started lookin' as if you need to take a ride on the washin' machine during the spin cycle," she answered.

7

TAKE AND BAKE

I looked up at the sign, disapprovingly.

"What's yer problem?" Fitz asked.

"Seriously, Take and Bake? You are aware that the name of this place is a type of pizza, right?"

"What would you prefer it was called, the little shop of dildos, perhaps? It just means they don't let ya use their stuff here."

I made the ewww face, "What?"

She giggled at me. "Never mind the name. I asked around, and everyone said that this was the place to go. It's legendary."

"To whom?" I asked under my breath.

We had found ourselves in a seedier part of town, than I hoped for. But, if I really thought about it, you didn't see too many XXX sex shops in Beverly Hills.

Guys were selling wares, such as t-shirts and watches, on the corner. As we approached the door, a skinny white man about 40, in a baby blue leisure suit, white patent leather shoes and a pencil thin mustache (that was almost as greasy as his hair) greeted us with coupons. '30% off of all electronics' it read. I stared at the flyer.

"Ladies," he said, in a super slimy voice.

Fitz, who had been walking in front of me, got the once over, twice. I mentally thanked God that I wasn't nearly as hot as her. It had some advantages. But when I looked back over my shoulder, Creepy was leering at my ass too. I squinted my eyes at him, "Hey, buddy! Eyes on your own paper," I said, and disappeared into the store.

"Calm down," Fitz said to me, as we entered the block long Sodom and Gomorrah. I started to fidget again. "What the hell is the matter with ya?"

"I just feel out of place," I answered, looking around.

"When the hell did you become Prudey-Prude-ington-of-the-Prudeshire? I swear Janie, yer actin' like you've never rounded the bases. I repeat, what the hell is wrong with ya?"

I took her aside, "Okay, here it goes. You know that I have been dumped, in every single relationship I've ever had."

"Yeah," Fitz said, shaking her head like she didn't get it.

"What if...what if it's because I'm bad?"

"Bad?" Fitz repeated, still shaking her head.

"Bad in bed Fitz! What if I SUCK in bed?" I blurted out.

"Well if ya do, I know lots of men that would want to date ya," she laughed.

I let out a sigh.

"Is THIS what's had ya so...not you?"

"You have to admit, all the guys I've dated, have had one thing in common."

"They were all assholes!" she pointed out.

"No me! What if it's me?"

"Look Janie, ya didn't have sex with half of the men who dumped ya," she said, as if that would cheer me up. "I refuse to believe that the same girl, who flashed a cop, is bad in bed."

"Shhh!" I looked around to see who was within earshot. "You said you'd never repeat that!"

"I think ya need a reminder of who ya really are. Ya had just found yer Barrymore, only a couple of weeks ago. What the hell happened to it?"

"Self reflection, that's what happened to it."

"Well, I want my old friend back. This is bull-shite! From here on out, were gonna find the old you, if it kills one of us."

"Did you just threaten me?"

"Aye," she said, stepping towards me.

"Fine," I backed away, a little. She was a scary little red headed fairy at times.

The store carried everything. And I do mean everything. I was almost certain they had zoo animals in the back, for the true pervert. Fitz held up items for me as we made our way through. Finally, she came to one that had strobe lights that changed color with rotating pearls.

"What the hell?" I asked. "Who would buy something like that?"

Fitz stared at it, before saying, "Women who like bling?"

I finally made a purchase, and let's just say, I didn't require any bling. Fitz offered to buy my first "Friend," stating that it was quite the occasion. I declined her offer, saying that would make it all the more awkward.

We then hit Saks, Barneys and Macy's. This was more my kind of shopping, even if I wasn't buying. The limo driver, Addison, who looked like he was a 'Heavy Hitter' for the Mafia, informed us that he had to go pick up Mr. Callaghan and the boys. Fitz wanted to get some more shopping in, so she said we'd just take the subway back to the hotel. I started to protest, but she said, "We may as well find yer sense of adventure while we're at it." My eyes rolled around in my head. Fitz could shop from sun up, to sun down, but I bored easily with clothes and fashion. Still, this was a new adventure for us, so I zipped my lip and trudged onward. I did find myself fancying a pair of Tiffany earrings, but couldn't justify spending that kind of money. Close to what I assumed was dinner time, Scotty called to ask when we would be back at the hotel. "Dinner at eight, then?" he said. That gave us just enough time to get back and changed.

As we read the subway map, we planned our route home. Pretty much a straight shot. On the subway, I finally got to rest my sore feet and weary ass. Fitz was rifling through her bags, trying to figure out which one of her new outfits would be worn to dinner that evening. I had let my eyes close when I heard, "Geb me you bugs!"

I opened my eyes and saw a tiny Oriental fellow holding an even tinier knife. He was dressed like a 1980's break dancer, complete with bandana tied around his head.

I'm sure I looked startled, but Fitz looked up for a moment, then looked back in her bag, "Bite me, short shit."

"I said..." he began to repeat himself, when Fitz cut him off.

"And I said, BITE ME, SHORT SHIT!" her green eyes flashing.

There were men on the subway who were busy pretending not to notice the 'would be' mugging.

Short shit, was sizing Fitz up. "You do as I say!" he yelled, jumping up and down.

Fitz seemed to be losing her sense of humor. "No," she said calmly, but through a tightened jaw, "What I will do is...take that tiny little knife...out of yer tiny little hand...then shove it up yer tiny little ass! Are we clear?" Short shit turned to look at me, "She really will," is all I could say.

Fitz had a slew of bags surrounding her that she had gone back to inspecting. She seemed less than interested with his threats. He must have been thinking about how this could end for him. Turning towards me, he quickly reached out, grabbed the solitary bag off my lap, and took off running. Fitz unpiled her bags from her lap and stood to go after him, but I stopped her, "Fitz it's fine, don't worry about it."

"But he stole from ya," she tried to pry herself from my grip.

"Fitz," I yelled and looked her right in the eyes, "He stole a rubber penis from me."

After a moment, Fitz and I both began to crack up.

Back at the Ritz, on an elevator heading North, Fitz was chastising me. "I just don't see why ya didn't beat his ass. Seriously, not what I expected from a woman named, 'Ground and Pound O'Connelly'."

"First of all, that's a nickname that you and Bacon gave me. Second, he was a mugger!"

"He was the Oriental version of a Keebler Elf," she retorted.

"A Keebler Elf with a knife!" I reminded her.

"Janie, it was a pocket knife. With yer arm span being twice his, ya could have held him at bay, by his head while he swung madly, never touchin' ya!"

"Well, he didn't get much," I said, trying to be grateful I hadn't bought the Tiffany earrings.

"Not much, indeed," said Fitz, "A tiny little penis, for a tiny little man!"

The same elevator operator from the night before looked sidelong at me. I let out a sigh. I wondered how many embarrassing conversations he had heard during his employment. Or were they all just mine?

We each went to our rooms to change. Martin was having dinner catered in his suite, so I didn't have to worry about dressing for a five star dining experience. I did put on a nice pair of black slacks and a white silk blouse that had ruffles down the front with capped sleeves, and a black pair of what looked like ballerina slippers. It was the only nice outfit I brought. But after looking at myself sideways in the mirror, I came to the conclusion that I looked like a cater waitress. I put all my long blonde hair in a bun and clipped it up. The whole look took less than twenty minutes, and looked like it took ten. I went to Fitz's suite and she was still in her bra and panties.

"Why are you taking so long to get dressed?" I asked.

"I want to look good," she said, eyeing me. "Not like I'm serving the meal," she added, looking me up and down.

I let out a sigh. "Should I change?"

"No yer fine. If there are any pictures taken, we won't get your ballerina slippers."

"Good, I didn't bring anything else. Why would there be pictures?" I asked, finding a seat on one of the overstuffed captain's chairs.

"Just in case Scotty proposes tonight," she looked at me like I had gone crazy for not knowing this.

"I thought the two of you agreed to take it slow, after the 'Push' thing? (Not the same as drugging or so I've been led to believe.)-

"Well, just in case he springs a ring on me, I want to look my best."

"So, you're just dressing to the nines, every moment you're together."

"I have to, Janie. I don't want to be caught off guard. I'm even touching up make-up and hair before bed, then getting up before him to re-apply...just in case. After all, I don't want to look like I'm catering a party in our engagement photos," she eyed me again.

I looked down at myself, "I prefer to look matronly, for the time being."

"Well, ya pulled it off."

"Seriously, you're an asshole."

She grinned and pulled on a tiny, body hugging, black dress, and red, four inch heels.

"Oh, so you're going 'hooker' instead. Those should be lovely photos for your unborn children to see one day."

"Well, what do you know? Yer an asshole, too," she grinned. "I need ya to do my hair, quickly. Can ya make it look a mess, like yours?"

I gave her a shitty grin, "Sure."

Hair done, we headed to Martin's suite, the life-like depictions of good and evil. Or cater waitress and hooker, same thing.

Martin's suite was twice as big as ours. Everything about this room screamed luxury mixed with comfort. From the overstuffed chairs, plush carpet, incredible artwork in gold scrolled frames, huge mahogany dining table, to the deep red and gold accents of the drapes and throw pillows. I was mentally taking decorating tips and trying to figure out how to make my two room bungalow, look like a suite.

As we entered, Martin and the boy's conversation ceased. "You look lovely tonight ladies," Martin came to kiss our cheeks. Scotty's eyes bulged out of his head, "You look amazing," he stammered, wrapping an arm around Fitz. He seemed a little off, as if we had interrupted something of importance.

"Oh, I just threw something on," she winked, not noticing the weird energy in the room.

"And Janie," said Scotty, looking me up and down, "You look lovely, as well." I smiled and said, "Thank You." I was used to being the Doris Day, to her Sophia Loren.

Cecil was less than his jovial self, as he stepped forward, "Yes, just lovely," he said, putting a kiss on our cheeks, as well.

As we sat to our four course prime rib dinner, very little was said.

Fitz had finally honed in on the energy crisis in the room. Looking from person to person, she finally said, "We had a wonderful day exploring New York."

"Yes," said Martin, "What did you ladies do today?"

Fitz looked sidelong at me, "We went shoppin'."

"Oh yes, great city to shop. Did ya find some lovely things?" Martin asked her.

"Oh I did."

Martin smiled and nodded then the room went quiet again.

"But Janie," she looked at me, "She was mugged."

All of the gentlemen put their forks down, and Cecil turned to me, "What? Are ya okay? Why didn't ya say anything?"

"I'm fine," I reassured him. "It was no big deal, really," I said, through a tightened jaw.

Martin stood and reached for his phone, "Damn hooligans. Imagine the cowardice it takes to rob a woman."

I glared, wide eyed at Fitz, who gave me a palms up?

"Who are ya callin', dad?" Scotty asked.

"The chief of police and I are old friends. I'm going to have him send over his best detective. Would ya be able to give a full description of the items stolen?"

My eyes were coming out of my skull as I turned to Fitz again. "Really, you don't have to go to any trouble. I'm sure the gentleman in question is really regretting his actions as we speak."

"What stores did ya buy from?" Cecil asked. "I'll take ya back to 'em myself. I feel horrible that I wasn't there to protect ya."

I had a mental image of Cecil and the Oriental Keebler Elf, each holding onto one end of my vibrator, and tugging back and forth. Sick, I was going to be sick.

"Ah, no," I reassured Cecil, "I only bought the one thing, and it wasn't anything I need replaced. Was kind of an impulse buy," I said, panicking.

Martin was on hold.

"Do ya remember the name of the store?" Scotty asked.

Before I could stammer out some made up name, Fitz said, "Take and Bake."

"Like the pizza?" Scotty asked.

Scotty and Martin nodded their heads. Cecil, on the other hand, grinned from ear to ear.

I let my head drop.

"Dad," Cecil said, "Why don't ya hang up the phone? Janie has been through enough today, I'm sure," he winked. "She can give a detailed description of the mugger tomorrow, if she wishes. She's well and safe. No reason to disrupt this wonderful dinner."

"Yer right son," said Martin. "Let's enjoy our meal and try to relax. I do hope it was nothin' expensive, Janie."

I looked at Fitz, "No, it was just a small thing," I said, avoiding Cecil's non-stop grin.

"A very small thing," Fitz added.

Cecil choked on his wine, trying not to laugh out loud.

Kill her! I was going to kill her!

Dinner was awkward, to say the least, with me shooting death rays at Fitz. After which, she followed me into the hallway. "I'm so sorry, Janie."

"Yeah?" I huffed. "What the hell, Fitz?"

"Didn't ya feel how..." she searched for a word, 'Wonky', the room felt?"

"Of course I did, but, could you have thought of anything else to say? I bought a new dress! I saw an Elvis impersonator!" I did a palms-up.

"All good examples," she said, nodding. "I am sorry," she winced.

"What's worse, Cecil obviously knows what 'Take and Bake' is!"

"Yeah, I caught that, too."

Cecil came around the corner, "Now Janie, can you give me a description of what the mugger stole?" he smiled.

I sighed, letting my chin fall to my chest.

"Quit torturin' her, Cecil. Isn't it bad enough that she's Dream horny?" Fitz said.

I turned my closed eyes to the heavens, "I'm good with you not coming to my rescue right now, Fitz."

Back in our suite, I asked Cecil, "So what's on the agenda for tomorrow?"

"Another meetin' for us. You and Fitz may want to take in some of the sights."

I waited for a joke about rubber penis, but it never came.

I slept like the dead, no dreams at all. Turns out, having a tiny Oriental man steal your rubber penis, can disrupt a Dream horny cycle. I was awoken by Fitz jumping on my bed. "Wakey-wakey! I want to go down and have breakfast in the dining room. Come on, get up!"

Since when did Fitz wake before me? What was I doing still asleep at almost 8am? Ah, my internal clock was off, and she was still waking before Scotty, in case he proposed at 6am.

I threw on a pair of 501's and a black baby T, then put my Rune in my pocket.

"Really Janie?" she looked me up and down. "We're in New York!"

"Yeah, and I'm going to breakfast."

"In one of the most prestigious hotels, wouldn't ya like to dress up a bit?"

"Gee, I don't know Fitz? I didn't bring clothes for dress up," I said sarcastically. I was still a little mad at her for the penis-mugging announcement. "What do you want me to dress like?"

"Funny ya asked. There's this place downtown that dresses ya up and takes pictures of ya."

I stared at her for a moment. "I bet there are lots of places that dress you up and takes pictures of you. It's how women get led into doing porn, isn't it?"

"No. they dress ya like fair maidens, or fairytale princesses, or pinups," she said excitedly.

"You're a model. Don't you do this for a living?"

"Come on, Janie. I want to do a portrait for Scotty, and this place specializes. Plus you should do it before yer old and lose yer attractiveness."

"Oh, so before the hump on my back gets any bigger?"

"Come on," Fitz whined at me.

Just then, my phone began to ring. I looked at the number and let out a sigh, showing Fitz the word 'MOM' illuminated on the screen.

"Well, ya have been away over forty-eight hours," she laughed.

"It's 4am at home, Fitz," I said, answering the phone, "Hi mom."

"Oh good, so you did make it to Ireland, after all. I wasn't sure, when I didn't get a call."

"Actually, we're in New York still, mom."

"What are you doing in New York? she sounded panicked.

"Martin had some business here, so we're staying at the Ritz."

"I wish someone would have told me."

"You mean me, mom! I'm the only one who would have told you, so just say you wish I would have told you."

She huffed, letting me know that I had already exhausted her. "Well, you know, people in New York get mugged every day. It's an epidemic. I saw it on the news."

"So I hear," was all I said.

"Maybe you should just stay in the motel."

"Hotel mom! It's a very nice hotel. One of the best in New York."

"Well, maybe you should just stay inside."

"Gonna do some sightseeing, mom. Don't know when I'll ever see New York again."

"Well, thank God, you dress like a boy. That way, those sex traffickers won't try and kidnap you."

My brows, arched, "And don't forget how tall I am. They may just think I'm a cross-dresser," I added.

Fitz, who could hear the whole conversation, began to laugh behind her hand.

"Good point," mom said, finding peace in my misery.

I shook my head at Fitz. "Okay mom, lots to do. I'll call you later."

"Wait, when do you plan on coming back? I want to have Sunday dinner planned."

I stared at the phone, "I don't know for sure, mom. I haven't even made it to Ireland yet."

"Well let me know, as soon as you know," she said. "I know a nice man. He's Lois's son."

"Lois, is seventy, mom. Unless she had him at forty, I'm not interested."

"Well, he's a little older than that, but very nice and well off."

"Okay, I'll let you know. Love to you and dad," I hung up the phone, sat back in my chair, covering my eyes. "So I can be a princess, huh?" I asked.

Fitz nodded, excitedly.

We went down to breakfast, and looked up a slew of photography studios, that specialize in theme photos.

"Oh, look at this one called Cherrydumplins'," Fitz showed me her phone. In a world where "Take and Bake," was a sex shop, I wasn't sure what to make of the name.

"That doesn't sound like a porn studio, to you?" I asked.

"I think yer confusin' dumplins' with turnovers," she pondered.

"You really want to do this?" I whined.

"Ah, come on Janie. Live a little!"

Fitz started calling studios, as soon as the clock struck ten. Most places were booked up, but she did find one, in the garment district. The men folk met us downstairs to say their goodbyes, before the meeting.

"What do ya ladies have planned for today?" Scotty wanted to know.

"It's a surprise," Fitz said, winking at him.

"I love yer surprises," he said, with a kiss for Fitz. "We'll have the limo sent back to pick you girls up. I don't want ya on the subway," he blushed and looked away from me.

After they took their leave, I looked at Fitz, "You told him, didn't you?"

"I had to, Janie. He wasn't gonna let the "Muggin' thing" go. He said he wanted to pay for what ya had lost."

I stared at her, "Then you said...?" I asked, doing a palms-up.

"I told him, 'HE' couldn't replace it...seein' as how it was the big O and all!" she smiled.

"Great, now your boyfriend thinks I'm a pervert."

"No, no he doesn't! I swear it to ya!" A moment passed before she said, "He thinks ya need to get laid."

"Yeah, that's better."

8

I FEEL . . . PRETTY?

Addison, the limo driver, ferried us through the streets of New York. I would have preferred to see the sights like a true tourist: The Statue of Liberty, The empire State Building, Central Park, but no. I was going to go play dress-up, and be photographed. Two things I really didn't enjoy.

There was a lot of hustle and bustle on the streets. But I assumed that was everywhere in the City. We ended up in a warehouse off of Seventh Ave. It was like an open air loft with several different rooms, divided by sheets and backdrops. Racks of costumes lined one whole wall, with four dressing rooms in the back. Coming to greet us was a striking woman. Tall, with some curve, just like me! I automatically felt a kinship to this Amazon woman. From her black A-frame haircut, her smoky eyes and red lipstick, to her smart looking leather boots, she was amazing. As she approached, I told Fitz, "I want to look just like her!"

"Hello," she announced, taking Fitz in an embrace. Her Adam's apple protruding and her voice, several octaves lower than my own. "I'm Janice, and I'm going to take special care of you today."

Fitz raised her brows at me as I was taken into an embrace.

"You're a tall one, aren't you?" she said to me. "I can't wait to get you in heels. What are you...? 5'10?"

I nodded, "Yes I am."

"Exquisite!" she announced, walking around me. "I have just the outfit for you. Make-up," she yelled, and two women came and whisked me away to a chair.

They had me turned away from the mirror, but it seemed like they were doing a lot of cover-up. I wondered how bad my skin actually was, that they spent so much time on it. I knew they were applying fake lashes, it was the only time they really said anything to me. "Don't blink," was the extent of our conversation. It seemed like I was in the chair forever when they started on my hair. Soon, I was led into a dressing room, and told to put on the specially chosen outfit hanging on the back of the door. I assumed there would be a mirror in the dressing room so I could finally check out my make-up and hair, but no. As I unzipped the garment bag hanging on the back of the door, I assumed there had been a mistake. A big one. I held up a patent leather, what could only be describes as a Merry Widow, just short of bondage, suit. It had hooks, buckles and rings, everywhere.

"Umm...hello?" I called out the cracked door. "Hello?" I repeated, louder.

Janice appeared, "Oh, your make-up and hair are perfect," she rolled the purr.

"Great," I said, quickly, "Ugh, I don't know about this outfit. It's um, not quite...me."

"Oh honey, I disagree," Janice said. "I knew from the moment I laid eyes on you, that this," she grabbed the garment and held it up to me, "Was you!"

"Yeah, I don't really see myself quite like this..."

Janice cut me off, "Well you should. You are fierce! Like a crouching tigress," she made a pawing motion, and roared at me. "There is a beast in you, just waiting to be set free, honey!"

"Yeah?" I said, with more doubt than agreement.

"Yes honey, we're gonna bring her out!"

I deflated at the thought. "I'm not even sure how to put this thing on," I said.

"Let Janice help you," she said, stepping into the dressing room and closing the door.

I knew I looked apprehensive, but she assured me, "Honey, if I was interested in women, I wouldn't spend this much time trying to catch a man's eye." She had a point. I personally did want a man, and would never suffer what she does to look more womanly.

She pulled and I huffed. She yanked and I winced. "Ouch," I said, when something near my nether region, snapped me.

"Sorry honey, elastic," said Janice.

I was grateful that my full bum was covered. In fact, even though everything personal was covered, I still felt very naked.

"Voila," exclaimed Janice, after lacing up my black patent leather, knee high, four inch heeled boots.

All I could think of was, I was now 6'2".

I walked out of the dressing room, and Janice escorted me to a mirror.

Pin up Liberty Curls with long tresses down my back, very smoky eyes, complete with long fake lashes and big red lips, not to mention the bondage Merry Widow...I didn't look half bad...as a dominatrix. Not exactly a princess, unless the 'Princess of Pain', was a thing.

Finally, I could hear Fitz being struggled into her own costume. I wondered what she would look like. She emerged, and we stared at each other. I knew what I looked like, but she was dressed like 'Little Bo Peep', complete with plaid dress, braids, and a staff. I started to laugh. "What are you wearing?"

Fitz was led to a mirror for the first time. She stared at herself and her smile quickly faded, "What the hell is this?" she asked.

"You're the lonely sheep herder," explained Janice, trying to paint a picture for her.

"I wanted to be a princess," said Fitz, still staring in the mirror.

"You are," Janice said. "You're the 'Sheep Princess'," she added with a far off look. "You spend your days alone on a hilltop...just you...and the sheep...waiting for your prince to come."

Fitz narrowed her eyes, as she tried to take in Janice's vision. "Uh huh, and what is she supposed to be?" she pointed at me.

"I'm a crouching tiger," I said, clarifying it for her.

"Yes, she is!" added Janice, winking at me.

"Uh huh," Fitz said again. "Look, since I am payin' for this, I'd like somethin' different, please."

Janice looked taken aback, "What do you mean?"

"I'd like to be a princess," said Fitz, trying to remain calm.

"Well, honey I told you, you're the Sheep Princess!" Janice wasn't seeing the crazy that we were.

"No," said Fitz, through a tightened jaw, "I want to be a REAL princess, like Cinderella or Snow White. Not the 'Sheep Princess'."

"But why?" Janice asked, dreamily.

"Because my fiance does not have a 'THING' for sheep...or sheep herders, or Sheep Princesses!" she raised her voice.

Janice looked like she had been slapped, "Well, I aim to please. And if you aren't pleased, I guess I'll have to try harder, change my vision. But can I at least get a few photos before you send me back to the drawing board?" she asked dramatically.

Fitz seemed less than thrilled, but I told her, “Ah come on, Fitz. Live a little!”

She glared at me for throwing her words back at her then agreed to a few shots as the 'Sheep Princess'.

A gothic stone backdrop, with standing prop table, lit candelabras, a hanging chandelier and a throne chair completed Janice's vision for me. I was handed a bullwhip and asked to let my inner sex kitten...out. Danzig's 'Under Her Black Wings', began to play overhead. I really had no idea how to do this, but I started to get into the role as I followed Janice's instruction. I even straddled the throne and slapped my fanny for her camera. Fitz, forgetting her own ridiculous attire, began to hoot and holler at me. After the shoot, I felt empowered, sexy!

Fitz's backdrop was a Swiss Alp, with a giant fake rock and a stuffed sheep. She didn't look happy as she complied with her instructions. The 'Sound of Music', began to play for her shoot. Deciding to have fun, instead of pouting, she made the act of holding her hand over her brow, like she was trying to look out over the fake mountains. For my amusement, she straddled her stuffed sheep, while biting her finger seductively. I was dying laughing, thinking of this as my Christmas card for the coming year. That was until she started pretending to lick her fake staff. Then I decided this would be the one I'd send out to all our friends and family.

All of the sudden one of the women who had done my make-up ran up and whispered in Janice's ear, then hurried off.

Janice quickly said, “Okay ladies, that's all for today. I'm going to start developing these,” then grabbed the camera and ran. Her black boots, knees to chest, as she disappeared.

“What about my costume change?” yelled Fitz.

Fitz and I stared at each other, “That was rather abrupt,” I said. “Is that normal?”

“Hardly,” said Fitz, walking out of her backdrop.

We both looked around, but saw no one, until an officer yelled, "I got two over here!"

"Got two what?" I asked Fitz. Two officers emerged with a guy in a suit.

"What's going on?" I asked, as one uniformed officer pulled my arms behind my back and cuffed me.

"Yer makin' a huge mistake," Fitz said, as she too was cuffed.

"Our clothes and purses," I said, more to Fitz than the officers.

"Your personal belongings will be waiting for you when and if, you make bail."

"Bail?" I said to Fitz in a panicked voice. We tried to plead our case, but had no idea what we were being arrested for. I asked, but was read my rights instead. They walked us outside, 'Little Bo Peep', and 'The Dominatrix'. People on the streets stared and made cat calls. "You could at least let me change!"

"Yeah, you're the picture of modesty, lady!" the detective said.

As they loaded us into one police car, I saw Janice, wigless, being put into another. "Sorry for this, honey," he yelled to me. "You really do look fabulous!"

Fitz yelled to Janice, "Ya better hope they don't put you and me in the same cell. I plan on killin' ya'!" He blew her a kiss.

Down at the station, we weren't put in the cell with Janice, him being a man, and all. "I hope he's enjoyin' bein' dressed like a woman, in a man's cell!" huffed Fitz.

"He's gay, Fitz. I'm sure he's fine," I said.

"He's not gay," she said. "He's a female impersonator. He told me so himself. He's a boob man!"

This little piece of information rolled around in my head, "That asshole," I muttered under my breath.

Fitz cocked her head and began to laugh.

"Shut up!" was all I had.

After two hours sitting in a dirty cell, (with what I didn't want to assume were prostitutes, given my costume) the detective came and basically tripped over his tongue, apologizing. Sitting in the waiting room of the police station was a very angry Martin, Cecil and Scotty. Turns out, the limo driver, Addison, had been told to move his vehicle for the police. He parked on the next block, then walked back to the building in time to see us being brought out in cuffs. He tried to talk to one officer, but he was told by an overzealous rookie to "Stand down." He had immediately gone to find Martin. When Martin found out what had happened, he called the Police Chief, and now here we were, being released. Me, half naked.

"Can I change before I go out there?" I asked.

The detective said, "Well, uh, I have your purse, and shoes, but you're clothes are missing. I don't have any idea what happened to them, I'm really sorry."

I turned, "Fitz, the rock was in my pocket!" I said, panic rising.

"Oh no, Janie, are ya sure?"

"Of course I am. I'm positive!" I was trying not to freak out.

"Well, maybe we can get ya another rock?" she suggested.

"Dammit!" I let out a sigh.

The officer looked confused, so Fitz explained, "It's an actual rock...a stone...her good luck rock. Not cocaine!" she added.

"O-kay," he said, looking a little ruffled. I wondered what kind of hell he caught for this little fiasco. "I brought you this though," he handed me a man's white undershirt, known as a wife beater in some circles. I put it over my head, and pulled it down just past my ass.

"Great," I said, putting my hands on my hips. I was covered up top, but still in a leather garter belt with thigh high hose, and Dominatrix boots that came up to my knees.

Out we were led, into the station. The guys stood up as we

came out of holding. Scotty looked Fitz up and down, "What are ya supposed to be?" he laughed.

"The Sheep Princess," she said, doing a spin. Scotty smiled and hugged her.

"Yer adorable!" Scotty said.

Cecil looked me up and down and up again..

"Not a word," I threatened.

"I'm not sure I have any," he said, wide eyed. "Hug?"

I shot death rays from my eyes.

"No?" he asked, "Okay."

I turned to Martin, who was making sure he kept full eye contact, "Did anyone find out what the hell happened?"

"The...um, man? Jason..."

"Janice!" me and Fitz, said to each other.

"Okay," continued Martin, "He had stolen some cameras and equipment from his last job. He was selling the photos he took of women to black market fetish sites and shops."

"Well, that explains the outfits," I narrowed my eyes at Fitz.

"How was I supposed to know?" she asked.

"Anyway," said Martin, "They did develop the photos for evidence against, Jason...Janice...whatever, but I got both of yours back." He handed me an envelope. "Jason did ask the chief to extend his apologies to you ladies."

"Maybe to Janie, he did," said Fitz. "He didn't see me naked."

"I gave Fitz a look of pure horror, and all three gentlemen looked at me with furrowed brows.

"Whoopsie," she said.

"I am so sorry, Janie," said Martin. "It seems ya haven't had a great stay in New York. Mugged and now...this?" he said, not coming up with a word for what had just happened. "Let's get ya back to the suite. We'll be leavin' tonight for Ireland. Maybe a hot bath and some lunch will help ya put today behind ya?"

My eyes narrowed as Cecil grinned at his dad's wording but I said, "Sounds wonderful." I was ready to kiss this city goodbye.

As Martin, Fitz and Scotty piled into the limo, Cecil signaled with his hand, "After you."

"I don't think so," I pulled the shirt down as far as it would go, and forced a smile.

"Just so ya know," he said, pointing at the envelope in my hand, "My favorite one... is you smackin' yer ass," then he dove into the limo, for a quick retreat.

I looked up to the heavens, "I do have family up there, right?" The limo driver smiled, "I'm sure you do, Miss."

"Thanks for getting us help," I leaned over and kissed his cheek. "I guess you don't usually get kissed on a street corner, by a woman in a dominatrix outfit."

"Please Miss, this is New York!" he blushed and smiled, before shutting the door after me.

I waited down in the limo, while Fitz went to get me a change of clothes. Changed, I put my dominatrix outfit into a bag, and headed for my suite. The boots wouldn't fit in the bag so I just carried them. As I stepped into the elevator, the young operator looked at my extreme make-up and hair, then down at the boots and raised his eyebrows, before quickly turning away.

Turning on the tub, I added some bubbles to my bath water, pulled the bobby pins from my hair and sank in. I needed this, I thought to myself, as the door knocking began.

"Janie, are ya decent?" Cecil asked.

"I'm in the tub. What do you need?"

"I have somethin' for ya."

I rearranged the bubbles, "Come on in, I guess."

He entered with one hand covering his eyes, and the other holding a whiskey on the rocks.

I laughed, "It's okay Cecil, I'm covered. At least the parts of me that you haven't already seen are."

He came and handed me the drink, before sitting on the floor and resting his back against the tub, looking away from me, "How ya doin?"

I took a sip, "Better now."

"You've really had a hard couple of days," he said, looking at me over his shoulder.

"More humiliating, than anything," I said.

"Now see, ya can't feel that way. Nothing you've done was humiliatin'. Not in my book."

"Well, that's quite reassuring," I joked. "That makes you the spokesperson for normalcy. We're all screwed now," I smiled.

"No really, yer too hard on yerself. I guess yer not a New Yorker, then?"

"No, I can't say that I am."

"What about Los Angles, then? Are you an L.A. woman?"

I shook my head, "No, not really."

"Are ya then a girl without a home?"

"Oh no, I have a home. I'm a South Bay beach girl. I mean, since I'm grown now, I avoid the city and Hollywood, like the plague. But the beaches of Southern Cal? I don't think I could ever stay away from home too long."

He looked back at the wall, "I hope ya like Ireland. It's beautiful ya know. There's even an ocean to remind ya of home."

"You talk like you're gonna hold Fitz and me hostage."

"Hardly. But ya will be in Ireland for some time. I'm hoping it grows on ya, that's all," he smiled.

"You do know my bloodline is from Ireland, right?"

"Aye. I'm hoping ya feel some long lost ache for her that ya didn't know ya had."

He was being serious again. I never knew how to treat this Cecil. Do I ask him if there's something wrong, or make a joke...?

"Well, I better step out, yer bubbles are disappearin'," he smiled.

And he's back, I thought.

Out of the tub and dressed, I met Martin and the family for lunch in his suite. I had never had duck before and was a little worried, but it was fantastic and I ate heartily. Everyone was quiet again, the tension was electric. I wasn't sure what was going on, but Fitz kept giving me pleading looks. I couldn't fathom telling them more than they already knew about today, so I rerouted.

"So Martin," I asked, "You never told me what size paintings you want."

He looked up from his duck and finished chewing before saying, "I figured about three foot by six. Sound good?"

I was a little shocked. I had assumed they would be wall sized, especially for the price we had agreed on. "I thought you would want them larger," I stated.

Cecil broke in, "Yes father, you may want to consider a larger size. I mean, it would take ya longer, Janie," he said to me, "But I mean, go big or go home, right?"

Martin nodded, giving it some thought. "I think Janie and I will be able to find the appropriate size for the wall. I'll depend on yer expertise," he raised his glass to me.

9

OFF WE GO!

We left in the early evening for our almost seven hour flight. I was grateful for the exhaustion that would have me knocked out for the night. I barely remember boarding and making a bed out of one of the recliners, before I was out cold. Cecil woke me as we approached Dublin. I was apprehensive to look out the window, but when I did, all was bathed in greens, reds and golds. The country side was so beautiful. "Wow!" was all that escaped my lips.

"Welcome home," said Cecil, putting a kiss on the top of my head.

We flew a bit further, to Martin's private strip. Stepping off the plane, I caught a glimpse of our rides and took in a breath. Cecil saw me and laughed. "They're 1955 Silver Wraiths," he said, like that summed it up.

I shook my head.

"Rolls Royce," he added.

Two of these beautiful cars, one white, one black, waited on the tarmac for us. I had been in love with Baby (Fitz's 1959

Cadillac convertible) since we were teens, but this ran a close second.

"Dad loves his cars," Cecil said. "He had one for him, and one for mom."

"I think I may be in love with them too," I said.

"You'll have to see the rest of them before ya decide which you love most. He has a Lamborghini you may like."

I shook my head, "Nope. I only love classics."

"You are an original, I'll give ya that. What about a 1955 Austin-Healey Convertible?"

I grinned, "Now you're talking."

"One of your drivers is gonna have to make a second trip to get all of Fitz's luggage," I said to Cecil as they unloaded her five suitcases.

We wound through meadows till we came to a tree lined drive, and made a left through scrolled iron gates. Huge trees hung over the drive as we made our way two miles in to see The Castle before us. Five stories high and made of dark stone, stood what looked to me like a medieval hotel. I admired the moss covered face and an elaborate circular driveway with a garden in the middle. With the rising sun behind it, it loomed and enveloped us.

"It's circa 1700's," Cecil said. "It's been in our family for generations."

"This is home to you," I said as more of a statement, than a question.

Cecil looked dreamy eyed, "Aye."

As we pulled up out front Cecil saw the staff waiting, and began to grin. "What?" I asked, assuming he was checking out the young maids.

"Miss Elanor," he said.

Scotty, who had been in the other Rolls, jumped from the

car as did Cecil, to wrap their arms around who I now assumed was Miss Elanor.

As I swung my legs out of the car I looked back at Fitz, who had the same look of wonder on her face. We both approached Elanor and the boys. She was tall, I would guess in her late fifty's, with a huge, loose, salt and pepper bun atop her head. She wore a grey full length, early 1900's gown with lace and inlaid pearls, at the very high neck line. If she had shoes on, I couldn't see them. She reminded me of the Wicked Step Mother in Cinderella, only more matronly. Martin came to put a kiss on her hand and introduce us.

"Miss Elanor," he said with a small head nod, "This is Sarra Fitzpatrick," she extended a limp hand to Fitz.

Fitz smiled and shook the woman's hand, "You can call me Fitz."

She turned a disapproving eye to Fitz, and looked down her nose, "I'll do no such thing," said Miss Elanor, smugly. "Your parents, no doubt, gave ya a proper name? I will call ya Sarra, or Miss Fitzpatrick."

Fitz, sensing a battle of wills, put on her best fake smile and said, "Miss Fitzpatrick, will be fine."

Tension was visible to me, but the menfolk seemed oblivious. "You can call me Janie," I said, extending my hand.

"I assume you were named Jane?"

"Uh yeah," I nodded.

"Then I guess you know how you will be addressed? Unless you wished to be called Miss...?"

"O'Connelly," I answered quickly.

She raised a brow, "Irish. Was not my first guess!" she said, looking me up and down.

Miss Elanor turned and smiled at the boys, "Let's get ya settled in." She turned them away from us and walked inside, leaving Fitz and me standing with the maids we hadn't been introduced to.

"I don't look Irish enough?" I asked.

A bubbly maid, about my age, with a blonde ponytail, black and white uniform, and tiny features, stepped forward and smiled, "I am Mary, and will be yer maid, Miss," she curtsied. "Whatever ya wish, whatever ya need, call on me."

Her tiny and pleasant twin, stepped to Fitz, "And I am Carrie, and will be yer maid," she smiled and curtsied to Fitz.

We said some quick "Thanks," and tried to catch up to the men who had left us behind. The maids trailed behind us.

We caught up to our party in time to hear Miss Elanor announce, "I have your rooms freshened and awaitin' your return. Go get settled, lads."

She gave Fitz a disapproving look as Scotty put a kiss on her cheek, and took off with Cecil up to the right of the second story staircase.

Miss Elanor watched the boys disappear out of sight, before turning to us. "You ladies will be housed in the North Wing."

"And my boyfriend?" Fitz asked.

"Master Scotty will be in the South Wing," she said, turning her back to us and ascending the staircase.

"I'd rather be closer to Scotty," Fitz said, and was quickly turned on by Miss Elanor.

"No matter how ya were raised," she hissed, "In this home, I will require ya act like a lady."

I saw Fitz's green eyes, darken. To speak ill of her 'raising' was akin to smacking her mother's face. I knew this could only end badly.

"Now you wait one damn minute!" Fitz began. I felt both Mary and Carrie step away.

I cut Fitz off as quickly as I could. "This is a lovely house," I said a little too loudly.

Fitz bit her tongue, but she and Miss Elanor's eyes stayed locked on each other. After a moment, Miss Elanor began up the stairs again. "This isn't a house, Miss O'Connelly. This is a 'Manor'. I take great pride in how it is kept."

"Yes," I said, "You've done a lovely job."

Fitz looked like her head was going to explode, and I couldn't blame her. Miss Elanor led us up the stairs, down a long hallway decorated with what I assumed were old family portraits, medieval weaponry, candelabras on pedestals, chandeliers hanging from the ceiling, and even a few suits of armor that actually looked used. Heavy red drapes covered the windows, and made the walls seem even darker.

"The room at the end of the hall was Miss Margaret's private room. No one is allowed in there. And to make sure no busy bodies try, it remains locked," stated Miss Elanor.

Miss Elanor left us there, asking our maids to show us to our rooms. Directly across from each other, it seemed we would be neighbors, alone in the medieval North Wing.

Walking into my room, I assumed that Dracula was watching me from behind a portrait. A large canopied bed, rich with blood red fabric and bedding, looked dwarfed by the size of the room. A fireplace made of dark stone, an antique armoire, a full length mirror and dressing table sat against the opposite wall, complete with a beautiful pitcher and wash basin made of silver. Another small table held a bottle of Callaghan whiskey and two rocks glasses. I began to worry about how updated the bathrooms would be. I saw no chamber pot, but couldn't rule it out.

"Would ya like me to unpack for ya, Miss?" asked Mary, as I took in the room.

"No thank you," I said, staring at the strange painting above my bed. It was of a woman. She appeared to be in this very room, in this bed, lying with flowers on her chest, as if dead. "What the hell?" I said out loud, staring t it.

"Yeah, this one has always given me the creeps, too," said Mary at my side. We both shivered. Just then, I heard Fitz in her room let out a scream. Mary and I dashed across the hallway. There, standing on the bed, were Fitz and Carrie.

"What the hell are you yelling about?" I asked Fitz.

"Snake!" she yelled.

"There are no snakes in Ireland, Fitz," I said.

"Well, someone had better tell Saint Patrick, he forgot one!" she pointed.

There, lying as still as death, was a fourteen inch long lizard. He looked frightened. Mary walked over and picked him up as Carrie and Fitz "Ewwed and yucked." I squished up my face. Even though I didn't fear reptiles and vermin like Fitz, I wasn't happy about the thought of finding one like this in my room, either.

"That horrible woman put it in here. I know it," Fitz bellowed, "Hateful old crow!"

"Mary, would you mind taking that outside?" I asked.

Both Maids scampered off.

"Fitz, I know you don't like what she said about your raising..."

She cut me off, "I should have pulled her dress over her head and rolled her down the stairs!"

"I know how you feel. Mum is my Mum too, remember?"

"Then ya should have let me at her instead of complimentin' the ol' hag on her housekeepin'."

"You're right of course. But Fitz, did you see the way the boys greeted her? Martin? I think you may want to consider that this woman is more than a fixture in their lives."

She let out a sigh and climbed down from the bed. "I was

secretly happy that I wouldn't have to 'live up to' a mother-in-law's standards. Is that horrible of me?" she asked.

"A little," I said, honestly. "I know you two didn't get off on the best foot, but for Scotty's sake, you're gonna to have to make an effort to get along with her."

Fitz huffed. "Fine. I'll do my best. But if she says one more word about my 'raising', I'm goin' to pull out that bun of hers and strangle her with her own hair!"

"Well of course," I said, "You're only human." I looked around Fitz's room. It was done in deep blues and golds. Above her bed was a scene of a fair and ladies dancing around a wooden pole. "She already likes you more than me," I decided.

"How do ya figure?" she asked.

"The art work," I pointed to her painting.

She followed me into my room to check out the painting over my bed, of the apparently dead woman.

"Ewww," she said. "Check out the shadow in the background.

I leaned in closer and did in fact see a shadow that appeared to be overseeing the dead. I shivered again.

"Who puts shit like this in their home?" Fitz questioned.

"Well, the painting is well done," I cocked my head, trying to take it in from an artist's point of view. "It's the subject matter that's a little...frightening," I finally said. "How well do you know Scotty?" joking of course, but Fitz made a questioning face. "Oh, come on Fitz, I was just kidding. Your dad is an old friend of his father's."

"Well, ya do have to admit, he has been actin' rather oddly since we left L.A. All of them have. That weird electric...silence?"

"Really?" I started laughing, but she didn't. "You can't be serious? You're engaged to the guy!"

"Not yet I'm not!" she held up a bare ring finger.

"I'm pretty sure neither Scotty, nor his family, are psycho killers."

I unpacked my things into the empty armoire as she rambled.

Miss Elanor entered the room without a sound, making us both jump. "Since you ladies will be living here," she said with visible disgust, "Martin would like ya to meet the staff, before he breaks his fast."

Fitz narrowed her eyes and opened her mouth for what I knew would be a regretful retort, but I cut her off again. "We'll be right there," I said. Miss Elanor disappeared from the doorway.

"Ol' battle axe," Fitz hissed.

"So, the boys may not kill us...she, on the other hand...it couldn't hurt to keep an eye on her," I suggested.

"At least admit that you notice a difference in the way the guys are actin," Fitz said, as we were descending the staircase.

"Alright, I noticed, okay? Yes, something is going on," I said, under my breath, noticing all the people standing in line at the bottom of the stairs.

"Come ladies," said Martin, extending his hand. "This is my, and now your, staff. Ladies and gentlemen, this is Miss Fitzpatrick and Miss O'Connelly. Ladies, you've already met Miss Elanor,"(Fitz and Miss Elanor practically growled at each other) and you've made the acquaintance of Mary and Carrie," he went down the line. "This is Mr. Briggs, my butler," I nodded, as did he. Damn, I thought to myself, why did I have to have so much trouble remembering names? He was my height and thin, with the thickest eyebrows I had ever seen. I already knew, Mr. Briggs, to me, would be 'bushy brows', guy.

"Mr. Donahue, Scotty and Cecil's butler," Martin continued through my thoughts. I nodded again, "Mrs. Pole, the cook (Mrs. Clause to me) Mrs. Aimes, the upstairs maid (the Eagle, for her long face and beak like nose) Miss Collins, the downstairs maid (aging Princess Leah, because of the buns on the side of her head) Carlson, the driver (James Bond, Moore, not Connery) Ansel and Aaron, the mechanics who also drive for us at times, (awkward Fonzie in overalls, and old James Dean), Brewster and Holmes, the gardeners (Laurel and Hardy) and Danny, the stable keep (young, tall, Tom Cruise).

"Daniel," he stepped forward to shake our hands, never taking his eyes off me. He was a very handsome lad, 6'1", muscular, green eyed with brown hair and smile to die for. But I couldn't imagine he was even old enough to have a full time job. He held my hand even though we were no longer shaking. Cecil stepped forward, laughing, "That's enough lad," he smiled and moved him back to the line. Everyone laughed a bit, but I blushed. "I will also hire ya an assistant, Janie, to help with whatever ya need for your work."

I smiled, "That won't be necessary," I said.

"I can help Janie with whatever she needs," Cecil said.

"Fine," agreed Martin. "You two can work all of that out. So ladies, are ya ready to break-fast?"

The dining room had ceilings three times the height of a normal home, and a table that seated twenty-two. The Irish flag, family colors and coat of arms were proudly displayed. There were more paintings of family and what I assumed was the distillery. This Castle was dwarfing me, one room at a time. I was sure I was shrinking. Paintings done to fit these walls would take years, I thought.

We all sat huddled up at one end of the table, with Martin at its head. Fitz and Scotty were sitting on the same side, holding hands. Elanor stood by Martin's side, and stared disapprovingly. Fitz noticing her sneer, put a kiss on Scotty's cheek then smirked. Cecil and I shared a side, not holding hands.

Martin asked, "Ladies, would ya like a tour of the grounds, or would ya fancy a nap after yer journey?"

I knew I couldn't sleep during the daytime. And maybe never again, in my Dracula room. "I'd love a tour."

"I will meet ya in the foyer, in let's say half an hour?" he looked at his watch.

"Perfect," I said.

"And Fitz, what about you?" Martin asked.

"I think a nap sounds glorious," she grinned at Scotty, then smirked at Miss Elanor again.

Elanor butted in. "Don't forget Scotty, Cecil, the tailor will be here in fifteen minutes to fit ya for yer new tuxedos. That should give yer little friend time to nap peacfully," she smirked back at Fitz.

Ding, ding, round two, I heard in my head. By my account, Miss Elanor had won both so far.

Fitz and I headed for the stairs so she could nap, and I could get freshened up. Fitz cursed Miss Elanor's name all the way up. "She's the devil," Fitz announced. "Who the hell, does she think she is? Keep me from Scotty, I don't think so," she huffed.

"Just take a nap. Things will look better after you get some rest."

"Things will get better, when she's locked in a closet with a broom shoved up her..."

"Fitz!" I cut her off. "Relax and try to forget about Miss Elanor for a little while."

"What? Are ya on her side?" she bellowed.

"No, I just don't want your head to blow off your shoulders. Seriously, I've never seen you so ruffled." I grabbed her by both shoulders and faced her head on, "I need you to breath. You've had lots of women dislike you, usually based in jealousy. But you've never let someone get to you."

"I've never had to compete with a woman who was so dead set on ruinin' my happiness."

"Well, don't let her!"

"I'm just afraid."

"Of what?" I couldn't imagine.

It took a moment for her to choose her words. "She has some kind of pull with Scotty, and he's been actin' so weird. What if she turns him against me?" she asked, doing a palms-up.

I had never seen Fitz insecure about anything. I don't think she had ever felt insecure. But now she was. She was afraid to lose someone for the first time in her life. I hugged her close and said the only thing I thought could help, "He loves you, Fitzy."

She calmed a bit, and nodded.

"Now go get some rest, and try not to worry. I love you."

"Aye, and I love you," she headed off to her room.

The restroom was a door down from my room. And I'm happy to report that the plumbing was in fact, up to date. Standing in the middle of a room large enough to be my living room was a claw foot tub. I couldn't wait to sink in, but that would have to wait until after my tour. I headed back to my room and grabbed a sweater. I was warned that the weather could be unpredictable. I needed to call my mom. But we were eight hours ahead, so I'd have to wait until later.

I found Martin and Miss Elanor waiting for me at the bottom of the stairs. He had a thick head of hair, graying at the temples, and was still holding onto the sparkling eyes and nice build he had passed on to his boys. But the best of all the things he had gifted them, was that smile. He would be a handsome man till his last breath.

"I'm sorry, have you been waiting long?" I asked, descending the stairs.

Martin looked up and smiled, "Not at all. Plus," he added,

"A man should never rush a beautiful woman. She's always worth the wait."

I smiled, but Miss Elanor narrowed her eyes at me. I wondered what I had done?

"Would ya like an umbrella, Mr. Callaghan?" she asked.

"I don't require one, rain lover that I am," he said to me. "But maybe Miss Janie?" he questioned.

I smiled again, "Not for me, thank you. I love the rain as well." He offered me his elbow, "The front walk gets slippery." I put my arm through his, as we headed out. I swear I heard Miss Elanor hiss at me. When I looked back over my shoulder, she was sneering. I liked it better when she only showed open disdain for Fitz.

Off we went, Martin and me, through a meadow path. The sun was dipping in and out of big white and grey clouds. Lush green hills rolled as we made our way down the path that led to the stables, also a large stone building, like a miniature Castle itself. I could almost imagine knights from days long past, saddling up and riding off to war or on great quests. The 'Romantic' in me ran wild with thoughts. As we walked down the row, I got an idea of just how large the stable was.

"Before I had it renovated," said Martin, "The stable could accommodate twenty-four horses. But I didn't like them being so confined," he stopped to rub the nose of an absolutely huge horse. "So I had each stall opened up. Now it only holds twelve horses. She's an Irish Sport, or Irish Hunter," he said of the gentle beast letting me rub her nose.

"She's beautiful," I said.

From behind me I heard, "Yes, she is."

We turned to see Daniel the stable boy. "Sir," he nodded to Martin.

"Ah, good day!" Martin said, clapping him on the shoulder.

"Once again, this is Daniel. The young man I trust to keep well, my precious horses. How do ya do this fine morn, son?"

"I do well, Mr. Callaghan," he flashed his own amazing smile.

"And you, Miss Jane? How are ya kept?" he stared.

"I'm well," I answered.

"Have ya ever been on horseback?" he asked.

"If you count the ponies at the fair, then yes," I laughed.

"Maybe sometime you'd like to go for a ride?" the boy asked, locking his eyes with mine.

From down the row, I heard, "Yes Janie, would you fancy a ride?"

"Ah Cecil, my boy," said Martin, "I thought you were gettin' fitted."

"All done," said Cecil. "So Janie would you like a ride?" he asked again.

"I believe I asked her first, sir," Daniel said to Cecil.

Cecil was impressed by the boy's boldness."Why, yes you did, lad. Nice to see ya again by the way, it's been a few years! What were ya then? Fourteen?"

"Aye," answered Daniel, stepping forward to shake Cecil's hand.

"Janie may want to go with someone who has a little more...experience ridin'," Cecil said, cocking his head.

"Well sir, I'm no boy, anymore," Daniel fired back, with an amused smile.

"Yes but, I've been ridin' since before you were born," Cecil crossed his arms over his chest.

Martin and I watched the conversation go back and forth. What is happening? I thought to myself.

"Yes, but I ride every day," Daniel crossed his arms across his own chest, as well. "I'm guessing ya may need some refreshin', especially at yer age," added Daniel. "Ya know yer not as young as ya used to be."

Cecil grinned, "Funny ya mention age...tell me, are ya legal yet?"

"Believe me, sir, I'm old enough," Daniel's smile broadened. "Some would say...I'm at my peak."

Cecil, put his tongue in his cheek and nodded his head, "Once again, experience is required to handle some things. Or at least...to handle them well."

"But ya know, havin' a young man's stamina, and all...I can ride all day," his grin becoming downright cocky.

"Oh, I'm sure," Cecil said, "But it's actually more important to leave her satisfied at the end. After all, what good is it...to be at it all day...if she doesn't enjoy the ride?"

I felt like I was watching a different kind of cock fight.

"Well," Martin said, laughing and putting an end to the one upping, "I'm sure if Miss Janie chooses to go ridin' she will be well escorted, with either of you men." He turned to me, "Let's leave them to haggle, while we enjoy the grounds." I smiled and took his arm. "Remember boys, I have the most experience...with horses, and ladies," he grinned to them both, as we exited the stable.

Martin and I headed to the garage. "It seems you will be the recipient of some good old fashioned courtin'," he said.

I laughed, "Is that what that was?" I asked.

"Oh no my dear, that was male posturin'," he concluded. "I got ya out of there before one of them peed on yer leg, no offense."

I laughed, "None taken, and thank you for that."

We saw his car collection, and yes, his twelve car garage was impressive. But Cecil had been right about the Austin. It was by far my favorite. Off we moved to the gardens, where I kept seeing rings of stone. They had been mowed around and left to grow as they saw fit.

"What are the rings all about?" I asked.

"My girl, have you never heard of Fairy Rings?"

"I must admit, only in jest."

"Oh, make no jest of it. The Fairy Rings are very real," he smiled. "We never wander within them for fear that we will enter into the Fairy World, and stay there 'a year and a day', as the story goes." He pulled dried fruit from his pocket, and set it over the ring. "I leave them small gifts of food and such."

I smiled, "They are beautiful."

"Ya must see the large one at the bottom of the meadow. Perhaps Cecil could take ya?" he looked sidelong at me.

"Why Martin Callaghan, are you trying to get me to spend time with your son?"

"Hardly my dear. I am no maker of matches. Just an old man, who doesn't think he'll make it down the meadow and back, without ya havin' to carry him," he smiled.

I eyed him suspiciously, "Funny, you don't seem old to me."

"And if ya never have to watch me try to hike back up the meadow, hopefully, ya never will," he grinned.

Winding around the grass covered meadow, nestled down by the stream that ran through the property, stood the biggest Weeping Willow, I had ever laid eyes on. Even from a distance it was majestic. "Wow," I breathed, "What an incredible tree."

Martin smiled, and looked sidelong at me. "I had hoped you would see the magnificence of her."

"She must be hundreds of years old," awe filling my voice.

"Aye," Martin responded, staring at her. "She is magic, you know?"

I smiled.

"Tis true. My grandfather kissed my grandmother, for the very first time, under her branches," his mind wandered back in time. “He would tell me, when I was young, that he had been datin’ another from a very auspicious family. He was practically engaged. But then he met her,” his eyes went dreamy. “She was hired as a maid, and in that time most people treated the help, as they called them, differently.”

I nodded, thinking of the lines drawn between 'The haves and the have-nots', at that time.

“Well, it was obvious that he fancied her. He made excuses to be in her company...would spy, to catch a glimpse of her. At a lavish party, thrown on All Hallows, she disappeared into the night. He rode the property on horseback, and found here there,” he pointed to the Willow.

I too, became dreamy eyed picturing the scene.

“With the full moon above him, he watched her dance and sing around the willow's trunk. Well, his horse huffed and startled her nearly out of her skin, as she told it. Standin’ there, barefoot, she started to apologize and explain her flippancy. But he had been captivated by her. He lay his coat on the ground, and bid her sit. For hours they spoke of anything and everything he could think of to keep the conversation flowin’. Right before the sun rose, he asked if she would grant him one favor. A kiss. This whole night had been forbidden to her and she knew it may never come again knowin’ their stations in life. She leaned in, and their lips met. A kiss of pure innocence.

I smiled at the tree and the memories she held.

“With that one kiss my grandfather was smitten. He went straight to his father and told him he would love nor marry, any but she. His father wanted to know how he had come to this conclusion. Blushin’ the lad told his father of the night, and the kiss. His father asked, “Where was this kiss, received?” When he said, “Under the Willow,” his father smiled and nodded. A year later, on All Hallows, they were wed.”

I sighed, “How beautiful.”

"Yes," he looked fondly at her. "I too kissed the love of my life, for the first time under that tree."

I knew he had lost her several years ago, and could see he was still smitten, even if it was with a memory.

"I am sorry for your loss," I said, reaching out to squeeze his hand.

He squeezed back, "In truth dear girl, I feel lucky everyday to have had a love such as hers. She, just like my grandmother before her, was pure...magic."

It took nearly two hours for our walk, and both of us were ready for a rest. As we entered the foyer, Martin turned and removed my sweater, handing it to his butler. "You are a treasure my dear and I delight in yer company."

"And I, in yours," I nodded. "Thank you for the tour. I enjoyed it very much."

He cocked his head to me, "I can see why the boys make such a deal of your attentions," he smiled warmly. "You really are quite a beautiful young lady," he put a kiss on my cheek. "I must be off now, lots of work to be done before the meetin' tomorrow."

I watched him exit to his study. When I turned to head up to my room, I ran face to face with Miss Elanor. Having been caught off guard, I put my hand to my chest and took in a breath.

"Did ya enjoy yerself?" she asked, eyes flickering.

"Uh, yes," I said slowly.

"I'm glad Mr. Callaghan has taken such an interest in ya."

"Yes, he's very kind."

"Maybe I should take more of an interest in ya, as well?"

I said nothing, but something in her voice made my eyes widen and an ice cold chill went running down my spine.

"After all, what did Mr. Callaghan just say about ya? Yer

quite a beautiful young lady?" We stared at each other for a moment then she turned and stormed off.

I practically ran up the stairs. Dracula room or not, I'd rather be safely locked behind a door, any door, than have another run-in with Miss Elanor. At the top of the stairs, I decided to go wake Fitz and tell her that she was no longer alone on the chopping block. I grabbed the handle, but it was locked. Frantic whispering began. "Hide," I heard Fitz say, in a hiss. I guessed Scotty had also finished his fitting.

"It's just me," I said through the door, "I can come back later, if you're having...alone time."

Fitz opened the door in her silk Oriental robe, "No, it's okay. We're done," she looked at Scotty.

He finished buttoning his shirt and gave me an embarrassed smile, before kissing Fitz on the cheek. "I have to find dad," he said, and exited without looking up. I watched him disappear down the hall before I said, "What is going on with him?"

"If ya must know," said Fitz.

I reconsidered, "I mustn't," I said quickly.

"He can't perform!" she finished.

"Oh," I raised my brows.

"I gave him some of my best stuff, too," she huffed, beginning to pace.

I shut the door behind me. "How long has this been going on?"

"Just since we got here!"

"Seriously Fitz, one time and you're upset?"

"Ya don't understand! He and I have a very healthy sexual relationship."

I didn't know about healthy, per say. Active, I knew to be true. Very active, is how I would describe it.

"And he was great, I mean GREAT," she reiterated, "Last night on the plane. I was scared we would break the sink! And today? No matter what I tried, and I tried some stuff," she flared, "Nothin'! Not even a twitch! Somethin' weird is happenin' here, Janie."

"Okay, so maybe he's working through something. I'm sure it's nothing to worry about. Worst case scenario, we'll both be dream horny for a little while."

"Oh, the hell I will!" bellowed Fitz. "No offense, but I won't allow myself to become an uptight wreck."

I narrowed my eyes, "Thank you."

"Sorry Janie, but you get to row that boat alone."

"So what are you gonna do?" I asked, seriously. "I know you wouldn't cheat on Scotty."

"Of course not," she looked at me indignantly. "I'm gonna tease the hell out of him, till he can't take it anymore."

"Ah, come on Fitz. He may be too preoccupied with whatever it is that's bothering him to be able to...you know. Maybe you should just ask him..."

She cut me off, "Ya don't think I can do it?" she asked, walking towards me.

"Of course I do," I put my hands up to show submission.

"Ya bet yer ass I can!" she tightened her jaw.

"O-kay. I came in here to tell you something. Are you ready to move on to another conversation, or do you need to rant further?"

"I'm fine," she snapped, "Go ahead!" she waved her hand.

A few rants later she did calm down, and I told her everything. From the odd cock fight Cecil had with the stable boy, all the way to Miss Elanor's reaction to Martin's comments.

"What do you think?" I asked.

"It's so awesome they have Fairy Circles on the property."

"Yes," I said slowly, "But what about the other stuff?"

"Well, ya already know Cecil is interested in ya. It's not a big leap to think that he would try to mark his territory."

"I am not territory," I said, hotly.

"Fine," she raised her brows. "But, you have to admit, men are very..." she searched for a word.

"Territorial," I sighed.

She grinned, "Obviously, Daniel's crush is threatenin' him.

I nodded.

"But Miss Elanor's reaction is just strange. We may have to conclude that she's just batshit. A different kind of batshit than we're used to," she added, with a wave of her hand. After all, our lives were strewn with batshit crazy family and friends.

I nodded. "She's kinda scary," I admitted.

"I can take her," Fitz giggled.

"Don't be so sure," I answered.

"So, that Daniel guy...?"

"You mean that Daniel kid?" I cut her off.

"He's got a crush on ya, huh?"

"Maybe," I allowed.

"That may work in our favor."

"How?" I asked, truly confused.

"I'm workin' it out in my head."

"Alright, let me know when you're done," this couldn't be good, I thought to myself.

A loud gong went off and I jumped nearly out of my skin. Fitz laughed at me. "What the hell was that?"

"Lunch," she smiled.

`I wasn't used to assigned eating times, except for my weekly dinner with mom and dad. But it was the time spent there not the timing that drove me crazy. I mentally reminded myself to call my mother later.

Down the stairs again to the dining hall we went. I wasn't really out of shape but I assumed by the end of my stay those stairs would give me a great ass.

Tiny sandwiches and salads were served. “Where are Martin and Cecil?” I asked, looking at the empty seats.

“Mr. Callaghan is taking his noon day meal in his study,” said Miss Elanor.

Just then, Cecil arrived covered from head to toe, in what looked like mud, but smelled like shit.

Fitz, Scotty and me, squished up our noses.

“What the hell?” Scotty said, “Are ya covered in shit?”

Miss Elanor raised her brow to him.

“Sorry Miss Elanor,” Scotty said. “But for the love of God, what have ya been doing?” he asked Cecil.

Cecil put his hand on his hips, “I just had to show our young stable boy, that ya can't send a boy to do a man's job,” he winked at me. “He wasn't keepin' the stables as clean as he should be. So I showed him how a man takes care of things left in his charge.” He reached out to take a sandwich off the platter.

“Don't ya dare,” flashed Miss Elanor, slapping his hand. She grabbed a napkin and put a few small sandwiches in it. “You can take these upstairs and eat them AFTER you've had a proper shower!”

“Thank you, Miss Elanor,” he said, taking the napkin. “So yeah, showed the boy some things,” he said, resuming his dialog. “I had five stalls done, before he finished two. Then he sat on his arse, exhausted, while I finished another three.”

“So, you put the stable boy in his place, huh?” I asked.

“I sure did,” Cecil said, looking proud of himself and winking at me.

“Huh!” I grinned.

“What?” he asked.

“Nothing,” I laughed.

“No, what? Come on Janie, what do you have to say?”

“Do you like Mark Twain?” I asked.

“I do!” he nodded.

"Have you ever read Tom Sawyer?" I asked.

Cecil's cocky grin slowly faded as he pondered this thought.

Fitz and Scotty were stifling laughs behind their hands. Even Miss Elanor made a sound that was almost a laugh. Something I didn't think she was capable of.

Finally, Cecil said, "Well that little son of a..."

"Cecil," Miss Elanor cut him off.

"I'm goin' up to shower," Cecil said, and retreated.

When he left, Scotty asked, "What's that all about?"

"Seems Cecil and the stable boy are both clamoring for Janie's attentions," Fitz laughed.

"Really?" laughed Scotty, "This should be fun to watch!"

"Well," I said, "I have no intention towards either of them."

Miss Elanor sneered, turned on her heels and left the room.

"My only interest is in completing your father's paintings...to his liking," I added.

"Well, Cecil hasn't had to put in any effort where a woman was concerned. Or compete with anyone, for that matter, for quite a few years. Truthfully, I've never seen him this way," Scotty laughed again. "Prepare yerself for some real courtin', Janie."

I let out a sigh.

After a moment, I asked Scotty as Miss Elanor re-entered the room, "I hope you don't mind my asking, but has your father dated at all since your mother passed?"

Miss Elanor dropped a tray and went as rigid as stone.

Fitz and I shot looks at each other.

Scotty stood to help her, but she motioned him to sit, "I have it, lad," she said, bending to pick up the tray.

Scotty took his seat and answered me, "He dated a little in the past. But none of them worked out. I wish he would try again, but after all the accidents...?" he trailed off.

"Accidents?" I asked.

"Yeah, I swear he thinks he's cursed!"

"What kind of accidents?" I questioned.

Scotty finished chewing, "The first was a woman named Marie. They had only been dating a short time when she crashed her car."

"Lots of people have car accidents," I offered.

"True. But according to the detective, her brake line looked as though it had been cut through."

"Wow, that's a little scary," I said. "Did she...?" I didn't finish the question.

No, no, she's alive and well. But she left dad anyway, saying that she felt it was a sign of some kind. Next, was a woman named Frances. She was lovely. But within a few weeks of their dating, she would break out in a horrible rash, every time she was around him. It got to be too much for her, and they went their separate ways."

I nodded.

"The third lady..." he began, "Was a Miss Host. Never knew her first name. But she swore that she was drugged and left out under the willow, naked. When she was found she was babbling about seeing a woman standing over her. She said she couldn't focus well enough to make her out. The apparition supposedly told Miss Host, that "She didn't belong there" and it was best for her that she left for good. Scared the poor woman somethin' horrible!

Fitz and I both, found ourselves speechless.

"Anyway," Scotty said, "I do wish he would find love again. But until then, he has Cecil and me. Oh, and Miss Elanor," he said, smiling at her. "She's been a fixture in our lives forever. Long before my mother's accident."

Miss Elanor smiled at Scotty as he went back to his lunch, then she let her smile drop as her eyes turned to me. "Don't bore the ladies with talk of curses, lad. There was good reason for all of them to go," she added.

I did a shudder, as Fitz dropped her jaw.

After lunch, Scotty went to find Martin so they could get some work done. Fitz and I headed to her room and barely got the door closed before Fitz said, "Did you, too, get the feeling that Miss Elanor may have had something to do with Martin's love interests going away."

Truthfully, I had pondered the same thought, but came to the conclusion that the thought was insane. "I can see how it looks, but the Callaghan men are very smart. If that was the case, I'm sure they would have figured it out by now."

"Seriously?" Fitz asked. "Cecil just got duped into doin' the stable boy's job. Maybe they're not the brightest bulbs in the chandelier?"

I pondered, cocking my head.

"Not only that, you see the way they treat her. Almost like SHE'S their mother?"

I nodded. I had to agree, they did treat her with great reverence. "But she's been a part of their family for a long time?" I tried to reason with her.

"Yes...since before their mother's 'ACCIDENT'! I'm telling ya, Janie, somethin's fishy! And I'm gonna get to the bottom of it!"

Great, I thought. We weren't the brightest bulbs, either. And if Miss Elanor was a psycho, we were going to hand her the knife. "Paintings," I said.

"What?" Fitz asked, with questioning eyes.

I stared off, "I just came to do some paintings."

"Yeah, well now yer Watson to my Sherlock!"

"Yeah, that's how I see us." I said, blankly. "So, how do you wanna start this wild goose chase?"

She pondered, “I don't quite have that worked out yet, but I'm on it Watson.”

“Yeah, that's gonna get old, quick.”

Scotty spent the rest of the day with his father in the study. Fitz seemed fit to be tied. I wasn't sure if it was Miss Elanor's possible involvement in near homicides or a lack of sex that had her so wound. I did know one thing, though; A lack of sex would cause her to be overly focused on other things and that couldn't be good.

At around three, I heard someone knocking on my door across the hall. I opened Fitz's door and saw Cecil standing with his back to me. I could smell him, all clean and fresh. I took a deep breath of him before saying, “I'm over here.”

“That was my second choice,” he smiled. “May I?” he asked Fitz, stepping to her door.

“Sure,” she said, “But don't let Miss Elanor catch ya in here.”

“Yeah, she's very old fashioned when it comes to men in a lady's bedroom,” he answered. “I brought ya this,” he handed me a tablet of paper and a pen.

“Am I writing my own ransom note?” I joked. “You better address it to my dad. My mom wouldn't pay to get me back.”

“Who are ya kiddin'? She'd shove ya back in her womb if she could,” Fitz laughed, as I made the ‘ewww’ face.

“I thought ya may want to write down some of the things you'll need for the paintin's. So ya don't forget anything. The canvas will need to be delivered, most likely.

I nodded,” Yeah, depending on the size canvas your dad decides on.”

“I'll be goin shoppin' with ya tomorrow, for supplies. Dad said he wants to go with two, 6'x3', canvases. Dad and Scotty have business in the city, so they'll be out most of the day. Fitz, would ya like to ride along? Maybe do a little shoppin', too?”

I could see something brewing on her face. “So everyone will be out of the house tomorrow?”

“Everyone but the staff,” he said.

“I think maybe I'll sleep in...paint my toenails,” she added.

“Suit yerself. I guess it's just you and me, Janie,” he winked.

“Great,” I said, worrying what Fitz really had planned. Fitz suggested we get dressed for dinner. I raised my brow, “We have to dress for dinner?”

“Yeah, ya shouldn't go naked...or in yer bondage gear, to dinner.”

“Ha ha, you're so funny, Fitz. Seriously, why do we have to “Dress up” for dinner?”

“Yer at a Manor. Of course we're supposed to dress up a bit.”

It wasn't that etiquette was lost on me. I just hadn't really thought about it. I mean, we were in a private dwelling, even if it was a Castle. “I have a small problem,” I admitted. “I didn't bring any dress up clothes, except for the slacks I wore at the hotel, and they need to be pressed.”

Fitz made a face, “Lucky for you, I brought five suitcases of clothes.”

“Not so lucky for me. We're not the same size, Fitz.”

“I may have somethin' you can pull off.”

“I'm more worried about whether or not I can pull it on.”

“I have a spandex dress.”

“In my world, spandex and dress shouldn't go together. How classy, can a spandex dress be?”

“Look, the dress goes to my knees, and will stretch to fit ya. Do ya want to wear it or show up to dinner in a pair of jeans?”

“They are the Cadillac of jeans, 501's,” I reminded her. “Crap, just give me the dress.”

Fitz began to dig through one of her many suitcases that had been packed by situation: Dressy- sexy-casual-active-period. The last mentioned had less spandex and more cotton. She pulled out a blood red dress from the sexy case. With the spandex, not stretched by a human form, it looked like it would fit a ten year old girl.

I held it up against my frame, "Are you kidding me?"

"It's what I have. It's this," she pointed at the dress, "501's, or naked. Take yer pick."

I tried to think of any shoes I had that would match this dress. My choices were ballerina slippers, DOC's, Chucks, or bondage boots. "Shit!" I said, and started changing into the dress. I got it over my head and began to shimmy it down. I ran out of fabric way before my knees. About mid thigh was all I could hope for since the dress had to cover so much more body.

"Jesus, Janie," Fitz said, taking me all in. "You've got one hell of a body!"

I gave her a shit look.

"No, I'm not bein' an ass, ya really do." She moved me towards her full length mirror.

I was curvy, that was true. But this dress made my curvy hips, full butt, and long legs, look amazing. "But I still feel naked."

"You need to get past bein' so self conscious. This is what you look like," she said. "I'm not sure I want ya lookin' this good, in front of my finance," she giggled.

I hugged her, "Do you have a sweater I can wear over this?"

"Nope," she grinned.

"I'm wearing the ballerina slippers, you know."

"I know," she said still hugging me. "Yer legs don't need to be any longer anyway."

The gong went off, and I jumped again. "I'm gonna have a hard time getting used to that."

"I'm surprised we can hear it from here...locked away in the North Wing, like crazy ancestors," Fitz answered.

"We're probably hearing an echo," I laughed.

Down the staircase we went. I kept trying to pull the dress down to cover more thigh, but that only exposed more cleavage. "Tomorrow, when Cecil and I go to the city, I have to go clothes shopping, as well. Are you sure you don't want to go with us? I'm no good clothes shopping alone," I said, as we entered the dining hall. Fitz and Elanor, locked narrowed stares.

"Ya won't be alone, you'll have Cecil," she smiled.

"I don't think that is the kind of help I need," I gave her a worried look. "I need girl help!" I admitted.

"You'll be fine. I have some things I need to do." She paused and dropped her voice to a whisper, "And I need to be alone in the house to do them. With Scotty and Martin out for the day, and you takin' a day with Cecil, It'll be perfect."

I was trying to find a way off of Elanor's radar. But, Fitz wasn't backing away from her and whatever 'crazy' she was toting around.

The men stood as they saw us enter the hall. For the first time in my life, all eyes were on me. But I wasn't sure that was a good thing.

Cecil, let his jaw drop, "Damn!" he said.

His father turned to me, "What my son means is, you look amazin', dear," he kissed my hand. Elanor turned her cold stare towards me.

So much for staying off her radar, I thought.

"Yep, that's what I meant," Cecil gave me the once over as he pulled out my chair.

I was starting to feel uncomfortable and fidgety again, when Fitz said, "She's quite a looker," and winked at me.

We were served roast mutton. I wasn't particularly fond of mutton, but I ate most of what was put on my plate. Dessert was a cake made with stout beer and a cream cheese frosting. I really wanted a piece, but was sure the seams of this dress had been maxed out. After dinner we headed to the study for whiskey and cigars.

The boys lit up without even offering us womenfolk a smoke.

"May I?" I asked, as Cecil shut the humidor.

"Ya want a cigar?"

"I would," I said.

He cut the tip of a Cuban Cohiba Esplendido and put it to my lips before lighting a wooden match. I rolled the cigar in the flame as I puffed. Cecil stood watching long after the cigar was lit. Finally, the match burned down to his fingers and he let out a yelp.

Miss Elanor offered the men whiskey then put the tray down.

"Can I get one of those?" Fitz asked.

Elanor gave Fitz a look of disgust, "I'm sorry. I am not used to women actin' like men." She shot me a look as well, as I made rings of smoke.

"Why, my Margaret used to have a whiskey with me after dinner," he reminded Elanor. "She even smoked a good cigar from time to time," he smiled at me and raised his glass.

"I assume, you'll want a whiskey, as well?" Elanor asked me through a tightened jaw.

"I would love one. Thank you," I said, taking a rocks glass from her.

Martin regaled us with stories of when the boys were young. He was a proud father indeed. Pictures of his boys and their awards covered one wall of his study. Cecil had in fact won some awards for riding, and Scotty, for rugby and soccer, and both boys had taken and excelled in martial arts and fencing. I saw a picture of Cecil, racing a sailboat, and winced. I hated sailing, especially since I had tried so hard to enjoy it with the ex-boyfriend. But after a horrible sunburn, seasickness, and being struck dumb by the 'boom', I never acquired any love for the sport...or hobby, whatever. Story after story convinced me of the boy's very different personalities. Scotty: Was level headed, and did things only after great thought. Logic was at the forefront of his every action. Cecil: Was daring and impetuous. With little thought to the outcome of his ideas or actions, believing that all will work out as it should in the end. Some part of me envied people who didn't feel the need to try and control their situations, and just flow. But I was more Scotty, and Fitz was more Cecil.

Without trying, I couldn't help but wonder if that would make him the perfect match for me. After all, Fitz and I had been best friends almost all of our lives. I tried to pay attention to the stories, but was drawn to the curve of Cecil's lips, the blue of his eyes, the white of his perfect smile, the tiny lines at his eyes, when he laughed. I started to get pictures in my head of him shirtless, mucking the stalls of the stable. Sweat dripping down his chest...tanned muscles flexing with hard work. What the hell is in this whiskey? I wondered, staring dreamily.

"Don't ya think, Janie?" he asked.

Holy crap, I had been lost in him through a whole conversation. "I'm sorry," I said, shaking my head. "Could you repeat that?" I asked.

"Oh dear," said Martin, "You must be exhausted. You haven't had any real rest. And here I go on and on about my boys," he beamed with pride.

But Cecil saw through me. I could tell by the way he was looking at me, that he had caught me again. "Yes Janie," he said, "Maybe you'd like to go to bed."

He didn't say it as a jest though, something I could be irritated by. He said it with a longing. One that made me blush and look quickly away. "I would love to hear more, Martin," I said. "But I'm afraid I'm more tired than I knew, and I still need to call my mother."

Fitz laughed, "You sure you'll be able to sleep after that?"

She knew how conversations with my mother usually went. One of two outcomes was the side effect of talking to my mom: Exhausted, and couldn't hold my eyes open. Or: Stressed out, and couldn't sleep. "Keeping my fingers crossed," I smiled.

I said my goodnights and headed upstairs. Before I reached the landing I heard Cecil call my name. I turned as he was coming up the steps behind me. Here it is I thought, the 'come on'. But when he caught up with me, he took my hand brought it to his lips for a quick kiss. He held my gaze for a moment before saying, "Good night, Janie," and headed for the South Wing. I stared after him, chastising myself for wishing he had tried something. So dream horny was a thing of the past. Now I was just perpetually horny. Great.

I walked into my Dracula room and shivered. Maybe I should sleep with Fitz, I thought. But chances were someone else would be sneaking his way into her bed tonight. I grabbed my night clothes out of the armoire, toothbrush and cell phone. I figured if I sank into the tub, maybe I could relax a little while talking to mom. If not, I could drown myself.

The bathroom, also dark stone walls, looked more ominous at night. I tried not to let my imagination run away with me. Filling the huge claw foot tub, I had the feeling I was being watched. Another chill ran up my spine as I grabbed my phone and sank in. It was 2pm at home, and most likely mom was at home starting dinner. I had a message from Betty, my 60 plus year old Southern Belle, landlord. I decided to get my call to mother over with first. Taking a deep breath, I dialed my parent's number. "Hi mom," I said when the phone was picked up on the sixth ring.

"No Janie girl, it's me, Dad."

I was caught off guard, dad never answered the phone, "Hi dad!" I gushed. "How are you?"

"I'm well, missing my little girl already. How is Ireland? Does she miss me?"

"I haven't seen much of her yet, we just arrived. But I am sure she misses you. Is everything okay there?"

"Sure, why do ya ask, luv?"

"You never answer the phone," I laughed.

"Oh that, yer mom is at your house cleaning and such. She's been there since seven this morning."

We're eight hours ahead," I said blankly. "My house isn't that dirty that it needs seven hours of cleaning," I said.

"You know yer mom. She's probably bleaching the walls and stripping the floors."

I laughed, but he was probably right.

"You can call her at your house. I'm sure she'll answer," he laughed back.

We said our "I love you's" and rang off.

I wondered if a call to my parent's house was a 'good enough' try. But I came to the conclusion that I had to talk to my mom, or I'd never hear the end of it.

I reluctantly rang my house. Five rings, and finally, mom answered. I heard music in the background. Was she listening to Enya? A little spiritual for her, I thought. "Mom, can you turn down the music?"

I heard a male voice say, "Oh, are we done?"

My mother turned down the music and shushed someone. "Hello Janie," she said, like she was trying to let whoever was there know she was on the phone with her daughter.

"Did I just hear a man's voice, mom?"

"Oh, uh, I'm interviewing a gardener."

"Mom, I have two planters and some bushes. The rest is concrete slab. Why would I need a gardener?"

"Ya know what, you're right. You don't need a gardener," she said into the phone. "Thank you anyway," she said to the male voice I had heard.

"Oh, okay," said the voice, loudly. As if he had talked directly into the receiver. Then I heard my door slam.

"Mom, what is going on?"

"I told you," she said quickly.

My mind began to wander.

"How is Ireland?" she asked.

"It's beautiful. How is home?"

"Fine Janie, everything here is fine. I met your landlady today. I guess she thought she was supposed to be watering your planters, why is that?"

"Well, it's her house, and she planted the flowers. So when she offered to keep them alive while I was gone, I accepted."

"Well I am capable of watering the flowers, and I told her so."

My mind bent, "If you're capable, why were you interviewing a gardener?"

"Uh, I'm sorry, but I have to finish bleaching your tub, so I'm going to go now. Love you, bye Janie."

She didn't even wait for me to say goodbye, before she hung up. And she said "Love you?" I stared at my phone and decided that maybe I needed to hear the message from Betty, right now.

I played the message: "Hi Puddin! I sure am missin' ya! But I hope you're havin' a great time in Ireland." I smiled. "I ran into your mama and daddy today. I didn't expect anyone to be there, so I guess we caught each other off guard," she laughed. "She said she was pickin' up the mail and could do the waterin' as well. Give me a call if you get the chance. I would love to hear from ya, Puddin, bye now!"

I listened to the message twice through to make sure I had heard it right. She met my mom AND dad? That wasn't possible as my dad was firmly placed in his easy chair, watching boxing. Who the hell had I heard in the background? And who the hell did she see? I decided to call Betty.

Betty picked up on the third ring, "Puddin!" she yelled. "How the hell are ya?"

"Hi Betty," I said, realizing that I missed her and her Southern accent. "Ireland is beautiful, you should see it!"

"That's wonderful honey. Things are the same here. Larry and I are well. We swung by the house today to do some waterin'."

"Yeah, I heard you met my mom and dad?"

"Well, I met yer mom, but yer dad just peaked his head out quickly."

"Yeah?" I was wondering how to inquire about the mystery man without making it sound as though I was concerned. "So, who do you think I look like?" was the lame assed question, I came up with.

Betty was silent for a moment before saying, "Uh, well, I don't know. I didn't get a good look at yer daddy, my eyesight bein' what it is and all. But I don't think you look like yer momma, so I'm gonna say yer dad?" she said, like she was confused by the question. "I guess that's where you get yer blonde hair from?"

No I didn't, I thought. A blonde man? Who the hell was this guy? I was silent long enough to raise Betty's curiosity.

"Puddin'?" she called into the receiver.

I said, "Uh, yeah Betty," being pulled back to our conversation.

"I didn't see yer daddy, did I?" she asked. Betty was anything but stupid. Reading between the lines was a gift of hers.

"No," I said, "You didn't." I'm sure I sounded broken hearted.

"Now, just you wait a minute there, Puddin. There could be

lots of reasons why a man was there. Don't let yer mind wander off."

"Okay," I said, really wanting to come up with anything other than an affair.

"What did yer mama tell ya?"

"She said she was interviewing a gardener."

Betty was silent.

"What am I thinking?" I asked. "My mom isn't the type to have an affair. I mean, her and my dad, are totally happy. I'm being ridiculous!" I added, starting to laugh. "Seriously, I'd have to be crazy to even think such a thing."

"So ya want me to spy on her, huh?" Betty asked.

"Yes please." I said, without hesitation.

"If it'll put yer mind at ease Puddin, I'll do a little recon for ya."

"Normally, I wouldn't ask you to do something like this, but..."

"But yer mind won't rest until ya know, and yer too far away to do it yourself. I know honey. Don't ya worry, Puddin, I got this."

"Thank you Betty. I'm sure it's nothing," I said, sounding not so sure.

We said our goodbye's and I hung up. "There's no way!" I said to the empty room. I set my phone on the stool next to the tub and tried to relax. My mind had other ideas as it went wandering to places and thoughts that made me make the 'ewww' face. I couldn't believe my mom would have an affair, and in my home? Even more unlikely, I told myself. But then again, my mother knew I was out of the country, and she would never have expected anyone to drop by my house. The more I thought about it, the more my house seemed like the perfect place. Every time I came up with a reason why it wasn't possible, my mind found a reason why it was.

Just then I thought I heard a door close in the next room. But the next room was Margaret's private room. Fitz and I had been told that this room was not only locked, but off limits. Who would be in there? I wondered.

I quickly finished my bath and opened the door, just in time to run into Elanor coming down the hall from one of two rooms. One of those rooms being Margaret's.

"Miss O'Connelly, I thought you had gone to bed," her glare fixed and icy.

I stammered, "I needed to call my mother."

"From the bathroom?" she asked, as if she didn't believe me.

"I called while taking a bath. Two birds, one stone kind of thing," I said.

She just stared then walked away. As she disappeared, I ran back to my scary ass room and took refuge there behind the locked door.

I turned off the light and was enveloped in total darkness. Not even a sliver of light entered the room. There was a candle and matches on the bedside table. But all I could think was how grim the room would look bathed in candlelight. I turned the light back on so I could find the window hiding behind the blood red, black out curtains. Opening them wide to display a huge arched window, I thought I saw the glow from a candle in the courtyard. Someone was out there, walking the grounds in the middle of the night. Maybe Fitz had convinced Scotty to go on a walk. Hopefully one that would end in her 'getting some' so she would finally unfocus her mind on Elanor. I walked back to the light and switched it off. Now there was light in the room, but it was shining on the scary ass picture over my bed. Lovely, I thought. I pulled the covers over my head expecting to lay there thinking of what the hell was going on with my mom. Or possibly, what Elanor was doing in Margaret's room. Was she was a psycho who tried to get rid of any woman who came into the Callaghan men's lives? But in the end, horny won out again.

I was walking in the dark meadow. My white silk gown was flowing in the gentle breeze. A full moon lit my path as I made my way barefoot to the willow. Under its weeping branches I entered its sanctuary. Twirling around its trunk, spinning with abandon, I hum a tune that is both mournful and heartfelt. In the distance I hear hoof beats approaching. I hide behind her trunk afraid of being caught alone. I can see the legs of a black horse. Someone has dismounted the beast, and is coming towards the Willow. Her branches are pulled aside revealing the form of a man. He is cast in shadows, but without sight, I know him. "Trobhad," he whispers, holding out his hand to me. I move toward him, taking his hand. Face to face, silence and darkness, move around us, as our hearts scream. "Barry," I say. "No," he says. "I am yer love. Will ya not see this, Petal? Will ya deny me...deny yer own heart?" As I tried to pull away, he says, "Deny me later," and kisses me. I wanted to fight it, I did. But the kiss, ah, the kiss! I melted, I felt my whole body going limp with a surrendering...given, not taken. I was giving into, giving up, all that I thought I had wanted, letting go of the child's wants, and giving into woman's needs. "I choose you," I whisper, over and over.

I woke to the sunrise pouring through my window. I had a weird pulsing sensation in between my brows. A hang over, I wondered, from two shots of whiskey? Not likely. The dream was still fresh and alive in my mind. WTF, I thought. My thoughts were quickly interrupted when something behind me in the bed, began to stir. I jumped up and prepared for Dracula to emerge from under the sheets.

Fitz said, peeking out from under the covers, "Can ya please close the damn curtains? It's too early to be awake!" she whined.

"What the hell? When, or better, how, did you get in here? The door was locked."

"I found a skeleton key in the drawer of my changin' table."

"Well, that sums up how."

"Scotty came to bed with me, but snuck out at three saying that Miss Elanor was up at four. He wanted her to think we were being proper. So, after he left, I tried to sleep. But my room gives me the creeps, so I tried the key and it worked. You were so out of it, ya didn't even move when I came in."

"No, I had a weird dream," I said, furrowing my brow. Unless drunk, I was a light sleeper. How could Fitz have come in and gotten into bed without my waking?

"I guess ya did. You were makin' funny sounds, and once you said, "I choose ya!" It was almost weird enough to make me go back to my own bed. I had forgotten that you were dream horny," she added.

I explained the dream, all except for the part of calling out her brother's name. I had had a crush on her brother Barry since we were kids. But when I started dating my mind was preoccupied. Now that I was working on ME and not dating, he spent more time in my head than I enjoyed. Now Cecil had blown in, and quite a storm he was. I knew I was more than attracted to him. And after almost six months 'without', I was starting to feel what was once a 'wanting', move into the realm of 'needing'. If my dreams were any reflection, I should probably be locked in a tower, until I had finished the paintings I had been hired to do.

She thought for a moment, "Sounds like ya dreamt about Martin's grandparents, from what ya told me about the walk you two took yesterday."

I didn't want to say that it felt more personal than that, but it did. Was Cecil the man from my dream? I wondered. After mulling it over, I was convinced that it was in fact just me being dream horny, nothing more.

We better get dressed," I said. "That damn gong, is gonna go off any minute."

Fitz whined a little, but I convinced her that coffee was served at breakfast for us American girls. May not have perked her up, but it did get her ass out of my sheets.

I opened my armoire and took in a shocked breath. Fitz came to my side.

"Wow, what a beautiful dressing gown," she stroked the white silk. "When did you get this?"

"That's a great question," I answered.

"It's not yers?"

"Have you ever known me to wear anything so...beautiful?"

"So where did it come from?"

"Again, great question. It looks like the one I wore in my dream." We looked at each other. "What time did you come into my room?"

"About 3:30am," Fitz responded. "What are ya thinkin', Janie?"

"I'm thinking you weren't the only one in my room last night," I said, shivering at the thought.

We dressed quickly and headed downstairs as the gong rang out. Fitz was back on her suspicions of Miss Elanor, so I assumed that it had been another night without sex for her. Sad thing was, I was starting to become more suspicious of Elanor as well. After all, she had been the one in the hallway when I was bathing.

Breakfast was eaten in haste by Scotty and Martin, who had business in the city. Rushing off, Scotty put a kiss on Fitz's cheek. Martin, without thinking, came and put a kiss on my cheek, "Have a good day, Janie my luv. I should be home by six, and shall enjoy seeing what you've bought for the paintin's."

I smiled, loving that I was wished a good day as well. But Cecil, Scotty and Elanor stared at Martin, who took on a look of abashment before hurrying off. What was the big deal? I wondered.

"What?" I asked Cecil after Martin and Scotty had left the hall.

"He called you, "My luv."

"Yeah?"

"That's what he used to call our mother."

"I'm sure it didn't mean anything," I said with a laugh, "Undoubtedly just a slip of the tongue."

Cecil looked unsure and Elanor stormed out of the room. Fitz and I both exchanged looks. It was harmless to me but the way everyone else was acting was making me uncomfortable.

I needed to change the subject, "I hate to ask Cecil, but can we also go to some clothing shops?" I asked.

"Sure, I don't mind shoppin' with ya. Dad gave me his card and said to make sure ya didn't spend a pingin."

"What?" I asked.

"A penny."

"I can buy my own clothes. I just didn't pack anything but jeans to wear."

"Dad made it very clear, everything on this visit, is on him."

"The materials, yes," I said. "Everything personal, I will pay for."

We started to argue a bit then Fitz broke in, "Oh for the love of Pete! Cecil, you won't win this one. Just let her buy her own damn clothes!"

Fitz wanted us out of the manor, and wasn't hiding this fact well, as she practically shoved us out the door. "Off ya go now, lots to do, you two!"

10

TO TOWN, WE GO

The Austin had been pulled around to the front of the Castle. I smiled widely as Cecil held open the door for me. Two-toned red and white, the top was down and ready to go. It was going to take some getting used to. Even though the Healey had the left side drive I was used to, driving in the left lane? Not so much. Off we sped, heading for the city.

We wound through hills and meadows, passing smaller farms. Cottages hid among the trees and looked like fairytales come to life. I could see myself living happily in one of these small homes surrounded by open skies and green fields. As we made our way to the city, the architecture drew me in further. I could almost see in my mind how it must have looked a hundred years ago. There were also pubs on every corner. This was my kind of town, I thought. Tourists holding small maps and carrying umbrellas lined the streets. I smiled at Cecil who took my hand and gave it a squeeze.

"What do you think of her?" he asked loudly over the engine's purr.

"She's amazing! I think I'm in love," I answered.

Most of the stores and shops were already open. He asked me, "Where to first?"

"Materials first, then I'll worry about finding clothes."

We headed into a large craft store that had everything. It was the equivalent of a candy store for my heart and mind. Mentally, I was already painting. The canvas, not nearly as large as I had imagined, would still need to be shipped. I needed to find a sales person so I could maneuver my needs. As we walked to a checkout counter, a beautiful brunette woman raised her head. Immediately I was ignored. She had honed in on Cecil, and looked only at him as she spoke.

"May I help ya?" she said to him in a sultry voice that somehow held more than a hint of innuendo.

Cecil leaned on the counter, "We need to do quite a bit of shoppin' in yer fine establishment. Could ya assist us?"

And the flirt is on, I thought to myself.

The woman leaned on the counter as well, purposely using her arms to push her breasts, further up, out of her low cut shirt, "Oh, are you a painter now then?" she asked.

I had to look away so she wouldn't see my eyes roll at her blatant attempt at a come on.

"No, I'm not," said Cecil, grinning at her and taking a good look at her 'well advertized' assets. Then he stood up and said, "But my Petal here, is," he extended his hand to me.

At his calling me Petal, my eyes snapped to him. The dream came flooding back.

"Oh," she said, shooting me something between a glare and a smirk. "Let me show ya what I have," she said to him, making another clear offer.

Pushing a large cart she walked us down the aisles. Her ass was shoved in a black pencil skirt and swayed from side to side with great exaggeration. I decided to let Cecil walk in front of me, so he wouldn't drool on my shoulder. I looked at all the different color palettes and chose the best oils I could find. I still needed brushes, of all sizes, pencils, a good eraser, linseed oil, and drop cloths. I used paper plates to mix my colors. I know! A little 'low rent' but they worked just fine for me and were easy clean up. Cecil had wandered off to find a sketch book for himself. When he was out of earshot, the counter girl said, “Handsome man ya have there.”

I wasn't caught off guard by her comment. She was exactly the type of woman who would hit on a man, right in front of who she believed to be his woman. I stared at the tube in my hand, thinking I would need way more green to paint the meadows. “He's not mine,” I said, like someone who was watching a dog for a friend.

“Oh really?” she raised her eyebrows.

“Nope,” I said, wishing she would just walk away.

“But he called ya his Petal?”

“Yeah, well, I'm not.”

“Well, if I were you I'd put my leash on that right now. The Callaghan boys are quite the catch.”

This comment finally drew my eyes to her. “You know Cecil and Scotty?”

She grinned like the cat who ate the canary, “Oh, everyone knows Cecil,” she grinned at me. “And Scotty...although he's a little...” she searched for a word, “Pure...for my likin', but he's still worth his weight in gold. You are aware that the boys will inherit a fortune?”

I narrowed my eyes. She was everything I hated about some women. “I'm aware,” I said, wanting to scratch her eyes out.

“Have ya been to the Castle then?” she asked, totally unaware, or possibly unconcerned, that she had offended me.

“I'm staying there,” I said blankly. I turned down the next aisle and Cecil was at the far end picking out charcoals.

“How does one get an invitation to the Castle these days?”

"Not sure," I said, hoping to end the conversation.

"How did you get an invite? I mean, if yer not his petal?"

"Mr. Callaghan liked my paintings. He's my employer."

"Well aren't you a lucky girl," she sighed, staring at Cecil at the end of the aisle. "Yer already in good with the family, if I could just get in the door I'd tag one of those Callaghan boys."

"Well, Scotty is off the market, and the other," I said, "Is right there."

"Ya don't mind if I take a stab at him?"

Jealously was starting to rear its ugly head. I wasn't sure what I felt for Cecil that was true. But I hoped he wouldn't end up with this kind of woman. "I have no claim," I finally emitted.

Well if ya don't want Mr. Money Bags, you can just step aside. Hell, I'd even take a shot at the father, if it meant never havin' to work again."

She had done it. She had flipped my switch. "Listen here you gold digging whore..." Cecil was coming within ear shot, and looked at me with questioning eyes.

"Ible," I added. "Just a horrible color, I can't use this," I handed the paint tube to the counter girl.

She narrowed her eyes at me. "We have another shade of green ya may like. It's called ENVY," she smirked.

"You know what I'm really looking for?" I took a step into her personal space and stared down into her eyes, "Blood Red."

At first she looked as though she might challenge me.

"Would you happen to know where I can find any?" I asked. My eyes burning with a touch of 'you really don't want to'.

Cecil saw me do some posturing of my own, but just grinned at me as the woman sauntered away. "Did I miss somethin'?" he asked, cocking his head.

We finished shopping without her help. Before I walked out of the store, I said, "I may be back for that Blood Red. Keep me in mind, okay? Come on Petal," I said to him.

Outside, Cecil asked, "What was all that about?"

"Nothing," I said, putting the few materials that weren't being shipped, in the trunk. "There are just some females that I refuse to think of as women. They should have a separate gender... and know their place among the rest of us," I added.

"Do ya know yers?" he asked, then put his hands over his heart.

I laughed, as he made a heart beating motion. "Cecil, why did you call me Petal?"

"It's the most beautiful part of a flower," he said blankly. "And I didn't call ya Petal."

I cocked my head questioningly.

"I called ya MY Petal."

I wanted to kiss him so badly. I stared at his mouth and bit my lower lip. "Back in the car, get back in the car!" my brain yelled. But other parts of me yelled to my brain, "You're no fun at all!"

We drove to a boutique whose outside was misleading. Inside, the place seemed to go on forever. Rack after rack. I began to fidget. I was no good at dressing ladylike. Another fear hit me as I pulled a day-glow sweater from the rack. The 80's are back? I loved 80's music, and 80's movies, but the clothing and hairstyles were horrid. I let out a sigh of pure exhaustion. "Maybe I should wait until Fitz can come help me shop?" I said to Cecil.

"Excuse me?" he said, feigning offense. "I can help ya, after all, who better than a man to dress a woman?"

"I have a feeling I'll end up back in my bondage suit."

"While I did enjoy the leather, you would be underdressed to some people at the Festival. Not to me," he added, "But some."

"Festival?" I questioned, like I had no idea what the word meant. "No one said anything about a festival."

"Sure, you'll undoubtedly be here for the Lugh-fest!"

"When is that?" I panicked.

"August first. And you'll probably be invited to be a judge."

"A judge of what?" I couldn't imagine.

"We always have an art competition."

"Really? That's awesome. So can anyone enter?"

"Not you," he smiled, "Only amateur artists. We also have cookin', bakin', harvest, beer, and quiltin' competitions...then there's 'the games'."

I stared at him, "Games?"

"Yeah, ridin', and somethin' akin to joustin'."

"That sounds dangerous."

"Not really, yer lookin' at a winner two years in a row."

I laughed, "Will you be entering this year?"

"I have to. It's my first year back. Need to show the lads that I haven't lost my edge."

I probably had a month of work here, or so. I tried to think of how long the 6 foot pin-up painting of Fitz had taken me. A week or so, I assessed. And these paintings would be more in depth, with tiny flowers, individual stones on the Castle and distillery; intricate work.

"What is Lugh-fest, exactly?" I asked.

"It's the halfway point between summer solstice and fall equinox."

"So it's like a harvest festival?" I asked.

"It's like the beginning of harvest, basically," he laughed. "The whole town is invited to the Castle. Dad provides all the food and drink. We play games of strength, and matches are made. He grinned at me." He took on a childlike excitement. "Then, at midnight, all the people run through the meadow to a huge bonfire. We throw candy, fruit, and whiskey into the flames.

"Huh, sounds like fun," I nodded, wondering why anyone would throw away candy and booze.

"It's my second favorite time of year, after Samhain that is." he added.

I was still going through racks and getting super frustrated. Finally, Cecil walked me to the dressing room and told me to just wait there while he picked out outfits. So in the little stall I stood, awaiting his picks. Finally, he called out, and I put my hand up so he'd go to the right room. I opened the door and took half a rack of clothes from him."Ya are goin' to model these for me?" he questioned.

"Sure, I could use your opinion in lieu of having Fitz here. How did you know what size to get?"

"I lived with you. Of course I know your size, all of them," he grinned.

"Cecil, you stayed at my house for two weeks. We didn't live together."

"Closest I've ever been."

The first outfit had me raising my eyebrows. I walked out of the stall and said, "I can't help but notice, this is roughly the same skirt and shirt the girl at the craft store was wearing," I looked down at my overly exposed bosom.

"Yep," he said, staring and grinning.

"So, I see she made an impression," I tried not to sound bothered.

"No, that's not my type anymore," he said passively. "I just knew I wanted to see YOU dressed like that. Ya look amazin'."

I tried to hide the fact that I was flattered. "My breast are kinda..."

He cut me off, "Amazin'!" he said again.

"I'm a little more under-dressed than I'm comfortable with. Is this what happens when I let you pick out my clothes?" He just grinned as I went back to the drawing board, so to speak.

I tried on several more outfits. More dresses than I had owned during my whole lifetime. Finally, I came across an outfit, and said, "Nice try," I handed him the red corset with matching g-string panty.

"Ya really can't blame me for tryin'!" he smiled.

After I had picked out a dozen outfits, I had to get shoes to match. This for me was why shopping was so exhausting. After clothes, came shoes, followed by purses, and ending with accessories to match the purse, to match the shoes, to match the outfit. Shopping completed, we decided to have a little lunch and a well deserved pint, before heading back to the manor.

Stopping at a little pub and grill, I perused the menu. After deciding on the fish and chips, I dove into my Wiccan B Ale they had on tap. Up at the bar sat four men who kept looking over their shoulders at us. They were in their early thirties, I imagined. Dressed like warehouse workers. One in particular, seemed to have an issue with Cecil's button down shirt and jeans.

"Guess the little rich boy doesn't have to work," said the angry man, as the three others tried to quiet him.

Cecil acted as though he hadn't heard a thing, but the man continued his rant regardless of his friend's pleas. "Never done a hard day's work in his whole wretched life, I imagine." Turning towards us, he said, "Is that the way you like em Miss, little well-dressed pampered Petals?"

I got it now: When a man called a woman a Petal, 'compliment'. But when a man called another man Petal: 'not so much'.

Cecil very calmly said, "Maybe you've had too much to drink, friend?"

Again his friends tried to hush him, but he pulled out of their grasps and said, "Oh, am I yer friend, boy?"

"I am no boy, friend!" Cecil answered.

"That's what I call a man who lives off his father and never bothers to get his hands dirty."

"Why, my good man, you must think ya know me well, to make such a derogatory smear of my person," Cecil smiled. "Although yer opinion undoubtedly means somethin' to you, I can assure ya, it has no bearin' on my life. So ya may as well keep it."

I was starting to get an uneasy feeling in my gut as the man walked over to the table. Cecil moved his chair away from the table, but didn't stand. "So, my opinion means nothin' to ya?" asked the man.

"Less than that, I'm afraid," Cecil responded.

The man was huge, six foot five, and almost as wide at the shoulders. His bald head was shining with sweat. His red beard was wild as any Viking's. He had arms that looked like they had been borrowed from a gorilla. One of them bore a burn scar from his wrist to his elbow. His hands were as big as anvils, and looked as strong.

"Would ya like to stand like a man, then?"

"Cecil no!" I said, shaking my head. "Let's just go," I was panicking. The man's friends had turned their backs to the situation. I was busy looking for the quickest exit.

"It's okay, Janie," Cecil said, standing. He and the man were sizing each other up. Cecil fell horribly short in both size and girth. "Take yer best shot," Cecil said.

The man's eye began to twitch. Before I knew it, the man's hands were coming at Cecil. They were bigger than Cecil's whole head. I jumped up quickly with no idea of what my body had planned for the next two seconds. I grabbed my pint glass...and before I could do anything, the man and Cecil were hugging. A huge bear hug where Cecil was lifted off his feet and swung about like a rag doll.

"Ah, ya big Petal," the man said. "How the hell have ya been?"

"Grand!" Cecil said, having the breath hugged out of him. "How are ya, Big Dave?" he asked, being set right on his feet.

I was still trying to absorb what had just happened. The guys at the bar and the waitress looked relieved.

"I do believe yer lady was gonna crack my skull with the pint she's holdin'," Dave said.

Cecil smiled, "I do believe ya may be right. Were ya gonna ding his brow, Janie?"

"I don't know," I stammered, then downed my beer, hoping it would cure my fear induced adrenaline rush.

"Janie," said Cecil, "This is Big Dave. One of my school boy chums, and the greatest friend a man could have. Dave, this is Miss Janie."

I held out my hand, and the gentle giant took it to his lips for a kiss, "Lovely to meet ya."

"You as well," I said, finally finding my smile.

We sat with Big Dave, ate and had a few pints. He worked at Martin's distillery and was one of the nicest men I had ever met. A far cry from needing his head dinged. Dave said he was excited for the festival, seeing as how Cecil was home for the first time in many years. He showed us pictures of his wife and children on a cell phone that looked like a child's toy in his massive hand. I came to see how the two men adored each other.

"Ah, Miss, I could tell ya stories," said Big Dave.

"Don't ya dare," Cecil laughed. "I'm still tryin' to win her over."

"Ah," said Dave, winking at me. "A woman who'll put ya through yer paces? And put a ding on the skull of someone who messes with ya? I'd say ya found yerself a keeper. Don't screw it up!" Dave added, smiling.

"Doin my best," Cecil laughed.

"Well, I must be gettin' home to Hanna and the babes. Was wonderful to catch up, Hanna will be so sorry she missed this. But you'll see all of us at the festival, if not before."

Standing, the two hugged, "Tell Hanna, "Hello" for me," Cecil said.

I too, was hugged and damn near disappeared in his embrace.

Back in the car, heading to the Castle, Cecil said, "I'm sorry if Dave scared ya at first."

"I'm just glad I got to meet him. He's a nice man," I added.

"You were gonna clock 'em, weren't ya?"

"I just didn't want him to spill my beer while he was kicking your ass," I said.

Cecil grinned and brought my hand to his lips for a quick kiss. "Right," he smiled. I had to laugh. To think I was going to clock that sweet giant. I guess I should thank God that I'm not too quick on my feet. Not that I thought for one moment, that a beer pint to the head would have stopped Dave or fazed him in the slightest. Now...had Fitz been there, it may have been a different story. I couldn't help but wonder what Fitz had been up to all day. Thinking about it brought back that nervous feeling. Had she and Elanor banged heads? Fitz was overly focused, due to a lack of sex. And Elanor...I was pretty sure, was crazy, if not a homicidal maniac.

We drove back through the meadows, passing small farms and cottages, before coming to the wall and iron gates of the Manor. Cecil unloaded my bags and we started to my room when Elanor appeared from nowhere.

"Cecil my boy, I know yer NOT headin' up to Miss Jane's room, correct?"

"I was just helpin' her with her bags," he stammered, like a kid.

"Let Mary help her," Elanor sneered at me. "Proper women do not entertain men in their rooms."

Mary scurried up to him and took the bags from his hands.

Elanor had a way of making me feel indecent. I had always been the good girl. Now I knew what it must feel like for Fitz with my mom. Not a fan, I concluded.

Mary and I headed up to my room. Putting down my bags, I thanked Mary before heading to Fitz's room. I knocked, but there was no answer. Opening the door and stepping inside I wondered, "Where the hell could she be?" Scotty and Martin were still in the city. I turned to see her coming into the room, dressed in all black. She looked like a cat burglar.

I let out a giggle, "Why are you dressed like that?" I asked.

"This is what one wears to go snoopin'!" she did a little spin so I could get the full effect.

"In the middle of the night, yes. In broad daylight, you're just conspicuous," I pointed out.

She looked down at herself, "Yer right. I'm gonna change. Then we have somewhere to check out."

"Great," I said, realizing that she was Sherlock again.

"Come on, Watson," she said, after changing into normal clothes.

11

SHERLOCK, INDEED

"Fitz, seriously, I can't walk with you on my back!" I flared.

"It's not my fault that yer like a huge door blocking out all the light," she hissed.

"You are more than welcome to take the flashlight and go in front of me," I hissed back.

"No, I'm good. As usual, I have yer back."

"Very comforting, considering we already know what's behind us...a closed door...to a secret passageway...in a 300 year old Castle!"

As we descended the stairs, the tiny beam of light bounced off the grey stone walls. I was starting to have that trapped feeling I had in the Jet on the way here. I had Cecil to keep me calm then. This was a whole other 'bunch of scary' for me. Breathe, I told myself. How the hell did I get here?

Fitz brought me back from my slow dance with hyperventilation. "Well, I bet yer glad I grabbed the flashlight off the desk before we got trapped in here."

"Don't you mean before you called me a pussy, and pushed me in here?"

"It's always funny to me how two people can remember a shared incident, so differently," she asserted.

I was busy doing a slow count to ten, so I wouldn't strangle her. "This isn't funny, Fitz. Not even a little. We are currently stuck in a secret passageway, in a 300 year old Castle, and we have no idea how to get out of here. Not funny, Fitz. Not funny!"

"You are so dramatic sometimes. Do ya honestly think no one will be looking fer us?" she asked.

"And that's a whole other ball of shit...what do we say when we're found? How do we explain our snooping? I mean of course, in a way that doesn't end with your boyfriend's dad, kicking us out on our asses!" I could almost feel her eyes rolling around in her head, as I continued forward. I turned on her, "How the hell did you find this passage, anyway?"

"Daniel," she said.

"Daniel? Who are you talking about?"

"Daniel the stable boy."

"Why would he tell you about this place....and what makes you think he won't rat on us?"

"Because, I bribed him."

"With what?"

"He asked for a kiss, so I promised him one."

"Wrong on so many levels," I said, moving forward again. "First, you're dating his boss. That's a big one. And second, he's practically a fetus."

"I didn't tell him I would kiss him."

I stopped walking, and Fitz slammed into me. "What do you mean? You said you promised him a kiss."

"I did," she began slowly, "But I figured I'd give him a kiss on the cheek, and we'd be good to go."

"Yeah..."

"Well, as it turns out, he didn't want a kiss from me."

"I'm lost. That's saying a lot considering where we are."

Silence bounced off the walls.

"This is where things get muddled," she said.

"What do you mean muddled?" I asked.

"It means confused, jumbled..."

"I know what the word means, Fitz. What I'm asking is, to what extent have things become muddled?"

"Sorry, Miss Vocabulary, It's not like I've ever heard ya use the word in a sentence. How am I supposed to know, that you know..."

"Fitz!" I interrupted. "Explain please!"

"He wants a kiss... from the American," she said, slowly.

"You promised a kiss...from me? Are you kidding?"

"It's not a big deal," Fitz said, backing away slightly. "One kiss, Janie. It's not like yer seein' anyone, or datin' anyone, or have any intentions towards anyone so..."

I cut her off, "Yeah, you're not making it any better. And seriously Fitz, he's like thirteen."

"Oh please, he's eighteen. I made sure he was of legal age."

"Well thank God you at least did that before you prostituted me."

"He's a handsome lad, Janie, and nicely built. I didn't think you'd mind so much. Plus, like I said, he wants a kiss from the American girl."

"He does know I'm Irish, right?"

"Sorry honey, doesn't count," she said.

"What do you mean, it doesn't count? I'm of Irish descent!"

She laughed a little, "No, I'm Irish, born in Ireland. You, are like Guinness made in the states. Ya may be an Irish recipe, but ya were still made in America. At best, yer Irish-American."

I thought about this for a moment. "That seems somewhat...prejudice, I think."

"Sorry, but that's the way it works. He sees ya as an American."

"Outline this kiss for me. What is he expecting exactly?"

"Jesus Janie, really? He wants a kiss! Ya remember how to kiss, don't ya?"

I took in long deep breaths.

"Why are ya breathin' so weird?" Fitz asked.

"I'm trying not to kill you," I said, and kept walking.

"I need to snoop, Janie. Scotty's been actin' really strange since we got here."

She was right about that. Scotty was almost being secretive. But most women would ask their boyfriend what had him so preoccupied. Fitz wasn't most women, I reminded myself. And because of that...here we are.

Up ahead the flashlight caught something in its beam, and I stopped dead in my tracks.

"Ouch," said Fitz, running into me again. "What the hell?"

"There's something up ahead." There was a pause before I said, "I don't think you're gonna like it, Fitz."

"What?" What is it?" she asked, practically crawling on top of me. "Is that a...skeleton?"

I did a slow nod. "I believe it is."

"What the bloody hell?" she said, as we moved closer to the bones.

The skeleton was in a seated position against the wall, legs out in front of him, with his arms above his head hanging by shackles.

"You should probably take a closer look?" said Fitz.

"At what?"

"Maybe there's some clue as to who this was."

"Who the hell am I, Nancy Drew?" I squeaked. "I believe YOU are Sherlock!"

"Just take a closer look, Janie," she said, nudging me towards the bones.

I let out a sigh, and moved closer. "This is odd."

"What?" Fitz asked quickly. "What's wrong with him?"

"The obvious answer is, 'dead' is what's wrong with him. But..."

"But what?"

"There are no clothes around him. I mean, I know there must be rats down here..."

"What?" said Fitz, looking frantically at the ground.

"Well, there's rat shit on the floor next to the bones."

"Eww, eww, eww!" Fitz began to hop from foot to foot.

"Really Fitz? You don't "Ewww" at the skeleton, but the mere thought of a rat turns you into a giant pussy? You're one of the toughest women I know, act like it!"

"I don't do vermin," she began hotly, "I don't date it, hang out with it, or want it anywhere near me!"

"Fine, back to the skeleton, there are no clothes."

"And?"

"And, I don't know! Wouldn't there be scraps of clothing, like on the 'Pirates of the Caribbean' ride...the skeletons have clothes on!"

"I don't know," Fitz said, doing a palms-up.

"Neither do I. I'm not a CSI, but it seems odd. I mean, was he put here naked? Did the rats eat his clothes?"

Fitz "Ewwed" again.

"Wait...there's something on his ankle." I bent down and inspected the bone, 'Made in China'? I said out loud.

"Okay," said Fitz, "Now how did he get here from China? Was he a prisoner, left here to die?"

"Fitz, I'm gonna need you to think about this," I said.

"I am," she huffed at me.

"I'm gonna need you to think harder, Fitz."

After a moment or two, I saw realization dawn on her. "If ya tell anyone about this, I'll beat yer ass!"

"Seriously Fitz, do you think you have a 'Made in Ireland' stamp on your tibia?"

"No, you ass! I was thrown off by the thought of rats. Plus, I would have a 'Made in a 55 Bel Air' stamp," she said, with her hands on her hips.

I nodded slowly, "Yeah, I don't need to know that much about your procreation."

"Prude!" she exclaimed.

"So, I guess we move forward," I said.

"Guess so."

Onward we went, until we came to a turn in the passageway that led to another staircase. Up we went till we came to a landing that opened into a slightly larger room. At least the walls no longer felt like they were caving in on me. Breathe, I told myself again. Light was pouring in from two tiny holes in the wall covered by flaps of fabric. It looked like a door of sorts. As we moved closer, we could hear muffled voices. We each took a hole and looked into what appeared to be another office. Into the room, came Scotty and his father, Martin. They were mid conversation.

"I don't know what to tell her. This could end our relationship," Scotty said.

"Maybe you're not givin' her enough credit, son. Maybe she'll understand completely."

"I'm not sure I would, Dad. It's a game changer, for sure. All I can hope is, it's not a deal breaker."

"Well, if it is, you'll have to re-evaluate yer choice. That's all there is to it." Scotty nodded as his father came and put his arm around him, "Some things are more important." Martin then grabbed a ledger off the desk, and the two exited the room.

We waited until they were out of earshot, then Fitz said, "Did you hear that? Something is going on, something that concerns our relationship!"

"Yeah, I heard," I said, giving the door a push. It popped open and we stepped out from behind a painting of a mildly amused woman from the 1700's, I guessed, standing in an Oak Grove. "You shouldn't jump to conclusions though."

"Were ya hearin' the same conversation I heard? Scotty said it may be a deal breaker. That doesn't exactly sound good, does it?"

I had to agree, but there had to be a logical explanation. And snooping seemed like a difficult way to find it. "Can we get out of here, already?"

We pushed the door open, and came face to face with Elanor. She looked just as surprised as we were.

"What are ya doin' in here?" she asked.

"Looking for Scotty and Martin," I answered as calmly as I could. "We thought we saw them come this way."

"Really?" asked Elanor. "And how did ya find Master Scotty's office?"

I looked at the door we had just come through. It was a mock wall with no doorknob.

"You don't know what Scotty and I talk about when we're in bed together," Fitz answered.

My eyes shot to Fitz. Good Fitz, I thought. Throw fuel on the fire!

Elanor's lips pursed. Fitz's eyes narrowed. I prayed... "Our Father, who art in Heaven...

"The gentlemen are in Martin's office. Would you like to come this way...or go back through the secret passageway?" Elanor asked, smiling wickedly.

"Is there a secret passageway?" Fitz asked, returning the wickedness.

I just wanted to tell her everything, confess all of our sins and get it over with. But Fitz was going to play the cat and mouse game with her.

The two women held their stares, before Elanor marched off.

"We've been caught," I said. "I'm begging you, let's just fess up, and get it over with."

"No," Fitz said, "Martin told us to treat this place like home. I'm sure that included some exploring." She squinted like she was trying to do long division in her head. "She wants to catch us doing somethin' that can't be dismissed."

"Like what?"

"I'm not sure yet, but from here on out, no more snooping! She'll be watching us like a hawk. Circlin'...eyein' us...huntin' us...choosin' her time to strike," she continued.

"Yeah, I get it Fitz," I interrupted. "Can we get the hell out of here already?"

I was more than happy to hear Fitz say, "No more snooping." With my clumsiness, inability to lie, and good old fashioned Catholic guilt, I was more circus clown than spy.

We headed back to my room to dress for dinner. Finally, I got to tell Fitz about my day.

"Boy, that Big Dave guy sounds like a lot of fun."

"He was. You'll get to meet him at the Lugh-Festival."

"Oh, I can't wait. Dad told me what a blast he always had at the Lugh-Fest. Sounds like a great time."

"So you already knew about it?"

"Well, yeah. It's an old tradition here."

I nodded, "Huh."

"Huh what?"

"It just seems like it's a really big deal, and no one told me about this huge Festival. I mean, I understand that it's like a huge celebration?"

Fitz's eyes got hazy. "The tradition is as old as the trees. We celebrate the beginning of Harvest and the slow dying of the summer sun."

I nodded my head, like this all made perfect sense to me. It didn't, but any excuse to drink and make merry was usually welcomed.

"So, did ya really threaten the craft store girl?" Fitz asked.

"I seriously couldn't believe the audacity of that woman, Fitz. And to say she'd even "Take a shot at the father, if it meant never having to work again." Who says shit like that?"

"The nerve! I'da cracked her pretty little face," Fitz responded. "After all, Martin is to be my father-in-law. If Scotty ever proposes, that is. I'm startin' to worry, Janie."

I stopped unloading my bags. "Fitz, whatever is going on, everything will be fine. I promise."

"Pinky?" she asked, sticking out her little finger so I could lock mine with hers.

"Pinky," I said. "Now, stop your worrying and check out my new duds."

"What? Are we at a 70's disco? Duds? Really?" she smiled and started going through my bags. "Wow, ya got some really cute things. I was expecting...well I don't know exactly, maybe a 501's leisure suit."

"Oh you're so funny."

"Really, did ya pick all this out, yerself?" she asked, holding up the black pencil skirt and satin top.

"Well, no. Cecil picked the clothes, had me try them on then vetoed what he didn't think looked good."

"I'm surprised there's no lingerie then."

"Oh, he tried," I laughed.

"Have ya given any more thought to him?

I nodded, "I'm trying not to be won over by his charm but, it's getting harder."

"That's what he said." she joked.

I gave her a shitty grin.

"Am I wrong?" she asked.

We dressed for dinner. Me: in my pencil skirt and red satin top, with a pair of black heels and Fitz in a red Geisha dress. I loved this look on her. It was like Japanese/Irish fusion. The gong went off, and I didn't jump, so I was programming easily enough.

Down the stairs we went, through the long hallway to the dining room. The men folk, who usually arrived before us somehow, stood as we entered.

"Ladies," Martin said, stopping a conversation he was having with his boys. He walked over and put a kiss on each of our hands. Cecil and Scotty moved behind our chairs and pulled them out for us to sit. Taking my seat I noted the uncomfortable electricity was back.

The meal was served, salad first. Elanor looked like she was just waiting to pounce.

"So, tell me of yer day, ladies," Martin said, smiling.

Cecil and I told him of our outing, and having purchased all the necessary tools for the paintings.

"They should be here tomorrow," Cecil added.

Then we told him about meeting Big Dave.

"Janie was gonna crack him one with her pint glass," Cecil laughed.

Martin grinned, and raised his glass to me. "More and more, ya remind me of my dearest Margaret. If ever I was to find myself in harm's way, she would be right by my side."

Elanor sneered from behind his back.

"That Big Dave is a treasure. I wouldn't trade him for a hundred men," Martin added.

"He's a big man. I imagine not many people can do the work that he can," I said.

"Oh, it's not just that. He's a loyal man. Loyal to his job, his family...and mine," he said, looking at Cecil.

Cecil nodded to his father.

I felt something, in the way they looked at each other. There was a story behind Big Dave. I could feel it. But no one elaborated, so I decided not to ask. Even though I was now very curious I knew he and Cecil had been friends all their lives.

"To Big Dave," Cecil raised his glass. We all followed in turn, "To Big Dave!"

The Prime Rib was served. All I could think of was how much weight this place was going to stack onto me. Truth was, I wasn't used to eating so much, so often. Everything was full fat, real butter, cheese, cream and meat. Don't get me wrong, I loved every bite. But as soon as my jeans start to get tight, I'd have to monitor my servings. Unlike Fitz, my body stores fat.

Finally, Martin asked the question I had been dreading. "And Fitz, what did you do today?"

Elanor eyed Fitz with an evil grin.

Fitz answered, "I had a long bath, painted my toenails then Janie and I did a little explorin'."

I was trying not to panic, but couldn't help but wonder what the hell would come out of her mouth.

"So what did ya explore?" Martin asked.

Elanor looked like she had trapped a rat in the pantry. Almost giddy at the thought of us being cornered.

"Well, Janie and I," my eyes went wide, "We thought we saw ya go into yer office. We looked for ya, but ya weren't there. Then I saw that beautiful globe on the side table. I had to get a closer look."

Martin looked at Fitz and asked, "Did ya move the globe?"

"Aye," said Fitz.

"Then I imagine, you found the secret passageway?" he asked, straight faced.

"Aye," Fitz said again.

I started to take deeper breaths, so I wouldn't hyperventilate.

"Did ya go into the passageway?" Martin asked, before taking a sip of his wine.

"I did," said Fitz, with her jaw set. She wasn't going to let Elanor have the fun of telling on us. "Even pushed Janie in," she added.

I mentally started packing. Farewell Ireland.

After a moment, Martin smiled, "I love that curious heart of yours," he winked. "Did ya see my skeleton?" he asked, like a boy talking of his favorite toy.

"We did," Fitz grinned. I let out a breath I had been holding. Elanors face squished up, and she made a hasty exit.

"Oh, I was a young lad when I found the tunnels," started Martin. "My father was fit to be tied. He didn't want me playin in them since some of them locked at both ends. But he just couldn't keep me out of 'em," he laughed. "One night, I didn't show to the dinner table, so he and the staff had to search the whole Castle. He finally found me curled up in a ball, sleepin', in the very same passageway you two were in. I was too tired to walk, so he carried me to my bed. He tanned my hide I don't mind tellin' ya. But within days, he changed his mind, and had all the tunnels fixed so I could play in them. Dad said, "It's part of yer heritage. You should know the Castle, as well as its history. That very next day, I was to learn the Castle's long, hard and sometimes frightenin' history. Most of the tunnels, had been formed to save the women and children durin' times of war. A few even lead as far out as the next town. People would use them to find their way to the safety of the Castle's inner walls, if the countryside was under siege. One ends in the dungeon, although we don't really go down there. I was told when I was a boy that it was haunted. And I only needed one trip to the dungeon to believe that statement."

My brows met with fear. Fear that Fitz's curiosity had been piqued. Mental note: Do not go to the dungeon.

"The suits of armor," Martin continued, "That line the hallways, were all used durin' real battles, by real knights. Most wore light armor, but a few wore full. Those are kept here to remind us of our heritage. Of battles fought, won and lost. I have enjoyed falling in love with this place. I hope the two of you will as well," he smiled to Fitz and me. "Now, durin' the Samhain Festival, I give tours to kids and their parents. We decorate for the event. That's what Walter is doing down there."

"Walter?" Fitz and me, asked in unison.

"The skeleton," said Scotty."

Martin nodded, as if this summed up Walter. I decided not to ask. I was good with Walter, from China.

With dinner coming to a close, Martin announced that he was tired and was heading to bed early. Scotty and Fitz looked like maybe they were gonna try having 'alone' time again. So, Cecil asked me if I'd like to change and take a walk to the stables with him. I knew I needed to call my mother, and Betty, but I also needed to walk off dinner. Getting back into a pair of 501's also sounded fabulous, so I went up to change.

I passed by a suit of armor and shivered. I now understood that whoever had worn this had seen war here at the Castle. It was an amazing, and slightly horrifying thought.

In my Dracula room, I still had the feeling that I was being watched and wondered if there were any tunnels that led to my room. I had no way to explain the appearance of the dressing gown in my armoire. Changing as quickly as I could, I turned away from the scary-ass picture and faced the corner (Like you do when you don't when you think the boogeyman can see you). Hurrying downstairs, I met Cecil at the front door. It was only eight o'clock, so we had some time before the sun set. As the door opened, a slight breeze met me. 'Bushy Brows', or Mr. Briggs, as the rest of the world called him, handed me my sweater. Cecil took the sweater and ran the sleeves up my arms, giving them a squeeze.

"Alone at last," he said.

"We were alone together all day," I laughed.

"What can I say? I can't get enough of ya." He offered his elbow and I wound my arm through his. Down the walk we went to the stables. Only upon our arrival did I remember the scene between young Daniel and Cecil. I also was reminded of the fact that Fitz had pimped out a kiss from me. How was I going to explain that to Cecil? I was grateful Daniel was nowhere to be seen.

"Come," Cecil said, starting down the row, "I want you to meet my baby. Watch this!" he smiled. "Baby?" he called. One of the horses 'neighed' a response. "Baaaaby?" he said, again. Her huge black head poked out of the last stall on the right. She neighed louder, and kicked at the stall door. As we approached, she began prancing in her stall.

I knew nothing about horses other than they were huge. She was at least that.

"This is Babygirl," he said, petting her nose. "She's an Arabian, and faster than lightning. I've had her since I was 16. Say hello to Janie, Babygirl."

She looked at me, and I swear her eyes slit when she saw me.

"Go ahead, pet her!" he said.

I was apprehensive, but brought my hand to her nose. Her eyes widened as she pulled her head away from my hand.

"I don't think she wants me to," I said.

Babygirl shook her head as if she was answering me.

"Nonsense, she's just shy," he said. "Try again!"

I reached out again, and the damn beast tried to bite my

fingers. "You know what," I said, pulling my hand away, "I think I should leave her alone." At that comment, the damn horse, nodded.

"Be nice Babygirl," he said, in a babytalk voice I had never heard him use. It made me giggle. I had to admit, it was cute to see how he and Babygirl loved each other. She was nuzzling at his hand and trying to get him to pet her. But every time he stopped to talk to me, she gave me the evil eye. "Maybe tomorrow, we can go for a ride?" he said.

I shook my head, "I don't think that's a good idea. I've never ridden anything bigger than a pony!"

"You'll ride Babygirl." Both the horse, and me, snapped our heads at him.

"Oh I really don't think that's a good idea," Babygirl nodded in agreement.

"She's the best horse out of the bunch," he whispered so the other horses wouldn't hear. At that comment, she took on a look of contemplation. "I know she'll keep ya safe." Her eyes narrowed. Shit, I thought. We fed all the horses carrot and apple pieces. One of them, Buddy, a twenty-eight year old quarter horse, let me love on him despite sensing my fear. He was caramel colored with a white nose and chest. According to Cecil, he was the oldest in the stable. But he was definitely my favorite. If I had a choice of which beast to ride, it would be him. But I'd feel guilty about riding a horse that was enjoying his golden years. It seemed like I would be putting him out.

"So, 6am? Nothin' better than a sunrise ride."

I thought of protesting, but then heard Fitz's voice in my head, "Live a little!" What was the worst that could happen? When I thought about it that way, I was scared shitless.

We walked the property and watched the sun setting. Reds, gold, and purples lit up the sky with fire before slowly extinguishing themselves. A light rain began to fall and Cecil decided we should head back before we got soaked to the bone. He was right. By the time we made it to the front doors we were caught in a downpour that left us both soggy.

"Are ya tired?" Cecil asked.

"No, I'm soaked," I laughed.

"Would ya like to meet me for a nightcap? After you've changed, of course," he smiled at my soaked attire.

I knew Fitz was hoping to see God tonight, so I agreed. "Okay."

"Pajama party?" he winked.

"Sounds good."

"Meet ya in dad's study in twenty minutes?"

"Alright," I said and headed up the stairs.

"It's a date then," he added, heading to the South Wing.

I made it to my room and checked my cell. One missed call from Betty. I took a breath and pressed play for the message.

"Puddin?" Betty began, "I'm here, about two houses down from yours. I borrowed my cleaning lady's car, and I'm wearin' a big floppy hat, so your mom won't spot me."

The thought was funny. Betty was conspicuous no matter what she wore, or drove. It was part of her charm.

"There was some guy starin' at me from the bushes of the house next to yers."

Mr. Mendlebaum, my nosey pervert of a neighbor, I figured.

"He's kinda creepy, Puddin. I'm gonna have an electric fence put between yer two houses," she joked. At least I think it was a joke. I never knew with Betty. I'd kinda love to see that, though. ZAAAP! Bye pervert.

"Anyway, your mom showed up in that pimp Caddy she drives..."

Yep, I thought. That's how I described it, too.

"Then that guy from the other day showed up, the blonde guy. I swear he looks about thirty. He disappeared into the house for an hour or so then left. A few minutes later, your mom got back in the pimpmobile and left as well. I followed her to her house where she went in and stayed in.

I wondered how long Betty sat in front of my parent's house.

"I sat there for an hour or so, before heading back home. Okay, Puddin, that's all I have for today. I don't know if any of this helps. I miss ya, kid. Call me when you can. Bye now," she rang off.

A blonde guy, I pondered. About thirty? Either Betty's eyesight was really off and she didn't figure age well, or she was mistaken. I couldn't see my mother, in her mid forties, with a thirty year old. Even without the whole overly pious, prude thing she had going on. The more I thought about it, the more an affair seemed unlikely.

I put on my PJ's: A red plaid flannel night shirt that went to my ankles. I looked in the mirror. Not sexy, I surmised. Why would I want to be? I wondered. Maybe I should wear the dressing gown someone had left in my armoire? Maybe then I could find out where it came from. Part of me assumed it was from Cecil. But, what if it wasn't? I couldn't figure out what bothered me more about it, "Who?" as in "Who" was in my room, or "When?" I decided to change into the beautiful dressing gown. If Cecil did leave it for me he'd say something. I looked at myself in the mirror. The deep plunging neckline displayed the girls quite well. This was going to take some courage, I thought. I took a deep breath, set my jaw, and went for it.

Picturing myself as a beautiful Hollywood starlet, I glided down the stairs. Mr. Briggs saw me and raised his brows.

"Good evening Miss Janie. Can I assist ya in some way?"

"No, no," I smiled. "Off for a nightcap with Cecil."

"Very good, Miss," he bowed.

From the way Briggs looked at me, I knew I had hit one out

of the park. I felt gorgeous and powerful as I opened the door to the study.

"Wow," Cecil said, looking me up and down. "Ya look amazin'."

"So you've never seen this gown before?" I asked, raising my brows.

He shook his head, "No. I don't think ya ever got out of jammie pants when I was staying with ya," he smiled.

He was right about that. After the concussion I didn't move a bunch, much less play dress up.

"It kind of looks familiar, though, in a way. Maybe I dreamed it?" he said.

Now I was perplexed. He wasn't screwing with me, was he?

He was in a pair of grey sweat pants and a white T-shirt. Seeing him, I became aware of the fact that no matter what he wore, he would look sexy to me. This was unsettling in my current state of mind. Horny. He had already poured me a whiskey that sat on the table in front of the couch he was sitting on. So I guess I was expected to join him on the couch instead of one of the chairs. He patted the spot next to him, "I don't bite." I started to sit, "Often," he added.

"So, six am," I said, taking my seat and the drink.

"We ride!" he said.

"I'm not sure Babygirl is right for me. Maybe a slower horse would be more my pace?"

"I trust her...with my life," he added.

"Well, maybe with your life, but mine is the one in question."

"What makes ya think there's any difference between the two, to me?"

I stared at him for a moment.

"Surely ya are aware of how I feel about ya?" he finally asked.

My heart began to race. I took a big gulp of whiskey and tried to steady myself. "Actually, no, I'm not certain that I do."

"Do ya think I'm incapable of..."

I waited for him to finish, but nothing. "Of...what?" I pressed.

"Ya know," he said.

I shook my head, "Not really. I mean, if you can't even say what it is that you feel, why would you assume that I know?"

"Look, I'm not good at this," he said.

"This what?" I did the hand-roll, hoping he would elaborate. "I have no idea what we are. Or what you want from me. Other than the obvious, that is."

"Sex?" he questioned. "Is that what ya think all of this is about?"

"I don't know!" I answered, getting more frazzled than I wanted to. "Okay, yes! I assume your desire toward me...is based on sex."

He looked hurt, and even though I had said exactly what I felt, it left me feeling like an ass. "Am I wrong?" I asked, doing a palms-up.

"Do I want ya in my bed? Underneath me?" he asked.

I blushed at the thought and got a little tingly at his wording.

"Aye, I do. So sue me! I want ya! Have wanted ya, since the day we met. I absolutely crave ya!" He was frazzled now, too. "Ya drive me crazy, ya know? I get the feelin', that yer holdin' out for somethin', someone, that's never gonna happen. And because of that, ya won't even give me a chance, or let me in!"

"As what?" I fired back. "As a lay?" He looked like I wounded him, but I couldn't shut up because he had wounded me. "I don't want to be a fling?" I stated. "Or a conquest! Another notch on your already very full headboard?"

"Is that what bothers ya? I've had a lot of sex?"

"You are capable of having sex that doesn't mean anything, that's what bothers me! You were ready to bed me the very first night we met. I don't go around humping everything that moves, with no attachment! Sex has to mean something to me!" I exclaimed.

"Yeah?" he asked. "And how has that worked out for ya? I'll tell ya, it left ya not only dumped, but cheated on, broken hearted, and then assaulted! That's better, right?"

I stared at him for a moment before finishing my drink and standing. My eyes started to fill with tears, "Thanks for the nightcap," I said, and walked to the door.

"Janie, wait," he said. "I...I..."

"I put my hand up to stop him from whatever he was going to say. "6am," I said, and shut the door behind me.

I raced up the stairs and ran into Martin on his way down.

"Hello, Janie," he said, taking notice of my watering eyes. "Are ya okay, luv?"

The compassion in his voice as he reached out to touch my arm almost sent me over the edge. "I'm fine," I tried to smile, "Just overtired."

"Ah," he said, not believing me for a moment, but not pressing either. "That's a lovely gown. Margaret was laid to rest in a bedgown just like this one," he stared.

I looked down at the bedgown trying not to show my horror. But I now understood why it looked familiar to Cecil.

"I'm sorry, that must have seemed an odd thing to say. It's just so familiar. It's beautiful on ya, dear."

I tried to smile.

We held each other's gaze for a moment, before he shook his head and said, "Well, I am parched and didn't want the water Briggs left by my bed. A whiskey seems more conducive to falling asleep. Can I offer ya one?"

"No thank you," I said, "Sleep will find me quickly I'm sure."

"Good night, Janie," he put a kiss on my cheek, then headed down the stairs.

Tears started to fall the moment he was out of sight. They always made me embarrassed. Sniffling back sobs and snot, I headed to the bathroom to find tissue. Our first fight, I thought. I thought this shit was reserved for relationships. It seems unfair to fight if you're not having sex. I was waiting on something, someone that would never happen. Couldn't happen. I knew this. I blew my nose. Barry, I had a ridiculous crush on Barry, since I was a young girl. But, he never saw me that way. Not to mention, if we did by some miracle, date and break up, which was a pattern for me, (actually dumped was my pattern) what would happen between Fitz and me? I was LIKE a sister to her. But, he WAS her brother. And what about Mum, and the family I had been raised with? They were MY family. What about parties, family gatherings, and the pub? Not to mention, he was in love with another woman. What was I waiting for? Was I just using an inconceivable crush, to keep me from wanting someone else? I knew I wanted Cecil. My God, when he said, "Underneath me," I almost passed out. That one phrase sent a yearning to all the right places. Then, he wounded me with the truth, thus unleashing my mouth. I was mad at him for being right. He knew I was clinging to the thought, or hope, of someone. Now I was embarrassed on top of feeling like a complete ass. And what about this damn gown? I looked in the mirror. It wasn't from Cecil, like I figured it was. It obviously wasn't from Martin, which I was grateful for. That would have been awkward. But yet, not as awkward as hearing his wife had been laid to rest in one that looked just like it. It was a thought that gave me the creeps. I thought I heard a door shut in the hallway. Maybe Fitz and Scotty? I listened.

Nothing. This place was giving me the creeps. I couldn't help but wonder if the South Wing, where the men's bedrooms were, was any less...medieval-creepy. My eyes looked puffy and red from crying. I turned on the faucet and brought cold water to them. Again, I thought I heard a sound, but this time it was footsteps. A shiver ran up my spine. Opening the door, I peeked out slightly, to make sure there were no ghosts or goblins walking the hallway. Everything was quiet. No sign of anyone.

Quickly, I made it back to my room and closed the door behind me. This place was playing tricks with my mind, was exactly what I was trying to convince myself of when I saw an envelope on my bedside table. I looked around the room to make sure I was indeed alone.

'Dearest Janie', was printed on the front. I pulled out a card, revealing a black and white picture of a rose, losing a petal. Inside, it read; "Janie, please meet me at the stable at midnight. I will be waiting for you!" Something inside me fluttered and my heart began to race. "Cecil," I said out loud, holding the card to my chest. I knew I had been hurt by what he had said. But being honest, I think I hurt him, too. I needed to explain, needed to be honest with him, with myself. I grabbed my cell phone and realized I only had twenty minutes to make it there on time. There was no time to change, or I would be late for sure.

I grabbed my robe and slippers, and ran down the stairs. The pathway to the stable was dimly lit, but I could see well enough. Only then did it dawn on me, what kind of wild animals did Ireland have? Did they have wolves? Big cats? Bears? I began to pick up the pace. I was almost running, knees to chest, when I realized I couldn't outrun a wolf, big cat, or bear, so WTH was I doing?

The stable was aglow with candlelight. I walked in and removed my robe, tossing it on a bench. There I stood, in my beautiful gown, my chest heaving. Not just from the ridiculous running, but from the anticipation. I had thrown caution to the wind. I was going to let the moment take me. Possibly even let him take me. Wherever the wind takes us, I thought. I pulled out my ponytail, shaking my long blonde hair to make it look as wild and untamed, as I felt. There I stood in the middle of the stable. Where was he? I wondered. "Hello?" I finally said.

From behind me, I heard, "I knew you'd come."

I turned to see the young Tom Cruise look alike, Daniel, the stable boy.

"Ummm..." I said.

"I knew you couldn't deny me...us," he added, moving closer. He was wearing a pair of jeans and white T-shirt.

"Ummm," I continued, cocking my head and squinting.

"From the first moment I met ya, I knew I wanted ya. Did ya feel the same?" he asked, still making his approach.

I squinted harder and bit my lip, "Not so much," I said, taking a step back, as he advanced.

"We don't need to play these games," he shook his head. Pulling his shirt off, he revealed a nicely sculpted upper body.

"Shit!" I said under my breath. "Look," I said, shaking my head, "I wasn't expecting...this!"

"How could ya not have? Ya got my letter. Ya came. Ya want this! Ya want us!" he was advancing again.

"Well," I winced.

"Well what?" he asked. "Say you'll be mine. Say you'll give yerself to me...and I to you!" he said, dropping his jeans to his ankles.

"Oh my God!" I hadn't been expecting him to do that. I looked away, "Oh for the love of Pete, Daniel! Pull up your pants," I commanded.

I want ya to see me! I'm offerin myself to ya!

I let out a sigh, "Daniel look," I started. But then I heard

Cecil. He was calling for Babygirl. "Oh shit!" I said. "It's Cecil! You need get your clothes back on! Right now!"

"I don't care who knows about us, Janie!" he exclaimed.

Finally, I looked at him. What the hell? "Are you wearing frog boxers?"

He smiled, "I thought you'd like 'em."

It was too much of a flashback. Me...in my frog boxers...right before the rebirthing ritual...all the women laughing at me.

I heard Cecil call out for Babygirl again. She was neighing frantically.

"Seriously, you need to hide!"

"For yer honor?" he asked.

"Uh, yeah, sure, for my honor," I said, moving him toward an empty stall. "Wait, what does it say on your boxers?" I questioned.

He faced me and grinned, 'Don't croak on it'! was the caption.

I narrowed my eyes, "Not likely!" I said, and pushed him in through the gate door.

"Oh yer that girl," he said. "Lucky me!" he nodded.

My face squished up, "Just...just...

"You look beautiful, by the way," he whispered.

"Great, thanks, now please shut up!"

Cecil entered and stopped dead in his tracks, "What are you doin' here?"

I was trying not to panic, "I just, uh, just, uh...decided to go for a walk, and ended up here."

I heard Babygirl neighing loudly and kicking the stall door, with all her might.

"What's gotten into Baby, I wonder," he said walking down the row of stalls to hers. She saw us approaching and began rearing up. "What's wrong girl?" he asked her. Babygirl was throwing a fit. She looked me dead in the eye and squinted. "Calm down, girl!" Cecil put his hand out and stroked her nose. "That's my girl," he said, as she rubbed her giant head against his hand. "Janie," he turned to me, "I'm glad yer here. I wanted to apologize. I had no right to say all those things to ya."

My heart warmed again, "No Cecil, I need to tell you how...

There was a loud bang from the stall I had pushed Daniel into. Followed closely was a whispered curse word.

"What the hell was that?" Cecil began to walk back down the row.

I began to pray. Please God, let him have his pants on!

Cecil was looking into each stall. When he came to the first, there stood Daniel, shirtless, (but pants-full) holding a pitchfork.

"What are ya doing here at this time of night?" Cecil asked.

Daniel raised his jaw defiantly. "I am here to meet Miss Janie!"

So much for my honor, I thought.

Cecil's head spun in my direction, "Janie?" he asked, looking for an explanation.

"You see..." I began.

"I'm not sure I do," he answered, before I could finish.

"It's not what you think," I told him. "And it's not what you think either," I said, turning to Daniel.

"But ya came," Daniel winked at me.

Cecil shot me a horrified look, "What?" he raised his brows.

I caught how he took the comment, "NO, NO, NO!" I said, shaking my head.

Cecil turned on Daniel, "What do ya mean, she came?"

"In the note, I asked her to meet me here, and she came," Daniel said, not getting what had been implied.

Ah, to be young, cute and dumb as a rock, I thought.

Cecil was absorbing the information and processing. "So you

went to Janie's room, and gave her a note, to meet ya at the stable?"

"No," said Daniel, "Janie wasn't in the room. I left the note on her bedside table."

"You, uninvited, went into Janie's room?" Cecil took a step towards Daniel.

Daniel gave the defiant look again, "I did!"

Cecil looked as though he was considering decking the boy.

"Look," I said, raising my hands submissively, "No harm, no foul. Let's just let clearer heads prevail, here."

"He left ya a note...and ya came here...to meet him?" Cecil asked me.

"Well, not exactly. I mean, I did come here, but..."

"We're in love!" Daniel announced.

Cecil's eyebrows almost hit his hair line, at Daniel's comment.

"No," I said, getting flustered. "I'm not in love with you, Daniel!"

"Then why did ya agree to kiss me?" he asked, winking again.

"What?" said Cecil, turning another questioning look my way.

I rubbed my temples. "See, I didn't agree to kiss him. Fitz kind of offered me up, without my okay. I'm sorry," I said to Daniel. "I didn't know anything about the kiss! Fitz agreed to it without my consent."

"What? Why would she do that?" Cecil asked Daniel.

Here it comes, I thought. He's going to rat on Fitz. Of course everyone knew we had been in the secret passageway, but not WHY. We had been snooping, not exploring.

Daniel said slowly, "Fitz said that Janie was in need of a man."

My eyes bugged out, wondering if Fitz had indeed said

something to this extent, considering my current state of horniness. I blushed at the thought.

"So Fitz is trying to, what? Pimp ya out...after yer 'Take and Bake', fail?" Cecil asked.

My eyes narrowed at what I took as another verbal attack. I was silent, eyes darting from him to Daniel. I was so embarrassed and humiliated. I tried to regain some semblance of self respect. "I guess you'd have to ask her!" I said, over a lump in my throat. Hoping for a speedy retreat, I turned to leave.

"Aren't ya forgettin' somethin'?" Cecil asked, as I passed him.

I turned and let out a sigh, "What Cecil?"

"I think ya owe the boy a kiss, don't ya?" He folded his arms across his chest.

He was being ridiculous and rude, and I was not a fan.

"That's what you want me to do?" I asked, hoping he would say, "No!" Hoping one of us would just cave. Knowing that in light of new hurts inflicted, it wouldn't be me.

Our eyes locked, as I waited for an answer. "It's yer debt," he said, matter-of-factly.

I stared him dead in the eyes, "Fine!" I walked over to Daniel, who was grinning from ear to ear. "After this, consider my debt paid."

"Of course," Daniel smiled. I leaned in expecting a harmless kiss. Four lips, pushed against each other, a smack of them, then a retreat. Not what I got. The kiss started harmlessly enough, but when I would have pulled away, he gently pulled my head closer and went all in. I was tentative at first, but the kiss seemed never ending until Cecil cleared his throat, loudly.

I had to admit, the boy had a kiss that could do some real damage. When I pulled away, I was aware he also enjoyed the kiss. Some parts of him proudly displaying the fact, I noted. Ah, to be an 18 year old boy, I thought. Daniel looked dreamily at me as I turned and walked past Cecil saying, "Happy now?"

He stared with his tongue in his cheek.

"See you at 6am," I said, as I walked out of the stable.

"Son of a..." was all I heard Cecil say.

As I walked back to the Castle, I no longer cared what kind of wild animals roamed the Irish hillside. I was pretty sure I could take 'em. I was so angry. This wasn't the way it was supposed to go. I hadn't had all the details worked out in my head, but none of this was supposed to happen. Why hadn't I just told Cecil that I thought it was him who sent the card? HE was why, I told myself. I had gone from wanting him, to wanting to smack the Irish out of his bloodline in a matter of moments. "Dammit, dammit, dammit!" I said underneath my breath with every step I took. "Why are you such a stubborn ass?" I chastised myself all the way back to the Castle.

It was late in Ireland, but was a good time to call home back in the good ol' USA. Considering how bad tonight had gone, calling my mom couldn't make it worse, I told myself.

I picked up my cell, and hit speed dial number four. Fitz was number one, followed by my work, then Mum, then my mother. She picked up on the second ring. Now that was more my mother, I thought.

"Hi Janie," her voice rang. She sounded different to me, relaxed. I was immediately concerned.

"Um, hi mom," I said back. "How are you?"

"Oh. I'm wonderful. How are you?"

I pulled my cell from my ear and stared at the number. Yep, that was home. "I'm good. What's going on?"

"Oh, just making dinner."

"Yeah? Anything new happening?"

"Mmm," she thought. "No, not that I can think of."

"Huh," I responded. "How are you and dad?"

"Oh, fine. You know, same ol, same ol!"

"Uh huh." She wasn't killing me with her usual conversations. Normally by now, she would have offered some poor man as a fix up, accused Fitz of being the reason I wasn't a neurosurgeon, and criticizing my life as a whole. "Are you sure you're feeling okay?" I finally asked.

"Never better!" I could almost hear her glowing. "Well, honey,"

'Honey'? I thought.

"I hope you're doing okay, but I have to get dinner on the table now. I'll talk to you later, okay?"

"O-kay," I said.

"Love you."

"Uh, love you, too?" then she hung up on me. "What the..." I said, looking at my phone. After twenty-six years of my mother being a horrible pain in my ass, I had no idea how to react. I decided to call Betty.

"Hello Puddin!" she said. "How are ya, honey?"

"I'm good. A little curious about whether or not you found out anything more about my mom?"

"Actually, I followed her to the grocery store, the bank, the pharmacy then home. She didn't head to your house or meet up with the blonde guy today."

"And you're sure she doesn't know you're following her, right?"

"Oh Puddin, I'm wearing disguises and changin' cars...I'm fully undercover!"

I had a mental image of Betty in a trench coat and dark glasses, following my mother around the grocery store.

"Is she still actin' oddly?" Betty wanted to know.

I thought about the "Honey" and "I love you." Biting my lip, I said, "I'm not sure what the hell's going on!"

"Ya want me to keep followin' her?"

"I feel like it's a lot to ask of you, Betty."

"Look, Walter is in Australia for the next two weeks. As of right now, this and catching the sunset, are my only plans," she laughed.

"I don't know, as paranoid as she is, she's liable to see you, at some point."

Betty was quiet for a moment before saying, What if we were more obvious?"

I had no idea how this could help Betty spy, but just said, "Go on!"

"Like, what if I was having somethin' done to the house? Then I'd have to be there, since yer not."

I pondered.

"Well, I mean, if I was having work done, I'd have to be there to make sure someone was there for the workers. Ya know, so if the workers had any questions, or needed any directions."

"Really Betty, I can't even think of anything that needs to be done."

"Well, I was thinkin' about having the house painted. It's been over ten years, the color is faded all to hell. I was gonna have it done soon, anyway. Might as well do it while yer away."

I thought about that. "Ya know, that's a pretty good idea. I can pay for it, and you can pick the color."

"I'm still yer landlord, Puddin. I can pay for it, and you can pick the color."

I smiled, "Betty, if you insist on paying for it, you pick the color."

"Done Puddin! Now don't you worry. I got this."

We caught up for a while, then rang off. I really did miss her and the comforting, 'no bullshit' way, she had about her.

I changed back into my flannel nightgown, and curled up. I thought for sure I would be awake for hours, obsessing about

Cecil and the kiss from the young stable boy. But exhaustion won out in the end. Into dreams, I fell.

I was in the stable, darkness behind me. The glow of a candle before me, a scent of musk fills the air. I can smell...him. My whole body is alive with awareness. Where is he? I feel someone approach me from behind. I don't turn around. I don't need to. I know who it is. I know it's him. The man I crave. His arms wrap their way around my waist. His breath, warm and welcome, on the back of my neck. He moves my hair aside and puts a soft kiss just under my ear. Bumps, of the goose variety, rise on my flesh. I turn and see him...half man...half horse?

12

F-ING FIVE A.M.

Five A.M., my phone alarm went off. I was to meet Cecil for a sunrise horseback ride. Obviously, my dream combined my two biggest fears at the moment. That damned horse ride and Cecil. I didn't know if I even wanted to see him, but knew no matter how large the Castle was, I couldn't avoid him forever. I stretched as the lump on the bed next to me, stirred. I pulled back the covers to see Fitzy. Oh, I thought, she's so cute! All rolled up like a happy little kitty.

"For the love of Pete, Janie! If yer gonna get up at the ass-crack of dawn, can ya at least let ME sleep in peace."

"Well what the hell are you doing back in bed with me, anyway?"

"I couldn't sleep in my own bed, ironically," she added.

I pulled the cover back over her. "Apparently little happy kitty, has claws!"

"What are ya babblin' about?"

"Nothing, Go back to bed, Fitz."

I threw on a pair of 501's, and layered on a few tops before throwing on a hoodie and my black Chucks. Down to the stable

I went. Cecil already had Babygirl out of her stall. If it was possible, she looked even larger than she had the night before. She saw me and offered a cold stare.

"Good morning," I said, apprehensively.

"Good mornin' Janie," he said, never looking up from inspecting Babygirl's shoe.

I got the immediate feeling that my company was unwanted. I stood fidgeting, wondering how to handle the tension between us. After a moment, I said, "I'm just gonna go back up to the Castle. Let you enjoy your ride."

"Nonsense," he raised his eyes to mine. "She's almost ready for ya."

Babygirl narrowed her eyes at me. Great, I thought.

He saddled her back, and bridled her.

"Do you usually put that thing in her mouth?" I asked.

"No, I don't ride her with a bridle or saddle. But since yer new to bein' on horseback, I thought it may make ya feel more in-control."

She shot me another angry look.

"I don't want her to be uncomfortable. I mean, if she isn't used to it, wouldn't that make her...unhappy?" I searched for the word.

She nodded.

"Come on, Babygirl," he said, "You'll take good care of Janie. Then maybe next time, she can ride you without the bridle. Okay, ya ready?" he asked me.

Ready? No, I thought. "I guess," I said, against my better judgment. He pulled another huge horse from a stall. "This is Mac. I'll be riding him. Let me help ya mount Babygirl." I moved forward and he instructed me to put my left foot in the stirrup. Using the saddle horn, I was to pull my body up, then swing my right leg over her body. Mounted, I felt even more worried. It's not like I was afraid of heights. It wasn't like she was so very high off the ground. It was the fact that I had a one thousand pound animal beneath me, and these thin reigns in my hands were supposed to control her? Plus, I already had the feeling she didn't like me.

My stirrups were raised up to fit my leg length and Cecil went over how to use the reigns for control. He made sure I had it down before mounting Mac. We started out of the stable at a walking pace. This wasn't so bad, I thought. The saddle wasn't exactly comfortable. And let's face facts, I hadn't had my legs spread this wide for quite some time, but I was adjusting. This was actually 'freeing' in a way. Cecil, on Mac, was next to me. We walked our horses in silence for a short period of time.

"About last night," Cecil started, "If ya weren't goin' there to meet Daniel, who did ya think left the note?

I bit my lip and drew in a breath, "I thought you left the note."

"Ya did?" his brows raised.

I nodded to him.

"Why would ya think that?"

I thought for a moment, "Because you called me Petal. And the card had a picture of a rose...losing its petal...and we had that argument..."

"Wait, so you receive a card, with a rose losing its petal, and what? Ya think that I see myself as losing ya? Janie, I think it's clear, I never had ya. Truth is, yer not my Petal to lose, are ya?"

His voice was colder than I had ever heard. Clearly, my big mouth, in more than one way, had done some real damage.

"I just wanted to apologize," I said, "For my part in the fight we had. I said some very derogatory things."

"Aye," Cecil said.

I waited patiently for his return apology.

"And," I finally said, doing a hand roll.

"And what?"

"Were you going to apologize for the things you said to me?"

"Why would I apologize?"

"Because you said some hurtful things?" I started to get worked up again.

"No, what I said was true. Correct? What you said, were yer perceptions."

"Perceptions you, yourself, have fed. If I have any misconceptions of who you are, you're the one who gave them to me. And," I continued, "If I'm incorrect in any way, why don't you just say so, instead of getting offended by what you led me to believe?" I was starting to talk in circles as my pulse rate rose. His calm demeanor was agitating.

Babygirl's ears began to twitch.

"Ya never asked," he finally said, grinning at me.

I was infuriated by his smugness, and that stupid 'I won' grin he was wearing.

"And you assume as well," I retorted. "You never asked either!"

With that, Babygirl took off like lightning. I was so jolted by her bolt, I damn near fell as she broke into a dead run. I could hear Cecil yelling from somewhere behind me, "Pull back on the reigns, Janie! Babygirl, stop!

"Oh my God, oh my God! Stop Babygirl, stop!" you could hear me screaming all the way down the meadow. I pulled back as hard as I could, but she put her head down and did the impossible, in my opinion. She picked up pace. Things, I assumed were trees and bushes, went whizzing by as green blurs. I switched my screams from, "Oh God," to "Holy shit!" repeated as a mantra. I thought seriously about jumping from her back, but I wasn't sure about my landing. My ass was flying up and crashing back down into the saddle, over and over again.

Cecil was trying to gain on Babygirl, but Mac was no match for her speed. He yelled over and over again, but his instructions weren't working. We were now running down the meadow. The lake was getting closer and closer. I pushed my feet as far forward as they would go in the stirrups. Pushing my ass back in the saddle as far as I could, I braced myself.

Cecil yelled from somewhere far behind me, "Go limp, Janie! Lean forward and go limp!" At the last possible moment, I leaned in and went limp. Babygirl, head down, had dead stopped two feet into the water. I, on the other hand, took fight. Over her bowed head, I flew, limp as a rag doll. The water, not so welcoming, was a shock to my already shocked senses. Luckily, it was deep enough where I landed, that I hadn't hit the bottom. Struggling my freezing body back to the shore, I drug my soaked, clothing layered ass out of the water, crawling on hands and knees. Seeing Babygirl standing on the shore, watching me, my eyes narrowed at her. Cold wasn't the only thing I was shaking with. As I stood, I advanced on her. Her eyes rounded and started to show less contempt, and more fear.

"You!" I hissed through shivering lips. "You!" I finally yelled, finding my voice, as Cecil approached. He dismounted Mac quickly and came to check me.

"My God, Janie, are ya okay? Are ya bleedin'? Did ya hit anything? Can ya bend yer legs?"

I did all the ridiculous movements he asked me to do, while never taking my eyes from Babygirl. Every bit of my flesh was raised with goose pimples, but my ears were burning.

"Why didn't ya pull back on the reigns?" Cecil finally asked.

My eyes widened, "Are you kidding me?" I practically screamed. "Ya didn't see me pulling back as hard as I could? My God, my head almost touched her ass," I pointed at Babygirl.

"Jesus Janie, yer making it sound like she did this on purpose. She's a horse."

Babygirl shot Cecil a hurt look.

I shook my head vigorously, "Oh no!"

"Maybe she got mixed signals from ya... you bein' new at ridin' and all. I mean, she follows yer commands!"

"Not mine!" I said. "Or didn't you hear me yelling my damned head off?"I said, my Chuck high tops sloshing as I advanced on her.

"She's a good girl," Cecil said, in her defense.

She nodded to him and pounded the ground with a hoof.

"No," I hissed again. "She's the Devil's Mare," I said, one eye beginning to twitch.

"Janie, come on," Cecil laughed nervously.

I was now directly in front of her, "Horse of Hades!" I announced loudly. She took a step back, "Beast of Beelzebub!" my eyes wild.

Cecil said, "Janie stop! Yer scarin' her!"

I turned my wild eyes to him, "I'M SCARING HER?" I huffed. "Are ya freakin' kidding me? This...horse," I finally yelled, "Is a damn menace! And you!" I pointed to Cecil, "You," I yelled, "Ahhh!" I balled up my fists and stomped up the meadow, sloshing away from them.

Cecil began to laugh, "Janie, ya can't walk all the way back to the Castle. You'll catch yer death! Come back! I'll ride ya back up."

"Not a chance," I yelled over my shoulder.

As I squelched away, I heard him say to Babygirl, "That wasn't very nice."

I had walked off most of the dripping wetness, and was now just soaked to the bone as I entered the Castle.

Miss Elanor gave me a disapproving look as I entered, and then raised her brow, "What in heaven's name happened to ya, child?"

Her concern caught me off guard, but didn't change my mood. "Thrown by a horse," I said, as I passed her and headed upstairs.

Fitz's door was open and she saw me pass by. "Ya missed breakfast, Janie," she said heading to my room. She gave me the once over. "What the hell? Jesus, yer soaked to the bone!"

I grabbed my robe and slippers and headed to the bathroom. Fitz turned on the tub and added bubbles as I tried, with all my might, to fight my way out of my soaked 501's. "They won't come down," I whined.

Fitz turned to me, "My God, yer lips are blue. We'll get ya out of those jeans if we have to cut ya loose." She pulled and I wiggled. Finally, she had me get on the floor, pulling at my ankles as I pulled down from the waist. Freed from my denim hell, I sunk into the tub. "It's scalding hot." I chattered.

"No, yer freezing cold," she answered.

As my numbness subsided, I said, "I have a lot to tell you." I started with the PJ party Cecil and I had. "By the way, the dressing gown wasn't from him."

"Who's it from, then?" Fitz wondered out loud.

"Still not sure," I shook my head.

I explained about me and Cecil's fight.

"Who does he think yer holdin' out for?" she asked.

Clearly, I hadn't given a lot of thought as to how to answer this. I shrugged my shoulders, "I don't know."

I told her about the call to mom. "Yer mom?" she asked in disbelief. "Did she at any time metion' my goin' to either jail, or hell?"

I shook my head.

"Something's very wrong, here," her eyes narrowed. "Have ya considered the 'body snatcher's' angle?

"It's worth considering," I nodded.

I told her about Betty's involvement. "I love that woman," she giggled.

Then, I told her about the note, my assumptions, the truth

of it having been sent by Daniel, and the horror of running into Cecil. "How was the kiss?" she wanted to know.

"Pretty damned impressive. But not enough to make me forget that his mom was in labor with him, while I was in the third grade spelling bee."

"Oh, men do it all the time," Fitz replied.

"They also publically adjust their sacks."

She smirked at me, "You can too, ya know. Once ya find yers."

"Anyway," I continued. I told her all about the new argument, and how his horse had taken me for quite the ride. By the time I finished, she was rolling around on the ground.

"What the hell is so funny?" I demanded.

Fitz was having trouble getting her words out, through her laughing snorts. "I can picture it...hahahaha...you holdin' on for dear life...bouncin' in the saddle...eyes poppin' out of yer head...then...whoa...(she made a wobbling motion) "Air..."(she did the Superman in flight arms and wild, frightened eyes) "SPLASH!" she yelled. She rolled around on the floor holding her gut.

I stared, "YOU are an asshole. I could be really hurt, ya know."

"I'm sorry Janie," she tried to catch her breath. "Are ya hurt?" she did her sympathy eyes.

"My ass is sore," I said.

"I bet!" she broke into laughter, again.

"I have another question for you?"

"Shoot," she said, trying to calm her laughter.

"Did you tell Daniel that I was in need of a man?"

She acted like she was trying to recall the conversation, finger tapping her chin, as she looked off in the distance, "Hmmm?"

"Fitz, how could you?"

“Look, I needed info on the Castle. Truth is, he played me. He made it seem as if he were telling me grand secrets. But you heard Martin, he'd tell us whatever we wish to know.”

“But you promised Daniel, ME!”

“No, I promised him a kiss from ya, and said you were in need of a man, to get him riled up enough to give me information.”

“So, does that mean you played him, too?”

“Sure. That's one way of looking at it,” she accepted the notion.

I got dressed for lunch, and realized while walking down the stairs, that I was stiffening up. I guessed it was more from trying to hold on, and stay on, Babygirl's back than from hitting the water at a high rate of speed.

Small sandwiches and salad were served. It seemed that Fitz and myself were the only two in attendance.

“Scotty and Martin are in the city?” I asked Miss Elanor.

“You mean Scotty and Mr. Callaghan?” she raised her brows to me. “Yes, they are.”

I didn't feel like arguing the fact that Mr. Callaghan had asked me to call him Martin. I didn't, but Fitz did.

“I assume soon, I will be calling him dad,” she said.

Miss Elanor's lips all but disappeared.

Just then, Cecil entered and tried to pluck a sandwich from the tray, but Miss Elanor stopped him. “Those are for the ladies,” she smiled wickedly at us. “I will make you your own sandwich, if ya wish.”

Her comment had the desired effect of making me wonder about the food on my plate. Fitz, on the other hand, picked up her sandwich, stared at Miss Elanor and took a huge, angry bite. Ripping through it like a rabid dog. Cecil sat across from me, but neither of us said a word to one another. I could feel him taking quick glances at me. Fitz stared, back and forth, waiting for something to be said.

"Are ya both to be stubborn asses, then?" she finally asked.

My jaw tightened.

Cecil kept his eyes down.

"Ya know, Janie was going to apologize to ya. During yer ride!"

My eyes bugged out at her, "Fitz!"

"Well, it's true. Ya were, weren't ya?"

"I did," I said. "And it went fabulously," I clenched my jaw.

"Oh, but did ya tell her about the 'humpin' everything that moves' comment?" he flared.

"I apologized for that. Or couldn't you hear me, as you assumed NO responsibility for the argument?" I asked.

"You've made assumptions, fact," he shot back.

"Didn't you, yourself, lead me to believe you were a mad, humping letch, the first night I met you.

"So I like sex. What's the big deal? I'm a horrible man because I like sex, right?"

"Hey, I enjoy sex, too," I said, defensively.

"I seriously doubt that," he fired back.

My jaw dropped, "Now who's making assumptions?"

Fitz had been watching us fire comments back and forth. She looked nervous at the scene she had put in motion. "See, you two are talking, that's good, right?" she let out a thin laugh.

Cecil and I both ignored her, "Well, then maybe that's what ya need, a good roll in the hay!" Cecil said.

I was fuming mad, my chest heaving. "Maybe I do!"

"Great, now if we can just get young Daniel on board..."

Fitz winced at Cecil, "Damn."

"YOU, SON OF A..." I said slowly, while rising from my seat. "You have...you can't even...I can't believe...I thought, for even one minute...You piece of...," I yelled, and walked out. Miss Elanor quickly stepped aside as I rushed past her.

I heard Fitz say as I walked out, "Nice going, dickhead! Janie, wait up!"

Fitz caught up to me on the stairs. "Janie, I'm so sorry. Please turn around. Are ya cryin'?"

I spun around and she took a step back. "What the hell is happenin' to yer neck?"

"What?" I asked. "What are you talking about?"

"Yer neck is all red and blotchy," she moved closer. "Ya have tiny red...welts of sorts." She inspected them.

Running to the mirror in the bathroom, I saw what she was seeing. "Oh my God," I said.

"Did Miss Elanor poison ya?" Fitz began to panic, "Oh Lord...am I to break out, too?" She pushed me out of the way, so she could inspect herself in the mirror. "I don't see anythin'. But maybe I'm immune or somethin'."

"They're hives Fitz."

"Oh my God! Wait, what are hives?"

"It's a reaction to eating foods you're allergic to or, as I believe to be my case, a reaction to stress."

"Yer sure ya weren't allergic to anythin' ya ate? Ya know that one woman Martin dated, always broke out in hives, remember?"

"No. I'm pretty sure my body's fine with ham and cheese." I leaned in for a better look, and tried not to scratch my itchy red bumps.

"Wow, they're really spreadin' fast. Do ya have them, ya know, everywhere?"

I lifted my shirt to show the red bumps taking over my torso. "Shit!"

"What do we do?"

"I'm not sure."

"Scotty said that Miss Elanor was trained as a nurse. Nurse Ratched I assume. But she'll know what to do."

The bumps were spreading quickly. I was left without another option. "Fine," I said, still uncomfortable with seeing her after my display.

Fitz went darting out the room. "I'm on it!" she bolted.

I tried to breathe and calm myself, but I was still raging inside. I began talking to myself, "Tell me I don't enjoy sex. What does he know about my sex life? Nothing, that's what! Tell me to roll in the hay with young Daniel. He doesn't know...I'd break that boy!"

"Um, are we intrudin'? Fitz asked, Miss Elanor at her side.

The only good thing about the hives was, you couldn't see me blushing.

Miss Elanor came to the same conclusion I did; hives. She gave me antihistamines and told me, "I'm going to monitor ya for a short while, to make sure you don't have an adverse reaction." She told Fitz I needed my rest, and shooed her out the door. Fitz looked nervously at me, but I nodded an okay. Elanor and I sat in silence for almost fifteen minutes till I began to yawn. "They're going to make you groggy. You might as well lie down and get a nap. When you wake, they'll be gone," she told me.

She was being so nice, I was suspicious. "Thank you," I said, as I crawled into my bed. She pulled the covers up to my chin.

"I'm sorry for the way Cecil spoke to you," she said, not looking me in the eye.

"I appreciate you saying that," I yawned, again. I was starting to feel...groovy.

"I raised him better than to speak to a woman in such a manner. No matter the manner of woman he's speaking to."

"See," I said, a little wobbly, "Ya almost had me there. Then ya have to go...and say meanie head things like that," I slurred a little. "Exactly, what matter of manner, do you, uh, think I'm having?"

Miss Elanor's brows raised. "Excuse me?" she asked.

"You...you know...what I'm sayin' some stuff about!" I tried to sit up. He's mad because his sex, I don't want. I'm proper!

"Lie down," she commanded, with a look of concern. "You seem to be sensitive to antihistamines."

"Ya see? Yer, yer...pushy! Not nearly as nice as one of those stuffed things."

Her eyes rounded. "Stuffed things?" she repeated.

"Yeah, you know," I pointed my finger at her. "They are ALL nicer than you. Except that one."

"Which one, what?" she shook her head.

"The one with the clouds raining on his..." I patted my boobs.

"Chest?"

I put my finger to my cheek then pointed it at her. "Yep. I've been thinkin' that who was the one I thought it was."

Miss Elanor's brow furrowed, "Child ya better lay down. Yer not makin' any sense.

The last thing I remember saying, or trying to say, was, "Janie out!" I tapped my chest twice and threw up a peace sign, before passing out cold.

I woke around four, feeling very groggy indeed. Fitz was bedside, "How long have you been sitting here?"

"For about an hour, or so. Miss Elanor sat with ya for the first two hours."

I winced a little, knowing I had said...something to her. But I wasn't sure what, exactly. "I can't remember what I was saying to her before I passed out."

"Well, I think you called her an angry stuffed animal," from what she said to me. She also said you were overly affected by whatever it was she gave ya. But look! All of yer yucky bumps are gone, just like she said they'd be, so that's good."

"Oh my God, I'm so embarrassed."

"By what ya said to Miss Elanor?" Fitz made a dismissive gesture, "She knows ya weren't in yer right mind."

"Not that. Well, not only that. Cecil," I said. "I can't believe I got so worked up."

"Ya well, he and I had a little chat."

This couldn't have been good, I thought. "Oh Lord no! Tell me you didn't."

"I did," she said. "He came up here to talk to ya, and I told him that his talkin' to ya had done enough damage."

I put my head in my hands. "Great. What did he say?"

"He said he was sorry, about the fight, Babygirl, the whole thing. He apparently scolded Babygirl. She is to stay in her stall for a week. No ridin' for her."

"He grounded her?" My brows arched.

"I guess so. Don't ask me to explain. I don't understand it, either."

"He should have grounded himself," was all I said.

"Do ya need anything?"

"I'm parched. I'd really like something a drink," I made pleading eyes at her.

"Lord, put yer beggin' eyes away. I'll get ya some juice." She left the room, and I picked up my cell phone.

I wanted to do a little research on horses. Truth is, I had never had a pet. Not even a hamster. So really, I had no real understanding about their attachment to their humans. I wanted to know what normal horse behavior was like. I was amazed to read that these huge animals can become as attached to their owners as a faithful dog. They have a sixth sense about people, and can feel a person's fear. One article, in particular, said that horses are very sensitive to the emotions around them, and react accordingly.

Accordingly? I thought. Throwing me in the lake was acting accordingly? Cecil, her owner since birth, and I, had been having an argument at the time of her impression of the great lemming run. I started to feel bad for Babygirl. In her own way, I guess she was protecting Cecil.

I was dressing, when Fitz came back in the room with my juice. I swayed a little trying to step into my jeans. I was becoming more than aware that I was definitely sore in places that hadn't been sore in quite some time.

"Whoa," Fitz said, grabbing me by the arm to stabilize me. "Where do ya think yer goin' there, Janie?"

"I need to see Babygirl."

"This seems like a good idea to you? I want whatever it was that Miss Elanor gave ya."

"Really, I feel like I have to."

"Alright. I've never been one to let ya do something stupid, alone. I better go and make sure ya don't end up in the water again."

"I'm not going to ride her again, Fitz."

"What the hell are ya plannin' on doin', then?"

"I'm just going to talk to her," I pulled on my boots.

"Uh huh," she nodded her head. "Well, alright," she finally said.

We headed downstairs, Fitz holding my wobbling self, so I didn't take a tumble. I took an apple from the fruit bowl on the dining table, and down the meadow path we went.

As we walked into the stable, all the male horses moved to their gates, to get a look at Fitz.

"Really?" I asked her, "Even horses?"

Fitz smiled, "What? Ya don't think horses have good taste?"

Walking up to Babygirl's stall, she turned her giant head away from me.

"Wow, she is a bitch," Fitz said.

Babygirl turned to look at her.

"Fitz!" I said.

"What? I can respect a bitch, in all forms."

Babygirl nudged Fitz's hand, and nuzzled it.

"See, she's a good girl," Fitz smiled.

I let out a sigh. "Can ya give us a moment?" I asked Fitz.

"Sure, I'll go check out the other horses. You two play nice," she wandered off.

Babygirl turned her head away from me, again.

"Look," I started, "I know we didn't get off on the right...foot, so to speak."

She gave no response.

"I didn't understand how much you could feel. Or," I leaned in, "How much you do feel for Cecil."

She lifted her head but still didn't look at me.

"I've never had, a..." I didn't want to call her a pet, "An animal companion. I didn't know how attached you could get to a person, or them to you. I understand, at least a little more, that you were protecting someone you love. The same way I would protect someone I love," I added.

She looked sidelong at me.

"I know I called you some horrible things."

Her eyes narrowed.

"I know," I said. "And I meant them at the time. But I am sorry. I was mad, and acted very badly to you throwing me in the lake."

I swear, it looked as though, she was grinning.

"Well, even if you're not sorry for how you treated me, I am sorry for how I treated you."

I pulled the apple from my sweater pocket, and held it out to her.

She turned her head away.

"Okay, I'll just leave it here on the gate."

I started to walk away, when she neighed.

I walked back, and she picked up the apple in her mouth. Biting it in half, she nudged her nose at me until I put my hand out. She dropped half the apple in my hand and started chewing the other half. I stared at the half in my hand, dripping with horse saliva. She looked at me, waiting. She gave me a twitch of her ear and nodded her giant head. I brought the half chomped, icky apple to my mouth and slowly took a bite. Trying not to let my gag reflex take over, I chewed and forced a smile. When I had swallowed, she put her head down. Reaching out my hand, I rubber her long nose.

"Thank you," I said. "I'll try to be more understanding in the future."

She nodded again.

Just then, I heard Cecil talking to someone outside the stable. When they entered, my heart dropped. Walking on Cecil's arm was the horrible shopgirl. Her boobs were popping out of a white, 'oops I missed a few buttons' button down shirt, black skin tight leggings and black knee high boots.

"Janie, what are ya doin here?" he asked.

"I wanted to see Babygirl, and apologize," I rubbed Babygirl's nose.

Cecil smiled, but the shopgirl said, "To a horse?"

"You remember Alexandria," Cecil said, letting her arm go. I nodded, with my tongue in my cheek.

"Please, call me Alex," she nudged him.

"Yep, I remember," I said. "And yes, I was apologizing to Babygirl here."

Cecil looked uncomfortable, as Alex wrapped her arm back around his. "That's weird, isn't it?" she asked.

Fitz had come up to join the conversation, "About as weird as it is that yer the delivery driver."

"Oh, I'm not," said Alex, "I just wanted to make sure everything got here alright. Ya know, make sure Cecil didn't need anything else."

"Course ya did," Fitz eyed her. "I'm Fitz, as in, 'throws a mean ass fit'...but in plural form."

"Oh, this is Scotty's girlfriend," Cecil added.

"Oh, well that changes things," Alex said, extending her hand.

Fitz folded her arms across her chest, "Does it, now? And how's that?"

Alex let her hand drop, along with her fake smile and turned back to me. "So, why exactly are you apologizing to a horse?" she questioned, grinning.

"My Babygirl here," Cecil said petting her nose, "Took Janie for quiet a ride today. It didn't end well."

"Really?" said Alex. "How badly could it have gone? I mean it's a horse. Haven't you ever been on horseback?"

Babygirl and I, both, narrowed our eyes. "No, I hadn't... and her name is Babygirl," I said. "I ended up in the lake," I stated matter-of-factly. Babygirl nodded.

Alex threw her head back and laughed, "Oh that's a hoot," she said. "Some women just don't know how to handle a beast beneath them," she looked at Cecil. "Ya have to take charge," she grinned at him.

"Somethin' tells me you've had quite a bit of experience with beasts between yer legs. I mean beneath ya," Fitz corrected herself, like that sounded better.

Alex and Fitz held each other gaze's for a moment. "Cecil,

I'd like to borrow ya for a moment, if I could," Fitz said to him, and led him out of the stable by his arm.

Left standing with Alex, I said, "So, you found a way into the Castle after all, huh?"

"I wasn't going to miss this golden opportunity. You said Cecil wasn't yours. You had no claim, as I recall. So how about you stay outta my way, and things won't have to get ugly," she smiled.

Taking a step forward, "Just so you know, just because I don't have a claim, doesn't mean that I'm not protective of him. I do care for him, and we are friends. You do understand that? Correct?

"That has no bearing on me. I'm not a jealous woman."

"Just so we don't have a miscommunication, I know exactly what type of woman you are."

"Oh you do, do you?"

"Oh yeah," I nodded. "You made that very clear, when you referred to him as Mr. Moneybags."

Babygirl's head snapped towards Alex.

She put her hands on her hips, "You don't scare me. So why don't ya just run along and do yer little paintin's. Cecil doesn't need a babysitter. But if you feel the need to start a war, just remember, I have ways of making a man forget about everyone else. That includes you," she smiled.

With her boots on, she and I were eye to eye. I leaned in, "You've made a very powerful enemy today," I whispered.

"Please!" she guffawed. "As I said, I'm not afraid of ya," she shook her head at me.

"I wasn't talking about me," I smiled, wickedly.

"Who then?" she gave me an amused grin, "the red headed bimbo?"

Cecil and Fitz were coming back down the aisle.

I leaned further into her, "You ever say one word about Fitz ever again, and I'll rip your eyes clean out of your botoxed face. And just so you know, I didn't mean her, either."

"Ah, Janie, we should probably check the delivery," Cecil suggested.

"No Cecil, I can check it myself," I glared at him. "Why don't you go ahead and give your friend here, the rest of the tour. I reached out and rubbed Babygirl's nose, and she winked at me. I winked back then Fitz and I headed up to the Castle.

We started up the path, "Well, she's prowlin'," Fitz assessed.

"Yep," I agreed.

As we made our way into the Castle, Miss Elanor saw us, "Are ya well, Miss O'Connelly?" she asked, back to her old frigid self.

"I am thank you. I do appreciate your help."

"Fine," she answered.

I sighed, our moment, if we had one, was over. "I understand that the delivery is here."

Mr. Callaghan has set aside a room for you to work in. Follow me. We passed Scotty's office. Or what I assumed was his office. Having no visible door from the outside, I wasn't positive. Down another corridor, right, then left, then right again, at the bust of...Benjamin Franklin? Or so it looked like to me. I was never going to able to find the painting room again, without a map. Finally, she came to a door just past an 1800's painting of a woman in a blue gown, down at the willow tree.

Stepping in, I fell in love. I was to paint in a huge atrium. In the middle of the room was a glass incased dome that looked up to the blue sky. One whole wall was floor to ceiling glass. Down the grass hill I could see the stable directly in front of me, and the garage a bit further out to my left. Beautiful flowers and plants wound their way around the room in pots, vases, urns. Some hung from ceiling planters. The glass room was framed by dark woods, and the floors were white marble. Two large easels were set up with two blank canvases. Tables sat next to each with all my materials set on them. Drop cloths lined the floors directly beneath the easels. A special stool, that could extend from a normal seating position, to rising up three feet by the click of a button, was also at my disposal. Knowing I wouldn't have to stand to do the top of the painting was a wonderful perk. Martin had put a lot of thought into the lighting these paintings would need. Not to mention, the comfort of the person painting them. There was even a CD player and CD's left for me. I looked at them, Tychowski, Mozart, and Pachelbel. How did he know that I loved to listen to classical music while painting? A small bar was set for me as well.

"Thank you, Miss Elanor," I said, still focused on the room.

"Is there anything else you require?" she asked, as I checked out all my materials.

"No, not that I can think of," I looked around with dreamy awe.

"Good, then I will go be an angry stuffed animal, elsewhere," she said, exiting.

I winced, "Sorry about that," I yelled after her.

Fitz came to my side, "Ya should try the apple trick on her."

I gave her a shitty look.

"What? It couldn't hurt, is all I'm sayin'."

I couldn't wait to get started. But first, I'd need some snapshots of the Castle and distillery to work from. I had to decide which angle I wanted then see if Martin and I were on the same page.

I grabbed the digital camera Martin had left for I and Fitz and me, took off to take some photos. I knew I would need photos at sunrise as well, seeing as how Martin loved daybreak in Ireland. We headed to the front of the house, and down the driveway a bit. I wanted to get the tree line leading up to the Castle as well. I decided that I may need to actually climb one of the trees to get the shot I was picturing in my head. Then I moved down the meadow, towards the stable, to get a side shot.

I could hear that Alex was still here, and I got a sick feeling in my gut.

Fitz asked, “It bothers ya, doesn't it?”

I bit my lip, “If she wasn't THAT kind of woman, I don't think it would.”

“Hmmm,” Fitz said.

“What?” I asked her.

“I don't think yer being quite honest with me.”

“What do you mean?” I took another picture.

“I mean, I think any woman would bother ya.”

I took a deep breath, “Maybe. But her kind of woman...just makes it worse. Can't he see what she really is?”

Fitz nodded, but something in her look, said so much more.

“I care what happens to him.”

She nodded again, but said nothing.

“Fine, I care ABOUT him! Are you happy now?”

“Gettin' warmer.”

We could hear them talking now. I snapped off a few more shots, trying to seem unaware of their presence.

“So, when are ya gonna let me ride Babygirl?” Alex was asking, loudly.

He seemed nervous, and I could see him out of the corner of my eye, looking my way. “I, I, I don't know,” he stammered.

My lip went into a sneer. I had to forcibly return it to normal.

“Oh, come on. I swear it'll be a good time,” she leaned into him and laughed.

I wanted to vomit...on her.

“I won't take no for an answer,” she pushed harder.

Hate her, hate her, hate her!

"Well, 'hard to get' isn't her game," Fitz said, seeing my facial expression.

"Come on, take me," Alex whined, and stuck her bottom lip out, in a pout.

"Ah, how about tomorrow mornin'?" he said.

"Oh, I'd love to," Alex gushed and threw her arms around his neck. "So I will be ridin' Babygirl, then, right?"

"Well, Babygirl, um, she's not allowed to ride right now. I'm kind of punishin' her for the whole 'Janie-in-the-lake' thing."

"Well, that hardly seems fair, to punish her, because her rider couldn't control her. She was probably confused by Julie's inexperience."

I was fuming pissed now. She knew my name and purposely called me another, just to add insult.

"Well, Babygirl is kind of...special," he finished.

"Oh," Alex gave the wounded bird look. "I could be special, too," she smoldered.

"Damn, she's good," I said, to Fitz.

"Amateur," Fitz answered.

"Not from where I'm standing," I said. "He's gonna fold."

"Oh, he'll fold, no doubt. But, it won't end well for her."

Cecil looked from me, back to Alex, "Well, if it means that much to ya."

"Folded," I said, trying not to look wounded.

"Yep. I knew he would. But I stand by what I said, it's not going to end well."

Alex threw herself at Cecil and wrapped her arms around his neck again."You'll see. Babygirl and I will be the best of friends. So when do ya want to go?"

"Uh, tomorrow, 8am?"

"Perfect! It's a date," she shot a look to me, which I ignored.

"I have a lot to do, and it's almost time for supper, so..." Alex cut him off.

“Are you inviting me to dinner?” she asked coyly.

Cecil stood stammering again. “Uh, well, um, sure. I guess so. I better head up to the house to let Miss Elanor know we're having company.”

“I'll go with ya,” she suggested, wrapping her arm through his, and pulling him up the path. “I'd love to see the inside of the Castle.”

He looked over his shoulder at me, I pretended not to notice.

“Looks like there'll be one more for dinner,” I said to Fitz.

“Excellent,” Fitz grinned like the angry, red headed fairy she was. I could see the wheels turning.

13

THE ANGRY, RED HEADED FAIRY, EMERGES

Fitz and I went up to change. My mood had become somewhat foul, and I openly debated not going to dinner. Fitz was busy on her phone. So much so, that she barely heard a word I said.

Finally, she looked up and said, "What kind of pussy are you? Are you goin' to be run off, to hide in yer room, by that tart?"

"I'm not in the mood to watch her and Cecil making googly eyes at each other."

"Well, not standing yer ground looks pathetic."

"What ground? I have no claim to him, or intentions toward him," I said, in an almost believable tone.

Fitz stared, "Blow smoke up someone else's arse, will ya? I know ya. And, whether yer ready to admit it to yerself, or not, I know this little spat...hasn't rendered ya done. So how about ya stop tryin' to protect yer heart, and think about protectin' yer friend. Even if ya don't want him fer yerself, ya know he deserves better than her."

I was being schooled, and had to admit, she was right. I

pulled my pout back in and stiffened my upper lip, nodding to her.

"Now show me what yer wearin' for dinner," Fitz said.

I showed her a pair of black slacks and a modest silk blouse.

Fitz shook her head. "Nope," she put my clothes back in the armoire. "This," she said, pulling out a black wrap around dress, and black heels that Cecil had picked out.

"Won't that seem a little...obvious?" I asked.

"What? We dress for dinner around here. Now get changed."

The dress fit so well, and was a comfortable length for me. Fitz said after taking me in, "Hair up. Men like to see a woman's neck."

She helped me put my long hair into a clip and pulled down some strands at the side, for a messy 'windblown' look.

The gong went off. "You have to get ready, too," I told her.

"No offense to ya Janie, but it takes me no time at all to be fabulous." She crossed the hallway and emerged looking stunning in a green satin dress and matching pumps, all in three minutes. "Ta da," she announced, doing a little spin.

Odd how much I loved her, given how much I shouldn't, I thought, and said as much.

"It's my sparklin' personality," she grinned.

We headed down the stairs, and the fidgeting began. Fitz put her hand on mine, "Tonight, yer Grace Kelly. Ya got that?"

"What?" I asked.

"How do ya think some models do it? We take on a persona. It gives us power when we need it."

"You could of and should of, shared this with me years ago."

"Ya know how to Barrymore? What did ya think that was all about?" she asked like I was dense.

"So why am I not Barrymore-ing, then?"

"Too sexy. We want all class, no sexy. When I think of ultimate class, I think Grace."

"She was drop dead gorgeous, Fitz."

"Yes, but she was also diplomatic. Get it?"

I nodded. "Okay. Who are you gonna be?" I asked.

"Me?" she smiled, "I'm gonna be a bitch."

"So...yourself," I grinned.

"Nothing less," she blew me a kiss.

Cecil, Scotty and Alex were seated when we entered. Scotty stood and laid a kiss on Fitz before pulling out her chair. He shot a look towards Alex then gave us a confused shake of his head. Cecil had rushed around the table to pull out a chair for me. Turns out, Alex was sitting in my chair sitting next to Cecil. Round one: Alex.

"You look lovely, Janie," he said.

"Yes, Janet, was it?" Alex started, "I'm having so much trouble keeping yer name straight. You clean up nicely. I hope ya didn't go to too much trouble on my account."

Grace Kelly, I reminded myself. "Not at all, and you're too kind," I nodded to her.

Fitz grinned, and now Alex was the one who looked confused.

Miss Elanor sneered, but I wasn't sure to whom she was sneering.

Martin entered and made his way to me first, putting a kiss on my cheek, "Good evening, dear Janie."

"Good evening," I said. "You're looking quite dapper, Martin."

"Thank you for noticing," he bowed his head before moving to put a kiss of Fitz's cheek.

"This is Alexandria," Cecil said, as he moved back to the other side of the table.

She batted her eyes wildly, "Please, call me Alex," she said, as Martin kissed her hand.

"Nice to meet ya, Alex," Martin said bewildered, cocking his head to Cecil. "Welcome to our home."

Miss Elanor sneered again, but this time I knew to whom she was sneering. Alex was clearly moved to the front of the line for the chopping block. I smiled.

"Alex works at the art supply store and brought the shipment today," Cecil said. "Janie will be able to start paintin' now."

Martin smiled at me, "Lovely," he emitted. "I can't wait."

"I saw the room you provided for me. It's perfect, Martin," I gushed.

"I'm glad ya like it. But Cecil was the one who picked the room and had it set for ya. I'm embarrassed to say, I had no idea about the lighting or space needed. Any of it really! Nice to have my boy know so much about art," he raised his glass to his son.

My eyes softened as I looked at Cecil, "You did that?"

Cecil smiled at me warmly, and said, "Aye."

We held the smile until Alex sneered and said, "Yes Cecil that was so kind of you. I loved that room, as well. Really, the whole Castle is amazing. And Cecil," she looked at him, "Your room has such a comfortable feel about it. Don't ya think so, Janis?" she asked.

Miss Elanor spun around and looked as though she would strangle the girl.

Ding, ding, ding, round two: Alex. I tried to smile as naturally as I could. "I haven't had a full tour."

Alex put her hand on Cecil's knee, "Oh Cecil, ya should have given her a tour, too."

Fitz and Miss Elanor glared at her.

Cecil smiled uncomfortably, "I wanted to grab some photos of the Castle for you," he said to me. "Some were taken a few years ago, but ya may be able to use them." He stood, letting Alex's hand fall off his lap, as he pulled them out of his shirt pocket. Walking to the other side of the table, he crouched down in front of me and presented them.

I smiled as I looked through the pile. There were pictures of him (at about eleven years old) and Scotty in front of a large decorated tree in the front walk. Others were of the whole family, including his mother, Margaret. "When did you take these?" I held up what looked like newer pictures.

"I took some of these yesterday. The sunrise photos," he added, "Were taken before our ride this morn. And there's a few from...after. The others I found in old albums last night."

My heart warmed. Even after our fight, Daniel and the kiss, and the ride from hell, he went through old photos and took new ones for me. It was more than an apology.

"These are wonderful," I said. For a moment it seemed as if we were the only two in the room. "You have quite an eye for catching the beauty of this place."

"Yes, I do," he stared at me. "I see the beauty."

I blushed a little, feeling my cheeks go rosy and warm.

I could feel the stares from around the room. Martin smiled. Miss Elanor cocked her head, questioningly. Fitz and Scotty grinned. Alex was seething.

"So, Cecil is taking me for a ride tomorrow morning," she said. This broke the spell between our eyes, but not the warmth in my chest.

"Yes. I did say I would." Cecil sat back down next to Alex, who immediately put her hand back in his lap.

He took a deep breath and looked uncomfortable again.

"I can't wait to go riding. It's my favorite thing!" She gave her lower lip a bite. "Well one of them, at least." Alex glared at me.

Fitz saw the glare and piped up, "Ya know Alex, I checked out yer store online today. Well YOU, really."

Her face went tense, "That seems like an odd thing to do."

"Doesn't it?" Fitz agreed. "Anyway, yer on the website of course."

Alex stared, eyes narrowing as Fitz spoke.

"So I thought to myself, maybe we would be friends, ya know, on social media."

Alex's jaw tightened, "Really." It was not a question.

"Yeah, I found out that yer quite an experienced rider, from what I saw."

Their eyes locked. No one else at the table, including me, had any idea what Fitz was talking about. Alex was losing her battle with remaining calm and cool.

Martin, with the rest of us, not quite understanding the whole situation asked, "Oh, did ya ride competitively, then, Miss Alex?"

Fitz gave an amused smile, "Yes Alex, did ya?"

Alex turned her attention to Martin, and cleared her throat, "Not exactly," her smile visibly forced.

"It sure looked like ya did," Fitz nodded, innocently.

Alex's eyes could have melted steel.

Fitz smiled broadly, "Dinner looks amazing Miss Elanor."

Miss Elanor accepted the compliment with a head nod.

We small talked through the rest of the meal. When dinner was over, Alex announced that Cecil had agreed to take her home, since the delivery men had driven the van back to town.

"Janie would ya like to ride along?" he asked.

I started to answer, but Alex cut me off, "Oh, I was hoping we'd take the Lamborghini. You promised me a ride," she batted her eyes. "It's a two-seater. Ya wouldn't mind stayin' behind?" she asked me.

Round three: Alex, as well. "Not at all," I smiled.

Cecil turned to me, "I shouldn't be long," he said, and put a kiss on my cheek.

Alex's eyes slit, "We'll just have to see about that, won't we?" she smiled at him.

I headed upstairs, trying not to think bad thoughts. Fitz and Scotty had adjourned back to her room. Since things weren't back to normal with them, Fitz was still laying on the sexy. I didn't want to think about the lengths she was willing to go. I wondered if she still had her 'Sheep Princess' costume.

In my room, I felt more alone than I had in some time. Blue, I thought. Period's coming? It kind of did what it wanted, and sometimes the only pre-clue I had was a change of mood. Or, maybe it was the fact that Cecil was with Alex doing God knows what. Being overly fidgety, I knew sleep was going to be an issue. I decided on a hot bath. Taking my phone, a pair of yoga pants and a bra top to change into, I headed to the bathroom.

Sinking into the tub, I tried to picture all my fears melting like candle wax. I submerged. Coming back to the surface, like a crocodile, I heard more noises in the hallway. Maybe the Castle was just settling? I mean, old homes do that, right? Do stone Castles do that? I wondered. How much more settling could a 300 plus year old Castle do?

I dressed and made it back into my room without running into anyone. Now, everything in my mind came at once. I was excited thinking about painting, especially in that beautiful room. How sweet Cecil was to provide and take pictures for me. What did platypuses do for fun? Like I said... everything. I looked out the window. Had Cecil returned home yet? Turning off the light, I forced myself to sleep.

Late into the night, I was awakened by a noise. It was the sound of a door. I assumed, in my state of sleepiness, that it was most likely Scotty sneaking out of Fitz's room. But then it dawned on me, I was facing my door, but the noise came from behind me. I felt a whoosh of air and heard a clicking noise.

Like a gun I shot out of bed, through my door, to Fitz's room. I knocked, without stopping. FINALLY, Fitz answered the door, sleeping mask pulled up to reveal one half-shut eye.

"Is Scotty here?" I asked.

"No!" She looked grumpy, but I couldn't tell if it was from being woken up, or another night without.

"Come on!" I grabbed her by the arm and pulled her to my room. I threw open the door and turned to Fitz. She was standing but both eyes were closed. "Damn it Fitz, wake up!"

"She whined at me and opened her eyes, "This had better be good."

"I think someone was in my room!"

"We already know that, hence the dressin' gown," she turned to stumble back to her bed."

"No! I think there's a passageway in my room."

She stopped and turned to me, "Where?" she whispered. I pointed to the wall, with the chest of drawers, next to the bed.

We both walked to the other side of the bed, cautiously, expecting the boogie man to jump out and eat us. She ran her hand around the dresser. She tried to move the chest away from the wall. That's when she realized the chest was built into the wall.

"There has to be a lever or switch of some kind. Remember what Martin said? They were all fixed so he wouldn't get stuck in one. So it must open from both sides, right?"

I shrugged, "That would make sense."

Fitz moved her hand further out from the dresser, "Right here, you can feel air passing through."

Reaching out my hand, I could feel it as well. The wall looked absolutely seamless. We touched and moved everything we could think of.

"What if the lever isn't on this wall, but somewhere else in the room?" I asked.

"Seems farfetched, then again, so does someone sneaking into yer room through a secret passageway in a 300 year old Castle, yet, here we are."

We touched and moved every last thing in the room. Running out of ideas, I almost convinced myself that I was insane, and that Castles were just drafty. Fitz and I sat on the bed, pondering. At the same time, we both looked over our shoulders at the creepy picture.

"You think?" I asked.

"Only one way to find out," she replied.

We stood on the bed to move the painting, "This damn thing gives me the creeps," she said, reaching out her hand.

"Yeah, I'm aware. I sleep underneath it, remember?"

"So do I most nights," she giggled.

We moved the bottom of the painting to the right, and voila! The wall, dresser and all quietly sprung open.

I looked at Fitz, "We don't have a flashlight."

"Hang on," she said, and ran out the door. She returned a moment later with the candelabra from her room.

"Yeah," I said, "Only one thing could make a secret passageway in a 300 year old Castle more 'creepy' and that would be to see it by candlelight. What if it goes out?"

She held up a lighter, "Always prepared!" she grinned.

"Now you're thinking, I guess." I looked at the black passageway, "You should probably go first, since you have the candle and all."

Fitz smiled and handed it to me. "Have at it."

Taking the candle and a deep breath, I entered the passageway. I was immediately met with grey stone walls and floors. I hadn't expected to see a window, but there it was, bringing in moonlight. From its vantage point, if I looked to my far left, I could see the stable in the distance. The garage was even further to the left but well out of my view. A short ways down the passageway was a door.

"This must be Margaret's room," I whispered to Fitz. We both did obvious shudders.

"Do ya want to try the door?" she asked me.

I thought for a moment then shook my head, "Not really. You?" I asked.

"No, it's kind of taboo, isn't it? I mean it's locked for a reason, right?"

I nodded at her. I knew the truth, we were both pussies, and assumed that Dracula slept in Margaret's locked room.

We continued down the hall soon coming to a spiral staircase. "Are we up to this," I asked, starting to get fidgety.

"Look, someone HAS been in yer room. I'm pretty sure it wasn't Margaret."

I did a shudder at the thought of Margaret, in specter form, visiting me as I slept.

"We have to follow this passageway, to figure out where it ends, so we can figure out who's sneakin' about yer room."

"What if it goes down to the dungeon?" I asked.

"I won't have to worry about that. Neither will you."

I looked at her questioningly.

"I'll be be back up those stairs in the click-of-a-heel."

I nodded, resigned to the fact.

"Try and keep up," she smiled.

Down the staircase we went. The ceiling was tall enough that I didn't have to duck, but the steps were made for much smaller feet. It felt like we wound down forever. I almost expected to end up in Hell or at the very least, Purgatory. Rats squeaked away from us and scurried into black crevasses. Fitz hopped from foot to foot, and "Eeewwed!" behind me. Darker and darker, the candle did it's best to produce enough light to see three feet in front of us. The air changed, grew cooler and moved around us. If I came across a skeleton down here, I'd pee myself for sure. The staircase came to a straight away and on we trekked.

"Holy crap, it's getting cold. Are we outside?" Fitz asked.

I shivered, "That would be my guess. Martin did say that one of these tunnels, led all the way into town."

"Well, if we don't find a door or outlet soon, we better head back."

"Agreed," I said, but on we went, fueled by a need to know.

After a short while a ladder appeared, but the tunnel continued on.

"What should we do? Up? Or forward?" I asked.

"Up!" she was shaking from the cold, "For the love of God, up!"

Handing her the candle, up the ladder I went, hitting my head on a trap door. "Ouch!"

"Quit playin' Janie. Open the damn door!"

I pushed and pushed. "I think it's locked. I can't budge it!"

"Move over! I'm comin' up!"

I stood to one side of the ladder as Fitz worked her way up. Together we pushed and the trap door opened. Our heads popping up, we were in the middle of the stable. We climbed the rest of the way out to finally stand on familiar ground. I looked around, hands on hips. "Huh."

"So, basically, anyone could have used this passageway," Fitz said.

I nodded. "Anyone who knows about the passageway," I added.

"Well, that doesn't exactly narrow things down, now does it?"

"Not really. But I can't see Miss Elanor wandering around down there."

Fitz shook her head. "Me either, but we can't really rule her out, can we? I mean, she may be a psychopath. Psychopaths ARE unpredictable," she added.

I just stared at her.

Someone was coming. I could hear the whistling of "Oh Danny Boy."

"Hide," I whispered.

"Why?" Fitz asked. "We're just visitin' the stable."

"Right and we got our butts locked out of the Castle to do so? The only way were getting back in, is back through the passageway, or wake someone up!"

Martin knows we've been in the passageway. What's the big deal?"

"I don't want whoever's been in my room to know, that I know. Get it?"

"Gotcha!"

Fitz and I ran to the empty stall that Daniel had hid in the night before.

Within seconds of finding cover Daniel entered the stable. He was a little tipsy, I thought. He began singing to the horses. I heard a car pulling up the drive. It was the Lamborghini.

"Really?" I whispered to Fitz. "He's just getting back now? It's the dead of night!"

"Shhh! Hold yer tongue!"

Cecil entered the stable and saw Daniel, his back to Fitz and me, leaned up against a bale of hay. "Whatcha doin' there Daniel? It's late."

"Aye, just as late for me as it is fer you," he smiled and held out his flask to Cecil."

Cecil took a pull of whiskey from the flask. "So, what's on yer agenda for tonight?"

"Just singin' to the horses." His S's a little slurred. "I see ya took Miss Alex home."

"Aye," Cecil handed back the flask, as he took a seat next

to him.

Great, I thought, now they're blocking the trap door. I was pulled from my thoughts quickly though.

"She's quite a looker, isn't she?" Daniel said.

"Yes, yes, she is," Cecil sighed, almost dreamily. "And that body," he added, "Must have been gifted by the gods themselves."

I reached for the pitchfork that was leaning up against the stall wall.

Fitz shook her wide eyed head at me.

"And she's quite a kisser, too," Cecil added.

My eyes narrowed.

Fitz gave me the 'go ahead' hand movement to pitchfork him now, but I just sat listening and fuming."

Daniel took a swig then offered Cecil another drink. "Ya know, Miss Janie is quite a kisser," he said. "Almost knocked my socks off."

I nodded my head.

"It looked like it. Janie...is just so...difficult!" Cecil finally emitted. "She makes me crazy, ya know?"

"Aye," Daniel agreed. "But, I bet she's worth it."

"Maybe," Cecil started, "But Alex...Alex is just so much easier."

I nodded again. Easy was definitely one of the words I would use to describe her. Gold digger, tramp...

"I've always been attracted to women who were...fun. Could just enjoy the moment, ya know?'

Daniel nodded, "I do. I believe it's an Irish thing."

"But Janie is all, 'Sex needs to mean something', he mimicked. 'I need to be in a relationship', he made a whining voice.

My eyes rounded at his impression of me. Fitz sat wincing.

"Janie wants the relationship guy," he made air quote as he

said it. "But how can a man be sure he wants to be in a relationship, with someone he hasn't slept with?" he asked Daniel.

"I haven't slept with Miss Janie, and I'd take her hand tomorrow."

"That's because ya don't know how impossible she is," Cecil smiled. "The first night I met her," he sighed, "She was just so...in control. The more I get to know her, the more I think she's a control freak."

Wounded, I let my eyes dropped to the floor.

Fitz put her hand out and stroked my hair. Raising my chin, she looked me dead in my watering eyes and shook her head 'no'.

Cecil continued, "At first I thought she was just hard to get, making me want her more. But there is something to be said for a woman who wants you, ya know? Alex makes it so clear. She's easy to read. No guessing!"

I shook my head. Down the stable Babygirl began to neigh frantically.

"Wonder what has my girl riled?" Cecil said, both men standing to check on her. As they walked to Babygirl's stall, Fitz grabbed my hand and we darted, rabbit quick, out of the stable. We were half way to the Castle when we realized, there was no way to get back in. We were stuck out in the cold.

"Now what?" I asked. "Freeze our asses off?"

"No way," Fitz said, shivering. She looked around, "Come on."

"Maybe the front door is unlocked?" I offered.

"Would you leave the front door of a Castle unlocked?" she looked at me like I had no sense at all.

I followed her to the garage. Opening the door we used the lighter to find the Rolls. Taking the thick quilted tarp off the top, we climbed into the backseat and huddled underneath it.

Now, in total darkness but warming quickly, Fitz asked, "Are ya okay?"

It took a moment before I said, "Yeah, I'm fine."

"So no, huh?"

I couldn't talk. I was trying not to cry. Hearing how Cecil saw me hurt more than I thought it would. The first night we met I had been playing a part of the sexy seductress. He liked her, but the real me? Not so much. Hearing how he felt about Alex, hurt even more.

"Ya know he's not right."

"Sure he is," I said.

She pulled me into a hug and just held me. "It's okay, Janie girl," she soothed.

I'm really not sure why, but she began to sing High Hopes. I curled up next to her and the next thing I know I was woken up by the sound of the mechanic opening the electric garage door. Light flooded in, then Fitz and I were found, cuddled up under the tarp, in the backseat of the Rolls. Fonzie, (of the Fonzie and Dean duo, as I remembered him) stared through the window at us.

"Fitz!" I said. "Wake up. We have company."

Fitz, who was still holding me, woke.

Fonzie opened the door for us. "Uh, good mornin' ladies," he said, looking very confused.

"Good mornin' to ya," Fitz stretched.

I'm sure I looked guilty as hell, but not for whatever he was thinking.

"Are ya okay?" he asked us.

"Sure," Fitz answered. "Sometimes girls just need a place to be alone, ya know?"

He nodded his head, but the look on his face told me that this didn't clear things up for him. He helped us exit the car, and Fitz said, "The backseat is pretty comfy."

I noticed that Dean was putting the Lamborghini on the lift to check it out.

"Uh, yeah," Fonzie answered.

"Have a good day," she said over her shoulder as we walked away.

"You too, Miss."

We headed back up the path, the sun just coming over the horizon, I asked, "Do you suppose he thinks we're closet..."

Fitz cut me off, "Definitely," she grabbed my hand for his benefit.

"Great," I grinned. "Do you suppose he'll tell everyone where he found us?"

"Maybe, but it's easier to explain than the truth."

"I'd love to hear the explanation, myself."

"As soon as I think of one, I'll let ya know," she smiled.

Briggs was at the door, as we entered. He looked confused at our being outside in our apparent bed attire.

No time like the present I thought, looking at Fitz.

"Ladies?" he said.

"Good morning Briggs," Fitz said. "Went for a late night stroll, and locked ourselves out. We didn't want to wake the whole household, so we slept in the garage."

"Very well, Miss," he said, furrowing his brows. "We will be breaking fast at seven. Is there anything you may require?"

"We're good," she said.

"And just so you know, Miss's, the doors are left unlocked."

I shot a look at Fitz.

"How was I supposed to know?" she said and pulled me off to the staircase.

"That was what you came up with, huh?"

"The truth is easier to remember, and it's mostly that. Omittin' how we got outside, and the whole stable incident. Now go get ready for breakfast. I'm starvin'!"

14

ALEX, ALEX, ALEX

I dressed quickly and checked my phone; A text from Betty. When I opened it, there was a picture of a man who had a striking resemblance to Jesus, except with a blonde man-bun. I read the text below the photo, "This is the guy yer mom's been meeting at yer house. Does he look familiar?"

Of course he does, I thought. He's the Messiah...with a man-bun. What the hell is going on, I wondered.

I typed back, "Haven't a clue," then headed down to breakfast.

Scotty and Martin were already in the dining hall when Fitz and I arrived. I said my good mornings to them both. Fitz put a kiss on both of their cheeks then took her seat.

Miss Elanor entered the room and looked sidelong at me with a raised eyebrow. I, too, raised my brows. "Good morning?" I said to Miss Elanor as more of a question. She set down the tray of scrambled eggs, and asked, "Did you ladies sleep well?"

I began to stammer but Fitz cut me off, "Very well," she held Miss Elanor's gaze. "And you? Did you sleep well?" Miss Elanor didn't answer, but left the room.

Cecil dragged himself in looking haggard, unshaven and a little hung over. How long had he and Daniel sat drinking and making fun of me?

He walked over to me, and put a kiss on my cheek. "Good morning, Janie."

I stiffened and forced a smile, but said nothing. We all helped ourselves to eggs, sausage and potatoes. Cecil ate like he was trying to kill a hangover. Ravenously!

I picked at my food.

"Aren't ya hungry?" Cecil asked.

"Not particularly," I answered.

"Yer gonna start paintin' today, right? Yer gonna need yer energy."

"Oh, don't you worry about that" I said, picking up my glass of juice, "I have it under control...like always," I added.

Fitz tried to kick me under the table, but the table was too wide. So she swung her leg out and slid down off her seat, catching herself on the chair arms before going under the table completely.

"Scotty caught her arm and helped her up to a sitting position, "Whoa there luv, where ya goin'," he asked.

"I slipped," she rounded her eyes at me. "I won't slip again," she warned.

"Martin," I said, "I'd still like to go to the distillery. Take some photos and just get a feel for the place."

"I can take you," Cecil said.

I continued, "Until then, I'd like to start the painting of the manor. I have some photo's you can look at. Choose which view you want, or time of day?"

Martin smiled warmly, "I actually want yer vision of the manor. How you see it. I adore yer paintin's and want one that is 'all you'."

I smiled, "I'm honored. Thank you."

Miss Elanor went stiff as a board.

"I have obligations already today, but I can take you to the distillery maybe tomorrow," Cecil added.

"Yeah, well, I know you don't really enjoy planning things, so we'll see tomorrow. Okay?" I excused myself, saying that I wanted to start painting. Before I could leave the room, Briggs announced Miss Alex's arrival. "Shit," I said under my breath, as we met face to face. She was in skin tight jeans, riding boots, and of course a red tank top that was having trouble holding in her sizable assets.

"Well, good morning to you too, Jamie," she fake smiled.

Fitz stood, "Her name is Janie. If yer having a hard time remembering it...I can help ya!" her eyes flickered.

Alex looked amused, "I have such a hard time remembering the small things," she answered.

Fitz's smile became frightening, as she came closer to Alex and whispered almost inaudibly, "The only thing small in this room, is yer self respect. Try remembering that. I know I will," she added.

Fitz and I left the room, with Scotty in tow.

"I have to go to the City with dad," he said. "Another long one, I'm afraid. Kiss me for luck?"

"What exactly do ya need luck for?" Fitz asked.

"There's nothin' for ya to worry about, it's just business stuff."

Fitz was still trying to entice him into a sexually successful interlude. She wrapped her arms around her man's neck and laid a kiss on him that could have been the cause of global warming. I turned to the stairs and exited to give them their privacy.

I changed into my jean painting overalls that were damn near threadbare in the knees, and wrapped my long hair into a bun. Fitz joined me a few moments later, grinning from ear to ear. “I've got him,” she announced. “He'll think about that kiss all day!”

“No doubt,” I agreed with her.

“Can I go with ya to the paintin' room?”

“Sure, but I think you're gonna be bored stiff.”

“I'll bring myself a trashy novel and enjoy the view of the meadow.”

“Fine by me, but I'm listening to Mozart,” I warned her.

“Fine,” she said, sullen. “I'll have the kitchen make me a bloody mary.”

“How can you drink and read? Do you remember anything?” I asked.

“It keeps me busy at the moment. The memory of it doesn't have to keep me busy later.”

I cocked my head at her, “You and I read for totally different reason,” I concluded.

“It's a trashy novel, Janie. I'd rather live it than read it.”

Off to the atrium we went. Once again the house dwarfed me, as I tried to find my way. I kept wondering, where is the Ben Franklin bust? We finally found it and made all the turns that eventually led us to the painting room.

A knock at the door brought our maids, Carrie and Mary, holding a tray full of goodies, a pitcher of Bloody Marys and another of water.

“Good morning, Misses,” Carrie said, setting down the tray.

Mary smiled, “Yes, good morning.”

“Hi ladies, ah look what ya brought me. Yum,” Fitz grabbed a glass and poured her first drink.

The maids giggled. “Did ya need anything else?” Carrie asked.

“No, I believe I'm good,” Fitz said, warming up to her glass. “This is fantastic. Seriously the best I've ever had.”

“Well, don't tell Mum that,” I joked.

"Seriously Janie, you have to try this."

"I need to decide which picture I'm using, and start sketching."

"No really, come on, one taste! I swear, ya can't turn this down, or you'll look back from yer deathbed and it'll be a regret."

I was busy going through the stack of pictures, "Well, I think I'll risk it."

"I don't know why ya just can't take one little drink?"

"Because I want to be present," I explained.

"Present? And one sip...of the best Bloody Mary ever, is goin' to make you un-present?"

I looked at her, "I don't think that's a word. At least not the way you're using it, Fitz."

"Fine dis-present then."

I smiled and shook my head. Mary and Carrie giggled behind their hands.

"One sip," she brought the glass to me.

"If I take one sip, will you let me get to work?"

She stuck her pinky out at me, and I locked hers with mine," I pinky swear."

"Fine," I took the glass.

Carrie had moved to the window, "Um Misses?"

I didn't really hear her as I tried the Bloody Mary and said, "Damn, that's fantastic!"

"I told ya, huh?" Fitz smiled as I took another sip.

"Oh, for the love of Pete!" Mary exclaimed, meeting Carrie at the window.

"Now I'm going to crave these. I hope you're happy!" I told Fitz.

"Right? I can't even imagine what's in here." She stared down at the half full glass I handed back."

"It looks like those may be feta stuffed olives," I said.

"No, I think they're blue cheese. Oh, wait, I think there's one of each," I looked down in the glass.

"Misses!" Carrie and Mary called out in unison, breaking us away from the heaven sent drink.

Fitz and I startled by their yell, walked to the window to see whatever it was that had the maids so upset.

Looking out, at first I saw nothing. I looked at Mary and Carrie, "What's up ladies?"

Mary pointed, "Out there Miss."

While we stood, trying to figure out what the hell they were looking at, I saw Babygirl bolt into view. On her back was a brown haired blur of a woman. She was barely holding on. Now, into view came Cecil on horseback racing behind.

"Holy shit!" I said.

"Fitz brought the drink to her lips and said, "Damn, that Babygirl is fast."

All three of us turned to look her.

"What? I'm just sayin'," she shrugged and turned away from the window to go refill her glass.

"Where is she heading? The lake isn't that way?" I shook my head.

"No Miss, it looks like she heading to the farm," Carrie said.

"There's a farm?" I asked.

"It actually belongs to Mr. Callaghan. But he bought the property when the man, who once owned the land, was going to lose his home."

"Yes," said Mary, "Mr. Callaghan owns the land, but lets the man live there. All the money he gets from the farm, Mr. Callaghan lets him keep."

"So is there a fence or a gate, something to stop Babygirl?" I asked.

"Nothing will stop that horse," Carrie said. "She's a verter!"

I looked at her, "What does that mean, exactly?" I asked,

watching Babygirl run past the window again. Cecil was several hoof beats behind, yelling wildly at Babygirl to stop.

Brown hair, no longer in a ponytail, bouncing in the saddle and legs flailing, Alex was on the ride of her life.

"It means, she's a hurdler," Mary said "And a damn good one, too!"

She covered her mouth, embarrassed for cursing in front of me.

"Crap! Can you get me through this maze of hallways to the front door, and quick?"

"It'll be faster if we go out the back door from the kitchens," Carrie announced.

Carrie and Mary led the way, with me in tow. "Fitz are ya coming?" I yelled to her.

"Fine," she said, setting down the drink.

All four of us ran through the Castle. I couldn't believe this was a shorter route. As we sprang from the back door we headed out over the meadow behind the house. We had to race up a hill of green grass. I thought I was going to die. The maids had their skirts pulled high on the sides and were far ahead of me and Fitz. Suddenly at the top, they stopped and brought their hands to their mouths.

Catching up, I realized that they were stifling giggles behind their hands. I stopped, bent and grabbed my knees for stability as I panted.

Coming back up the hill, was a very pissed off Alex, covered in mud. Cecil was trying to help her, but she was slapping his hands and screaming wildly. "Don't you touch me! You should have that beast put down! Made into glue...or dog food!"

My eyes widened. "Oh my God, Babygirl threw her in the mud!"

"I don't think that's mud, Miss," Carrie grinned. "Before you made it up the hill...I saw her sitting in the pig's shitpile."

Fitz laughed so hard she snorted through her panting.

Mary said, "It took her a bit to get her footin'. She fell back into the pile...a couple of times," her lips disappearing, as she tried not to laugh out loud.

"Oh shit!" I winced.

"I think that's accurate," Fitz fell to the ground.

I wasn't sure if we should head back to the Castle or not. Seeing Alex, covered in shit, smacking at Cecil as he tried to apologize, was like watching a train wreck. I started walking down the hill towards Babygirl, leaving Fitz and the maids behind. Alex was making a B-line at me.

"You!" Alex yelled, pointing a shit covered finger.

My eyes widened, "Me?" I asked.

"You!" she growled, again. "You made this happen!" she then yelled, closing the distance between us angry-tramp-style. "You told me yesterday that I made a powerful enemy!" She was seething with hate and a smell so putrid, it burned my nose. "You didn't mean you...or your redheaded bimbo friend! You meant her!" she pointed at Babygirl.

My eyes narrowed, "Well if you remember that conversation so well, you also remember what I said about Fitz. I pulled back my hand to smack her, but her shit covered shoes slipped on the damp grass and she landed on her ass.

Fitz and the maids on the hill began to yell, hoot and applaud.

"Twice!" I looked down at her. "There won't be a third warning."

"Well go ahead!" she lifted her jaw. "What's stoppin' ya!"

"Shit splatters," I grinned.

"Janie!" Cecil yelled, running to Alex's side.

She batted at him again. "Away! Step away!"

"I'm so sorry, Alex," Cecil offered.

"Give me a break," I said and headed down towards Babygirl.

"Janie," Cecil yelled at me, "Are ya crazy? Get back here and apologize!"

"For what?" I yelled back. "And, not a chance!"

Alex, noticing that she had created a divide between us, began fake crying.

"Alex, are ya okay? Let me help ya up," Cecil said.

"I can't believe the animals you surround yerself with. You know, she threatened me yesterday."

With that, I stopped dead in my tracks and walked back towards her. "Tell him why."

"I have no idea," she said, dramatically.

"Tell him WHY!" I yelled at her.

"Janie, I don't think there's any reason why you should threaten, much less hit Alex."

"She's just crazy," Alex whispered.

My chest was heaving, "If you believe that, Mr. Moneybags," Alex's eyes narrowed and her fake crying stopped, "Then you know what, you two deserve each other!"

I walked down to the farm and climbed the gate to where Babygirl was pacing. "Are you okay, girl?"

She nodded, and pawed the ground. "Let's get you back to the stable, okay? Grabbing her reigns, I walked her to the gate and led her out. Walking back up the meadow with Babygirl at my side, she began to nudge me with her nose.

"What?" I asked her.

She stopped walking and folded her front leg, bowing.

So I bowed back. She shook her giant head. She went into a deeper bow.

"Oh God," I finally caught on. "You don't want me to ride you?"

She nodded.

"I'm not sure that's a good idea."

Babygirl nodded again.

"I'm not sure I can even get on your back," I tried to rationalize with the giant beast.

She bowed till she was almost lying on the ground.

"I just..."

She stared at me.

"Okay!" I put my hands up. "But please be careful. My ass is still sore from yesterday."

I climbed on her back, with absolutely no grace, and she stood.

She began walking, and I started to calm down. This was kind of awesome. She started to trot, and I found a rhythm to it, so my ass wasn't slamming in the saddle. I held on tighter.

"Don't hurt me Babygirl," I said, as she broke into a run. Just as I was starting to think that I had been crazy to get back on her, I pulled a little on the reigns and she slowed some. I pulled a little more and she slowed again. I gently pulled to the right and she followed. I believed it was her way of letting me know that she would actually let me ride her.

I smiled broadly and whispered to her, "You feel like a run?"

She nodded her big head and took off. I was startled at first. She was so fast. I leaned down into her and just let her run. Fitz and the maids were cheering again. As I rode past them, I yelled out a yee-haw! Riding on Babygirl's back was like riding the wind. After a short while we headed back to the stable. Sitting on a bale of hay, was Cecil.

I dismounted Babygirl, and gave her a pat. She walked to Cecil and nudged him. "Go to yer stall, Babygirl. I want to talk to Janie."

She looked hurt, but walked to her stall, with her giant head hung.

"It wasn't her fault entirely," I started.

"Not entirely. But she did throw Alex in the shitpile."

I tried not to laugh, "Where is Alex?"

"She went home." He stood and looked at me. "Why did ya threaten to hit her, Janie?"

"Can't I just say she had it coming, and leave it at that?"

"No, I'm afraid I require an explanation," he stared.

"You require an explanation?" I repeated. "Who do you think you are, my father?"

"I deserve one then," he raised his eyes to mine.

"It wasn't about you."

"What was the Mr. Moneybags comment about?"

"That's between me and Alex."

"Ya better start tellin' me somethin', Janie. I'm startin' to think..." he trailed off.

"What? What are you starting to think?"

He let out a sigh, "That yer jealous and tryin' to sabotage somethin'."

I nodded, "That's what you think?"

"Aye," he dropped his eyes to the floor.

I took a deep breath, "Ya know what? Fine! If that makes sense to you, then you don't need an explanation from me." I turned and walked away.

I made it halfway back up to the Castle when I heard him behind me, "Ya know what? No! I want ya to explain! How do you justify trying to hit another person."

"Look, I told her point blank, that if she said one more word about Fitz, I'd hit her. Actually, I said I'd tear her eyes out of her botoxed face! I think she got off light, falling on her ass," I huffed, picking up my pace.

"So yer tellin' me, this is all about Fitz?"

I overshot the front of the house in my desperate attempt to get away from him.

"I'm saying I would hit her because of what she said about

Fitz." I looked around and was closer to the kitchen door, than the front of the Castle. I started walking, with absolute determination, to the back of the Castle.

"So that's the only reason?" he asked.

"That I'd hit her? Yeah. It's the only reason I'd hit her."

"Ya just can't admit it, can ya?" he said, on my heels. "Ya just won't let yer damn guard down. Say what ya really think or feel."

"What are you talking about?" the back door was within view.

"You! You are so damned..." he was looking for a word.

"What? Impossible?"

His look changed to one of question.

"How about control freak? Does that sum me up?" I asked, walking through the kitchen door and not knowing where to go from there.

Cecil caught me by the arm and I spun around, "Why would you say those things?" he asked.

I tightened my jaw. "It is what you think of me, right? I have to be in control of everything, right?"

"Where did ya hear that?"

"I don't see you answering the question," I stared into his eyes. Rage building between us, "I'm afraid I require one!"

Our eyes locked, "Yes," he answered. "Now tell me why ya were gonna hit Alex."

"I did tell you why."

"There ya go again. You refuse to say how ya feel. That's what I'm talkin' about. You spend so much time controllin' yerself that ya just let things pass ya by. Just like that guy?"

"What guy?" I demanded.

"The one that has ya so wound, ya won't even look at another man. But while yer busy holdin' on, is he busy holdin' his life for you?"

I grinned, "Wow, are you off." I pulled away, turning to walk out.

"He's engaged, Janie."

I stopped dead in my tracks.

"He's goin' to marry another."

I spun on him, my heart beating wildly.

"Why don't ya just deal with it, instead of running? He's in love with someone else, and there's nothin' you can do about it."

I pursed my lips, trying to 'will' my tears away. "I don't know who you're talking about!"

"Yes ya do. I've seen the stares. I know the longing in yer eyes every time you look at him. I'm surprised Fitz never caught on. How the hell have ya kept this from her?"

Just then, down the galley, the refrigerator door closed. There stood Fitz, with a fresh Bloody Mary in her hand. "What's he talkin' about, Janie?" she asked.

My eyes fell closed. When they opened tears had made their way to the surface. Cecil looked from Fitz to me. I stared at him.

"Seriously Janie, he's not talkin' about Scotty?" she laughed.

I dropped my eyes and shook my head.

She pondered for a moment, "Barry?" she asked.

I nodded

Cecil said in a whisper, "I didn't know she was there. I swear it."

I met his eyes and just went cold as ice.

"Yer...in love...with Barry?" she asked while walking towards me.

"It's a crush," I said weakly.

"How long?" her face had turned to stone.

"A ridiculous crush," I added.

"How long!" she demanded.

I took a deep breath, "As long as I can remember."

"Since ya met? Since we first became friends?"

I nodded.

She stuck her tongue in her cheek, “So I have two questions. First, how could ya keep this from me?”

“You knew I had a crush on him when we were young. It just...never went completely away. I wanted to tell you, but it was complicated, and...”

She cut me off mid sentence, “Yeah, I bet!”

“Fitz, you don't understand...”

“Second,” she practically yelled at me, “Was yer crush...why we became friends? So you could get close to him?”

I was shocked, and my face showed it, “Are you kidding me, Fitz? We've been friends for over twenty years!” I was pleading.

“Yeah...as long as you've had a crush on my brother, right?”

“I can't believe you would even ask that. You know how I feel about you. I think of you as my sister!”

“But, you don't think of him as yer brother though, right?”

“Fitz, yes, I've had a ridiculous crush on him...practically my whole life, but I'd rather have you as my sister, than have...anything with him.”

“I asked ya point blank who Cecil thought ya had a crush on!”

“I know, I just couldn't bring myself to...”

“Ya lied to me!” she yelled. “You looked me right in the eye...and lied.” Her stare filled with rage, “Ya told me “No one,” you had feelings for no one!”

I was having trouble breathing as I tried to swallow back my tears.

“Did ya ever think,” she started, “That if ya had gotten together...with yer horrible man problems...and ridiculous track record...you could lose me as a friend? Did ya ever even consider that?”

“Of course I did. Why do you think he's just been a crush all of these years?”

"Because ya knew ya had no chance with him!" she replied viciously, then turned, and walked away from me.

Tears fell and a pain hit my chest that I hadn't felt in years. It felt like my heart broke in two. Not just because she said something so hurtful, but, because I knew my truth had hurt her. Hurt us. "Fitz...Fitz, please!" I was begging for her to hear me but she just kept walking.

I let out a heart crushed sob. Cecil dropped his head, and said, "Janie, I'm so sorry. I swear, I never meant to cause a fight between ya."

I turned on him, "Well, you wanted it out? There you go, I guess."

"Janie..." he started.

"Just so you know," I cut him off, "None of this...had anything to do with him. None of it!" I repeated then walked out the back door.

Across the meadow I went, with no idea where I was heading. The big open grounds, now felt like a prison I couldn't escape from. Just then, I looked at my phone and saw an incoming call from Betty. I debated on whether or not to just let the call go to voice mail but needed to hear a friendly voice.

Taking a deep breath, and trying to steady myself, I flipped open my phone.

"Hi Betty."

"Hello there, Puddin."

"How's it going at home?"

"I'm good! How are you?" the question real in her voice.

"I'm okay."

"Uh huh," she seemed to be zeroing in on me. "Ya sure?"

"Yeah, just homesick," I answered. In a way it was true.

"Well, I met that gentleman today. The one yer mom's been meetin'."

For the moment, I was done focusing on my problems. "Really? How?"

"Well Puddin, I set up a painter and decided to meet him at yer house. Your mom wasn't happy when I told her that the painter, and myself would be there for the next week or so."

"Hmm," I said.

"Well, then that guy showed up, the Messiah look-a-like."

"We need to find another name for him," I suggested. "I was raised Catholic. Something about referring to him as the Savior, just seems...sacrilegious," I finished.

"Man-bun?" she suggested.

I rolled this around in my head, "Yeah, that's better."

"When he walked up the painter, yer mom and I were outside lookin' at the house. She tried to pretend that he was a beggar, saying, "You look like you could use a warm place to sit." He looked confused, but yer mom was givin' him the eyes, and he finally caught on. Then she handed him a five and said there was a coffee house a couple blocks away and to have a cup of coffee on her. She then blessed him and sent him on his way."

I had to laugh, "Really?"

Betty was laughing too, "Yer mom sure is determined. I told the painter what color I wanted, and she tried to railroad me saying that you would prefer blue."

"What color did you pick?" I asked.

"Yellow. But not a mustard yellow, a sunshine yellow."

"Yep, I would prefer sunshine yellow."

"I thought so. I went with yellow' much to yer mom's dismay. She doesn't like not gettin' her way, does she?"

I was still laughing, "Not really. She thinks of her opinions as facts."

"Well, after she and I bickered a bit, I left and went down to that coffee shop."

"Was Man-bun there?"

"Yep, I went in and started up a conversation with him. Just some "Talk about the weather" kind of stuff, but he kept staring at my bosom as we spoke."

My eyes rounded, "What? That's weird...and uncomfortable," I added.

"Well, Puddin, that's what I told him. I said, "It's not polite to stare at a woman's breasts, when she's lookin' ya in the eye." He began apologizin' and said that he was sorry, but my 'shakers' were off."

"Ugh...what?" I had to ask.

"Then he said he could align my shakers."

My eyes damn near popped out of my skull.

"I was just about to clean Man-Bun's clock, when he put up his hands and tried to explain. Apparently, shakers are some kind of portholes in the body?" she sounded confused.

My brow furrowed, as she continued.

"He said they were supposed to spin, and that when they weren't spinnin', somethin' was off."

"I finally got it, and laughed, "You mean chakras?"

"Yeah, that's what he called 'em."

I began laughing.

"Then he grabbed my palm, and told me I would be gettin' married soon."

"If that guy only knew just how close he had come to an ass beating!" I shook my head.

"Tell me about it. I wasn't sure what to grab from my purse, the pepper spray, taser or the gun," she laughed.

"So, did you get anything else from him?"

"He seemed to be one of those spiritual guys, from what I gather. I still prefer my religion the old fashioned way, 'Hellfire and Damnation', but he was enlightenin'. Once I realized he didn't want to play with my boobs, that is."

"He just doesn't sound like someone my mom would be spending time with."

"He received a call during our talk and said he had to go. I followed him back to yer house where he met yer mom on the porch. They bowed to each other then went inside. You don't think maybe yer mom has joined a cult, do ya?" she asked.

"No, I can't see that. She also enjoys the 'Hellfire and Damnation' approach to God. Although...even that seems more likely than an affair. Did you get a name?"

"Ya know, I was kickin' myself in the ass for that. It's just not Southern to have a conversation and not introduce yerself. I told him my name, but he just smiled and shook my hand. I'm sure he'll tell yer mom that I met him at the coffee shop and started a conversation. My cover is blown, sugar."

"So now what?" I asked.

"Now? I just make myself a menace," she laughed. "All kinds of things need to be done to that house."

I winced. I liked my house, just as it was. A new coat of paint, was one thing, but I didn't want my house completely changed. "Don't go to any trouble, Betty."

"No trouble, Puddin. I was thinking of adding some equity to the house, anyway."

Crap, I thought but said, "It is your house."

"Oh, I have to go Puddin, I'm gettin' a call from Larry. God, I miss that man!"

I smiled, "Okay Betty, thank you," I said and rang off.

Great, I thought, this created more questions. What would my mother be doing hanging out with a thirty-something year old spiritual guy with a man-bun? And, what the hell was Betty going to do to my home? On the bright side, her home was beautiful. Maybe it wouldn't be so bad.

I walked a bit, stuck in my own head, but I was pulled back to

Fitz. The look on her face was breaking my heart over and over again. I wanted to be mad at Cecil. But the truth was, I had been keeping this secret, longer than I had known him. It may have been his fault that it came out but not that it existed. I understood where Fitz was coming from. Ex's of the Fitzpatrick's, didn't hang out at the house, or the pub. They didn't go to family gatherings or parties. They were exes! She was also right about my track record, sixteen break-ups in ten years. And always, I was the dumpee, not the dumper. My track record as it stood showed a likelihood that if Barry and I had dated, this would have been the outcome. I would have become just another ex, to the Fitzpatrick brood. I tried to think of life without them. No Mum. No Da. No brothers. No crazy Aunt Marble. The thought made me feel like an orphan. Then I thought of no Fitz. The air was sucked out of my lungs again. I shook my head. I couldn't even handle the thought.

I ended up at the stable. Babygirl was in her stall, looking sullen.

"Hello," I said, as I approached.

She stuck her giant black head out of the stall and neighed. Reaching my hand out to her, she rubbed her nose against my palm.

"Well, at least you're happy to see me," I said.

She nodded her head.

"I enjoyed the ride this morning. Actually, I enjoyed the ride you took Alex on too," I smiled.

She nodded her head again.

"She's not a good person. Then again, maybe I'm not either."

Babygirl put her giant head against my chest.

I rubbed her ears, "Thank you," I said, as a tear fell.

She lifted her head, and licked the tear from my cheek.

I tried not to gross out. Not being exactly fond of dog kisses, horse kisses held the same icky factor. Really, I didn't like anything licking my face, but I smiled none the less. She let me wrap my arms around her neck, and I stood hugging her.

"He makes me crazy, you know?"

She neighed and nodded.

"Even if I don't want to, I have real feelings for him."

She nuzzled me, again.

"Impossible relationships... I am the queen of impossible relationships."

Just then, I heard something strange. The trap door was being opened. I climbed Babygirl's stall door and hid behind her.

Out of the hidden passageway popped Daniel's head. I watched him climb out, look around, close the trap then walk down to another gate. He took a horse out of its stall and walked it out to the meadow.

"Hmmm," I said to Babygirl. I gave her a quick hug and snuck out of the stable.

Back up the path I went. Was Daniel the one then that had been in my room? He did tell me that the gown looked beautiful on me. And...he had left me the note that had brought me to the stable. Still, I couldn't be positive, but he seemed the most likely.

As I entered the Castle the gong went off for lunch. I knew I didn't want to eat. Knew I couldn't eat, so I headed to my room to see if anything had been left in there by Daniel. I looked around my Dracula room. Nothing was missing or out of place.

I still wasn't one hundred percent sure it had been Daniel. Either way, I was now even more uncomfortable in my room. I knew I couldn't relax. I was going to sit and obsess over everything that was taking up space in my head. Fitz, Cecil, Alex, Daniel, and my mom had invaded. I decided to go to the painting room.

After taking every wrong turn you could possibly imagine, I

finally found the right door. The room was flooded in sunlight. I grabbed the pencil and a ruler, and began marking out where the Castle would be. How big would the Castle be in comparison to the grounds? Did I want it centered, or to capture the meadow land behind it?

There was a small bar in the room (as there was in most of the rooms in this Castle). I looked and there sat a bottle of whiskey with a tag that read, 'For Janie, enjoy!' Cecil had thought of everything I mused. Well, as it pertained to the painting room. I cracked the seal and poured myself three fingers. Taking a sip of pure heaven, I then walked back to the chair in front of the giant blank canvas. I rarely painted while drinking. It changed my mental focus, not to mention, blurred my vision. But I wanted a drink to steady the nerves, no matter what it did to the senses at this point.

I looked through the pictures Cecil had given me. There he stood with his family, all of maybe eight years old, grinning wildly. I smiled despite myself. It hit me all at once. Barry may have been my longest running crush, but he wasn't my only crush. I did have feelings for the giant ass that was Cecil. No matter how mad I was at him.

I put the picture down, and closed my eyes. I was envisioning the Castle the very first time I saw it: Bathed in the sunrise...moss covered grey stone...being kissed by reds and golds. I opened my eyes and the picture I wanted to paint was clear. I began to trace out the lines. Every detail, small or large, seemed to pop and stand away from everything else. I was moving madly. Time didn't exist as my hand moved quick, but precise, across the canvas. Forming, the lines of a pencil...became a picture. Soon enough, I was ready to start painting. Long into the night my brushes flowed. Shadow and light danced before me. I stopped only to turn on more lights as the sun faded in the sky. Even my drink had been cast aside. Pachelbel's Canon in D began as I stood back to admire my work. There before me was Cecil, the first night we met. Done completely from memory, he sat reclined in a chair at Fitzpatrick's pub. Fingers locked behind his head, leg folded at the knee to cross the other, grinning from ear to ear.

I was going to need to order another canvas, was all I was thinking, as I downed the rest of my drink.

I clicked off the lights and started my journey back to my room. After finding many wrong turns, I finally found the entry hall and ascended the stairs. I paused at Fitz's door and debated knocking, but I could hear her and Scotty, so I moved on.

As I entered my Dracula room, I heard the secret passageway shut again. Panicked, I looked around the room. Was anything out of place? Anything disturbed? Anything new? Not a note or piece of clothing. The dressing gown was missing from the armoire. I stood there pondering...why would whoever put it there, take it back? I decided I was going to catch whoever this was right now! I was a little tipsy, but warm tipsy. Not drunk tipsy. Whoever it was, would have me right on their heels, I assessed. I quickly threw on my jeans, boots and a sweater. Grabbing a candle from the hall, the lighter out of my other pair of jeans, I pushed the creepy assed picture to the side. Open sprung the secret passageway and in I went. I lit the candle and moved quickly till I hit the staircase. I took the stairs cautiously, considering how tiny they were. I had planned on taking the trap door to the stable, but I heard something echo further ahead in the tunnel. I had to keep going even though I couldn't help but wonder if I had been a little hasty in my choice to follow the unknown intruder. I even stopped and thought of turning back, but I was tired of wondering and thought maybe at the end of this, I'd have answers. I walked and walked, the tunnel wider, then smaller, then wider again as it went. "I am not afraid. I am not afraid," I said out loud as a rat scurried underfoot. "I am not happy, I am not happy!" opting for a new mantra. It seemed I had walked miles, and aside from squeaks from rats, no other sound emerged. Just as I had decided on turning back, another staircase emerged. As I climbed, I became aware that this may have been the stupidest thing I had ever done. What if there was a crazy person at the other end? What if I ended up having to put the lotion on the skin? I would have felt better if I had had Fitz with me. I could tackle the rats, and she could tackle everything else that went boo in the night. I was way too sober now not to think straight, but I had come this far. Cautiously, I opened the door at the top of the landing, and was in another darkened room. Music was playing above me. I could see light through cracks in the ceiling. A small maze through cases of beer and kegs made a path to another staircase. I climbed again, thinking that maybe I was in the distillery. But I couldn't imagine the distillery having a live band.

I opened the second door, and light came through a crack from a third door on the other side of the room. Was I in another storage room? Passing by more kegs and even more cases of beer, I realized I was in a pub. The passageway goes to a pub? What the hell, I thought. No one seemed to notice me emerge from the closed door.

It was an old building, three stories high of dark wood, old stone and brick. Black and white pictures of the town and family members adorned the walls. Huge steel chandeliers hung from the ceiling in places where the ceiling was high enough. Small tables were fit into six separate arched brick cubbies against one wall. Opposite that, was a long hand carved bar, with twelve occupied stools. People were everywhere and seemed not to notice or care where I had come from. I was still getting my bearings when I heard a deep voice calling my name. I turned to look and there was Big Dave and a blonde woman, sitting at a small table close to the bar. I smiled and walked over, "Dave, nice to see you again."

"And you!" his Viking head nodded. "This is my wife, Hanna," he said standing. "This is Cecil's girlfriend, Janie."

Shaking her hand, I corrected, "Cecil's friend."

"Well, I can hope for the man," Dave said. "Please sit. Where is Cecil?"

"I came alone. Rather unexpectedly," I added.

"Well, ya must join us for a drink," Hanna said, smiling.

"Yes, what are ya havin' Janie?" Dave asked, his Irish accent thickened with drink.

"I'm afraid I didn't bring my wallet," I admitted.

"You'll never need that here," Dave smiled. "This is my pub. Well, ours," he said, leaning in to put a kiss on Hanna's temple. "We insist on buying ya a drink."

I smiled, surprised. "Well, if you insist, I'd love a Black and Tan."

He looked confused.

"I'm sorry, a Half and Half," I corrected.

"Done!" he headed to the bar.

His wife, a beautiful woman with my own stature, a little thicker in the hips, being a mother several times over, asked, "Are ya enjoyin' Ireland?"

"It's truly amazing. I know I'll miss it when I head back to the states."

"So you won't be stayin'?" she looked saddened.

"Well, no," I was confused. Did she think I was someone else? I wondered.

"It's just...Dave said you and Cecil seemed...right for each other. Cecil and Dave have been such good friends for so long. He's the Godfather to our children, ya know. A good man indeed, despite the incident."

"The incident?" I questioned.

"Yes, he shouldn't have let the opinions of others run him off. This is his home and if Dave has any say, he'll be home for good."

"I'm at a disadvantage here. I don't know about the...incident," I said, as Dave sat back down with our drinks.

Hanna looked at her husband, "I'm afraid I've spoken out of turn," she said to him, blushing. "She doesn't know."

Dave patted his wife's leg to reassure her that she had done no wrong. "It's quite alright my love," he told her. "It would undoubtedly come to light at some point. Better she hear it from the mouth of truth than of those who speak with forked tongues."

Dave began, "Quite a few years ago, Cecil left home due to some rather unfavorable opinions."

"I knew he left home feeling that he had 'blighted' the family name for something he had done. But I never asked what that was all about."

"Again, better ya hear it from me," he began. "So, it was over eight years ago now," he looked to his wife for verification of his facts.

Hanna nodded in agreement.

"Cecil had just finished college and was home for the first time in many months. We met up here, which used to be my father's pup, before he passed, God rest his soul." Dave and Hanna both bowed their heads. I bowed mine quickly, as well, trying to keep up. Dave continued, "We were drinking most of the night when Cecil told me that he and his girl had parted."

"Cecil had an actual girlfriend?" I'm sure I looked shocked.

"Aye, they had met in his freshman year and dated for the next three."

Cecil dated someone for over three years? I rolled this around in my mind. He had had a longer relationship than I had ever had? I took a moment to feel bad for myself.

"Well, the girl had been cheating on him if you can believe that. He had caught her red handed in her dorm with his dorm mate. They had been shaggin' since her and Cecil had started datin' apparently. He was broken, he was," Dave nodded his giant Viking head. "We drank most of the night, as I said, but before we headed to our homes, Cecil said that he needed to light a candle for his mother. As if this night hadn't been hard enough on him, it was also the anniversary of his mum's passing."

I winced. A shitty day indeed, I nodded in agreement.

"We stumbled to the church. I'm not sure who was holdin' who up."

I was sure, I thought, there was no way Cecil was holding up Big Dave. I actually visualized Cecil squashed underneath a passed-out-drunk Big Dave.

"The church was so lovely," Dave recalled. "I did love that old church."

His wife took his hand and smiled.

"My parents had been married there...my father's funeral held there. It was over two hundred years old. The tapestries that hung on the walls were said to be twice that. But I was to wait outside. Give him his privacy, ya know, with his mum."

I nodded, tears beginning to form at the corner of my eyes.

I heard a little commotion and a damn cat came flying out the door like it had seen a ghost. I hoped the cat hadn't scared the life out of him. After all, my friend was drunk. I walked down the lane a little to find a tree."

"To relieve himself," his wife added.

Her husband smiled at her, "Yes, to relieve myself. When I looked back, the whole church was aflame. I ran as fast as I could, not seeing Cecil anywhere outside. I was panicked. I went through the flames and found my friend, bleeding from the temple and unconscious."

"He pulled Cecil to safety," his wife gave her husband a look of pure admiration.

"She brags on me," Dave put a kiss on her cheek. "I did for him what I know he would have done for me."

I smiled, knowing it would take a lot of adrenaline for Cecil to have accomplished that feat.

"You said he was bleeding from the temple? What happened?"

"Turns out, a cat had jumped on the altar when Cecil entered the church. He was caught off guard as the wee beast jumped onto his shoulder, causin' him to knock the lit candles to the ground. Cecil spun with the cat clawin' at his skull. Not knowin' what had attacked him, he fought and flailed tryin' to remove the beast from his head. The cat made a hasty getaway, but Cecil, dizzy and disoriented fell and hit his head on the front pew. Knocked himself out cold, he did! The old rugs, wood floor and altar cloth went up like the devil himself had thrown the flame."

"Oh my God!" I said.

"Exactly," Dave said. "By the time the fire trucks and police arrived, there wasn't much left of the old church. Cecil had to be taken to the hospital where he was treated for smoke inhalation and a concussion. Before he was released, he found out that he was bein' charged with arson."

I sat dumbfounded and wide eyed.

"His father, of course paid his bail and he was left in Mr. Callaghan's charge till the trial. After the doctor presented his case, the smoke inhalation and the concussion, not to mention my side of the story, he was found not guilty. But some of the town wagged their tongues anyway. Some said he was despondent over his break up and had tried to end it all. Others said he was just a spoiled boy who started a fire and then his daddy paid people off to lie for him. They even tried to say that I had lied to pay back a debt."

"A debt?" I asked, confused.

"After my father died, most of the money the pub made went to his hospital bills and his funeral expenses. We owed too much and were goin' to have to sell to stay alive. My father and Mr. Callaghan had been old friends. When Mr. Callaghan found out the state we were in, he paid off all of my father's debts."

"Oh, I see." I was starting to really love Martin. What a wonderful man he was.

"Not to say I wouldn't have lied for Cecil, because on the cross, I can't say I wouldn't. But I can for damn sure say that I didn't!"

I nodded again, "Your scar, it's from the fire?"

"Aye," Dave said, raising his arm to show the burn scar that went from his wrist to his elbow.

"So Cecil just left then?"

"People weren't going to give him a fair shake. In fact, some were downright horrible. The things they said...the way they treated him to his face. Then Alex came back."

"Alex?" I repeated.

"Alexandria," Dave said, with great exaggeration. "She was always over the top. She was a drama major in school but a shitty actress if you ask me."

"Well, give her some credit dear," said Hanna, "She was able to convince yer friend that he was the only one for many years."

I sat absorbing. It couldn't be the same Alexandria, could it? This was bending my mind. Was that why he was so mad that I almost slapped her? Is that WHY he thought I almost slapped her? Because she WAS his ex! Why he accused me of being jealous? Was that why he had introduced me as his Petal? Just to get her goat?

"So what became of this Alex?" I asked, hoping she lived far away, happily married with a few kids.

Dave and his wife raised their eyebrows at each other. "She tried her hand at actin'," Hanna said.

"But as I said, she wasn't a good actress," Dave added. "She ended up in soft core porn from what I've heard."

My eyes widened, "Porn?"

"But, she's working back in town now," Hanna added. "It seems she couldn't even act well enough by porn's standards."

"She works at the art supply store." I said. "Doesn't she?"

"Yes, she does," said Hanna, furrowing her brow.

I let out a long sigh and covered my eyes. "You're fucking kidding me!" I said to the heavens.

"No!" Dave said, "Yer kiddin', right?"

I shook my head.

Hanna said, "Oh for the love of Pete, no!"

"We're gonna need more drinks over here!" Dave said to the barmaid.

"That must have been what Fitz meant when she told Alex that she had seen her riding?"

Dave and his wife stared at me, "Huh?" they said in unison.

A second round came and I relayed the whole story to them: From the art store to the shitpile.

"Oh my!" Hanna laughed.

I nodded, "Splat!"

"That Fitz sounds like a wild one," Dave laughed too.

"Yeah, she is," I answered. I did wonder though, if Fitz had known about Alex's past, why didn't she tell me?

"I don't like that woman bein' back," Hanna said to her husband.

"Nor I," Dave shook his giant head. "I hope he can keep his senses about him."

"Seriously? Cecil isn't that..." I didn't want to say dumb.

"She's always had a hold on him," Hanna said. "Even after

everything she had done, he asked her to come to the courthouse when he had his trial. He was brokenhearted all over again when she didn't show."

"You're kidding? How could he forgive her, much less want her around?"

"I won't call my friend a doormat, but where she's concerned, I have a hard time comin' up with another word."

I was shocked. Shocked they knew each other. Shocked they had a history. And most of all, shocked that he could even be in her presence. I was mulling for a while. Why didn't he tell me about her? Doormat indeed, I thought. But who was I to judge. In all truthfulness, I should have known that my ex, John, was up to no good. I too became a doormat as well. John wasn't exactly the first man, or only man, I had held that status with.

"Are ya in there Janie?" Dave asked.

All I could do was nod and let out a loud sigh.

Dave asked how Cecil and I had met. It was a long story considering we only had a month or so of history. The two of them laughed as I told the story of our first meeting, then his beating the crap out of my ex when he hit me.

Dave said, "Cecil may not be a big boy," (I spit beer out my nose thinking, I thought he was a pretty good sized man, till I met Big Dave) "...but," Dave continued, raising his glass in a toast to Cecil, "I trust that man to have my back like no other. He's quite the scrapper when need be."

"Here here," said Hanna, raising her glass as well.

"Well, I really wouldn't know," I laughed. "I was unconscious for the show."

Dave, Hanna and I closed down the bar. I had to admit the drinks here in Ireland, packed quite a wallop. Hanna and Dave insisted on riding in the cab with me back to the Castle (which was greatly appreciated since I didn't want to go back down in the secret passageway). I wondered if Dave knew about the passage. He'd have to, right? I wanted to ask, but Dave started singing a rowdy Irish drinking song and my attention was diverted.

As we pulled up to the circular drive in front, Cecil stepped out of the shadows and opened the cab door. I, not expecting the door I was leaning on to be pulled open, promptly fell out. Hanna leaned forward and covered her mouth, worried. When I began to laugh, she did as well.

"Oh my, ya are alright, aren't ya?" she asked.

I lay on the ground laughing my ass off. "Fine, fine," I slowly stood, Cecil taking my arm.

"Thanks for bringing her home, you two," Cecil said, and paid the cab's fare for their ride home as well.

"She's a definitely a delight," Dave said out the window as the cab pulled away.

"Ya hear that?" I said to Cecil, "I'm a delight," I slurred a little.

"Maybe." he said.

"No, Dave said I was definitely a delight," I told him.

"Well, ya MAY be a delight...but yer DEFINITELY drunk.

"Let's get ya to bed," Cecil said.

"You can't take me to bed," I shook my head. "Miss Elanor will kill you if you're in my room. Actually, she'll kill me."

"I think she'd make an exception,"

"I think she'd tell you to take me to the stable before she'd let you in my room. She'll be pissed," I added.

"I'll risk it," he said and swept me off my feet, carrying me to my room.

"He opened my door and knocked on the light switch with his elbow. Laying me on the bed, he looked around. "This room is... downright creepy."

I did a drunkin' nod, "Look at the painting over the bed," I hiccupped.

"Is this a trick? Are ya trying to get me into yer bed?" he grinned. He leaned over and looked at the picture. "This is truly frightening. My God, how do ya sleep in here?" he asked.

I shrugged, "It's more comfortable than the back of the Rolls."

"What?"

I shook my head, "Never mind."

"So, I have some questions, like what were ya doin' at the pub with Dave and Hanna?"

"I didn't start out with Dave and Hanna."

He waited for me to elaborate. "Okay, then how did ya end up with Dave and Hanna?"

"Dave saw me and called me over. Then I met Hanna and had drinks and then I came back here."

"Okay, let's try another approach. How did ya get to the pub?"

"Oh," I said. I looked up at the picture, "Move the...the...the scary ass picture."

He stood on the bed, and moved the frame. The secret passageway popped open. "Huh!"

"Are you gonna to tell me you didn't know it was there?" I asked.

"Truth be told, I did not."

I eyed him suspiciously. He seemed genuinely surprised.

"Where does this one lead?"

"Well, near as I can tell," I curled up on my side and pulled my covers around me, "It goes to your mom's room, the stable, and Dave's pub."

"The stable?" he repeated.

"Um hmm," I said as I started to doze off.

"Have you taken the passage to the stable? The other night, were ya in the stable? Janie?"

I answered him with a snore.

15

HOLY HANGOVER

I woke with a tiny burrowing headache between my brows. Sitting on my side table was a pitcher of water, Ibuprofen and toast. A note by the toast read, "Eat me." And the water pitcher had a note that said "Drink me!" The IBU had another little paper that said, "Take me." I did what the yellow sticky notes said to do, then closed my eyes and went back to sleep. I had just fallen back to sleep when it dawned on me: The picture I had painted...I didn't want Cecil to see it. Correction, I didn't want anyone to see it. "Shit, shit, shit!" I dressed as quickly as I could and sprinted downstairs. I prayed all the way down, "For once, let me find the damn room on my first try." I passed Miss Elanor in the entry hall.

She gave me a stern look, "I didn't expect to see ya today," she said snidley.

"I'm sorry, I didn't expect to see you either," I breezed past her.

I made the right, left, right, passed Ben Franklin and into the atrium. From behind me, on the chaise lounge, I heard, "Do ya want to explain this?"

On the chaise, Bloody Mary in hand, sat Fitz in a silk kimono.

"Explain what?" I asked, eyeballing the pitcher of Bloody Marys.

"Explain to me how you're supposed to paint pictures of the Castle and Distillery, and end up painting this?" she pointed to the portrait of Cecil.

"I don't know," I said hopelessly, then sat on the floor facing the picture.

"Okay, how about this then, is it my brother or Cecil ya want?"

I rubbed my temple, trying to figure out how to answer the question.

"It shouldn't be that difficult," she said.

"Well, it's not that easy to explain, and I have a serious hangover to boot."

She stood, filled a glass with the red heaven-sent concoction and handed it to me. "Drink up!"

I downed half the glass, and the churning in my stomach began to subside. "This really is the best," I looked at the glass.

"How do ya feel about my brother?" her green eyes burrowing into me.

I let out a sigh and began, "When we were young..."

"Oh for the love of Pete, are we to go that far back?" Fitz eyes grew wide.

"...he was a good boy," I continued. "He made sure no one picked on me. The boys who pulled my ponytails got one warning."

She smiled slightly, remembering our childhood. "That's true."

"As I grew, he became a good young man. Smart, funny but most of all, kind." I paused a moment, "Do you remember Jeff Goldberg?"

"Aye," she nodded. "He was an angry boy."

"I'm sure it didn't help that he was the only Jewish boy in our Catholic school. Or that he had been held back twice. Back then you and I weren't in all the same classes like we had been in younger grades."

"Aye, ya took those advanced Latin courses."

I nodded, "Well, Barry and I weren't in the same classes either. Neither was Jeff Goldberg but he had singled me out. Every day as I left Latin class, he would find me. He would pull my braids, knock my books out of my arms and on one occasion he spit in my hair. I started to cry. I wasn't tough like you, Fitz. And you know what happened if we tattled. We all got the knuckles. I swear nuns love the knuckles."

Fitz nodded in agreement.

"So I just stood there...crying. But then Barry came out of nowhere. He used his shirt to get the spit out of my hair, handed me my books then wiped away my tears. That was the day..."

"That was the day Barry beat up Jeff Goldberg on the way home from school!" she interrupted.

I nodded.

"I remember that," Fitz said. "Jeff was so much bigger than Barry, and everyone thought Jeff was goin' to beat his ass. But Barry pummeled him, knocked him Kippah first, to the ground."

"Jeff never picked on me again. Barry had grown into a good young man. I didn't have a lot of those in my life, just my dad, yours and the brothers. But all the other brothers treated me like a sister. Chased us around, scared us every chance they got, tormented us. But not Barry," I shook my head. "Barry always protected me."

Fitz nodded.

"Then Barry grew into a good man. Still smart, and funny and kind..."

"Ya forgot gorgeous."

"Oh believe me, I've never forgotten that." I smiled, "Smart, funny, kind and drop dead gorgeous. How could I not have a crush on someone like that?"

Fitz was mulling this over and began to nod, again.

"I never told you that my crush had continued on for two reasons. One, you and the family mean the world to me. I wouldn't jeopardize those relationships for... Well, I almost did at what I thought was my lowest," I grinned. "But the universe reminded me that he...us...not an option."

"Oh yeah, when was that?" she raised her brow.

"That would be after John dumped me but before Henry went psycho on me. To be exact, it was when Barry's 'eighty's reject' ex-girlfriend went batshit crazy on me at the pub."

Fitz was trying not to laugh. "And two?" she asked.

"Like you said, I would have never had a chance even if I wasn't like a little sister to him."

"I only said that because I was hurt. Ya know I don't believe that."

"Does this mean you're not mad at me anymore?"

"I wasn't mad."

"The hell you weren't!" my eyes rounded.

"Yer right," she admitted. "Scotty put it all in perspective for me. He made me realize that I was really mad at the thought of losing ya as my sister. I was pushing you away to keep from losin' yoa, or something like that. I can't really explain it but either way, it actually made sense. What Scotty said, not what I'm sayin' now. I wasn't even thinkin' about how painful this all must have been for ya. But, I don't like bein' lied to," she said sternly.

I nodded, "I know, and I am sorry Fitz. I'll never keep anything from you again."

"Pinky?" she said.

"Pinky," I locked mine in hers and we hugged.

"Now, I have some information for ya about Alex," she began.

"You mean that she's Cecil's ex, who cheated on him, then turned to a life of soft core porn before coming back here and making my life pure hell?"

"Okay! Scotty told me. How the hell did you find out?" she asked.

"Boy, do I have some things to tell you." We refilled our glasses and got into gossip position on the chaise lounge. I started at the secret passageway, and ended when I ran to the atrium to find her.

"Wow," she said when I finished. "I can't believe that ya went through the passageway alone. Atta girl!" she added. "But I still have two questions. First, who the hell would give ya the nightdress, and then take it back. It doesn't make sense. I mean, did Daniel give it to ya and takin' it back is his way of sayin' he's over his crush on ya?"

"Seriously, I have no idea," I said, doing a palms-up.

"Okay, second: Why am I looking at a giant paintin' of Cecil?"

"We're going to need more of these," I said, pouring the last of the red heaven mix into our glasses.

I really wasn't sure how to describe how I felt about Cecil, but I tried. The very thought of him pushed the ranges of my sanity. One minute, I was attracted to him. Like the kind of attracted that occupied my every thought. The next moment, I wanted to knock him on his ass.

Fitz sat grinning the whole time. "Well, you may have a crush on my brother, but I don't think he's the only one."

I sighed. "I don't think Barry is an issue anymore. The whole getting married thing, best friend pissed at me, kinda killed my crush."

"Well, maybe you should tell Cecil?"

"Tell him what? Sometimes I want to kiss you and other times I want to push you down a flight of stairs?"

"Somethin' tells me that he feels the same way about you."

"My bigger problem is Alex. She's been his 'drug of choice' for years."

"Oh come on, drug of choice? She doesn't have that much power."

"What do you call something that threatens to destroy you anytime you're around it? Even if Cecil doesn't want me, I can't stand the thought of what she'll do to him."

"Maybe you should tell him about the porn stuff?"

"Right, I'm sure that would turn him off. The chance to sleep with a porn star isn't every guy's dream?"

"First of all," Fitz began, "She's no star! Porn or otherwise! And you believe me, it's not for a lot of guys. Makes them feel insecure. She has more experience. Not to mention, most likely had bigger and better durin' her career. I imagine most men would be intimidated."

"He already knows she cheated on him for years, yet she's still here."

"Well, we may have to save him from himself," Fitz said.

"In the meantime, what do we do about this?" I pointed at the picture.

"We order more of these," she looked at the empty Bloody Mary pitcher.

After another pitcher, we put the picture of Cecil in the closet with a tarp over it. Not exactly the most helpful idea. But short of starting it on fire, I didn't know how to get rid of it without it being seen.

"Out of sight, out of mind," Fitz said, closing the door.

"I don't think that really takes care of the problem, Fitz."

"We're goin' to have order another canvas," she said. "Shall we?"

Since neither of us should have been driving, we had the Fonzie look-a-like drive us into town after we changed and I brushed my tongue.

16

LOVE THE BRITS

We stood out in front of the art supply store. "Well, here I am again," I sighed. "Let's get this over with."

We walked in and went straight to the front desk. No Alex. Was I really going to get off that easily? A larger woman with big rolled black bangs, black horn rimmed glasses and arms that were completely tatted down, asked sullenly, "Yeah, whotcha need?" in a thick British accent.

I looked around, "I need to buy a canvas and have it delivered."

"Fine," she answered, pulling out a shipping clipboard. "A've we delivered to ya befo'?"

"Actually a few days ago. I need one canvas, the same size, sent to the same location. I'll pay cash for it."

"Whot name was it shipped under?"

"Cecil Callaghan, I think?"

She looked down the roster, "Ah, yeah, ere it is."

She was so monotone, I couldn't help but wonder if she was high. Fitz and I just looked at each other with questioning eyes.

"So," Fitz said, looking around, "No Alex today, huh?"

With this comment, she put her hands on her hips, "Oh, are ya friends of Alex's then?"

"Not exactly," Fitz answered.

"She just helped me last time I was in," I said.

"Well, at least she's 'elpin someone," the lady started to get fired up, and I wasn't sure how this was going to go. "Ya know, she called me not twen-ee minutes before 'er shift. The woman began to mimic Alex, "Oh Rosey, at's me," she pointed at herself, just in case Fitz and I weren't following the conversation. "M so sick," she continued, "I cun't make it ta work," she made a pouty face. "Then I ere im, in the back of er, "Oh Petal, I want ya...com back ta bed!" Like I dun't know what's she's up to? Whor!" Rosie Added. "Like I a've nuttin' bettr ta do than cover 'er ass, while she gets 'er brains boffed out!" she concluded.

Fitz was smiling from ear to ear, "I fuckin' love Brits!"

"Ya know, I go ta school online!" Rosie said. "I a've a life. I shouldn't be spendin' it coverin' 'er, every time 'er eyes roll back in 'er head. Whor!" she repeated.

I nodded, "Agreed," I said.

"Ya wouldn't happen to know who she's whorin' with, would ya?" Fitz asked.

"A've you been listenin'?" her eyes went wide. "She and I, we aren't friends! I'd more quickly throat punch 'er, than listen ta 'er go on and on 'bout her vaginal visitors. Whor'."

"Yeah I get it," I said, nodding my head.

"This address tis the Castle?" asked Rosey, abruptly changing the conversation.

"Yep," I said.

"Right on, I'll be there for Lugnasadh. Cun't wait. Gonna be epic."

"O-Kay. It'll be nice to have a...you, there." I concluded.

"Yeah, definitely," she nodded her head. "Wicked party!" she made finger horns at me.

"Uh, we have to go now." I said, handing her cash for the canvas then Fitz and I made our way out the door.

"Wow, she's fun!" said Fitz.

"Yeah, did you happen to catch that?"

"Oh, yeah, sometimes it's hard for you Americans to understand the British accent, ya see, what she was sayin'..."

"No Fitz, I understood what she said. I meant that part about Petal?"

"Ya. So?"

"That's what Cecil called me the other day."

"Ya don't think...?"

I shrugged and did a palms-up, "I kinda think...maybe."

"But he was there when ya got home last night."

"That doesn't mean he didn't leave later. Did you see him at breakfast?"

Fitz made a face, "No."

I let out a sigh, "Well shit."

We went back to the car and the Fonzie look-a-like asked if there was anywhere else we needed to go.

Fitz had her arm around me, "Pub!"

"Very well miss. Any particular pub?"

"A close one," Fitz answered.

He nodded at us and closed the door behind us before getting in himself. He pulled the car up a quarter of a block. "Here we are, misses," he announced. Fitz and I looked at each other.

Stepping inside, I got the feeling I had been there before. I was in Dave and Hanna's pub. Just being there, my hangover came back. We took a seat in one of the cubbies. The waitress came and handed us menus.

"Can we start off with two Bloody Marys, extra spicy, please," Fitz requested.

The waitress wandered off.

I was holding my head and trying to wrap my brain around how things had gotten so muddled when I heard a familiar voice. It was Hanna. I looked around, but couldn't see her. Her voice was coming from the cubby behind us.

"Yer gonna have to talk to her about it, Cecil," Hanna said.

"I just can't. Maybe it would be better just to let it go. After all, if things go the way I think they will, Scotty's problems have to take precedence. After all I've put him and the family through...I owe it to 'em."

Fitz and I sat, quiet as church mice trying to listen. The happy waitress came back and announced our drinks. We both hushed her and sent her on her way. She looked offended. I told Fitz in a whisper, "She's gonna spit in our next round."

"You hush, too," she hissed. We went back to spying.

"After all, this could ruin Fitz and Scotty's relationship, if it doesn't work out," Cecil said to Hanna.

"But what about..?"

"I don't know," he cut her off. "I didn't expect to fall in love...again! I mean, seriously, after all she put me through...I swore never again...and now? Shit! Here it is...stronger than ever! She's a cruel joke, ya know?"

"So it is love, then? Yer sure?" Hanna asked.

"Afraid so. I wish I could deny it, but I'd just be lyin' to myself."

"So what are ya goin to do about the other one?" Hanna asked him.

"She'll be gone in a couple months. I guess I'll just try to avoid her. Won't be easy, she's there damn near every time I turn around."

My heart sank. Fitz saw the look and reached out her hand to mine.

We downed our drinks, dropped some money on the table, with a generous tip for the waitress we had offended, and snuck out.

Back in the car heading back, I was mulling everything over. "Well, this sucks," I whispered, so Fonzie wouldn't hear us.

"Not to overshadow what's happenin' with you, but what do ya think Cecil meant when he said, this could ruin me and Scotty's relationship? Fitz whispered back.

"Well, now through our snooping, we've heard this twice, once from Martin, and now from Cecil. I think maybe it's time you just confront Scotty."

"And say what as to how we heard the conversations in the first place?"

"Well," I pondered, "Couldn't you just say that you've noticed a change in him...and wondered if you could help him through something?"

"Believe me, if the things I did, didn't work, there's no way talkin' will. Plus, I already asked if anything was wrong and he said, "Just work stuff, don't ya worry about it."

"Well, maybe it is," I gave her a palms-up.

"Why would work threaten our relationship?"

I shook my head, "I don't know. This is maybe what you should ask?" I tried to reason. The tiny hairs on the back of my neck began to rise. Oh crap, I thought. Something I'm not gonna like is coming. I knew even before she said it. I was picturing me, throwing myself from the car, in flight mode, when she said, "I think we need to do more snoopin'!"

Shit. I knew it, I knew it, I knew it! I thought. "While I have nothing to lose, you do. Are you sure you want to run on assumptions, and become that stalker kind if woman we make fun of?" I hoped putting it like that would make her back down.

A moment passed while she pondered. “Yes!” she said.

Again, shit! “So where do we go now? I mean, where do you think the answer is hidden?”

“We have to go to Miss Elanor's bedroom.”

My eyes rounded and my brows disappeared into my hair line, at the thought, “First, why? Second, this seems like the worst idea you've ever had...ever!” I added. “Do you even know where her room is?”

“I had assumed at one point that she just hung from the rafters.”

I nodded, “Kind of what I thought, too.”

“Think about it, she knows more than anyone about this family.”

“And you think she writes it all down, then what? She just leaves it lying around her bedroom? Seriously Fitz, that's the most ridiculous thing I've ever...”

“Yer brilliant,” yelled Fitz.

“I was being facetious, Fitz!”

“Well, yer big unnecessary words aside, ya may have hit on somethin'.”

I shook my head, “Lost. I. Am. Lost!”

“A diary,” Fitz grinned. “Don't most matronly women with no life, keep a diary?”

“I keep a diary, Fitz,” I looked sidelong at her.

She squished up her face, “Oh Janie, don't ya worry. We'll get ya a life soon.”

I just stuck my tongue in my cheek.

“So, we know that Martin, Scotty and Cecil are all out of the house. So, one of us has to keep her busy while I search her room.”

“Um Fitz, I caught that.”

“I knew ya would. It's easier if I just come right out and say it.”

"But you didn't, you..."

She cut me off again, "Now how do we figure out which room is hers, without arousing suspicion?"

I asked the Fonzie look-a-like, "Could you please pull off at a pharmacy?"

"Yes, ma'am," he replied.

"What's wrong with ya?" Fitz asked.

"I feel a headache coming on."

"Well pull yerself together, Watson. We have work to do!"

Opening the bottle of IBU, "These pills look strange," I said.

Fitz was in her own world, but answered. "What's wrong with 'em?"

"They're capsules. I asked the tech and he gave me these."

"So?"

"I don't know. I'm just used to tablets."

"Ok, are ya really going to focus on whether yer pills are in capsule or tablet form? In the grand scheme of things, you wouldn't think that this would even make the list."

"Fine," I said, trying not to sound too bitchy. I brought the water bottle to my lips and washed down two capsules.

17

GETTING TO KNOW ELANOR

The plan was to keep Elanor busy while Fitz snooped around. In theory, this sounded like an easy thing to do. And if we had actually been Sherlock and Watson we would have had this down to an art. Unfortunately, we were more Lucy and Ethel. Fitz assumed that Elanor's room was most likely in the South Wing with the menfolk based on the fact that we didn't see her in the halls much in the medieval North Wing. It was the only real selling point to the North Wing. Fitz would start her search there.

My job: Find common ground with Elanor and create a conversation with a woman whose only real emotion towards me is open disdain.

I watched Fitz disappear up the staircase. Taking a deep breath, I headed to the kitchen. There she stood over what looked like a small cast iron cauldron. I flashed back to Mum and Aunt Marble over the cauldron. There she stood, grey bun pulled tight and neckline higher than ever. Whatever she was making smelled God awful, but pointing that out wouldn't meet my purpose. I was going all in.

"Wow, it smells...really good," I said, startling her.

"What are ya doin' in here, Miss O'Connelly?"

"I was just bored, and thought that I'd, ugh, check out the kitchens. I love to cook, ya know. I've been kind of missing it since I've been here."

She looked sidelong at me, "I would think doin' the paintin' you've been hired to do, would keep ya busy. Busy enough to keep you out of my kitchen!" she added.

I forced a smile and an awkward laugh that made her eyebrows furrow. "You're so funny," I said.

"What is the matter with ya, child?" she asked.

I stammered, "Ugh, I just...missed my mom?" I said it as a question, to feel her out.

Her eyes rounded at me, "Well, I am not yer mother," she snapped.

"Yeeeah," I said slowly. "But," I had no idea where this was going, "I'm really homesick?" I asked it as a question again.

"Well," Elanor said, "I guess I can understand that. Ya are quite a ways from home."

Had I done it? I wondered. Had I found a way to bring out her nurturing side? Had I..."

She cut my thought off, "Just think, the sooner ya finish yer job, the sooner you'll be gone!"

So, maybe not, I thought. "Can I get a taste of what you're making?" I asked, inching closer with caution.

"If ya want to die," she turned her head toward me.

My eyes rounded, "Ummm..."

"I'm not making food, ya daft girl. Do ya really think my food smells like this?"

"Well, um, no, not really."

"It's medicine, if ya must know. A poultice for Mr. Callaghan."

"Oh. So what's in it?"

"Seriously? It's an old family recipe. Why in the world would I share it with ya? Have I given ya any reason to think that I approve of ya? Or that you and I are to be girlfriends who do each other's hair and that sort of thing?"

"No ma'am, you have not done that," I agreed.

"Good. I would hate for ya to get the wrong impression. Now please remove yerself from my kitchen."

I knew Fitz needed more time, but the bonding thing wasn't happening. Flattery sprang to mind. Maybe she would succumb to flattery. "So, you're a healer?" I asked.

She looked at the wall in front of her, the way I do when I'm counting to ten to keep from killing Fitz. "Child, I have one nerve left, and it's a small mess of a mass with yer name on it."

"I'm just amazed. You do so much around here," I started. "And now, you have this amazing knowledge of, like, plants and stuff. I just think you, ya know, are kind of awesome."

Her face relaxed a little, "Well, it does take many years and a lot of love to become an herbalist."

"Yeah, I mean, wow!" I answered. "I would love to learn how to...do what you do."

"How many languages can you speak? Read?" she asked, turning on me. "Without that knowledge, ya can't learn much in this field."

"You speak other languages?"

"Speak...read. Several."

"Wow," I said. And I meant it. "I wish I could learn another language."

"Well, ya can't go around muddlin' the mind with whiskey, and Bloody Mary's and expect to retain any of this knowledge," she waved her hand dismissively. "My medicines and remedies are very powerful," she took on an air of smugness. "An inexperienced practitioner can cause real damage. Even death!" she raised an eyebrow to me.

"Yeah, that would...suck."

"Child, ya are in dire need of a dictionary. Ya don't say 'suck', in polite conversation. You say horrible, wretched, dreadful, terrible, appalling...not suck!"

"This is a polite conversation?" I said under my breath.

"What was that?" Miss Elanor asked.

I shook my head, "Nothing. Anyway, is that camphor I smell?"

She eyed me, "You have a good nose."

"Not really, it smells like the menthol. My mother used to put on my feet when I was young."

"When ya were sick," she nodded.

"Nope, all the time," I said.

She furrowed her brow.

"My mother was more about preventative care."

Miss Elanor just looked at me.

"So what is the poultice for?"

She let out a sigh of exhaustion. "How is that any of yer concern?"

"I just want him to be well," I smiled.

She turned narrowed eyes to me, "I bet ya do," she hissed.

My mind was screaming, abort! Abort! I had to try one more time, "So the flowers in the painting room? Did you grow those?"

"Actually, Miss O'Connelly, the gardener grew them. Maybe you could go bother him with inane conversation?"

"Inane, meaning not significant, foolish, stupid or lacking point," I recited.

"What are ya babblin' about, now?" she was taking those deep breaths again.

"I was showing you that I knew what the word meant."

"Well, bully for you!"

"And that means..."

"Go," she pointed a wooden spoon at me.

I backed out of the kitchen, hoping Fitz had enough time to do her snooping. There was no way in hell I was going back in the there. I made it to the bottom of the landing, and Mary hissed at me from the top of the South Wing staircase. "Pssst, Miss Janie!" I looked up and she motioned me with her finger. "Miss Fitz asked me to fetch ya."

I headed up the stairs and followed her down the long hallway to where Fitz was standing. This hall wasn't nearly as creepy. Done in royal blue and gold, it was more majestic than medieval. No suits of armor or scary weapons of war, just beautiful paintings and sculptures. A giant metal lion's head sat on a pedestal, and captured my eyes. It was an amazing piece, with so much detail. Whoever crafted this was an artist of the highest caliber. I was busy 'oohing' when Fitz said, "Would ya mind gettin' yer ass down here, already?"

Carrie and Mary stood in a huddle with her. "So Carrie showed me where the room was."

"Uh, what part of snooping meant to get them involved?" I nodded towards our maids.

"Don't ya worry Miss," said Mary. "We're pullin' for ya," she winked.

"Yeah, yer secret is safe with us!" Carrie added. Her ponytail bouncing as she nodded furiously.

I looked at Fitz, what had she done now? What "Secret" had she told them?

"We'll keep her busy for ya, Misses," Mary whispered. "Good luck," she added, before the two of them scampered off down the hall.

"O-kay," I turned back to Fitz. "What have you done?"

"Well, I was sneakin' around the hall, and I ran into Mary and Carrie."

I gave her a hand roll, "Get on with it.

"Well, my mind had to work quickly."

"SOOOO?"

"So I told them that you were lookin' for Cecil's room."

"For what?"

"Well, so you could try to seduce him, with a love note."

My eyes rounded, "That's what you came up with?"

"Yeah, this is Cecil's room," she patted his door. "But during the tour, they also showed me where Martin and Scotty's rooms were."

I bit my upper lip, "How does this help us get to Miss Elanor's room?"

"Oh, yeah, Miss Elanor's room. This hall turns left and dead ends into her room. I brought this!" she showed me the skeleton key she had used to sneak into my room.

"Yeah that's great, so," I went immediately to my line of questioning, "Why didn't you just tell them that you wanted to know where Scotty's room was, or that you just wanted a tour of the South Wing?"

"Whatdoya mean?"

"Why, in the name of all that's holy, did you tell them that I was going to try and seduce Cecil?" I was trying not to yell and doing the mental counting thing again.

"Oh...because ya really should," she smiled.

I ran my fingers through my hair, "Yes, but now they think..." I trailed off. "Can we just put a pin in this? I mean, I don't think this is a good idea."

"Such a pussy, come on kitty kitty," she said like I was a cat.

I followed her, but for the life of me I couldn't explain why. At Miss Elanor's door, I pleaded again, but Fitz pulled out the key and put it in the lock. A twist to the right and the latch clicked open. Some part of me really hoped it wouldn't.

As she pushed the door open, a familiar scent met my nose. What was that? It reminded me of something, but what?

We stepped inside the large room and clicked on the light. Both of us stood and stared. It was a beautiful room, done in purples. Even the canopy over her bed was a rich purple satin. All of the furniture was deep cherrywood. I couldn't help but notice that the picture above her bed was a little strange though. Three women in witch's hats stood around a cauldron in an open field at night. Given the cauldron I had seen her using and her admitting to being an herbalist, combined with the painting of witches, I couldn't help but wonder. In a corner near the window was a set of shelves containing plants that were so healthy, they were in dire need of repotting. None of mine ever made it to the repotting stage before the plant gods took them. I moved closer to inspect them. Sitting on a shelf was a horticulture book opened to a page containing poisonous plants. There was Abrus Precatorius, Aconitum (otherwise known as Wolfsbane) Atropa Belladonna (commonly referred to as Deadly Nightshade). My eyebrows rose-up almost to my hairline. Why would she be studying poisonous plants? Chills ran up my spine as I backed away from the book.

Fitz had been doing her own snooping and was thumbing through the diary she found on the bedside table.

"You should see this," Fitz said.

"Honestly, I think I've seen enough. Can't we just get the hell out of here?"

"That old prune is writing horrible things about me! Listen to this, "Who does she think she is?" Fitz began reading. "How in the world can he take any interest in such a banal woman?"

"Yep, that's her wording all right," I said.

"There's more," she continued. "She can't be any good for him, little tart that she is! I won't let this happen to him. I'll see her gone if it's the last thing I do!" Fitz concluded the reading then looked at me, "Who the hell does she think she is?"

"All I'm sure of at the moment is I want the hell out of here," I said again.

Fitz put the diary back then said, "Oh crap!"

"Oh crap, is not something I want to hear. What is "Oh crap"?"

Fitz winced, "I can't remember exactly which way the book was layin'."

"You really don't get this whole snooping thing. The point is not to get caught!"

"I know that! Ya think I don't know that?" Fitz was shaking the book at me.

"Just put it down and let's get the hell out of here!"

Fitz put the book down and changed its position a few times while I tried to breathe. "Come on, already," I said.

"Fine," she said, then moved it another quarter of an inch.

We started back down the hall when I asked her, "Did you lock the door?"

We were turning to go back, when we heard the maids very loudly asking about getting new bath towels.

I was panicking, "Shit, shit, shit!"

"Stall her!"

"Again? Are you kidding?" I said, as Fitz ran down the hall and disappeared to the left.

"That's absurd," I heard Miss Elanor answer them. "We have all new bath towels. They're in the same place they always are. I swear you two are actin' oddly!" She rounded the corner as I was coming down the hall.

"Oh Miss Elanor," I yelled, "I was just coming to look for you!"

"Oh wonderful, Miss O'Connelly again," she sighed. "Why are ya in this hallway? Ya saw me not half of an hour ago in the kitchen."

"Right!" I nodded my head at her, but gave her no other

explanation. I walked around her so she would have to turn around to face me.

"I was wondering..." I started.

"Why are ya yellin' at me, Miss O'Connelly?"

"Oh, am I yelling?" I yelled.

She stared with a look of pure irritation.

"I'm sorry," I dropped my voice to normal. "I'm having a little trouble hearing. I think I may be getting a cold."

She covered her mouth, "Well, I don't want it, do I?"

"No, ma'am, of course not," I covered my mouth. What I was wondering is...if you could make something for me? Ya know, like a poultice...or a tonic, or something."

She let out a heavy sigh, "What are yer symptoms?"

"My throat is a little scratchy and like I said, having a little trouble hearing out of my right ear."

She nodded, "I'll have something for ya at dinner," she turned around, as Fitz was coming up the hall.

"What are you doing in this hallway?" she asked Fitz.

"I was looking fer Scotty," Fitz said.

"Neither Mr. Callaghan nor the boys are home. And I shouldn't have to say this, but I think ya may need reminding, ya don't belong in this hallway or the boy's rooms. Do I make myself clear?"

"Crystal!" I said, grabbing Fitz and taking our exit before she lost her temper.

We made it back to my room, "Look," I said, as I closed the door, "I don't think we should be snooping. That was too close!"

"Nonsense, we have to find out what's goin' on."

"You only say that because you don't know what I know!"

"How bad could it be," she reclined on my bed.

"Let's just say that our 'witch-hunt' may be a more accurate word than you think."I started to explain the cauldron, the picture above her bed, the book of poisonous plants, and the fact that I had just asked her for a remedy of sorts for an imaginary illness.

"Fitz's eyes rounded, "So, do you think she's a good witch?"

"Do you really feel that you need to ask? She's gonna know," I said, pacing. "She's gonna know and she's gonna poison me."

"Now yer bein' ridiculous," Fitz said.

"Am I? What about all those accidents that happened to those women Martin was dating? One broke out in hives just like me!"

"You said that was because of you and Cecil's argument."

"What if it wasn't? What if I just assumed I got worked up over the argument but it was really something she gave me?"

Fitz's laugh was thin but I could tell that she was pondering. "I don't know Janie. It doesn't seem likely."

"Neither does some woman 'passing out' in a fairy ring, naked no less, talking about spirits threatening her! But that shit happened!"

Fitz began to nod. But I wasn't sure if she thought it was Miss Elanor who was crazy or me. "Ya need to calm down before...oh no, not again!" she said, looking at me.

"What?"

"Did ya eat or drink anything while you were with Miss Elanor?"

"No!" Then I felt the itching begin. I ran to the mirror, "Oh shit! You've gotta be kidding me!"

"I think we can rule out Miss Elanor!"

"The hell we can. What if her room is cursed to anyone who enters without her permission?"

"Uh, I don't have any bumps."

"What if you're immune?"

Now she was looking at me like I was crazy. "Ya don't believe in curses, remember? Now, I'm gonna go get the anti-itch pills from Miss Elanor."

"Antihistamines," I corrected.

"Really?" Fitz asked, "Ya have to correct me?"

"If I don't, she will!" I told her. "No, I don't want them!" I was panicked.

"Janie, you have to take them, or go to the hospital," she reasoned. "Now, do ya want to go to the hospital?" she raised her brows at me.

Fitz knew me well. There were only a few places that were so dreadful to me that I would almost rather die: Downtown L.A. during rush hour (so ANYTIME that is), followed closely by any mall (anywhere, anytime, ever), and finally, the hospital. I shook my head.

"Okay, so I'm off to get yer itchy pills, then you'll go night-night and you'll be fine, okay?"

After a moment, I nodded in agreement.

Fitz came back with Miss Elanor in tow. Miss Elanor came to the side of my bed and ordered me to open my mouth. I was a little reluctant given my new knowledge of her. I pursed my lips like a petulant child. "Open!" she commanded then she put a thermometer under my tongue. She then broke one pill from its foil and handed it to me.

"I'm putting the rest of these in the medicine cabinet. No reason for ya to call me every time ya get a rash," she sounded stern, but her eyes showed...compassion? Maybe even concern. After a couple of minutes, she checked the thermometer. "No fever. Now take that," she pointed at the pill, "And go to bed. There's no reason for me to babysit ya this time. I will leave that to Miss Fitz," she left the room.

"Are ya hungry?" Fitz asked. "I'm hungry."

"I'm not sure you should leave me."

"Janie, yer not gonna turn into a toad. I promise."

I nodded.

"So, how about some cheese and crackers?" she suggested.

I nodded again.

"Okay?" she stood and kissed my forehead before leaving.

I sat there and tried to rationalize my thoughts about Miss Elanor. Obviously, I didn't believe in curses. Yet both times I had broken out in these horrible itchy spots, I had been doing something she either didn't, or wouldn't, have approved of. (Fighting with Cecil and sneaking into her room to snoop). Maybe I had cursed myself by caring what she and others might think. Round and round I spun these thoughts till I started to yawn. My head would no longer concentrate on a single thought. I started to giggle at my own imagination. I was picturing Miss Elanor as a witch with a crooked nose, complete with huge hairy wart at the end. She was still wearing her usual schoolmarm outfit which made me laugh even harder. She DID look like a witch I concluded. I was rolling with laughter when Fitz came back in the room. She asked what was so funny but I guess I wasn't making sense, because not only was she not laughing, she went to go get Miss Elanor. When they both came back in the room, I saw Miss Elanor and laughed so hard I almost peed.

"Why is she doing this?" Fitz asked Miss Elanor.

"Shaking her head, she said, "She's overly sensitive to antihistamines. She'll be fine."

"Are ya sure? She seems really...off."

"She gets this way about half an hour before she's out cold.

I let out an impressive witch's cackle.

"Annoying, but fine," Miss Elanor added,

I pointed to her and said in a gravelly voice, "I'll get you my pretty, and your huge wart, too!"

With that, Miss Elanor stormed out of the room. That's the last thing I remember.

When I woke five hours later, Fitz had her arms folded across her chest and looked positively pissed off.

"What's wrong?" I asked, groggily, trying to sit up.

"Oh, so ya don't remember, huh?"

I shook my head at her, "Please just tell me Fitz. I still feel weird."

"Okay," she said with a huff. "Ya asked me where my boobs were. Then when I pointed to my chest...you asked if someone had stolen them."

I pursed my lips together.

"Then, ya pulled my shirt out, and yelled "Hello" down it."

I winced, "Fitz I'm really..."

"Not done yet," she announced, putting her hand up to quiet me. "Then ya put yer ear up to my shirt. When I asked what ya were doin, ya said you were waiting for an echo!"

I closed my eyes, "I'm so sorry Fitz. I don't remember any of that."

"Ya also called Miss Elanor a witch."

"I did?"

"Well, you implied it. Then ya made me play airplane to get ya to finally eat some food. I had to make plane noises and tell you to open the trap door. Then ya pouted when I wasn't 'plane-y enough' as you put it.

"Great," I rubbed my head. "Look I am sorry. Those pills just...mess me up something terrible."

"Well, keep this in mind, the next time this happens, I'm takin' ya to the hospital. I don't get paid to deal with that shite."

"Understood," I agreed.

"Ya better dress for dinner. We have about half of an hour or so before that damn gong goes off.

I really didn't want to go to dinner, but I was super hungry. I slipped on a pair of slacks, a sweater and my ballerina slippers, thinking heels to be a bad idea at the moment. Into a bun went the hair. I didn't look impressive in any way.

Down the stairs Fitz and I went. Miss Elanor eyed me as I

took my seat. In filed Scotty and Martin. Scotty kissed Fitz hello.

"Oh, Miss Janie," said Martin, "I heard ya had another episode with the hives. I sure hope yer not allergic to us?" he smiled and kissed my hand.

"No, I don't think so," I smiled.

"Maybe yer a little homesick?" he suggested.

"Maybe a little," I allowed the possibility.

"Well, we love having you and Fitz here. The two of ya just light up this old place."

Fitz smiled, I said, "Thank you." Miss Elanor slit her eyes so hard they all but disappeared.

We were having ham with a mustard sauce, scalloped potatoes, and asparagus spears. Only then did I realize I hadn't eaten breakfast or lunch. Just however many crackers Fitz had been able to get into my mouth and Bloody Marys. I tried not to eat as ravenously as I wanted for fear of scaring the menfolk.

Cecil entered and I was reluctant to meet his eyes. I didn't know if it was shame, anger, or humiliation but when I did, he looked away from me quickly. So at least the feeling was mutual.

The odd electricity was back as we sat in silence.

"So, what has everyone been up to today?" Martin asked.

"Janie and I went to town," I immediately shot a look at Fitz. She had thrown me under the bus a few times when this strange energy took hold of the room. "We did some shoppin' and found a cute little pub."

"What did ya ladies buy?"

"Nothin' really," she said, "Just wanted to check out the town."

Cecil was eyeing me, "Which pub did ya stop at?"

I knew he could ask the driver where he had taken us. There was no point in lying. "I took her to Dave's pub."

"Did ya?" he asked, nodding his head. "I was there too, I didn't see ya."

"Well, we didn't see you either," I said. "Shame, you could have joined us for a Bloody Mary."

Silence took the room over again, but I could feel Cecil eyeing me.

"So Martin, I'd like to go to the distillery tomorrow and take some photos. Would that be alright?"

"I'd love that! I can arrange to give ya a full tour."

"I would love that," I smiled back.

Miss Elanor huffed at me.

"Fitz, say you'll come too. You'll be doing yer layout there, maybe you'd like to see it. I could get your professional opinion, like where ya think the shoot would best be staged?" Martin suggested.

Fitz looked proud to be asked, "I would be happy to."

"We have meeting' in the mornin', so maybe have the driver bring you around eleven. We can grab lunch afterward?"

"Wonderful," I said.

Cecil piped up, "I can drive 'em."

I stared at him.

"I said I would take ya, so I will."

I wasn't sure what to say, so I just said, "Thank you, I'd appreciate that."

When dinner was over, I excused myself saying that I was still a bit groggy.

Before I could leave the room Miss Elanor handed me a vial and asked, "Are ya allergic to anything?"

"Penicillin?" I answered, gulping back my fear.

"Miss O'Connelly, is that a question, or a statement?"

"Statement," I clarified.

"Fine," she nodded at me. "Put two drops in yer ear before bed."

I stared at the vial, "Thank you?"

She let out a sigh.

"I mean thank you!" I said quickly.

Back in my Dracula room, I was thinking of calling my mom when my eyes were drawn to two items sitting on my night table. I inspected them. One was a button about as big around as a dime. It was a dome shape and it had what looked like a fox hunt scene etched into it. The other was a flat gold coin. It also had a rider on horseback, but the rider was wearing a helmet and brandishing a sword, I thought. The picture had almost been worn away. The date on the coin was 18--something; not quite the size of a quarter but heavier. Where had they come from, and why?

I was going to call Fitz into my room but she and Scotty were almost to her door, so I figured I'd wait till later. With any luck she would just ask Scotty what the hell was going on now. Maybe she could save me another round of hives and give herself some peace of mind.

I went back to my bed and sat on the edge inspecting the items. I thought I understood the dressing gown. I figured someone wanted me to wear it. But then when I did, no one seemed to recognize it or fess up to leaving it in my room. But these items had me confused. What the hell could they mean? Why were they left here? And most importantly, who was leaving things in my room?

I rolled every possibility around in my mind until I finally gave up and called mom.

One ring, two rings, three rings. Finally, she answered.

"Hello Janie, how is Ireland?"

"Ireland is good mom." She sounded relaxed and calm. Who the hell was this woman?

"How's Fitz?"

I was silent. Never in twenty-one years had she asked about

Fitz in a way that wasn't derogatory. As in: "Did Fitz start that fire?"

"Janie," mom called, waking me from my thoughts.

"She's good," I said slowly. "Um, how's dad?"

"Oh he's wonderful. We went for a long drive yesterday up the coast. It's been years since we did that."

I tried to remember the last time they had. I knew that I had been in the backseat. Mom had been complaining about how fast dad was driving. But when I looked out the back window a trail of cars were behind us, hoping my father would pull over. "That's great mom," I had no idea what to say.

"We stopped at a little BBQ place and had a wonderful lunch. Then we went and put our feet in the water before we headed home."

Was my mom dying? I began to panic. I had heard of people's attitudes changing rapidly when faced with mortality. "How are you feeling mom?" I asked.

"I feel amazing! I feel totally refreshed!" she said almost giddy.

Usually the word amazing was used to describe one of my bigger screw-ups. As in: "It's amazing that you are still alive after doing something so stupid!" I didn't know how to talk to this mother.

"How is Cecil? Dad really liked him when they met. I hope I get to meet him?"

Aliens? I pondered. Did aliens take my mother? "Uh yeah, he's good. I hope you get to meet him, too," I was flabbergasted.

"Have you started painting yet?"

"Well, kind of," I answered, thinking of the huge Cecil painting.

"Well, I just know they're going to be amazing. I got this new cell phone and you can send me pictures."

What. Is. Happening? "You got a cell? What for?"

"Well, so you can contact me, even when I'm not home. It's so great! I'm thinking of setting up a page and getting one of those E-mail things. Here, let me give you my number."

I found a pen and took it down, my head spinning.

"Well, honey, I have loads to do today. I'll call you later, or you can call me. Love you!"

"Love you, too," I murmured. Then she hung up, leaving me dumbfounded.

I rubbed my face, was I dreaming? Was this the left over effect from my antihistamine daze?

Bath time, I assessed. Everything was better in a claw-foot tub. I grabbed my night clothes and headed to the bathroom. Sinking in, bubbles everywhere, I tried not to wonder about everything and everyone in my life. Turns out that 'clear your mind' crap, was more difficult than they would have you believe. I had finally attained oneness, or whatever the hell it was called, when I heard Fitz at the door.

"Are ya decent?"

"Does it really matter if I'm not?"

"I don't want to see ya on the pot."

"Just come in."

She looked sullen.

"Again?" I asked.

"If what you really mean is "Not again," then yes. I swear I need to know what is happenin'."

"Don't you mean you need to understand why it's not happening?"

She nodded. "I called Mum. I explained what was NOT going on."

"What did she say?"

"She put me on speaker phone with Aunt Marble."

I tried not to laugh. "What did the vaginal guru say?"

"She told me to 'up my game' Fitz said seriously.

"O-kay. How?"

"She told me to buy some cuffs, a blindfold and a feather."

"Ah ha," I nodded. "She doesn't have any idea that some of us don't..."

"I told her, I'm not twenty-one anymore, Auntie," she threw her hands up in the air. "Obviously, I've already tried those things," she expelled. "She could have told me to try a champagne bath, like I was a 'nubie' for God sakes."

I wasn't sure what to say now.

"I've tried everything! Strip tease, lap dance, food..."

I nodded, thinking this seemed normal enough.

"...cuffs, role playing, leather, toys, foams, jellies, creams...

My eyes rounded.

"...ice cubes, peppermint drops, edible undies, and yes, the blindfold, cuffs, and feathers!" She was almost frantic, pulling her long red hair through her fingers.

"I ugh...I've got nothing," I said, shaking my head. "Except...ASK HIM!"

"I tried. He said it was nothin' for me to worry about. I asked about the daily meetin's. He said that they were in negotiations and that it makes him a little edgy. Then he said he had an early mornin' and kissed me on the forehead. ON THE FOREHEAD, JANIE! I was naked, and he chose to kiss my forehead!

I winced. Me being shot down, that was one thing. But Fitz...this was unheard of for her.

I felt really badly for her, but had nothing comforting to say at this point. "My mom is crazy. Like a different kind of crazy than before."

"Go ahead," she said. "It'll take my mind off not gettin' laid," she pouted.

I told her about the conversation. "Is she dyin'?" Fitz asked.

"Funny, that was the first thing I thought, too. But she says she feels better than she has in years."

"Wonder if she's gettin' some?" Fitz said, sullenly.

"Yeah, I don't want to wonder about that, ever!"

"Jesus, ya act like ya don't know how ya got in her womb."

"Stork," I said, grabbing my towel.

"Meanwhile, my friendly neighborhood penis is on strike."

"Well, I'm right there with ya."

"No, no, yer not! You could get laid right now if ya wanted. Actually by two men if I'm reading them correctly."

"Two?"

"Cecil and young Daniel."

"First of all, I can't even get Cecil to look at me."

Fitz grinned from ear to ear, "Yep and there are several positions where he doesn't have to."

"Second, Daniel is NOT an option for me."

"Alright, calm yer knickers."

Shaking my head, I got dressed and took Fitz to my room to show her the newest addition of things left there.

"Okay, I get the dressing gown," Fitz said. "But a coin and a button? I can't even think of what that's all about."

"Me either," I said. "Are you staying with me tonight, then?"

"Are ya still dream horny?"

"Not for a couple of days. Not since Cecil and I have been fighting."

"Then yeah. I don't want to have to fight ya off of me. I may be goin' without against my will but my 'will' is still men."

"Very funny. Asshole!"

I stared at the vial Miss Elanor had given me. I wasn't about to touch that stuff.

We crawled into bed and fell fast asleep.

18

SORRY FITZ

There we were, midnight, in the stable. He turned to me; his hair blowing in the wind. His shirt was clinging to his body with sweat. His scent was intoxicating. Me: milking the cow, as he draws near. I can't get any milk from the teat. I am distraught, how will I get the milk? My eyes; pleading with him. Suddenly, he is behind me, hand clasped over mine. Ah he will show me how to get the milk. The bucket begins to fill with champagne, "Yes, yes!" I scream.

"No, No," I woke up screaming. "What the hell!"

"What the hell, indeed!" Fitz said. "I thought ya were done with dream horny?"

"I swear, I don't have any idea what the hell that was about." I reluctantly explained the dream.

Fitz narrowed her eyes and shook her head, "Not right Janie. What the hell has Ireland done to ya?"

We dressed and went down to breakfast. The men were already present when we sat. Fitz kissed Scotty good morning, Miss Elanor sneered. Everything was normal, until Mr. Briggs entered the room with a bouquet of wildflowers. Rounding the table he handed them to me, "For you Miss Janie," he bowed and walked away.

Everyone looked surprised, but not as much as me I'm sure. I read the small card to myself: To the most beautiful woman in the world, love Daniel.

"They're lovely," Fitz said.

I was trying not to wince, and forced a smile. "Yes, they are." I tried to drop the conversation.

Cecil sat, taking glances at me. "So, who sent the flowers?" he finally asked.

I took a deep breath.

"Do ya not want to say?" he asked.

Martin, seeing my discomfort said, "I'm sure Miss Janie several courters, son."

Miss Elanor made a small growling noise.

"I'm sure she does." Cecil smiled, "So which one is this?"

"Son, if you are so worried about who sends Miss Janie flowers, maybe ya should send some of yer own," Martin schooled him.

This had the desired effect of shutting him up. Fitz, knowing that Cecil had apparently not sent them, didn't ask. She was pretty sure who they came from without my saying.

"Miss Elanor," said Martin, "Maybe ya could ask the maids if they have seen my coin and button. They seem to have gone missing."

"Coin and button?" I asked, shooting a look at Fitz.

"Yes." Martin said. "I've had them for years, and well...years. Although I am afraid that putting it that way makes me feel quite old."

I smiled.

"The button was from my boardin' school jacket. It came off durin' my last year. When I wanted to have my mother put it right, she said "No." She said that long after I had graduated, it would be a constant reminder of the boy I had been and the young man I grew to be. She told me to keep it with me to remind myself to be young at heart."

My own heart warmed as it so often did when Martin spoke.

"The coin," he continued, "Was from my grandfather. It was the first money he earned with his whiskey. It was payment for a whole night's worth of drinking by a group of poets and philosophers. When he handed it to me he said it was important to know a man's worth, as well as his own. No coin, dollar, diamond or gold, has such worth, as a pure soul. It's a reminder to surround myself with, and be, the best man I can. Whether I be a rich man or poor in earthly possessions, rich of soul and heart, are the only things of true value. I keep them in my pocket every day. They've become like good luck charms," he smiled.

I knew how he felt. The Rune Diane had given me, wasn't nearly as sentimental and I had felt naked without her since she got lost in New York.

My eyes were welling. One: Because it was a beautiful speech. Two: I was pretty sure someone was trying to frame me as a thief. Fitz was looking sidelong at me. Martin and Scotty had another meeting to attend and Cecil went to the stable to check on Babygirl. As soon as they were gone, Fitz and I hauled ass back up to my room.

"SHIIIT!" I breathed, as I closed the door.

"What the hell?" Fitz asked. "Who would try to set you up to take this fall?"

I shook my head, "I don't know. But who has access to his room? He said he keeps those," I pointed at the coin and button, "In his pocket."

"Okay, so Mr. Briggs, for sure, the maids, that's a given," she counted on her fingers. "Miss Elanor of course. In fact, we may be the only two people in this house that didn't know about 'em," she said.

"So should I give them back to Martin?"

"And say what? They wound up in yer room and ya haven't a clue how?"

"It's the truth," I began to fidget.

"I know," she said. "But ya have to admit, it sounds nuts."

"So what do we do?"

Fitz was mulling, and that rarely worked out well for me. "We have to sneak them back into his room!"

My eyes rounded, "How?"

"Well, we know which room is his now and we do have the skeleton key..."

"Oh God, I don't want hives again!"

"Then just stay calm. We can do this!"

I shook my head, "We can't. This is a horrible idea."

So there we were in the South Wing, I had the coin and the button wrapped firmly in my hand. We knew the men were out of the Castle, and Fitz had made this mission sound like an easy undertaking. Oh how I wanted to believe that would be true.

We made it all the way to Martin's door unseen. The beauty of a Castle is that everyone is so spread out. Or at least you'd think. We came to the door, when Fitz started fumbling around in the pockets of her skinny jeans.

Looking up at me, she said, "Yer not gonna believe this."

"What?" I was starting to panic.

"I forgot the key," she winced.

I started shaking my head, "Are ya frickin kidding me? How?"

"Look I had it in my hand and set it down when I went to change clothes. I must have forgotten to pick it back up. We'll just go back and get it. No harm, no foul!"

Just then, we saw Miss Elanor coming down the hallway. I

don't know what I was thinking, but I had no pockets, so I turned my back to Miss Elanor and shoved the button and coin down Fitz's bra top then turned to greet Miss Elanor.

"What are ya ladies doing in the South Wing?" she asked.

"We were hoping to catch Martin and Scotty before they left," I said. "I've forgotten what time we were supposed to meet them."

"Why didn't ya ask Cecil? He's drivin' ya," she said sternly. Her gaze left me and landed on Fitz. She didn't seem to be looking at her eyes though. She made a face of concern as she tried to listen to Fitz going on and on. I followed her gaze, and my eyes bugged out of my head. She was looking at Fitz's top. There, underneath her bra top, she had two horribly misshapen, unaligned nipples. One looked as if it was pointing to the angels, the other pointing to the devil. One bubbled up and the other looked like a tiny flattened pancake. Miss Elanor tried to look away from what she must have thought was Fitz's 'trainwreck' of female anatomy.

"Well, the men are not here, as I've already said," Elanor stumbled over her words.

Fitz, not seeing what I and Miss Elanor were seeing, put her hands on her hips, further displaying her deformity. "Well, I guess we'll just wait for Cecil to fetch us, like ya said."

Miss Elanor tried to look everywhere but Fitz's chest. "Fine, fine," she said," a look of pity, tinged with disgust.

I was trying not to freak out. We had to get back to my room. As we parted, Miss Elanor was shaking her head to clear the image.

"Oh my God Fitz, you have no idea."

"That was a close one."

"No," I said as I walked her into my room, and placed her in front of the mirror. "Look."

"At what?" she said.

"Just look!"

"Okay. It's me," she blew herself a kiss.

"Put your hands on your hips and look again."

She did as I asked, "What the hell?" she yelled, taking a closer look. "It looks like I have crazy nips!"

I nodded.

"Do ya think Miss Elanor noticed?" she dug out the coin and button.

"Oh yeah," I said.

"Why did ya shove 'em in my shirt?"

"I don't have pockets in these damn slacks. They're supposed to make my ass look good."

"Well, good news for yer ass, meanwhile, I'm crazy nipple girl!"

"We have to get these back to Martin's room," I pleaded.

"Fine," Fitz pursed her lips, but you go put on a pair of jeans with pockets, right now!"

After I changed, and Fitz grabbed the key, we again made it to Martin's room unseen. I crept in and put them on the floor next to his bed so he would think they had fallen on the ground. I exited and locked the door. Fitz and I were back in my room faster than lightning.

"Okay, part one, done. Now all we have to do is figure out who put the damn things in yer room in the first place," Fitz said.

"Whoever it is wants me gone in the worst way."

"Miss Elanor," Fitz offered.

"Cecil?" I asked.

"He wouldn't do that to ya. No matter how bad the two of ya have had it. He wouldn't ruin ya. I have a question off the subject," she met my eyes, "Who sent ya the flowers?"

I had completely forgotten about the flowers. I handed Fitz the card.

"Daniel? I thought he had given up on ya?"

"I did too."

"This is so strange. Do ya think maybe Daniel...?" she trailed off.

I shook my head, "He would need a key to get into Martin's room."

"Or know of another secret passageway?" Fitz concluded.

"I guess, but if he was set on pursuing me, why would he want me thought of as a thief. Undoubtedly Martin wouldn't want a thief staying in his home. Seems like that would defeat Daniel's purpose, don't you think?"

Fitz nodded, "Well, we're back where we started from."

19

THE DISTILLERY

Cecil sent for us at half past ten. Fitz and I piled into the back of the Rolls, and Cecil sat up front with the old James Dean look alike. A gentle rain began to fall, and I voiced my concerns as to how to paint the distillery.

"I wonder if I should paint it is sunny or rainy weather. I mean, Martin loves the rain. Maybe he would prefer a picture in the rain?"

"Ya seem to know an awful lot about my dad," he said.

"Just what I've learned since I've been here." I was a little confused as to why my wanting to get to know his dad bothered him.

"He seems to take quite an interest in ya as well."

"I should think he would. We're staying in his home."

"Yeah, I guess that's a good enough reason. Those flowers ya got were sure lovely."

Crap. Here we go, I thought.

"I guess you have an admirer," he said, and dropped the conversation.

We pulled up in front of the massive distillery. Three stories of stone and brick were accented by large arched windows and a huge wooden door (big enough to drive a Mack truck through). I was immediately drawn back in time. I could almost feel the generations of history pouring from the walls. As I exited the car, I stood in awe. There was a sense of deja vu, leaving the tiny hairs on the back of my neck standing on end. Had I seen this place in dreams? Or was it just my Irish heritage calling me home. After all, whiskey was made here. Before I even turned my head, I knew Fitz was smiling. Flower beds worked their way around the massive structure. We walked the long wooden entry way before stepping inside the building.

Cecil was smiling again at my reaction. "Do ya love it?"

"I can't even express how much I love this place," I said, not knowing where my eyes would be drawn next.

I stepped into a room big enough to be an airplane hangar. The coat of arms and the family crest, on fifteen foot wide by twenty-five foot long banners, hung from the three story walls. Large rows of wooden barrels formed aisles and had signs saying five years, up to fifty (by five's), stacked twelve high and half a block long. My mind was blown by the sheer size of the place, and this was just the aging room. We found Martin and Scotty through a door that read, 'Mr. Martin Callaghan'. A man caught my eye as I watched him scratching Martin's name from the glass. I looked back at Fitz, who raised her brows to me.

Martin noticed what I was focused on and called my attention away. "Come ladies, to the 'Mash Room'."

We were led to a very warm room with vats that a small family could live in. Heated to perfection, you could smell the whiskey on the air. It burned my nose, but what a good burn it was. I looked at Fitz, and she was tearing.

"I know, the fumes are something," I said.

"It's not that," she sniffled. "Look at all the whiskey. I'm so happy. I need a moment," she turned away from us.

I couldn't help but giggle, as Scotty wrapped his arm around her.

"I'm good, I'm good," she said, dabbing her eyes with Scotty's sleeve.

Martin laughed, "I feel the same way, Fitz. Every time I walk into this room, I get overwhelmed," he looked dreamy-eyed. "From the floors, walls and ceilin ’," he extended his hand, "To the grounds and all the flowers Margaret herself planted."

"She planted all of those flowers?" Fitz asked.

"Aye," Martin smiled. "She was a hard workin' woman, always. She said I needed remindin', that she would always with me, and doing her best to brighten my day. I eat lunch out on the bench among her flowers most days," he began to well up.

Cecil walked up and rubbed his father's back. "It's okay dad."

"Yes my son," he smiled. "It is grand. Let's move on, shall we?"

I was not just confused, I was concerned. I decided not to ask, but whatever was happening, I was aware now that the daily meetings had something to do with Martin's name being taken off of his office door and his rising emotions. I assumed whatever was going on was also keeping Fitz from getting laid. I started to think of the poultice Miss Elanor was making. Was Martin sick? He looked healthy. But he had said he wouldn't be able to make it back up the hill, on my tour of the Castle grounds. Shit, everything was adding up to something I didn't even want to think about. I could tell by her stare, Fitz had questions, too.

I snapped off picture after picture. The place held me in awe. At the end of our tour, we walked the grounds, so I could take photos of the whole building. I was already envisioning the painting I would do.

We filed back into the Rolls and headed to a little grill for lunch. It didn't look like anything special from the outside, but the food was amazing. I had the ham and brie on a demi-baguette. Cecil, Fitz and Scotty all had steak and heavy food. I couldn't imagine eating that for lunch. Neither could Martin I noticed. He ordered a salad and only ate half. Martin said he was done for the day, so we all headed back to the Castle.

As we pulled up out front a delivery truck was blocking the circular drive. I shot a look to Fitz. We hadn't thought this far ahead. Standing outside of the truck was Alex. FML was all that went through my head. Cecil, too, didn't exactly look thrilled, but I wasn't sure why.

"Is that another delivery?" Martin asked. "I thought ya had everything ya needed?"

"I bought a new canvas," I admitted. "Seems the first canvas...broke." I looked at Cecil.

Martin smiled, "If you needed another, I would have paid for it."

"No, No, this was my...mistake. The next picture will...be perfect."

Cecil was eyeing me but said nothing.

As we stepped out of the Rolls Alex grinned from ear to ear.

"I saw that ya needed another canvas, so of course, I wanted to get it to ya as soon as possible."

Fake ass bi---, I thought. But then I smiled my fake ass bi--- smile, too. "Well, thank you."

"Miss Elanor wouldn't accept the delivery and asked me to either wait outside or come back later."

Martin stifled a grin, "Well, thank ya for waiting. Please, come in."

Two large men exited the van and grabbed the canvas. Cecil and Alex, her arm wrapped through his, led the men to the painting room. Fitz, Scotty and I walked in tow. The men set the canvas up on the easel and Scotty gave them a generous tip before walking them out.

"I just love this room," Alex said to Cecil. "Wouldn't this room be lovely for a weddin'?"

Cecil's eyebrows shot up as did my lip. I tried not to growl.

"Can't ya just picture it," she continued. Chandeliers hanging there and there," she pointed. "Then you'd have a trellis over here. A wrought iron trellis with flowers climbing it," she smiled. "Underneath it is where the vows would be exchanged. White chairs in rows, here," she motioned, "Divided for a pathway to the altar. A string quartet over there," she pointed toward the back of the room. "It would be so beautiful," she said dramatically.

Fitz's laugh drew Alex's attention.

"What's so funny?"

"You've givin' this a lot of thought, haven't ya?" Fitz asked.

"Well haven't you given any thought to yer weddin?"

"A little, I guess. But I don't like to put the cart before the horse. Do ya have a man in mind to play the groom at this weddin' yer plannin'?"

"Well, no," she smiled coyly at Cecil, "Not exactly. But that doesn't have to stop a woman from dreamin', does it?"

"No, I agree," Fitz answered her. "I think ya should keep dreamin'."

The implication of how she said, what she said, made Alex's eyes slit. "You are so clever," Alex said.

"Huh. I was goin' for transparent. I think I've done a wonderful job. Don't you?"

Cecil abruptly changed the subject, "So what happened to the other canvas?"

I was enjoying Fitz ripping Alex apart so much that I had forgotten that this question would eventually arise. "I ugh...I ugh..." I was blank. I didn't want him to see what I had painted. Even less in front of Alex.

"I fell on it," Fitz said.

We all looked at her.

"What?" Cecil asked.

"Yep, fell on the damned thing."

"How?" Cecil continued.

Fitz crossed her arms across her chest and sighed, "I was twirlin'," she said blankly, like this summed it all up.

"You were...twirlin'?" he repeated.

"Yeah, I twirl from time to time. I'm a twirler," she nodded like this was a very normal pastime.

I just stared at her. What the hell was she saying?

"It's such a beautiful room, as Alex pointed out. I couldn't help myself. I began twirlin'...lost my balance...and fell into the damned easel. The frame survived me, but the canvas sadly, did not. Ripped right through the damn thing."

"Those canvases are made very strong," Alex interjected, as though it was unlikely.

Fitz grinned, "Yeah...but I'm stronger."

Cecil began nodding, "Okay," he said to Fitz. "So what are ya gonna paint first, Janie?"

"The Distillery, I think. Both are so beautiful. I just hope I do them justice."

"I'm sure you will," Cecil said, smiling.

"Well, if you'll hand me your camera, I'll go and print those pictures out for ya. They'll be much easier to see that way. I can blow them up a bit, l too."

"That would be a big help actually. I 'd appreciate it," I added.

It almost felt like all the weirdness between us had melted away. I guess now that I knew where I stood and he knew where he was at (In love with the horrible whore of Ireland), we could just get back to normal.

He took the camera and I showed him which pictures I liked the most. He headed off to Martin's office with Alex in tow. She turned to Fitz and me before taking her exit.

"Lovely to see you two again," she said.

"Ya don't let the door hit ya in the..." Fitz started.

I cut her off, "Yep, you too."

Alex shot Fitz a look, but Fitz just grinned from ear to ear.

After she was gone, I said to Fitz, "Grace Kelly, remember?"

"No, you be Grace Kelly. I told ya, I'm gonna be a bitch."

"Well, mission accomplished," I smiled. "By the way, 'I was twirling', is what you came up with? Really?"

"I'm sorry my explanation wasn't as good as yer 'uh...uh...' answer. Plus, I'm the one who now has to twirl in front of him to sell that shite!"

I got a mental image and began laughing at the picture in my head. "I can't wait!"

"Yer an asshole," she concluded.

"What are we going to do about the picture? Seriously, the closet isn't the best hiding place. Cecil didn't ask how we got rid of it, but it's bound to come up at some point."

"Give it to Alex as a wedding gift?"

I just stared at her.

"Too soon?"

"And now you're the asshole!"

We thought and thought, and Fitz suggested my room.

"But someone has been visiting my room, remember?"

"Do ya think it's Cecil?" she asked.

"Well, no. Really, I don't."

"We could put it under the bed," she suggested.

I started to nod my head, thinking about its size. "That's a possibility. It is a huge bed," I agreed. "But how do we get it there, unseen?"

Fitz was thinking and thinking, and then she grinned, "How creepy do ya think this place is in the middle of the night?"

I closed my eyes, "Shit!"

20

OH, FOR THE LOVE OF . . .

I went upstairs and changed into my painting overalls and pulled my long blonde hair into a bun. I was ready to start painting. If I could keep my mind on that, instead Fitz's and my impending covert operation, all would be well.

Fitz had gone to speak to Martin about her shoot. She had some great ideas and took the time to write them down, so she could present them to him.

Back in the atrium, I looked at the blank canvas. This was always my favorite part. Nothing would turn into something underneath my brush strokes. I couldn't help but smile. If I took a moment to really think of where I was standing, and how I got here, I was both amazed and proud. I had finally found the courage to shoot for my dreams. And here I was, doing what I loved to do. I was just so happy, proud and grateful for the opportunity I was given. I put my arms out, head back and did a little spin of my own.

Just then I heard, "Careful, that's how the other canvas got damaged."

I stopped twirling to see Cecil and Alex watching me.

"At first," he said, "I wasn't sure I believed the twirlin' story, but now...I get it."

I just smiled as he handed me the photos. "These turned out great. Thank you."

"Well, they're from yer eye," he smiled.

It was so nice to not be fighting, I just enjoyed his presence. Until I was reminded by a throat clearing sound that we weren't alone.

"Well, I better get started," I said.

"Do ya need anything?"

"Don't let me miss dinner. I get kind of carried away when I paint. If I don't hear the gong, I won't remember to eat."

"You got it. I'll come get ya at seven-ish."

I nodded then Cecil and Alex left.

I needed to push everyone and everything out of my head. Mozart, I concluded as I loaded the CD. To work I went. Standing in front of the easel, I closed my eyes, and got the image I wanted. Opening them, I picked up the pencil and went to town.

Everything was just unfolding in front of my eyes. Slowly a picture began to form. It was exactly how I wanted the Distillery to look. The angle was perfect to capture the beauty of this old building and its surroundings. Including the flower beds Margaret had planted for her husband.

Fitz came back after a few hours and was very pleased to announce that Martin had found his beloved coin and button. I let out a sigh of relief and I high-fived her.

"One less thing to worry about," I said. "But I still wish I knew who was trying to set me up for a fall."

She nodded. "Also, he loved my presentation and said that my ideas were perfect for what he wanted," she rocked back and forth on her heels.

"I am so proud of you!" I hugged her. "So when's the shoot?"

"He set it up for this Friday! Ya are comin', right?"

"Do you even have to ask?"

"Well, I didn't know if ya'd be too busy paintin'."

"Wouldn't miss it," I smiled.

"Wow," Fitz said, looking at my outline. "That's so cool. It amazes me that ya can do that," she shook her head.

I smiled. "Well, thank you, Miss Fitz."

"No really, I'm a fan."

"My biggest, I know."

"I'm gettin' hungry. It's almost dinner time. Did ya want to change, or are ya going in yer overalls."

"Cecil was supposed to come get me."

"Fat chance of that happenin'. Alex is doing her best to keep him occupied."

I sighed again. "Well, you better get used to her. She may be family to you someday."

"Not a chance in hell of that happinin'. I can make it look like an accident."

I put my arm around her and we headed out of the painting room. We ran into Cecil and Alex coming down the hall. He looked like he wasn't feeling well.

"You alright?" I asked.

"I have a headache," he forced a smile. "Maybe dinner will help."

The gong went off and Cecil covered one eye with his hand.

We filed into the dining room, meeting up with Scotty and Martin. Scotty put a giant kiss on Fitz's cheek before pulling out her chair. I stood wondering where I should sit since Alex was there. She walked to my seat and Cecil pulled out her chair. I started to grab a chair on the other side of the table when Cecil ran to my side and pulled it out for me then took the seat next to me. Alex burned holes into me with her eyes. Miss Elanor looked sidelong at Alex. Fitz grinned. I was just really uncomfortable. But I was good at dealing with it by now.

Salmon was served and Alex looked at Miss Elanor, "I can't eat that. I'm allergic to fish," she said.

"Unfortunately, I was just as unaware of yer dietary needs as the fact that you would be joinin' us for dinner this evenin'," she gave Cecil a stern look."

"I was unaware as well," he said under his breath.

"I can make you a ham sandwich," suggested Miss Elanor, sternly.

Alex painted on a fake smile, "I'm sure the salad will be enough for me. I don't eat much," she said, eyeing my full plate.

Martin broke the silence that was gathering, "So Janie, did ya get started yet? I saw that ya practically ran to the paintin' room."

"I did," I smiled. "I started on the distillery. It's such a beautiful place Martin," I added.

He took a deep breath, "Ahh, that she is." The nostalgia was back in his eyes.

"I would love to see the distillery," said Alex.

Martin just smiled and nodded.

"Cecil, I would love a tour," she said to him.

He also smiled and nodded.

All eyes were darting around the table as the fish was served.

After dinner Alex announced that she would need another ride home. I wasn't going to give her any reaction as she batted her eyes at Cecil.

As I walked back up the stairs, I heard him say, "Of course."

I made it to my room and was wondering if I should nap until Fitz came to get me for our covert operation: Retrieve and hide giant Cecil painting.

I looked at my phone, one missed call from Betty. I wasn't

sure if I wanted to know. I grabbed my pj's and phone then headed to the bathroom.

After filling up the tub, I grabbed my phone and sank into the bubbles. Dialing Betty's number, three rings passed.

"Hello," Betty said. She sounded exhausted.

"Hi Betty. Are you okay?"

She let out a sigh, "I spent the day with yer mother."

"Ahhh," was all I had to say.

"She's somthin, honey. Look I had a question for ya, and there's no polite way to wrap this particular piece of crap in sugar."

Like I would have expected her to? "Go ahead."

"How the hell are you so normal?"

I started to laugh. "I wouldn't exactly call myself well adjusted."

"Ya know, I don't believe in all that psycho mumbo-jumbo 'blame yer mom' crap! But the fact that yer not in a cute little white jacket that zips up the back, is an impressive feat."

I laughed harder, "She's making you crazy?" I asked sympathetically.

"It takes the patience of Job to deal with that woman. Now don't get me wrong, I try to love all people, but she's testin' my Southern manners. Do you know she actually buttoned up my top when the workers showed up, saying, "We don't give the milk away for free!"

"Oh my God!" I could see my mother doing this to me, but to a grown ass woman, older than herself?

"I undid the button and told her that "Looks are free. But if someone tries to steal my milk, I'll shoot the petals off their daisy."

I giggled. "I am so sorry. Maybe we should call all of this off. It's not your problem."

"Oh no, Now...it's a battle of wills, and my will is good, Puddin!"

"Well, they should be done painting the house soon, right?"

"Ugh, well yeah. The paintin' is comin' along."

There was silence. Silence was a questionable thing with Betty.

"That's all you're having done, right?" I asked.

"Well...ya see, I was in yer kitchen..."

"Yeah?"

"Ya know I was just not happy with those old linoleum floors. I mean they're really shabby lookin'. So I decided that I would have new floorin' put in, ya know."

"O-kay. But once that's done...?"

"Well Puddin ya can't really fix the kitchen floors, without doing the living room. I mean it's all connected."

"But the living room is wood."

"Yeah, it just needs a little work. I figured while you're gone, I'd go ahead and get those little things done. It'll add equity."

"Ugh, okay." I liked my house the way it was, but I did rent from Betty. She kind of had final say. I told her not to put herself out. And if she was going to be spending time with my mom, Ibuprofen was a good thing to have on hand. The 'family size' was how I bought mine. We said our goodbyes and rang off.

Just as I put the phone down, it rang. "Hello mom," I said.

"That landlady of yours is impossible!" she exclaimed. "Every time I turn around, there she is."

What could I say. That was the plan, I thought.

"And the way she dresses? Just today I tried to show her how proper women dress a little more discreetly and she said something about shooting at flowers. I think she may be crazy!"

I was trying not to laugh. Mom was back. "Maybe you should just avoid her. You know, stay away from the house until it's finished?"

"I will not! She may own the house, but everything inside, you own. I will be there to make sure the workers don't try any funny business."

"Funny business?" I asked.

"Some of those men are thieves! And some are even worse than that!"

"Worse than thieves?"

She whispered into the phone, "Perverts, Janie. Those men aren't going to go through your underwear drawer. I won't have it!"

"So you're going stand guard over my panty drawer?"

"If need be, of course."

"Well, okay."

We caught up a little, and I said my hellos to my dad, then we rang off. All I could do was shake my head. Some sick part of me was happy to have my batshit crazy mother back to her old batshit crazy self. I was worried for Betty, though. A battle of wills with my mother wasn't easily won, and usually left me wounded. God speed Miss Betty, I thought as I got into my jammies.

It was past eleven by now. I had no idea when Fitz and I would be performing our recon mission. Cecil and Alex kept bouncing around in my head. He didn't seem too happy to see her this afternoon. But after everything she had put him through, I could see him trying to fight his feelings for her. He had admitted to Hanna that he was in love again and against his better judgment at that. Sitting and mulling was making me crazy, so I went to Fitz's room. She cracked the door so slightly, that I was sure she and Scotty were in 'flagrante delicto'. Quickly I let her know that I would be in the painting room. She rushed me off and closed the door.

As I turned away from the door I couldn't help but smile. I

didn't want to even think about all the circus-crazy-crap she was willing to try just to get a rise out of Scotty.

I headed down the stairs, passing Miss Elanor on my way. "I guess you'll be heading down to get a warm up from a whiskey bottle."

Oh sweet venom, I thought. I had a bottle in my room if that was all I wanted. And if I had stayed there I would have missed our pleasant exchange. "Actually, I was heading to the painting room."

"Well, you may want to close your robe," she looked me up and down. "There's no one here to impress with your nakedness."

I looked down at my attire as she headed up the stairs. Men's jammie pants and a black tank top, complete with robe and slippers. Didn't seem improper to me. "You'd love my mom," I said.

"Excuse me? What was that ya said?" she asked.

"My mom," I repeated. "You'd love my mom."

"Oh ya think?" she said smugly. "And why is that?"

"You're just so much alike," I smiled.

She eyed me, trying to figure out how to take this statement. "Well, please don't forget that I'm not yer mother." She continued on her way.

"Emotionally interchangeable," I said under my breath as I made my way to the painting room. I was getting better at making my way through the Castle. No wrong turns this time.

I admired my work for a few moments. If I buckled down, I could have the distillery painting done in a week or so. Miss Elanor had had one good idea. Pouring myself a drink, I sat on the chaise lounge by the window. A little relaxer couldn't hurt given how sure I was that my nerves would soon be put to the test.

Just then, I heard a voice coming down the hall. It was Cecil.

I hadn't wanted to spend time alone with him since hearing that he had fallen for Alex again. I didn't want to hear about her, him, or any of it. I looked around, eyes darting for a hiding spot. I ran to the closet and just made it inside when he came through the door.

I was busy chastising myself when I heard him say, “Where do ya think ya left it?”

I listened carefully. Who left what, where? I wondered.

“I'm checking,” I heard. His voice was coming towards the door.

Oh shit, oh shit, oh shit! Not really the best prayer, but it was all that was going through my mind. Just then I heard Fitz.

“Hey, is Janie in here?” she asked.

“Hang on,” he said to whoever was on the phone. “What was that, Fitz?”

“Sorry. Didn't realize ya were on the phone. Have ya seen Janie? I was supposed to meet her here.”

I slowly opened the door, just a crack. Cecil had his back to me as I waved frantically to get her attention.

Her eyes rounded at me. Cecil turned to look at what Fitz was seeing. “What is it, Fitz?” he said.

“Mouse!” she yelled. “I thought I saw a mouse,” she blurted.

“A mouse?” he started for the door.

Hanging in the closet were long rows of plastic covered drapes on hangers. I assumed were backups or seasonal. I squished myself between two rows and practically disappeared.

Quickly the light was flicked on and I heard Fitz yell, “Oh no, there it is.” Cecil clicked the light off and headed to wherever Fitz had pointed. “Out the door, out the door!” she yelled.

Cecil spoke back into the receiver, “Ah here it is. How did it get in here?” he asked, picking up something from behind the door.

"I'll look for the mouse, Fitz," he whispered as he left the room.

Slowly, I opened the door.

"I never thought I'd see the day," said Fitz, hands on her hips.

I looked at her questioningly.

"You...comin' out of the closet," she grinned.

"Ha ha," I said, trying to fix my static raised hair.

"So, ya wanna tell me what the hell is goin on now? And whose purse did Cecil find behind the door?"

I shook my head. "I don't know anything about a purse. Alex's?" I posed the question.

"Why would Alex's purse be in here?"

"Maybe when she delivered the canvas," I offered.

"Maybe," Fitz allowed, but she was rolling this over in her head. "Seems like an odd thing for a woman to forget, though. Have ya ever left yer purse behind?"

"Drunk or sober?" I asked.

"Exactly," said Fitz. "And she wasn't drunk." She went back to mulling for another moment then said, "Okay, so riddle me this, whatcha doin in the closet?" she asked while rocking back and forth on her heels.

I huffed, "I was hiding because I didn't want to see Cecil."

"Well that's mature. I wonder where we can hide ya for meals, work, the festival, the shoot," she counted all the ways I couldn't escape him on her fingers. "Perhaps if I get a purse big enough, I can drag ya along in there?"

"I didn't say it was mature, or smart. It was just a reaction. When he came to the closet door I was sure he was going to see the picture, even if he didn't see me. I almost peed myself."

I walked back to the closet and flipped on the light. "Um, Fitz, we have a problem."

She walked over to the closet and took a look inside. "What the hell? Where's the paintin'?"

"No, I asked you first," I said, hands on my hips. I began to look around the room like it had moved itself. "I'm freaking out, Fitz. Who the hell would have taken it?"

"Cecil?" she offered.

I shook my head, "No, he would have already tormented me with it. I'm sure of that. He would want to know what it meant," I made air quotations. "Shit, shit, shit," I pulled my fingers through my hair. "It had to be Alex. I can't think of anyone else. If it was her purse in here..."

"What's the motive?" Fitz asked. "Plus, we were in here with her when the shipment came."

I pondered. "I don't know. The only other person I can think of is Elanor. But why?" I did a palm up. "At least if she took it I know it's been set on fire by now."

Fitz nodded, "Agreed."

I poured Fitz a drink, then myself a second.

"Okay," Fitz said, putting down the glass and taking my hands in hers to stop my fidgeting, "Whoever has it, there's nothin' we can do about it right now. At the moment, it's out of the way and moved. If Cecil hasn't seen it yet, I venture to say whoever has it doesn't want him to see it, either."

She was talking in circles now but, I was calming down. The whiskey may have been helping, too.

I let out a sigh. "This place keeps me on edge. Cecil...Alex...Elanor and whatever the hell is going on with Martin and Scotty at the distillery. Not to mention, whoever's been in my room, leaving and taking things. What the hell is going on here? I was sure when we first arrived I would be the safe one. I mean, Elanor being so openly hateful when it came to you. No offense."

"None taken," Fitz said without so much as an eyebrow raise.

I was holding my skull. "Can I sleep in your room tonight? It's really creeping me out."

"I see that. Of course I can give Scotty the boot. I'll just say I need girl time. He's good about girl time. But first, I say we finish our drinks."

"Good plan," I nodded, and poured us another.

Back in her room, after Scotty was roused and sent on his way, we began to gossip. Maybe gossip wasn't the word for it, since it was all true.

I told her about mom and Betty's battle of wills.

"Ya know," she said, "I think Betty can take 'er!"

"Oh yeah, Betty doesn't back down from anyone. As bad as I feel for her having to deal with my mom's crazy, I think if anyone has a shot at handling her, it's Betty."

"Oh see, yer talking about handlin' your mother, as in 'being able to put up with the crazy'. I was talkin' about a cage match."

I got a mental image of the two of them in wrestler's outfits. Betty, with her full head of bleached hair in a ponytail, boobs popping out over the top of her leopard skin leotard. My mom, wearing a nun's habit and leotard with a turtleneck built in, nothing popping out from anywhere, growling at and circling one another. "I'm not so sure," I said. "Let's hope it doesn't come to that."

"So whatever happened to Manbun?" she questioned.

I shook my head, "I really don't know. Seems mom's been too busy trying to save Betty's virtue to meet up with the odd hippie. Betty's having a lot of work done on my house," I said somewhat sullenly.

"This is a bad thing?" she said slowly, trying to understand my crazy.

"I knew she wanted to paint, but now she's putting in new hardwood floors," I shook my head. "It just seems like a lot."

"Oh, boohoo, ya get to go home to a new house."

"That's just it, though. I like my house."

"I know ya get comfortable, Janie, and ya like things as they are. But change is necessary and can be a good thing." Fitz used her hand like a game show hostess to display where we were sitting at the moment. "All of this was brought on by change. Yer grand metamorphosis...and mine! Did ya ever think I'd go head over heels for a man? Any man?" her red mane flowing as she shook her head.

I shook mine in return, "No. I hoped someday...but no, I never ever saw this coming."

She grabbed my hands in hers, "I say we enjoy it and let it take us where we need to be."

I smiled. This was the calming side of Fitz. This was the Fitz that others didn't always get to see. The side of her that soothed my soul, and was one of the many reasons she would always be my best friend.

I nodded to her, "You're right. I need to enjoy this more." I looked around, "It would be a little easier if this place wasn't so..."

She cut me off, "Creepy, it's for damn-sure creepy!" she nodded.

"Yeah, that's the word," I nodded. "So any ideas about how Martin's things ended up in my room? Or the nightdress or how the painting of Cecil went missing?"

"None that I can think of," she shook her head. "I mean none other than the ones we've already explored."

"Hmmm," I pondered, coming up with ideas for 'WHO' possibly, but not 'HOW'.

"Ya paintin' tomorrow, I take it," she said.

"I am. But first, I'd like to go see Babygirl and take her an apple."

"So ya made friends with the great beast? She is truly magnificent," Fitz nodded. "Plus," she raised her glass, "Alex in the shitpile...Exquisite!"

I raised my glass as well, "Yeah she's pretty cool. I haven't been to the stable in a couple days and I miss her."

"Well, what are we waitin' for? Are ya tired?"

I shook my head at her, "Not really."

"We already know they don't lock the doors," she giggled remembering our sleeping in the Rolls so we didn't get caught out and about, sneaking around.

"It's raining though. Do you want to go out and about in this?" Fitz's red mane was a little 'more lively' when wet, than my own.

"We can take the passageway," she suggested.

Upstairs we went, to put on shoes and sweaters. I went down to the dining room and stole an apple from the fruit bowl. Fitz and I met back in my Dracula room, candle and lighter in hand. She said, "You get to touch the scary-ass painting."

I stood on the bed and moved the scary-ass painting to the right, and open the wall sprung.

Fitz and I made our way past Margaret's room, down the tiny footed staircase, and wound our way through the passageway till we hit the rung of stairs that went up to the stable. Standing on the same rung, we worked together to open the trap door. Popping my head out, I didn't see anyone. After I climbed out, I grabbed Fitz's hand and helped her up. Babygirl had heard the door trap open and looked out from her stall. As soon as she saw us she began dancing and neighing. Fitz and I made our way to her and I presented her with an apple. She nudged her giant head against our hands, the way a cat does when they want you to scratch them.

"Hi Babygirl, how are you?" I asked. Fitz looked at me oddly.

"Are ya expectin' her to answer ya?" She asked.

I nodded, "Yeah, watch this. How are you Babygirl, are you good?"

Babygirl nodded her giant head.

"See," I smiled.

"That's a coincidence, Janie. I don't think that the horse actually understands anything yer sayin'," she laughed at me.

"Of course she does! You understand, don't you girl?"

Babygirl nodded again.

"See," I said.

Fitz made a face, "It's more likely that she just nods to...I don't know...whatever."

"No she doesn't. She understands."

"Right." Fitz was humoring me.

"She does, dammit!" I was starting to get worked up. I really hated being humored.

Fitz got a look of disbelief and asked Baby, "Do ya think I'm an asshole?"

Babygirl's eyes narrowed and she nodded her head.

"See," Fitz and I said at the same time.

"No, she didn't understand the question," Fitz said, "She just nods at everything, like I said."

"Is that right? Okay Babygirl, do you think I'm an asshole?" I asked.

Babygirl looked Fitz right in the eye and shook her giant head, "No".

Fitz stuck her tongue in her cheek. "You two think yer funny, don't ya?"

Both Babygirl and I nodded our heads.

Fitz narrowed her eyes at us and pulled her arms across her

chest, “You two deserve each other. I'm goin to play with someone else now.” She wandered off to another stall.

I smiled and gave Babygirl the apple I brought her. She bit it in half, and offered me a piece. “Nope, that one is all for you.” She threw her head back and happily pranced. I was just enjoying her company when I heard the passageway door opening. Fitz, who was down at the opposite end of the stable, turned questioning eyes to me.

“What do we do?” I mouthed to her.

Fitz threw me a palms-up, “About what?” she mouthed back.

She was right. I could go down to the stable to see the horses.

Daniel's head poked through the trap door, not expecting to find others around, he started to climb up the ladder.

“Hello Daniel,” I said, catching him off guard.

He caught himself on the rail and stammered at me, “Oh, uh, Miss Janie, hello,” he said loudly.

Fitz walked up from behind the trap door, and said, “Wow, ya act like you've seen a ghost, Daniel.”

Her voice behind him made him jump again, “Oh yer here too, Miss Fitz!” he offered, even louder than before.

“Exactly why are we yellin' our hellos?” Fitz yelled back, as he closed the trap door behind him.

“I ugh, I ugh...ya surprised me is all,” he answered.

“So, the tunnel huh?” Fitz said, her green eyes flashing. “Where ya been, Daniel?” Fitz crossed her arms across her chest.

“I ugh, use it to get to the pub. It leads to...”

“Big Dave's pub,” I answered eyeing him.

“Yeah. You know Big Dave's?”

“I know Big Dave,” I answered.

“Ah! Right! He's old friends with Cecil.”

I nodded, “Best friends,” I added.

“Right, yes, well, I can walk there in the tunnel. No fear of 'drunk in public' and no rain," he offered with an awkward laugh.

I nodded my head, "Makes sense, I guess."

"So you were at Big Dave's?" Fitz asked.

"Well, fer a while I was. But I ended up at another pub. I went back to Big Dave's just before closin', so I could take the passageway home. Silence took over for a moment before he said, "So what are ya ladies doin' out so late?"

I reached out my hand and petted Babygirl's nose, "Just here to see her...bring her an apple."

"Yer gonna spoil her!" he grinned, relaxing a bit.

"Well, speaking of being spoiled," I started, "I should have thanked you earlier for the flowers. They really are beautiful."

His brow furrowed, "Flowers?"

"Ugh, yeah, I received a bouquet of flowers the other day...from you."

He looked completely dumbfounded, "I wish I had sent flowers. I really do," he nodded. "But I didn't send them, I'm sorry to say."

"Oh," my face began to flush. "I'm so embarrassed...the card said they were from you, and I..."

"No, please," he raised his hands, "I should be embarrassed," he said, looking back at the trap door.

"Not from where I'm standing," I said.

"If I had thought that they would have, ya know, changed things..."

"No really, you don't have to explain," I cut him off.

"I really DO wish I had," he said.

I smiled, "Well, the rain has stopped. I think Fitz and I should probably get to bed."

I grabbed Fitz's arm and we headed back up the path to the Castle.

Back in Fitz's room, she walked out of the bathroom and I

nearly jumped out of my skin. "What the hell?" I yelled, jumping backwards. She looked like she had hardened guacamole plastered to her face.

"Ut?" she said, trying not 'crack' the hardened goo. "Is iz ow I aay eautiful!" she pulled back the cover and sat down.

"I have a whole new respect for Scotty. That must be terrifying to wake up to," I laughed.

"Ee asn't een ee ike is! Aven't een able o oo is, in onths!"

"Yeah, I wouldn't do this in front of anyone. I should be included in that statement," I grinned.

"Uck ooo!" she said, and turned out the lights.

"Yep, love you, too."

I was woken by knocking on the door. Fitz was hiding by the armoire, trying to decide if she could fit in there with all of her stuff. "Ell im oo oh oway!"

I groggily made my way to the door, "Fitz is, uh, not dressed," I said, through the closed door.

"I hate to break this to ya, Janie, but I've seen Fitz undressed before," Scotty said.

"Yeah, but ugh, she ugh..." I couldn't think of anything. "I'm not dressed either!" I finally blurted out and winced.

Fitz shook her head at me, "Ut uh uck?" she whispered.

"I'm sorry, what?" Scotty said.

"Yeah, we're both ummm...naked."

There was a long pause. "Well...would ya mind puttin' on a robe or...somethin'? I have an early meetin' and really need a kiss for luck," he said.

Fitz let out a huff. "Ove," Fitz said, and pushed me out of the way.

When she opened the door, Scotty jumped back, just as I had the night before. He began to laugh. "I guess since yer face is covered in goop, and Janie is dressed, this is why ya weren't openin' the door?"

"I idin't ant oo oo ee ee ike is!"

"Says the most beautiful woman world," he picked her up and spun her around. "Ya couldn't think that you'd be anythin' less than that to me, ever?"

"Elll," Fitz tried not to smile and crack her goo. "I oov ooo!"

"And I love you, with all my heart," he moved in for a well placed kiss.

"Ave a ood ay, i ove!"

"You have a good day, too, my love." He smiled at me, "Naked huh?" then shook his head. "Good try!"

As Fitz shut the door, she leaned against it and got all misty eyed, "E oves eee!"

"He must!" I laughed.

21

BLUE BALLS, OR . . .

I walked into my room to change for breakfast and took a good look around. No Dracula, and no weird 'items' lying around. I was taking a breath of relief when I heard Fitz's scream coming from the bathroom. Rushing to her I wondered if the lizard, mistaken for a snake, had Fitz pinned on the potty. I threw the door open and stopped short, "Your face is..." I was in shock.

"It's fuckin' blue!" Fitz yelled! "What the hell?" she yelled again into the mirror. She looked like the angry, red headed, Irish version of Smurfette.

"Oh my God...what...happened?"

Fitz shook her blue face, "I took off the mask...then put on my skin toner...then...blue!"

I looked in the trash and the cotton balls she had used to apply the toner were almost black. Grabbing her toner bottle I removed the lid. It too was black. "You didn't notice this?" I asked.

I've used the same toner for a hundred years, I don't have to look anymore when I apply it!" she yelled at me.

"I…I…" I stammered, shaking my head. "Okay, okay! You're right! I'm sorry," I put my hands up, submissively.

"The shoot is tomorrow'," her eyes showing that the 'crazy' was seeping in.

"I'm gonna go get Miss Elanor!"

"What the hell can Miss Elanor do?" Fitz said, almost hissing. "My face is fuckin' blue…and my shoot is tomorrow!" she repeated, her accent getting stronger with agitation.

"I know, I know," I inched toward her and put a comforting hand on her shoulder, "But she, ya know, makes medicines and all. Maybe she can…I don't know…help!"

Fitz was taking deep breaths to keep from losing it completely. "Fine!" Fitz said through a tightened jaw.

I took off like a bat out of hell, down the stairs, and into the kitchen. There Miss Elanor stood, chastising a young female Saucier chef. "Does this," she pulled a spoon full of runny fluid from the pan in her hand, "Look like Hollandaise Sauce to you?"

"No mum," said the chef, taking the pan and scurrying out of eye shot.

"Miss Elanor, I need your help," I said frantically.

Without looking in my direction, she said, "What ya need to do is go change for breakfast. I'm not busy slaving away so that ya can make even more demands of me and my time!"

"I wouldn't ask, but…" she raised her eyes and saw the look on my face.

She read me for a moment, before saying, "Fine."

I took the stairs two at a time, and Miss Elanor was right on my heels. Back in the bathroom we could hear Fitz before we could see her. "If that woman did this to me…she's dead!" we heard her say, loudly.

Fitz had a wash cloth and was going to rub her skin raw. When she turned to face us, Miss Elanor's face showed sheer shock.

“What the hell have ya done?” Miss Elanor said.

“Me?” Fitz looked fit to be tied. “Ya think I did this...to myself? Are ya crazy, woman?”

Miss Elanor hardened her face, “You will not be disrespectful to me and ask for my help in the same breath, child!”

Both of them stared daggers at each other. I tried to break the tension, “Okay ladies, this is obviously a tense moment. But,” I turned to Miss Elanor, “We really do need your help.” Then I turned to Fitz, “And we will both be very grateful,” I nodded at her until she did the same.

“Right,” Fitz agreed, “Miss Elanor...will ya please help me?”

Miss Elanor, finding Fitz's humbling moment acceptable, nodded. I handed her the bottle and she took a look. “It's been tampered with. When was the last time ya used this?” she asked Fitz.

“Yesterday morn,” she answered.

The look on Miss Elanor's face made me wonder if she had someone in mind for this devious act. “Follow me to the kichen.”

After Miss Elanor ran off the cook staff, she went to her room to retrieve what she would need.

“Hopefully, Miss Elanor can help,” I said to Fitz, rubbing her back.

“Maybe she's the one who did this!” Fitz shot back.

I shook my head, “Unlikely Fitz. She seemed genuinely shocked when she saw you.”

“Yeah,” Fitz let out a sigh. “I thought she was goin' to pee her bloomers. That would have almost made it worth this,” she pointed to her face.

“I know you don't like the woman, but try to be nice. She really is our only hope at this point.”

Elanor returned with a small cauldron, book, and a basket of herbs and flowers. “This,” she said, handing Fitz a book opened to page 124, “Is what I think was put in yer toner.”

Fitz and I read, then with squinted eyes, said, “Woad?”

“That flower was often used to create a blue dye for clothin’. Certain bloodlines also used in battle to paint their faces.”

“Okay, so can ya...remove it?” Fitz posed the question.

Letting out a sigh, Miss Elanor said, “We'll see.”

When the concoction was at full brew, horrible fumes began to waft through the kitchen. Kind of a sulfer mixed with Lavendar smell that made my nose burn. I could almost taste it.”

“Lord almighty, that smell is horrible!” Fitz said, pinching her own nose.

“Yes, and it won't be any better during the twenty minutes it will be on yer skin,” Elanor explained. “It's done, but we have to let it cool. Also, it may take many passes to get it to work. And that's if it works at all.”

Fitz nodded, “I understand,” she seemed resigned to the possibility that this wouldn't work.

Miss Elanor applied the smelly gunk with gloved hands and cotton balls. “Now we'll have to wait. I'll be back. Try not to move around too much or it will drip.”

Fitz wouldn't open her mouth, for fear that a dollup of yuck might find its way in. I couldn't blame her. I heard two voices enter the kitchen.

“What is that horrible smell?” Mary asked Carrie.

“I haven't a clue, but the shit pile smells better than this,” Carrie said.” Coming around the corner, the girls jumped back when they saw us. “Sorry Misses,” Carrie and Mary curtsied.

Fitz rolled her eyes, “No problem,” I said to our maids.

“If ya don't mind my askin', what happened?” Mary asked.

I wasn't sure how much information Fitz wanted divulged, given the fact that we still didn't know who had done this to her. She nudged me and nodded her head, so I explained the story.

"Oh that's awful," they both said in unison.

Fitz pinched my arm, "Ow!" I said, and rubbed what I was sure would be a bruise. She rolled her hand at me. "Um, have you ladies seen anything?"

The ladies furrowed their brows, reaching out to pinch me again, but I moved this time. "Okay!" I yelled at her. "Have you ladies seen anything...odd?" Out of the normal? They went into a huddle and quietly discussed something.

Finally, Mary shook her head, "Go ahead if ya want to."

Carrie shot her sister a look, "Well, Misses, I came in the kitchen yesterday...I heard someone go out the back door, and quickly at that! By the time I crossed the kitchen to the door, there was no one there," her eyes rounded.

"So whoever it was ran away?" I asked.

"Possibly," she said.

I shook my head, "They ran or..." I let the question hang in the air.

Carrie bit her lower lip and looked to her twin for support. Mary held up her hands, "All you!" Mary told Carrie.

Carrie looked tormented, but said, "Or maybe no one was ever there."

I was waiting for her to tell me she had sight issues, or possibly, hallucinations. But what she offered next was just as good.

"Maybe...it was a spirit?" she said in almost a whisper.

I bit my own bottom lip trying not to tell her that maybe she needed mental help. Fitz, on the other hand, eyes wide, gave her the 'keep it coming' hand roll.

Mary was rolling her finger next to her head letting me know that she thought her sister was crazy.

"I'm not crazy!" Carrie defended herself. "This place is very...active. Strange and unexplainable things happen here all the time!"

When she put it that way, I'd have to admit, she was right. But I still wasn't ready to think that the nightdress, Martin's good luck charms, and Fitz's blue face were done by an unhappy or malicious specter. Then again...thanks to The Ladies of the Moon, and the two gatherings I attended, I'd have to agree that I had definitely felt...something.

Carrie had continued talking during my mind warp. "Then, there's talk about Miss Elanor." Hearing that, snapped me back to reality.

"What about Miss Elanor?" I asked her.

"Well, people talk, ya know," her ponytail bobbed as she nodded.

"What do they say?" I prompted.

Mary was shaking her head ever so slightly.

Carrie looked from her sister to Fitz and back at me, before lowering her voice to a whisper, "They say she's...a witch."

Mary slapped her head with her palm, and I had to cup my hand over my mouth to hold back a laugh. But Fitz was all ears. She listened to all the things Carrie had heard during her time at the Callaghan's Manor. Before she could finish the laundry list of reasons she believed this to be true, we heard footsteps coming. Miss Elanor turned the corner and stopped short.

"Ladies!" she said to the maids, "Surely ya have something else to be doin', other than gawkin' at our guests! Be on with yerselves!" she waved her hand in a shooing motion.

The ladies scurried off, as Miss Elanor wet a washcloth and started toward Fitz's face. Fitz leaned back a little, considering her newfound information. She was leery to say the least.

"Hold still," Miss Elanor commanded. As she wiped away the 'yuck', I could see that there was a difference.

Fitz held her thumb up at me, with a hopeful look.

I winced and turned my thumb upside down. Fitz had gone

from Smurf Blue, to Wicked Witch Green. "It's green," I told her.

Fitz huffed at Elanor.

"Don't ya give me that look, child. I told ya, it may take more than one pass, if it works at all."

Another round of ingredients were added into the freshly scrubbed cauldron. Within ten minutes, a new smell emerged. Kind of a camphor mixed with dead seafood smell. I hadn't eaten and wasn't sure I ever would again.

As Miss Elanor gloved up, I saw a look on Fitz's face I had only seen when she had the stomach flu. She looked positively vomitous, but sat still as Elanor applied round two. Afterwards, Elanor left us to sit and wait.

When Miss Elanor was out of earshot Fitz played charades to communicate her thoughts. Normally I would torture her by pretending I didn't know what she was trying to convey. But looking at her with all the horrible smelling gunk on her face, I decided to play fair.

"You really think she's a witch?" I asked.

Fitz pointed at me, then to her own face.

"I know, when I had my itchy bumps, I did say that Miss Elanor may have cursed me. But I went a little crazy there. I mean, they're hives and I was seriously on edge. You have to know she didn't do that to your face."

Fitz pointed again to the cauldron, then to her face.

"So because she is trying to help you, now you think she's a witch?"

She raised her gunky eyebrows to me.

"Does Miss Elanor strike you as a captain-save-a-hoe? Like she would do...this," I pointed to her face, "So what? She could fix you and then we would like her? That doesn't even make sense, Fitz. I don't think she cares if we like her."

She pointed to me again.

"Yeah, I know a lot of strange things have happened to me, but I don't think they're witch related. Next you'll be blaming Scotty's lack of sex drive on her cursing his manhood."

Fitz's eyes almost popped out of her skull.

Great. Apparently she hadn't thought of that until 'little ol me' put it in that head of hers. "No!" my head shaking furiously. "No, Elanor did not put a spell on Scotty!"

Fitz cocked her head and raised her eyebrows to me again.

"Yes, I know Scotty has been...off, but it has something to do with Martin and the distillery. Not Elanor. I'm sure of it!" I added.

Foot steps announced Elanor's return. Another clean washcloth was dipped into a bowl of water, as she washed the second round of gunk off Fitz's face.

Fitz held her thumb up again. This time, she was jaundice yellow. "Yellow," I told her.

Fitz let out the breath she had been holding.

"You could probably cover that with make-up," I pointed out the silver lining around the cloud hanging over her head.

She nodded, sullenly.

"Or," Miss Elanor said, "Ya could let me finish and then make that face!"

Another batch was made, more flowery this time but with a hint of burnt wood. As it was applied I said a silent prayer. I wasn't sure how to address this one to God. I was, however, pretty sure he didn't usually get a lot of, "Please, don't let my friend's face be yellow...or green...or blue."

This time, when the goop was removed, I was worried she would be pink with orange polka dots. But as the cloth moved, the real Fitz emerged. She was absolutely perfect. I didn't wait to give her the thumbs up. Instead, I jumped up and down in full grin.

"Really?" Fitz said, rushing to check out her complexion in

the toaster. "Oh my God! I'm ME again! I'm Fitz-tastic!" Without thinking, she ran and hugged Miss Elanor, pouring out "Thank yous."

For a split second, I thought Miss Elanor was going to hug her back. I thought I saw the beginnings of a smile too. But she quickly regained her composure, and said, "Yes, yes, it's all well. Now out of my kitchen. I need to fix lunch," then she walked out.

"You still think she's a witch?" I asked.

"Of course I do. Only today, she's a good witch!" Fitz beamed.

I shook my head and we headed upstairs. Having missed breakfast, I was changing out of my jammies for lunch. When I stepped into Fitz's room, she was on the phone and taking notes.

"Janie's here too. I'm gonna put ya on speaker."

"Hi luv!" Mum said. "Hello, sweet girl!" said Aunt Marble.

I beamed. In truth, I missed Mum more than my own mother. And even though Aunt Marble was batshit crazy, I missed her, too. "Hi Mum! Hi Aunt Marble!" I said.

Mum began, "I've given Fitz the instructions and list of everything ya may need for yer ritual."

My brow furrowed as I turned to Fitz and mouthed, "What?"

Mum continued, "It's very simple. Easy to follow. You ladies should have no problems."

Aunt Marble broke in, "Remember to go clockwise in the circle, tis where most people go wrong."

"Right," I said, dumbfounded.

Ah crap! What was Fitz going to have me doing now?

"Oh," said Aunt Marble, "Before I forget myself, I have some other help for ya, Janie. Take me off speaker. I can be more candid that way."

More candid? Aunt Marble? Oh shit, I thought.

Mum wished us love, and said her goodbyes. Clicking off the speaker I put the phone to my ear. "Okay," I said into the receiver.

The next five minutes of Aunt Marbles dialog had me turning a beautiful shade of green, myself. She was back to being the sex therapist. On and on she went, about how I needed to take my dream horny into my own hands, so to speak. Fitz laughed behind her hand at my changing expressions. "Yes ma'am, thank you. Yeah, yeah, love you, too," I said, with a blank expression, and hung up the phone.

Fitz broke out in hysterical laughter and rolled around on her bed.

"Why?" I asked, shaking my head at her.

She stifled her laughter, "It'll help. I promise."

"How?" I asked, still green around the gills. "How, for the love of all that's holy, could that have helped me. Ya know I picture her...and Benny, when she talks about this stuff?" I shuddered.

"I know."

I shook my head at her, "Then why?"

"Are ya horny now?"

My stomach flipped, "No! Maybe not ever again!"

Fitz did her evil fairy smile and winked, "Yer welcome."

I shook my head, "You're a horrible person. Just wondering, why doesn't it gross you out?"

"I'm not uptight," she answered blankly.

"I'm not uptight!" I rebutted.

"Ugh, yes ya are." Fitz made the face that lets me know that she can't believe that I don't know myself as well as she does. "Janie, I know where I came from...and out of. And even more so...how I know how I got in there."

I scrunched my eyes.

"See, right there!" she pointed to my face. "That says it all. I was made...by love. And my parents love each other ALL THE TIME! For God sakes, I was the fifth child in her womb! Ya act like ya can't see yer parents as sexual creatures..."

I shook my head.

"...but they are!" she continued. "Or were, whatever the case may be these days. And some part of ya still wants to believe you were left on a doorstep. Now I'm not sayin' I want details of their sex life, but knowing that my parents have one makes me feel secure in why I'm here. Ya know?"

It was a good argument. It really was. And some part of me was impressed by her take on the subject. But still, I did a shudder. "I'm good."

Fitz just shook her head, "Fine."

"So, what do Mum and Aunt Marble have us doing?"

"A ritual," Fitz changed her shirt.

"Umm, I don't know if this has escaped your understanding, but we don't know how to do a ritual."

Fitz held up the paper, "That's okay. It's all here."

"Okay, let me put this another way, we're not capable of doing a ritual."

"Why? It's just like prayin'!"

"So... why don't we just pray then?"

"We will be. While saying this," she handed me the paper. "Then we walk with a candle in a clockwise circle."

"So...are we trying to do a spell on Miss Elanor?"

"Well, I did relate some of what's been going on...with me...with you. And Mum and Auntie do think she may be dark. But THAT is a protection spell we're puttin' on us...and the men, instead."

I thought of all the things wrong with this idea. "I'm not sure about this. In fact, I think maybe we should get Miss Elanor a...Gift Basket or something. Ya know, for that whole changing you from a Smurf, back to Fitz?"

Fitz nodded, "That would throw her off our scent."

"Not what I meant."

Fitz ignored me, "What should we get her?" Fitz was in her own world, rolling this around in her mind. "I've got it!" she announced, finally acknowledging that I was still in the room. "We'll get her a book."

"O-kay!"

"No, ya don't get it. We'll get her a book on herbs, and magic."

"So, you think she may be a witch...and you want to get her a spell book?" I did the palms up. "This makes sense to you?"

"Of course. If she uses it, we'll know for sure."

"Because we'll be toads, right?"

Off to lunch we went. Miss Elanor served roast beef on demi-rolls with dijon and swiss cheese and potato salad. In walked Cecil. I was just as sure that he had been avoiding me as I had been avoiding him. He looked positively delicious though, from the one second glance I took. It was funny to think that women don't get caught staring as often as men. I attribute this to how quickly our minds take in the whole picture instead of processing the view piece by piece. In one second I took him in; jeans that fit really well, a white button down shirt (two top buttons at the neck undone), with sleeves rolled up to the forearm. Since I already knew how blue his eyes were and how white his smile was, I could forgo those things and concentrate on the apparel. Again I felt this yearning toward him as his Polo cologne wafted toward me. Mentally, he rounded the table, pulled me from my chair and put a lip-lock on me that made my toes curl. I was lost in this little fantasy, when Cecil called my name. Snapping to, I looked at him the way an animal whose been caught in a trap looks at the trapper.

"I'm sorry, what?" I asked.

Cecil smiled, cocking his head, "I asked what you had planned for the day."

His smile was so gorgeous, it made me blush like a newbie. "Ugh, Fitz and I are, ugh, going into town. "To do some shopping," I added. Like there was any other reason we would go to town. "You?" I asked.

"I have to go to the craft store. Can I catch a ride with you ladies?"

I wasn't going to the craft store so I could watch him and Alex fawn over each other. The thought made me physically ill, but I said, "If you'd like. We're going to a bookstore, so we can drop you at the craft store and pick you up afterwards."

He nodded, "Sounds like a plan."

That was the extent of our conversation. The rest of lunch was eaten in an odd silence with Fitz shooting looks from Cecil to me. I could tell she wanted to say something, but for once, held her tongue. I was grateful.

We dropped Cecil off at the craft store and went on our way to the bookstore. When we pulled up, I was a little thrown. It didn't look like a bookstore, and had a Celtic name I couldn't pronounce.

"Are you sure this is it?" I asked the Fonzie look alike.

"Only metaphysical bookstore in town," he answered, never looking my way.

I saw the sign looming above, 'Universal Moon'. "Why did we want a metaphysical store?" I asked Fitz.

"It's this, or the religious bookstore. I have a hard time believing the latter of the two would carry herb and spell books."

"And you're sure about this idea? I mean, if you're right, we're giving her some ammo," I said quietly.

"You don't even believe it, so what do you care?"

"Right," I said, but not with any real certainty.

As we walked in, the lighting changed so drastically, that for a moment I was almost blind. Dark curtains covered every window. The smell of incense practically choked me. Old shelves packed with books, statues, crystals, stones and candles filled up each wall. A huge desk sat on the far side of the room. I saw the rings of smoke from his pipe, long before I saw the little man dwarfed by the desk he sat behind.

"Hello," he said, popping up from behind the swirling smoke.

He was a slight man. Maybe five foot tall, dressed in what I assumed a Leprechaun would wear on rainbow-less days. His beard was well trimmed, but yellowed from nicotine. His gray shorn hair was parted on the side, making his big circle glasses seem off-center.

It was when he raised his bushy gray brows that I realized that neither Fitz, nor I, had spoken to the strange man. "Hello," I said quickly, nudging Fitz.

"Hell-o," Fitz added, trying to make her face less surprised looking.

"What can I do for ya ladies?" His voice, high, like I would expect from a Leprechaun.

"We were, ugh, ugh..." I said.

"We're lookin' for a book!" Fitz saved me.

"What kind of book?" he cocked his head in such a way, that he seemed almost animated.

"A unique book...for a unique woman," Fitz answered, while I still searched for my voice.

"A unique woman, huh?" he blew out a swirl of smoke. "What kind of unique?" he raised his brows.

"Somethin' to do with herbs and flowers," Fitz offered.

"Ah," he nodded. "Follow me," he put up a wrinkled old pointed finger and bid us follow. Disappearing behind a huge curtain, I nudged Fitz to walk behind him. We were led into a huge stone room with no windows. There in the middle of the room, stood a long table strewn with books. They looked old and well read.

"I'm not sure what Elanor would want, much less, like," I said.

"Well, if she doesn't like it, she can drag her ass out of the Castle, and, I don't know, exchange it?" she posed the question to the old man.

"Elanor," he repeated. "What a beautiful name."

"O-kay," Fitz said. "Can it be returned if she doesn't like it?"

"For store credit, yes," he answered.

"Good enough," she nodded to me.

"What is Elanor like?" he asked, in a hiss that made me take a step backwards.

"I don't really know," Fitz said. "Proper, matriarchal, stuffy, ya know."

His eyes twinkled, his brow rose, "Oh, I know just the book!" He riffled through a few, before pulling out an old leather bound book that looked as though it was several different books combined. Fitz thumbed through it, as I looked over her shoulder. Every page seemed to be in another language. There were moon symbols, pyramids, hearts, worms, cats, trees, snakes, half breeds of man with legs of goats and horses, I think. I didn't understand any of it.

"Huh," Fitz said, "I'm just not sure. I can't understand any of this."

The little man's mouth stretched in what I assed was supposed to be a smile, "If this Elanor is as unique as you say, she will love this book."

I shrugged, "I know she speaks several languages."

Fitz nodded, "Okay, how much?"

"For you?" he considered, "$200.00."

Fitz laughed, "We may be in the wrong place," she put the

book down. "She and I, we're not 'buy each other expensive gifts', friends."

Fitz and I turned to walk out and the little man made a second bid, "Fine, $150.00!"

"Why would ya mark it down, if ya thought it was worth $200.00?" she asked.

"I really want yer friend Elanor, to have this book!" his eyes flashed.

Fitz gave him a skeptical look, "Right."

He was giving me the creeps, and I wanted to run out of that store like my ass was on fire. But Fitz, thinking she had made a fine bargain, said, $150.00 it tis!"

The little scary man looked positively elated as he walked us back up front to the cash register. "Would ya like this gift wrapped?" he asked.

"Um sure," Fitz nodded.

He took a length of purple ribbon, wrapped it around the book twice then ended with a double knot. "There ya go!"

I raised my brows at his gift wrapping job.

As we turned to leave, the little man said, "Tell Miss Elanor to enjoy." Fitz and I nodded. "And remember ladies," he turned to Fitz, "The Blue Goddess is alive in you." Then he turned his attention to me, "Remember yer dreams!" He broke into hysterical laughter as I high-tailed out of there with Fitz right on my heels.

22

ESHA'S ACKBAY

"What the hell was that all about?" Fitz asked when we were safely outside.

I shook my head, "I have no idea," I admitted.

"How could he know I spent the mornin' in Blue Face?"

"I'm not even sure that's what he was referring to. He said to remember my dreams. That can't be good right? I mean considering my dreams lately."

It was Fitz's turn to shake her head. "Will ya put the book in yer purse? I, ugh, don't want to carry it."

"I bet," I said. "You want me to carry the scary assed cursed book, right?"

"It's not that," Fitz said, unrealistically. "My purse is just too small."

"Right," I said. "But if I turn into a frog, I want the best life you can give a frog...and french fries," I added, putting the book in my bag.

"Done," she agreed to my demands. "Ya wanna check that floral store ya got the flowers from? They may have a record of who ordered em."

This piqued my interest. "I would kinda like to know."

We entered the Bloom Room, which was your standard floral shop. Refrigerated glass coolers held vase arrangements from the single rose with baby's breath, to the hundred plus dollar variety.

The owner/manager was easy to find, as she was the only person on the display floor. Her name was Avril, according to her vest tag. She was about fifty-ish (not that I would ever guess a woman's age out loud), a little shorter than me and squishy in the middle, with big blue eyes and curly shoulder length blonde hair.

"How can I help ya?" she asked.

"Actually, I wondered if ya had any record of a delivery made to the Callaghan Manor in the last week," Fitz said.

"Actually, I do. It isn't often that we deliver to the Manor, since they have their own garden and gardener and all. Usually, their flowers are grown on site." She nodded to us, like she wanted to make sure we understood. I nodded back. "Then...there was the oddness of the transaction."

I perked up, "Oddness?" I questioned.

"Yeah, we usually get either calls or walk-ins. Since I brought us into the twentieth century, we even get e-mail."

"Right," I nodded again, prodding her to continue.

"Well, let me show you." She walked to a file cabinet and pulled out an envelope then handed it to me.

"Normally, we wouldn't give out any information...but seeing as how this has none...I figure it's okay."

I read the typed letter. It contained where the flowers were to be sent and what the card should read. "This wasn't mailed to you?" I asked, looking for a return address.

"No, I found it under the door. Just that note," she pointed to it, "and $50.00." There was also one of those little sticky notes," she nodded, "that said to send a thirty dollar bouquet, fill out the card and keep the rest for a delivery charge. I kept that note too, if ya want to see it?"

"Was it typed as well?" Fitz asked.

Avril nodded.

"Then never mind," Fitz smiled at her.

"Is one of you ladies, Janie?" Avril asked.

"I am," I said.

"Oh how lovely!" her eyes getting dreamy. "You have a secret, well very secret, admirer."

"So it would seem," I forced a smile.

We went back to the craft store and Fitz ran in to find Cecil so I didn't have to see Alex. When Fitz returned, she said Cecil was at Dave's pub.

Walking into the pub I didn't see Cecil automatically. I did, however, see Alex. I assumed that Cecil was in her booth facing away from us. Alex looked in my direction and grabbed the hands of her lunch date. Fitz led the way as we walked to their booth. Cecil seeing us moved his hands back to his sides.

"Oh hi, ladies, Cecil told me you were in town. I was lucky enough to convince him to have a drink with me while he waited for you."

I put on my fake ass smile, "Oh, how nice."

"Are ya ladies ready to go," he asked us, trying to scoot out of the booth."

"Oh, but Cecil, ya haven't finished yer drink. Surely the ladies will give ya time to do that. Come on, finish yer drink with me," she pouted.

I was going to be sick at her sugary display. She had won. Did she have to rub my nose in it?

Fitz started, "Actually, we have a lot to do today, schedule, and all."

"Well Cecil, I can drive ya back later," she offered.

"Actually, I have a lot to do today, too," he said.

"Oh, just one drinky-poo," she pouted some more.

"It's okay Cecil, I think I need a drinky-poo as well," I said, turning and walking up to the bar.

I left Fitz standing with the stomach churning duo, and ordered myself a whiskey on the rocks and a Bloody Mary for Fitzy.

"Why didn't ya tell him we were leaving? Why did you give him to her on a platter?" Fitz asked, taking the seat next to me at the bar.

"Oh Fitz, he's in love with her! My sheer existence makes him uncomfortable. You saw it, didn't you? How uncomfortable he was? Why would I make it harder on him? It's not fair to him! I said I wanted to be his friend, and I'm trying. Just give me credit for trying," I relaxed my jaw.

"O-kay. I give ya credit, okay?" she said raising her hands submissively. "Yer handling this very well, given the way I know ya feel for him." There was a small silence while we took sips of our drinks. Then Fitz said, "But ya still hope her implants fall to the ground, right?"

"Well, of course I do," I blustered. "I'm not a Saint."

Fitz raised her glass and we toasted. "That's my girl."

"I can't stand the thought that he feels...sorry for me. The unloved! Unwanted! It's humiliating!"

"What are ya talkin' about? First of all, he doesn't know that ya have feelings for him. And he knows ya never told Barry how ya felt for him. So why would he assume you were unwanted?"

"Maybe because of my 'dumped' number?" I suggested.

"Well, I never told Scotty about all that, ya know, ritual stuff. So he can't even know yer 'dumped number', unless ya told him?"

I shook my head, "No, pathetic wasn't really what I was going for," I answered.

"Okay, so stop letting yerself feel pathetic. This is on you, ya know. Ya can't NOT admit yer feelins' then get hurt when someone you have unsaid feelings for, moves on."

"I know," I nodded. "It's just gonna take a while for this leopard to change her spots."

Out of the corner of my eye I saw Cecil exit the booth. Alex stood and wrapped her arms around his neck, embracing him. As he walked over to us, I downed my drink. "Ready?" he asked.

"Yep," I said, letting out a sigh.

As we turned to leave, Alex blew him a kiss. I forced another smile and waved. Fitz held up her three fingers. I didn't know what that meant, but Alex's face took on an expression of hate.

It was almost time for dinner when we got back to the Manor. I took off upstairs to change. Fitz stayed behind with Cecil.

When I was changed and started back down the stairs, Cecil met me halfway. "I wanted to talk to ya for a moment," he said.

"Okay. What's up?"

"I don't want things to be weird between us, anymore. I think of ya...as a good friend. I enjoy how we used to be, before all of...this. I know how ya feel, I mean about Barry."

"Well, ugh..." should I let him think that 'in love' was how I felt for Barry, instead of an infatuated crush? Should I disclose that I had feelings for him?

"Ya don't have to," he insisted, shaking his head. "I understand. I too, know what it's like to love someone even if there is little or no hope. You and me...we're in the same boat."

I wanted to clarify that me having feelings for a wonderful man like Barry, wasn't quite the same as him falling back in love with a woman who cheated on him with his friend for three years, then became a porn star. But regardless of how good Barry was, or how bad Alex was, it didn't change the 'love thing'. Or at least it wouldn't have, if I thought I was truly in love with Barry.

When he put it that way, him admitting his feelings for Alex,

I decided to let the leopard stay spotted and not confess my true feelings for him. It could only make him more uncomfortable. And I didn't want him to feel like he had to let me down easy.

"You're right. I have missed our friendship. I've missed you!" I smiled, knowing it was true.

He took me into a big bear hug. It was a longer hug than I had anticipated. We were still holding tight to each other when Alex was announced by Bushy Brows. She saw us parting our embrace, "Did I come at a bad time?" she asked. She had changed into a slinky, emerald green dress that apparently hugged everything so tight, that it was trying to escape through the top.

"No," I said, dabbing the corner of my eye and smiling at Cecil.

"What are ya doin here?" Cecil looked truly baffled by her arrival.

"Oh, ya left yer supplies behind at the bar," she lifted a bag. "Or, were ya hopin' for a home delivery?" she smiled and winked.

"I'll leave you two to talk," I said and headed down to the dining hall. As I turned to go down the hall I saw her embrace Cecil out of the corner of my eye. Once again, I let out a sigh. It was so nice to hug him. To feel his body against mine, it just felt...right. But he had made it clear, she was his choice and I had to accept this and move on. So he thought my feelings for Barry ran deeper than they actually did, so what? He didn't know that every day since Barry's impending marriage was announced, my feelings had been changing. And Cecil didn't know that ever since he and I met, my thoughts turned to him more often than I would even admit to myself. As a friend, a real friend, I had to be happy for both of them. This 'trying to mature' shit was overrated.

Sitting at the dining table, Scotty and Martin entered. Scotty looked confused, as he put a kiss on Fitz's cheek. "What is that woman doin' here, again?" he asked us.

"I imagine she's here to see Cecil," I answered trying to sound happy about her existence.

Miss Elanor looked infuriated, "Is she to stay for dinner?"

All of us shook our heads and did the palms-up?

Martin let out a sigh, "Ya may have to set another plate," he looked apprehensively at Miss Elanor. "I hope it's no trouble," he added.

It was the first time I had ever seen a genuine smile on her face. Her features softened and warmed as she spoke to Martin. I didn't know she was even capable of making her face do that. I smiled at her and cocked my head. When she turned her gaze to me, daggers from her eyes flew in my general direction. They had the desired effect, I assumed, of making me gulp...hard.

Cecil, with a green clad living version of a brunette Jessica Rabbit, entered the dining room.

"I hope I'm not intrudin'? Cecil invited me to dine with ya."

Cecil looked at his dad and forced a smile, saying nothing.

"Umm, of course," said Martin, standing and extending his hand to a chair.

"Oh, I hoped I would be sitting with ya," she grabbed Cecil's arm.

"Here ya go," I said and changed seats.

Fitz looked like a dog about to attack. Scotty shook his head ever so slightly. Martin forced a smile. Cecil looked oddly strained. And Miss Elanor narrowed her eyes like she was planning on putting Alex into a stew. Nope, not uncomfortable at all, I thought.

After dinner was plated, Alex got the ball rolling. "So Martin, what's new at the distillery?" Alex asked.

Martin seemed confused by her line of questioning, "Business as usual," he offered.

"Oh, see I've heard some scuttle-butt...about the direction the distillery is headin'?" Alex eyed him carefully.

"Well, small minds have always had large mouths, I'm afraid." Martin's words had the desired effect of closing her mouth firmly.

I was even more confused now. What had Alex heard? Why did Martin shut her down? Why did he seem upset by her question? I knew one thing, whatever was going on at the distillery, or with Martin, it had affected Scotty as well. He set his fork down and sat staring at his plate. His ears were turning red. Fitz's eyes narrowed at Alex. The rest of dinner was held in a big ball of heavy silence.

After dinner, Fitz asked me to join her in the kitchen to present Miss Elanor with the book she had bought her. "We can share the credit!" Fitz said. Not knowing what the book entailed or the implication of the book, I wasn't sure I wanted any credit.

Finding Miss Elanor in the kitchen, Fitz tried to hand her the book. I forced a smile hoping this would go well.

"What's this?" Miss Elanor looked like she was being handed a poisonous snake and recoiled.

"It's a gift," Fitz said, trying again to hand her the book. "It's for you...for helpin' me...I'm tryin' to thank ya!" Fitz finished through a tightened jaw.

Miss Elanor took the book and removed the purple ribbon. For a moment I thought she was going to smile. Her expression was changing, but I quickly noticed, not for the better. As she thumbed through the pages her face was turning to stone, "What is this?" she shook the book at Fitz.

"A giiiffftttt?" Fitz said slowly.

"This is what ya think of me? That I would want somethin' like this? Am I a joke to ya then?"

I took a step back and shook my head.

"No," said Fitz, also taking a back step. "Look, I don't even know what the book is about, for the love of Pete. The man at the store said that this would be a good book to get ya."

"What store?"

"Universal Moon?" Fitz looked at me and I nodded.

"You girls," she hissed, "Should not be playin' at things ya don't understand!" Miss Elanor huffed and exited the kitchen swiftly.

"Well, that went well," I said.

"That's one hell of a way to accept a gift. I mean, seriously, even if she didn't like the damn thing, she could have at least been grateful for the thought with which it was given. Rude, just rude," Fitz folded her arms across her chest. "I am gonna do that protection spell, after all. Anyone that bitter shouldn't be trusted."

"Okay. But you have your shoot tomorrow. Shouldn't you get some...I don't know, beauty sleep?" I asked.

"What are ya tryin' to imply? I'm a hag! Bags under my eyes?"

I shook my head and began stammering.

"I'll be fine, once I know we're protected. Plus the shoot isn't until eleven. I could go to bed at midnight and still get my beauty rest, as ya put it." She raised an eyebrow at me.

I wasn't sure where Cecil and Alex had gone. I knew Martin had gone to bed. And Scotty had been purposely sent to his bedroom so Fitz and I could sneak out and do our ritual.

She did a secret knock on my door, which sounded a lot like 'Shave and a Haircut, Two bits'. I opened the door and stifled a laugh. Fitz was in her hippie dress, red hair in a bun, and sandals. "I feel a little...wrongly dressed," I said, looking down at my 501's and Chucks, with a zip up hoodie.

"I'm getting into the part!"

"Okay. So what exactly do we need for this protection spell?" I asked.

"I have all of it, swiped it from the kitchen." She opened her bag and pulled out a candle, powdered cloves, a bottle of ground cumin, garlic powder, chopped hazelnut, dried rosemary, salt, and a plastic bowl. I looked at all of it and bit my bottom lip.

"Ugh, what exactly are you making?" I asked skeptically.

"We!" she corrected. "We are making a protection spell."

"This is what Mum told you to get?"

"Well, she said all of them are used for protection. Her spell only called for salt, rosemary and clove, but she gave an alternate list, in case I couldn't get those three."

So if you do have those three," I went through the bottles, "Why do we have all of the other ones, too?"

"Fitz looked at me like I was stupid, "Extra protection!"

"I'm not sure it works that way," I furrowed my brow. "Are you SURE you wanna do this?"

"Yer not wimpin' out on me, are ya? Have ya no faith?" her eyes a little wild.

I remembered how long it had been for her. Her sex drive, usually quite active, had come to a screeching halt. Madness seemed to be taking over. I wanted to clap my hands, and say, "I do, I do believe in horny." Instead I just nodded, "I'm with ya."

We headed down the trail toward the Willow tree. It was close to full moon, but my eyes were still having trouble adjusting to the country darkness of Ireland. We came to a large bush, about a hundred feet above the Willow, when Fitz covered my mouth and pulled me down behind it. She pointed. Under the hanging branches of the Willow was a glowing light. Moving silently closer, I could make out legs from the knees down. Or at least I would have seen legs, if a floor length gown wasn't present. I could hear low words being spoken. Were they words...or was someone singing? I listened as carefully as I could. Suddenly, I knew what I was hearing. It was chanting. A shiver ran up my spine and ice prickled behind my eyes. The words weren't English of any kind. Around the huge trunk of the old tree she went, clockwise, chanting the whole time. I knew who it was, not a question in my mind. Minutes passed, but seemed like an hour, as I sat crouched and entranced. Thoughts bounced off of my gray matter: What was she doing? Why was she doing it? Did she get a spell from the damn book we gave her? Was she really a witch? Should we be scared? Would I in fact, be turned into a toad? I had lost myself in my own mind when she emerged from under the Willow's branches and blew out her candle. A memory connected some dots in my head. One of my first nights here I saw a candle glow, moving down to the Willow's path. Had that been Miss Elanor? She hiked up her skirt, and started up the hill. When she was directly across from the bush we were hiding behind, she stopped. It looked as though she was sniffing the air. Her eyes turned toward the bush. For a split second, I was sure she saw us. But after a moment, she turned away and continued on. We waited until she was well out of sight, before we scurried to branches of the Willow.

Fitz lit the candle, "Did I tell ya? I told ya that woman was up to no good."

I didn't want to let my mind run away with me. But I was having some trouble reigning it back in. "She kind of seemed like she knew what she was doing," I finally said. Making it even more clear that we had no idea what we were doing. Would our protection spell even have a fighting chance against whatever she had done? I didn't have any craving to eat flies, or hop, as of yet.

I was busy looking at her footprints around the Willow's base, when Fitz said, "Holy shit!"

I looked at her, my eyes followed her gaze. Pictures had been hung from tree limbs.

"Huh," was all I could muster, as Fitz raised her candle to the branches. "Here's Scotty. On the next branch is Cecil. The next," she moved to get a better look, "Is Martin! Holy crap! She does have them locked in some spell."

My eyes had been drawn to the other side of the tree. "Um, Fitz," I called. Coming to my side and raising the candle, I saw my own face staring back at me.

"Oh my...where did she get a picture of ya?"

"Of us," I corrected, pointing to a picture of her.

"When was yours taken?" Fitz asked.

"Breakfast...Oh my God, before my horse ride!" I answered.

"Ya mean before the horse ride that could have killed ya?" Fitz leaned in with the candle, her eyes rounding at her picture.

"Do you know when yours was taken?" I asked.

Fitz nodded slowly, "It was taken at dinner. Last night. Before I was turned into a smurf," Fitz looked sidelong at me.

"Look, I know we're supposed to do some kind of, uh, ritual? But I think maybe it would be smarter, to get the hell out of here!"

"Yeah, ya may be right," Fitz said, as we slowly backed out from under the Willow's branches.

We made it back up the hill in record time. Well, more like our asses were on fire. As we came to the front of the house Cecil was saying goodnight to Alex.

We skirted the duo, trying not to be in their personal space. Cecil had his back to us, and we almost made it to the door unseen. But Alex caught a glimpse of us, and planted a lip lock on him that cemented my thoughts of what was going on between them.

We closed the door before Fitz said, "The nerve of that bitch, trying to add salt to a wound. I'm sorry, Janie," she said and took me into a hug.

"Well, like you said, nothing ventured, don't expect the gain."

"I didn't say that!"

"Nope, but it is what you meant, right?"

I nodded and we headed upstairs for bed.

23

THE DAY OF THE SHOOT

I was so excited, I could barely eat. I had been on more than one shoot with Fitz, and it was always amazing to me. I know a lot of people probably think all you have to do to be a good model, is be lucky enough to be beautiful. It's not true though. There's a "Presence" necessary to be a good model. To me, it's harder than acting. Your eyes and smile have to convey unspoken words. They have to make you feel what is not being said. And Fitz...she's a pro at doing just that.

I sat with her while her make-up and hair were being done. Big pomp on top, and long ringlet red tresses down the back, eyes winged by black liner, and big red lips, she disappeared into the dressing room. I anxiously awaited her big reveal! Out of the dressing room door, she oozed. Fitz wore a silk, emerald green, form fitting dress, cut low on the chest and high on the thigh. She radiated something I would always be happily jealous of; Raw Confidant Sexuality!

Scotty's eyes bugged out of his head, and I noted, tied his tongue. He actually put his hand to his heart as he took her in. "This is mine!" he said, with an air of awe. Or was it a warning to the other men present, whose eyes had popped from their skulls.

I smiled at his reaction. This man, I knew was in love.

Scotty walked over to her, “I just want to smear yer lipstick,” he said.

Fitz knew she had him, heart, soul and then some. All of her fear and insecurities of the last weeks disappeared with that one look.

I was amused at how Cecil reacted to the other men's dropped jaws. “Hey, that's my sister, yer staring at! Clean the drool of yer chins!” he said, then winked at Fitz.

Fitz was placed on barrels of whiskey, in several different poses. Then, an hour later, she was placed in front of the Irish Flag and pictures were snapped of her toasting with Callaghan's whiskey.

Three hours and dozens of pictures later, Fitz was done. As the crew cheered and clapped, she took a bow then went to change. I noted that Scotty had disappeared as well. Twenty minutes later, Fitz emerged from the dressing room with smeared lipstick, a crooked pomp, and a smile I hadn't seen in a while. If Miss Elanor had put a spell on Scotty's manhood, Fitz had broken it. Scotty too, looked like he had “Released” some long standing stress.

As I went to grab Fitz's purse, I ran into Alex.

“So I guess the better woman won, huh?” she said.

“I didn't know you were competing with someone? But congratulations.”

“Get off it! I know you want Cecil, and he's made his choice. Instead of hangin' around us, tryin' to woo him, maybe ya could find a man of yer own? Clingy isn't a good look.”

“That's funny,” I grinned.

“What's that dear?” she made a mock sympathetic face.

"I didn't think 'used-up-bargain-basement-porn-star' was a good look either. But if the silicone fits...?"

Her eyes slit so hard they almost disappeared. "I'm warning ya. Back off, or I'll make ya sorry ya ever met me!"

"Oh you're too late," I grinned, "I'm already sorry I met you." With that, I turned and walked away.

On the way back to the Castle Scotty, Fitz, Cecil and I were in the back of the Rolls. Martin stayed behind to finish some work. I was trying desperately to let go of what Alex had said. Even though Cecil and I had admitted we missed each other, maybe it would be better for his new relationship, if I did make myself scarce. I remembered their kiss from the night before, and my stomach churned. I needed to get the paintings done, so I could go home and face whatever batshit-craziness awaited me there. On a good, somewhat uncomfortable point, Scotty and Fitz were busy making out like Cecil and I weren't even in the car. I couldn't fault them, really. No sex for a week or two was like dog years to Fitz.

As soon as the car stopped, I went to change into my painting overalls. Down to the painting room I went. Mozart played as my brushes began to flow. The last two weeks of July I would dedicate myself to finishing my task. A week and a half flew by, painting, eating, showering sleeping. Occasionally, I took a call from Betty, or my mother. They would both amused me with stories of each other. Maid Carrie brought me lunch and dinner. I had coffee instead of breakfast. Fitz came in from time to time, trying desperately to tempt me into taking a much needed break. But, I was a woman on a mission. Two, to be exact: 1.) Finish the paintings. 2.) Avoid Cecil and Alex.

Finally, at 6a.m., the paintings were done. Usually not one to toot my own horn, I was quite proud of what I had accomplished. The angle...perfect. The colors...impeccable. I debated twirling, but I was afraid a 'lie' would become a truth. I believe in Karma.

That morning, the Callaghan family was at home preparing for the festival. After breakfast we all headed to the painting room for the big reveal.

Martin had tears in his eyes as he took me in an embrace. "You've made an old man, very happy! Thank ya dear Janie."

Miss Elanor, who usually would have given me the evil eye for such a display, I noticed, was also fighting back tears.

Cecil smiled from ear to ear and bowed to me.

Scotty and Fitz had to force themselves to notice. Did I mention that things were back to normal? Neither of them could pass the other without groping, grabbing, touching, pawing, or kissing.

I did get a chance to pull Fitzy aside and ask her about the protection spell, and her thoughts on Miss Elanor.

"Oh, I'm not worried about that anymore," she made a dismissive gesture.

"So, because you're getting laid again, Miss Elanor is no longer a powerful witch?" I laughed.

Fitz shrugged, "If she's not, no big deal. And if she is, she's lost the battle. So either way, I'm good."

I was happy to hear that she had let the whole witch thing go, and was more...Fitzy, than she had been in the last month.

I decided to walk down and take Babygirl a treat. I knew she could be temperamental, so I wasn't sure if she would be happy to see me, or shun me completely. Gratefully, she began prancing and neighing as soon as I called her name.

"Hi Babygirl," I said, presenting the apple. While she enjoyed her treat, I rubbed her neck. "So I won't be here much longer," I told her. Her eyes rounded and she stopped chewing. "I know. I hate leaving you, but I'm done with my job here. I need to go back home now." She rubbed her giant head against my chest. I wasn't sure, but it looked like her eyes were watering. Even the thought made my eyes water, as well. "Just so you know, I think you've been the best part of this trip," I smiled. "I guess what I'm trying to say is, I love you babygirl." I wrapped my arms around her neck.

"Is this a private conversation?" I heard from behind me. I turned, tears streaming down my face. Cecil's face took on a look of concern.

"Are ya okay?" he walked forward and dabbed my eyes with his shirt sleeve.

"I'm just gonna miss her, ya know?"

"So, ya are leavin'?"

I laughed, "Of course I am."

"Well, I haven't seen ya much in the last couple of weeks or so. I guess I hoped you'd decide to stay."

"I'm afraid I have to go back home."

His face became very serious, "Why?"

I laughed, "Because...that's where my home is. And I miss my family...well, Fitz's family and my dad," I joked.

"So when are ya leavin'?"

"I was thinking Saturday."

"That's tomorrow," he informed me.

I nodded. "I'm aware."

"But the Festival? Won't ya at least stay for the Festival?" he was just short of pleading. "It's a big deal...and lots of fun...and you should be a part of it. Yer supposed to be a judge for the art competition. I mean, I know I didn't ask ya, specifically, but I did imply..."

I couldn't help but laugh, as he went on, "Okay, okay," I put my hands up. "I'll stay for the festival!" I wasn't sure how much more I could take of Alex, but figured I could make it through one more day.

"That's great! What are ya gonna wear?"

My brow furrowed, “Wear?”

“Yeah, a costume!”

“I don't have a costume. How am I supposed to dress?” I asked.

“1700's. Like a fair maiden, a queen or a priestess!” he threw out suggestions.

“Yeah, I don't usually pack costumes.”

“That's fine! We'll go to the costume shop, and we'll get somethin’ that fits ya perfectly!” he said, excitedly.

24

PLEASE, CAN I HAVE SOME MORE

"Well...it does fit...kinda!" I said, squishing up my face at my reflection. The last dress they had in my size was a serving wench. Made of cotton, the red skirt went to the ground, the white cotton off the shoulder shirt, was topped off with a black suede-leather tie up corset. My C's were somewhere up near my throat. This may very well have been the most naked I had ever felt, while being fully covered. It was worse than the dominatrix costume, 'boob-wise'. But at least my ass was fully covered. I kept wondering where the chastity belt that went with this outfit had gone.

Fitz sprang from her dressing room. "Well, mine is spectacular!" Fitz did a spin in the last size three red silk princess dress.

As usual, she looked fabulous. I, on the other hand, could use this costume to be a serving wench, pirate, or an 1800's British street walker.

Cecil added his two cents, "Ya look beautiful!" he said to me.

"I look like an old timey, hooker," was all I could muster. "Is there any way to, I don't know...cover these things?" I pointed to my neck boobs.

Cecil smiled and came at me with his palms.

I grabbed his hands, "Not what I meant."

"I was just willin' to offer my assistance," he shook his head at me. "But if ya don't want my help..."

I laughed, Cecil was back to normal.

When we arrived back at the Castle, the whole yard and lawn were bustling with people. Tents were being erected, tables were being set up, and a jousting run was being measured and dug out. Poles were set up and topped off with several strands of ribbon that Cecil explained was for winding around the pole. "It's more of a May Day thing, but the kids love it so much we do it for Lugh as well." He was really getting into it. I couldn't help but wonder what his costume looked like.

The kitchen was crazy as well. I heard Miss Elanor, long before I entered. "Don't scrape that pan," she ordered. "If ya do, it will ruin the taste, and I will ruin you!"

At that, I almost backed out, like a mouse that has gone unseen by a hatchet carrying trapper.

"Miss Jane? Did ya need somthin'?" she asked, with pure exasperation.

"I ugh, I ugh..." I was having a lot of trouble finishing my sentences.

"I haven't got all day," she stressed.

"I came in to offer help. Is there anything that I can do?"

"Well, it's very nice of ya to offer," she said, in a tone of surprise. "But I have all the help I need. And then some," she looked at the cook she had been terrorizing. "I hear you'll be leaving Sunday?"

"Yes ma'am."

She took a moment. I almost thought she was going to say something nice. "Good," she finally spat.

I let out a sigh. "Fine," I put my hands up submissively and shook my head, before walking out.

I was gonna be out of her hair. No more having to see me at the dining table, medicating me, or commenting on my attire...well, maybe one more day of that. I reminded myself of the 'Whore of Babylon' dress I was lucky to get, according to the costume shop keeper.

As I turned the corner to the hall that would take me out of all this agitation, I ran face to face with Alex. I said a word under my breath (four letters...rhymes with duck.)

"Oh, hello there, Janie," she said, her fake-ass-bitch-smile stretching from ear to ear.

"Hello," I said and tried to pass her.

She took a step to the side to block my exit. "I just wanted to thank ya for bowin' out gracefully. These last two weeks without ya, pathetically hangin' around hopin' Cecil would notice ya, have been good for Cecil and me."

"Your welcome," I said, and tried again to step around her.

Sidestepping again as I tried to pass her, "Not that you had much of a chance anyway. I mean, you knew that, right?"

I stared at her with eyes narrowed.

"I mean, I get what I want. And Cecil, well he's easy. He'll always choose me. No matter what I do...or say, HE'LL. ALWAYS. CHOOSE. ME! I've had my claws in him for a long time."

"Well, I can always hope he's smarter now."

She threw her head back and laughed. "That boy is as whipped as the day is long. And believe me, he's no smarter now than he was then."

She had done it. I took a step into her personal space. "I know you think you can say whatever you want to me, and because Cecil cares for you, I won't clean your clock...but keep this in mind...I'm leaving Sunday...and I have NOTHING to lose," I hissed the last part so close to her face I could see her eyes flash with fear. "You do anything to hurt him, or this family, in any way, I will end you!

"Do what ya want," she found her voice, squeaky as it was. "Because he knows yer in love with him, and he's in love with me! He'll believe you attacked me for that reason alone. Especially once I start the water works." She began dramatically fake crying, "Boohoo!" She pretended to dab fake tears.

Just as I started to think it was worth Cecil hating me to pop her one, or five, Miss Elanor came around the corner. "Ladies, is there a problem?" she asked hotly.

We were almost nose to nose, thanks to her heels. "No, Janie was just wishing Cecil and I luck," Alex said.

Miss Elanor cocked her head at me then turned a hardened stare on Alex. She was pondering something. Finally, she said, "I don't need ya blockin' the hall. Be on yer way," she waited until we walked away from each other in different directions, before she headed back in the kitchen.

Back in my room, I was fit to be tied but what should I do? "He's your friend! This is his choice. You should support him!" the angel on my right shoulder said. On my left shoulder, the little devil said, "But how much would you like to break her in half?"

As I was mulling, my phone rang. When I answered it, I heard two voices saying hello. One sounded like Betty. The other...was my mother! They conference called me?

"Hi Puddin!" yelled Betty.

"Hi honey," slurred my mom.

One eyebrow arched. "Hiiii. What's going on?"

"Well, yer mom and me...we got off on the wrong foot. The last week of having the kitchen redone, has been a real battle of wills!" Betty said.

"Kitchen redone?" I repeated.

"Yeah, but it's done now," my mom slurred again. "Two more margaritas," I heard her yell to someone.

"Ugh, what is going on?" I asked again.

"Well, ya know that Man-bun guy?" Betty started.

"Rooogger," mom said.

"Yeah, Roger," Betty confirmed, "Well, he's been givin' yer mom paintin' lessons. She was usin' yer paintin' room, so she could use yer...damn what is that thing called again?"

"Eeeesle," mom added.

"Yeah, that's it, easel. Anyhoo, she was learnin' how to paint again. Isn't that a hoot?" Betty asked.

"So...he's not some metaphysical, guru guy?"

"Oh yeah, he is. Nutty as a fruitcake. But your mama's not drinking the cool-aid."

There were so many things wrong with this conversation. I tried to roll with them, but there were too many questions. I had to ask, "Is mom drunk? Where are you?"

I heard mom in the background singing a Rod Stuart song with a jukebox.

"Well, yeah. She's a bit of a light weight. But damn, is she fun! We're at that little Mexican food place on the pier."

If it was six here, I began counting backward. "It's like 10am., there?"

"Yep. They opened at nine. See what I mean, lightweight! Anyway, she was really happy when she was paintin'. But she didn't want anyone else to know she was takin' classes. Then when I started hangin' around, she got all...well, yer mom, again. She needs to paint, Puddin. It'll keep her from bein' a B.I.T.C.H.," she whispered into the phone. "I think I should warn ya, yer mom...well she paints..."

"Nudes," I cut her off.

"Ya already knew?"

"Let's just say I found out recently," I grinned. "Have you seen any of them?"

"They're really good, Puddin," Betty said. "I'm even thinkin' about havin' her do one of me."

I was trying not to get a picture in my head.

In the background, I could hear mom belting it out, "If you really want me, just reach out and touch me..." Apparently 'drunk mom' forgot I was on the phone.

"Well, that sums it up, I guess. Make sure she gets home safe. Neither one of you drive!" I added.

"I already have a car comin' at two."

"That's quite a while from now," I laughed.

"Ah Puddin, she needs it!"

"I know," is what I said, but what I was thinking was, 'Lord, help them'! "You two have fun. And Betty, thank you."

"I love you, Puddin!" Betty said.

"I love you too," my heart warmed and I smiled from ear to ear.

"I love you!" I heard mom yell, but I wasn't sure if she was yelling to me, or Rod Stuart.

"Tell mom, I love her, too." I laughed before ringing off. It was hard to picture this scenario in my head. Would mom and Betty become...friends? Would mom become a day drinker? The thought made me laugh. More likely, mom would be horribly hungover tomorrow and would never drink again.

I was pre-packing my suitcase and getting ready for my departure on Sunday. I may not miss the scary ass picture that hung over my bed, the secret passageway that left my nerves frayed, Miss Elanor, or Alex, but I knew I would miss everything else. I thought about Babygirl, Carrie and Mary, Martin, just Ireland in general. I let out a sigh. I would miss...being here.

Oh well, is what I was thinking, when the dinner gong's echo made its way to my room. I scurried down the stairs.

Everything was still in full scramble with people everywhere. In the dining room, at least there was still some semblance of peace. Scotty and Fitzy entered hand in hand, followed closely by Cecil and Martin

As we sat, I noticed we were having a full-service dinner. In filed five servers carrying domed dinner trays. Usually, Miss Elanor, with the occasional help of another server, plated our meals. Miss Elanor was the last to enter. "Cecil has arranged a special last dinner meal for our guests. Miss Janie..."

She called me Janie! Not Jane, or Miss O'Connelly, Janie! Yeah, there was a "Miss" in front, but this was huge!

"...this was made especially for you," she said as the domed trays were set in front of each of us. I couldn't help but squeal with delight, when a bacon double cheeseburger and fries were revealed.

"I just wanted ya to know we can make these here, too. In case ya ever come back and visit," Cecil smiled.

Taking a bite, my eyes fell shut and happy noises emitted from me. "Ank U!" I said, covering my mouth. Halfway through I was full, but there was no way I was leaving a morsel on my plate. At the end of the meal, dessert was brought around, but there was no way I could fit another bite in my protruding tummy.

As we all stood to go for an after dinner walk and to check on the progress of the builders, Alex was announced by Briggs. One night, I thought, just one night without her, would have been great.

I heard Cecil tell her quietly, "Tonight was supposed to be just the family and our house guests, remember?"

Alex put out her bottom lip in a pout, "I know, I just needed to drop off my paintin' for the art entry tomorrow. And since the shop will be closed, I wouldn't have had the delivery men to help me. It's a rather large paintin'. I hope ya don't mind."

Cecil let out a sigh, and said, "We can put it in the painting room fer now. I'll come out help the guys get it there." He gave me a weak smile, "I'll catch up to ya later?"

I smiled, "Sure."

Alex shot daggers out of her eyes, but they meant nothing to me anymore.

Every branch of every tree sparkled with tiny glowing lights. The winding paths were lined with lanterns. Rows of wooden benches, with billowing silk sun shades in harvest colors, bordered the jousting field. Booths for food, drink and game were made to look like an old medieval town. The grounds had been turned into something straight out of a fairytale. The stables were still quite busy. Babygirl was having her mane and tail braided. I snuck in a hug, despite getting a disapproving look from her hairdresser.

Martin, Fitz, Scotty, and I, started back up the path towards the Castle. We could see Cecil and Alex in the drive. As we passed, I nodded to him. He was obviously going to be busy, so when he asked where I was heading, I said, "To bed. Tomorrow's going to a wild day."

"You could have a wild night, if ya wanted," Alex tugged on Cecil's collar.

I was gratefully out of earshot for his response.

That night, I slept in the most wonderful dream. I lay under the giant Willow. The sunshine was creeping through its branches to play hide and seek with me. I was comfortable and safe. I watched myself...from outside of my body. I was more than content, I was happy. Out of nowhere, tiny winged human figures with pointed ears and playful grins came to dance around me, play with my hair and kiss my nose. I had no concern about their existence. They were as real as I am. Leaning up from the grass I felt my own wings flutter. I smiled from my heart. Now I would have to learn to fly.

25

LUGHNAHSADH

When I woke, I was still in the glow of my dream. Everything seemed magical this morning. Walking to the window, I could already see the lawn full of the tents of people who would be selling and trading their wares. Stages had been erected. Martin had employed acts of jugglers, jesters, and actors who would be putting on plays. Bubble machines were in full force, iridescent orbs billowing into the sky. Off in a corner was a fenced petting zoo, and pony rides for the little ones. Food was already being cooked, smoked and barbecued. I watched a mountain of a man hefting kegs and delivering them to drink booths. It looked like Big Dave, but from here, I couldn't be sure. To me it seemed like a more magical version of a Ren fair.

Fitz burst into my room twirling in her red princess gown, complete with a golden crown and ruby lips. "I'm a princess," she elated.

Cecil came to my door, "She really does twirl, doesn't she?"

I took one look at him, and melted. I thought for sure seeing him in tights, would leave me in hysterics, but this? There he stood, sun lightened hair, dark blue eyes, big white smile and a kilt. The traditional tartan plaid, made of wool, was topped off with a white long sleeved shirt that laced up the front, a leather vest, knee socks and black leather riding boots. He looked like he belonged on the cover of a trashy romance novel.

Cecil caught the look and twirled himself, “Not bad huh?”

I was having trouble finding words. After making some sounds, I finally shook my head clear and produced a, “Wow!”

“That good, huh?” he winked.

“That good!” I confirmed.

Even Fitz was nodding her head. All of the sudden, she said, “I gotta go find Scotty!” and she was off like a streak.

Cecil and I both laughed.

“Okay, now you have to go so I can change,” I gently pushed him toward the door.

“Or,” he started, “I could stay in here and help ya with the laces. They're pretty tricky, at times.”

Seeing him in that kilt every part of me wanted to have him stay. But I knew he was kidding me, and in about ten seconds, I was going to lose control of my “Good girl” persona. “Out!” I laughed and shut the door behind him.

As I squished myself into the bodice, I remembered just how big boobs looked when they were cinched up to your chin. Looking in the mirror I bit my bottom lip. Miss Elanor was going to have something to say about this. And I knew it wouldn't be nice. Oh well, one more day, and she'd never have to look at me again. Plus this was traditional dress, so I was told.

I headed down stairs, and there at the bottom, were the three Callaghan men in their kilts. They were even more gorgeous if that was even possible. Fitz stood at Scotty's side and her eyes never left him. I noted her hair was more disheveled than it had been when she took off to find Scotty. I stifled a laugh.

The staff joined us at the front door. Everyone seemed to be in a jolly mood. Martin had brought in outside help so the staff could enjoy the festival as well. But where was Miss Elanor? She wasn't anywhere to be seen.

We all headed out to the fields. It was truly amazing to behold. Tents and stands were everywhere. People were in full swing, selling candles, oils, handmade chimes, paintings, carvings of wood and stone, jewelry made from stones, leather, silver and gold. All the food and drink were paid for by Martin. The tents included everything from meats to treats. People were arriving in droves, in full costume. I had never seen so many kilts and boobs in my whole life.

Cecil saw my smile and grabbed my hand so I wouldn't get lost in the crowd. "Do ya love it?" he asked.

"This is amazing!"

"You are amazing," he smiled.

It was a strange look he gave me that made me cock my head at him, wondering.

"I mean, ya look amazin'," he added.

I took my time at each tent looking through everything. The craftsmanship was mind-blowing. There was even a man doing portraits. Being an artist, I was amazed at how quickly he could do what it took me weeks to do. I had to bow my head to him.

As the morning wore on, I had eaten some fruit and some of the best nut cake I had ever tasted. I wondered if I could recreate it from memory. It was cooked over a fire and caramelized in an iron pan. I had never seen this done quite this way.

Only when Cecil said he had to leave to get Babygirl ready for the joust, did I notice his hand in mine. It had felt so natural. When he left my hand felt cold.

Trumpets were used to signal to the crowd that the games were in play. Most of us headed to the seats at the jousting field. I was put in a place of honor with the family and staff. I began to get nervous wondering how dangerous this was. The thought of anyone doing this, (much less Cecil) made my nerves spring into action. I reminded myself to stay calm or end up a hive-riddled mess. As the two horses made the line I could clearly see Babygirl all decked out. Her shining breastplate was worn like a badge of honor. Her head held high. She took on the air of a warrior going into battle. Cecil was wearing a breastplate of thick leather and gloves.

"Seriously? They don't have full metal armor or anything?" I asked.

Martin, who was seated next to me, said, "Don't ya worry, Janie. They are skilled riders and have done this since they were young boys."

More panic was rising. This seemed scary and dangerous to me.

I was more than shocked to see who Cecil would be jousting. There, also kilted and on horseback, was young Daniel. Both were handed lances, as their horses approached the line. My stomach was knotting. A trumpet blew and off the horses flew. At breakneck speed, lances set, they were heading directly at each other, full force. I held my breath as Daniel was hit. He was hit, but remained on his horse.

The crowd roared with cheering, as I tried not to turn green.

They set the line again, riding from opposite sides, their lances put into their other hands. This surprised me. I mean, how did you joust with both hands? I couldn't even write my name with my left hand. Another trumpet blew, and again they charged each other. I was going to be sick, I just knew it. Babygirl had dropped her head, her gaze was fierce as Cecil was struck. Again a hit was made, but both riders were still on horseback.

Again, the crowd roared and Fitzy whistled so loud I thought my eardrum would burst.

A third time, the line was set, the lances changed arms and I realized I hadn't stopped holding my breath. I actually felt faint. Again, the trumpet, the horses, the fear springing to my chest, Cecil was hit and unseated. To the ground he went, hard. Without even a thought I had jumped from my seat and was running at my own break neck speed to the field. Cecil leaned up as I was approaching. I went down on my knees in the mud, grabbing him in my arms.

"Cecil, Cecil," I said, looking into his eyes. "Please, tell me you're okay!"

He seemed dazed as I pulled him to my chest.

"Cecil please!" I said, brushing his hair back. Tears were pooling in my eyes. I kissed his forehead, "Please Cecil!" I begged one more time. Why was no one else coming to help? Where was the medical staff? I panicked and looked around to see smiling faces, and some people stifling giggles. What the hell was wrong with these people?

"This is a great view," I heard a voice say. Looking down at Cecil, his head held against my breast, he grinned from ear to ear.

"Are you kidding me?" I asked, tears running down my cheeks. "You're not hurt?"

"If I say no, are ya gonna pull away?"

"I watched you fall. How are you not hurt?" I said, still visibly shaken and confused.

"We use plastic lances," he snuggled in closer as the crowd began to snigger.

"But...they look like...steel."

"They're supposed to. We wouldn't use real lances," he smiled, and wiped the tears from my cheeks. "Someone could get hurt."

I pushed him off of my lap, and stood, covered in mud, I let out a huff. "That was a horrible joke," I stammered.

Cecil jumped up and caught me by the hand as I turned to

walk away. Pulling me back toward him, he took me in an embrace as the crowd cheered. "I'm sorry I scared ya," he whispered in my ear.

I nodded my head against his chest. No words would come.

After a moment, Cecil walked me back to the stands before taking Babygirl back to the stable.

I looked at Fitz, "Why didn't you tell me?" I asked taking my seat.

"Seriously Janie, I thought ya knew. When ya took off...I couldn't have stopped ya. You were like a flash. I didn't even know what you were doin'!"

For the first time, I saw Miss Elanor, seated next to Martin. She was wearing what she always wore, high necked grey dress that went to her ankles. Which I now realized, may have looked like a witches garb. She was looking at me with her head cocked questioningly. At least she wasn't laughing at me like the rest of the crowd.

Martin patted my leg, and said quietly, "All men should have a woman love them so."

I blushed, but couldn't smile. Had he known the whole time? Or was it my actions just now that made it apparent? I could still feel Miss Elanor's gaze, but I couldn't look at her. I was sure she knew now too and I was embarrassed. Cecil had chosen another and I could only make a play out of my acceptance, until now.

A few more matches were run and then some wrestling games. I found my voice again and cheered. Really at this point I just wanted to make the best of what was left of the day.

Around noon I went to find Cecil for lunch. Walking into the stable I heard voices. I was aware before I turned the corner, Alex was there.

"I didn't mean to interrupt," I said. Martin wanted to know if you wanted to eat with the family."

"We have things to talk about," Alex informed me. She was in an emerald green princess gown. Her fake boobs were well displayed. I had to give her credit, she looked beautiful. I looked down at my mud covered self and felt like a chipped piece of clay next to a a fine piece of china.

"I'll be up in a moment," Cecil told me.

I was truly uncomfortable. I wasn't sure what I interrupted but I knew I didn't belong there.

"I'm going to head back up," I told him.

I ate almost all of my turkey leg and brie, before I saw Cecil again. He looked upset and I didn't want to ask. Scotty looked at him with concern, and Cecil shook his head at his brother. Seems Fitz and I weren't the only ones who could communicate without speaking.

After lunch I was brought into an arena. As I stood, with a crowd staring back at me, I finally saw Hanna, Big Dave and their brood of four in the stands. The boys were already taller than any boys of their age. And their little girl was fairly like with delicate features. She sat on her dad's huge lap and looked like an animated red headed doll. I waved to them and they waved back.

Martin was on a microphone and introduced me, Cecil, and two others as the judges for the art competition. Everyone cheered and Fitz let out another high pitched whistle when my name was announced.

Five tarp covered art pieces had been set in a semi circle. The artists were brought out and introduced. I knew Alex would be among them. When she was announced, cat calls and whistles were heard. I wasn't surprised. She took a bow and blew kisses at the audience. I looked at Fitz to get her reaction to the 'bimbo extraordinaire' performance. I wasn't surprised to see her lip curled. Then I looked at Miss Elanor, she appeared to be mumbling something.

The art work was revealed one piece at a time. The first piece was a meadow painting, by a local, of his farm. It was beautifully done. I nodded and smiled. The second was a carving done in wood of a running horse. I was amazed by the craftsmanship. Every line was perfect. The third was also a carving, the coastline of Ireland with an Irish blessing inlaid. It was impressive to say the least. The fourth was a metal sculpture. It was an abstract of the universe. It had come to life through hand bending and welding. The last one, Alex's, was uncovered. My eyes rounded, my stomach lurched. I was going to lose my lunch or pass out cold. There, real as life, was Cecil staring back at me from the canvas. My painting had indeed been found by the wrong person. Everyone hooted and hollered as Alex took another bow. Cecil moved closer to the painting. He seemed to be examining it. I was having trouble breathing and controlling my face. Fitz stood up in the stands then whispered something to Scotty who also stood quickly. I looked at them and gave a small shake of my head. The look on Fitz's face started as shock then changed quickly to rage. That look...I had seen before...just before Fitz annihilated someone.

Cecil made a joke, "Now that's a handsome man!" he said to the crowd, who all laughed.

Alex grabbed the microphone from his hand, "I just wanted ya to know how much ya mean to me," she leaned over and kissed his cheek.

My heart felt like it would pound out of my chest, as I forced a smile.

"Well, I don't think it would be fair for me to be a judge," Cecil announced and picked someone out of the crowd to take his place. A young man stepped forward, and Cecil announced his name as Derrick. He couldn't have been more than 13 and was thrilled to be a part of the festival. After careful consideration, the other three judges voted for the picture of

Cecil. I voted for the horse carving, and it was given second place.

Cecil was announcing the gifts for each, and how they could be picked up that night after dinner during the award ceremony.

As the crowd began to disperse, I made my way to Fitz.

"For the love of God!" Fitz said, looking at me. "I'm surprised ya didn't break out in hives.

"I know, but I do have one hell of a headache coming on. I have to take something now, or I'll have a migraine in no time."

Scotty looked at me, "How did she get yer paintin'?"

I wasn't surprised that Fitz had told him. "I have no idea," I shook my head. "It was hidden in the closet in the painting room."

"I'm gonna tell em," Scotty started to move.

"Please don't," I begged. "Maybe it's better he doesn't know."

"If ya don't take care of that headache, yer gonna be miserable. I need to get ya back up to the Castle. Now!" Fitz added, letting me know this wasn't up for debate.

"I can go up myself. No reason for you to miss anything."

"Not a chance. I'll go and make sure yer okay. I'll be back right quick," she told Scotty, and gave him kiss.

"Okay. Feel better, Janie," he said, and embraced me.

Miss Elanor saw me holding my head, "Is she okay?" she asked Fitz, curtly.

"She's got a bad headache comin' on. I'm gonna get her pills and a cold wash cloth. If she lays down a bit in the dark she'll be fine, I hope."

"I can make her a tea that will help as well," Miss Elanor said.

I tried not to make an obvious look of fear, "I'll be okay, really. Thank you anyway."

"I'm goin' to make ya the tea, and yer goin' drink it!"

I gulped hard, “Yes ma'am,” I said.

Up the path we went, Fitz, Miss Elanor, and me. Fitz and I headed up to my room as Miss Elanor took off for the kitchen. Fitz sat me on the bed and wetted down a cloth for my head. I laid back and covered my eyes with it. The pounding had gotten stronger within minutes.

“Where are yer pills?” she asked.

“In the medicine cabinet in the bathroom,” I said. She took off to find them. “Hey, Fitz,” I called, “I'm a little freaked about the tea Miss Elanor is making.”

“Don't overreact. She can't kill us here, too many witnesses. Maybe she'll bring it and leave then I'll pour it down the sink.”

This sounded like a good plan, so I lay back and let the cooled cloth do its part. Fitz came back with the pills and a small glass of water, “Down the hatch,” she put them in my hand. I leaned up, threw them down my gullet, and took the water down in one gulp.

Miss Elanor arrived moments later with my tea. I cracked open one eye and the light pounded in my brain. “Drink it,” she said, putting the cup in my hand.

“I'm gonna let it cool off a bit,” I said as an excuse.

“Nonsense, ya don't want it to cool. It becomes more bitter as it does.”

Fitz winced behind her back and put her palms-up.

“Mmmm, o-kay,” I said, staring into the cup. I could smell whiskey and see sediment, swirling around. “So what is this?” I posed the question.

“Tea!” said Miss Elanor, sternly, not interested in playing this game with me. “Drink it,” she commanded.

“Alrighty,” I said slowly. “Bottoms up!” I drank part of the tea and gave her a weak smile.

“All of it!” she said.

I nodded, and gulped the rest down. It had the same taste as the whiskey herb concoction that Aunt Marble had given me at my rebirthing ritual. I immediately went warm from my ears to my toes. When I wasn't 'fearing for my life', it tasted pretty good.

"Yer headache should be gone in fifteen minutes or so. Come Miss Fitzpatrick, she needs her rest, "Miss Elanor told her.

Fitz came and put a kiss on my brow. "I don't want to leave ya."

I was already feeling a little grooviness kickin' in, "No it's fine. Go back to Scotty and the festivbal. I'll be right as rain in no time, "I yawned.

Fitz looked at Miss Elanor, "Did she just say festivbal?"

"She's fine. It's the whiskey and herbs. She'll sleep for a little while and feel perfect when she wakes."

Fitz looked back at me, "Sure?"

"Sure," I said. "I love you, Fitzy."

"I love you, too," she told me. Then I heard her telling Miss Elanor, "She better be fine," as the door shut.

26

W.T.F.

I 'came to' slowly. Drool on my chin, grass in my mouth. "Pthth pthth," I tried to spit it out. My eyes were having trouble opening. Where the hell was I? I could feel...air...and sunshine. Was I outside? I tried to sit up and became instantly aware that I was more than wobbly. My vision, 'off', but I thought I saw the Willow. As I moved my head, something dangled down in front of my vision. I tried to slap it away, but it came right back. Frantically, I tried to slap it away again before I realized it was attached to me. It was my hair. And it was braided. I felt my head and all of my hair was in tiny braids. I wasn't sure what to be more curious about first; The fact that I was outside somehow, or the fact that someone had braided my hair. My vision was returning, and for the first time I noticed I was in the middle of the big ring of stones. Before I could move, I heard Cecil yell, "She's over here!"

I heard people rushing toward me, and I was trying to make out faces.

There was Fitz, Cecil, Scotty, Martin, Miss Elanor, Alex, Daniel and the whole staff.

Fitz and Cecil tried to race to my side, but I yelled, "Stop!" and put my hand up to them.

"What the hell is going on?" I asked. "Is that mud you're covered in?" I asked Fitz. Her hair was a matted mess with chunks of clover in her ratty tresses.

Fitz voice softened, "I went up to check on ya and you were gone. I got Scotty, Cecil and the whole staff back up to the Castle to look for ya. We even went through all of the passageways. Oh my God, you've gotta see the dungeon! Crazy scary!"

Miss Elanor cleared her throat to Fitz.

"Right," Fitz said, "When we couldn't find ya in the Castle, we started on the property. No one thought ya could have gotten out here unseen, but we had to look. Cecil grabbed Babygirl and ran the grounds. She's the one who found ya," Fitz nodded to Babygirl. "I fell and rolled down the hill trying to keep up with her."

"My God! Are you okay?"

"I'm tougher than I look," she grinned, mud streaks down her face and princess dress.

I looked over at Babygirl, who was prancing. "Thank you, Babygirl." I called her to me, but she wouldn't come any closer. She just pranced in place. "What's wrong with her?" I asked.

"She won't enter the stones," Cecil said. "Let's get ya out of there."

"No! I have questions, and I'm not moving until I get answers!" I would have put my foot down, but at the moment, raising it would have been more impressive.

"Really, we can do this inside," Fitz started.

"I said no! I'm not moving until I get answers!" I was stuck in repeat mode. I was still groggy but determined to find out once and for all, what the hell was happening.

"First of all," I turned to Miss Elanor, "Did you poison me with the tea?"

Her brows raised, "Certainly not!" she looked like I had slapped her mother. "That tea has been used in my family fer generations. No one has ever had...this," she pointed to me, "Reaction!"

"The only thing I took besides your tea, was ibuprofen."

Fitz stepped forward, "About that..." she bit her nail.

Everyone turned their heads towards Fitz.

"Ya see, I may have mixed up yer IBU, with yer antiy-histy-mines," she winced. "I forgot Miss Elanor put them in there and...I may have given ya those instead."

"How many of those?" My eyes bugged out.

Fitz winced again, "Ummm...Three."

"Really? Three?" I couldn't believe I was still alive, given how they affected me. I took a moment to re-sort my thoughts. "Okay, but what about Fitz's blue face, and Martin's good luck charms?"

"My lucky charms?" Martin asked, brow furrowed.

When he said that, I giggled and snorted, "Lucky charms," I laughed. "I'm sorry, I'm sorry," I shook my head to regain some semblance of control. "I found your charms in my room next to my bed. I had no idea how they got there, but I figured that someone was trying to set me up as a thief."

"I'd never have believed that," Martin said, comforting my addled mind.

"I know...you're a great man," I added, a little slurry. "But that's why Fitz and I had to sneak them back into your room. I was worried about how it looked. I put them in Fitzy shirt, but then you saw Fitz's boobs," I pointed to Miss Elanor. The staff turned questioning eyes to her."But we still had to put them by your bed," I turned my double vision to Martin. "I hoped you'd think they had dropped. I'm sorry. We didn't know what else to do."

I wasn't quite making sense and everyone looked confused.

"In her shirt?" Miss Elanor looked at Fitz, understanding beginning to dawn on her.

"Tis true...I don't have crazy nips, after all," Fitz smiled at Elanor.

Miss Elanor began to slowly nod her head, "Oh."

Scotty shot a questioning look at Fitz, as did the whole staff. "I'll tell ya later," she patted his hand.

"So, someone had snuck yer charms into Janie's room," Fitz continued the story. "Then someone tampered with my toner, turning my face Blue." We both looked at Miss Elanor, as did everyone else.

"I didn't do it," she said indignantly, looking from me to Fitz.

"I may be able to shed some light on that," Daniel said, stepping forward. "The night you and Fitz saw me come through the trap door in the stable, I wasn't alone."

We all stared at Daniel.

"Someone was with me...someone who disappeared, while I was talkin' to the two of ya."

"Who?" we all asked in unison.

He shot his eyes to Alex, as did the staff. "When I came up and saw the two of ya, I didn't want ya to tell Cecil that I was with her. That's why I was talkin' so loudly. I was lettin' her know, we weren't alone. When ya left, I went back down into the passageway, but I couldn't find her. I headed toward the pub, to see if she was back trackin'. But then she called out my name from behind me. She would have followed the passageway up to yer room."

"When we came back up, we went to Fitz's room," I said. "I thought I heard someone in the hall. But when I opened the door, I didn't see anyone," I was putting it together. "So at that point, she was tampering with Fitz's make-up in the bathroom?"

"I believe so," Daniel said.

"But Martin's charms? That was before the blue face."

"Right," Daniel said. "But the day she delivered the canvas and was told to wait outside or come back later by Miss Elanor, she was parked by the kitchen exit."

I nodded, "Okay."

"See, I saw the truck, and saw her standing by it. Even came up and said hello. We weren't exactly strangers then, were we?" he winked at her.

Alex stuck her tongue in her cheek and let out a little huff.

Daniel kept going, "See we had met durin' her first delivery. We seemed to hit it off pretty well." he grinned at her. "Then she asked me to meet her at the pub. We had a good night, didn't we luv?" he said to her. "But not good enough to change my loyalty. The second delivery she made I said hello then headed back to the stable to finish workin'. When I walked back up, the truck was here, but she was nowhere to be found. Her delivery men didn't know where she had gone either. I walked the grounds lookin' for her. When I walked back up the path half of an hour later, she was standin' by the truck. I asked her where she had gotten off to, and she looked me in the face and told me she had been down by the Willow. Obviously she didn't know I had been there lookin' for her."

"That must have been who I saw, walkin' out of the kitchen," Carrie said.

"Ah, thank God," Mary emitted, "Yer not the ghost whisperer!"

"She couldn't have taken them then," I shook my head. "The charms were in my room the night before that!"

Alex smiled smugly at Daniel, "See, I couldn't have done it then."

"Maybe not then, but that wasn't the first time ya were in the Castle without anyone knowin', was it?" Daniel asked.

"No," said Fitz, "I think that was the day she stole the paintin'."

Everyone's heads swung back to Alex, except mine and Cecil's.

He stared at me, and I put my head down, embarrassed.

"Did ya really think I didn't know?" he searched out my eyes.

I bit my lip.

"That paintin'...was of the first night we met," he smiled. "I knew it...as soon as I looked at it." He shook his head, "Ya did the whole thing from yer memory of our first night together. For God sakes, the background was Fitzpatrick's. I love it, by the way. So I guess that's what really happened to the canvas?"

Tears were welling up in my eyes and I nodded at him.

"So when did Alex steal the charms?" Miss Carrie wanted to know.

Daniel smiled, "She knows all of the passageways. When she showed such an interest in me, and the Castle, I told her about them. I'm guessin' she used one of them to sneak into Martin's room."

"Ya can't prove it that I took the button and coin!" Alex said arrogantly.

"Except...for the fact that they've only been referred to as the charms and you just happen to know...that they are a button...and a coin," Martin pointed out.

She bit her bottom lip and tried to back away, saying, "Well, I guess it's time for me to leave."

Elanor stepped in front of Alex. The whole staff behind Alex, had formed a semi-circle around her.

"Wait!" I yelled! "I have more questions.

They all turned to look at me, "Alex, why did you send the flowers and put the dressing gown in my room?"

Her brows furrowed, "It's true. I sent ya the flowers, hopin' you'd fall for Daniel. Or at the very least, make Cecil back off of ya. But a dressing gown? What the hell are ya takin' about?"

"Oh, come on, we already know you've been playing in my room. Just admit that you put the silk dressing gown in there!" I practically yelled.

"Yeah, like I'd leave you a silk gown, really?" she raised her brows to me.

"I put the gown in yer room."

We all turned surprised eyes...to Briggs.

"Huh?"

"The gown is mine," he said.

We all went quiet.

"The truth is, I am a cross dresser," Briggs said.

Brows raised, and Carrie brought her hand to her mouth.

"Miss Margaret knew what I was. She also knew that the maids would find out if I left the gown in my room. She offered me her room to express myself. Even had shoes made for me, since finding a heel in my size, used to be hard to acquire." We all turned to look at his abnormally circus sized footwear. "She was a wonderful woman. And probably the only person I could ever confide in," he sniffled.

None of us were sure what to say. Martin walked over to Briggs and embraced him. "She was a wonderful woman, and you will be accepted here, just as ya are."

Sobs emerged from Mr. Briggs, as his secret was finally set free.

I gave a much needed moment of silence before I asked, "So, why did you put the gown in my room?"

Briggs dabbed his eye, "I was wearing the gown, when I heard someone come to the door. The lock was being engaged. I couldn't be caught that way!" His expression showed fear. "I had to escape and went to the passageway to change back into my uniform. I was panicked, and opened the passage that led to yer room. Seeing that ya weren't inside, I put the gown in your closet, and left out yer bedroom door. Later that night I saw you wearing the gown. You looked beautiful, as I said," he nodded and smiled to me. "But I had to get it back. It was a cherished gift."

We all just nodded.

"Okay, so who went into Margaret's room?" I looked at Martin, and he shook his head.

"It was me," Miss Elanor said, lifting her jaw. All eyes shot to her. "Margaret and I were best friends, long before she married Martin." Martin smiled and nodded. "She brought me to work here after a...well...bad relationship," she lowered her eyes. "I couldn't seem to shake the man. I wasn't strong enough. Margaret renewed me. I was happy here with her and her family. I was only supposed to stay here awhile, but when they wanted to hire a governess, I asked if I could fill the job. I was unable to have children of my own," Martin patted her hand. "My desires to be a mother were quelled by her sharing her family with me."

"So there was someone in the room!" Fitz said. "Janie wasn't goin' batshit, again!"

I shot a look to Fitz, and raised a brow. Yeah, I'm the batshit one, I thought.

"I go in often to talk to her. It soothes me. I talk to her just as I did when she was well."

"Okay," Fitz said.

"What does that mean, Miss Fitzpatrick?" Elanor asked.

"Well, if you've been soothed, you certainly haven't sent any our way," she motioned to herself then me.

"Yer right," Miss Elanor admitted. I had a hard time with you and Scotty. But can ya blame me? He's like a son to me.

He's off for a year at a time...in America...then he brings this woman home with him? And he's in love with her? I didn't know then...how much ya meant to him, and how he means to you."

"That's how relationships work," Fitz said. "Ya don't go around bein rude and cursin' people."

"Now what are ya on about? I'll admit I was...short."

Fitz and I both raised our brows.

"But what do ya mean cursin' ya. I've never cursed at ya!"

"No, that's not what I mean," Fitz gave her the prodding nod. "The day I gave ya the spell book ya went to the Willow and cursed Janie and I, to keep us away."

"What? First of all, that's no spell book," Elanor blushed.

"Well, what kind of book is it?" I asked.

It took her a moment then she said, "Do you know what the Kama Sutra is?"

Fitz's eyes rounded, Martin's brows raised, Scotty's eyes popped, Mary and Carrie looked scared and Cecil said, "Oh yeah" and nodded.

We all shot looks to Cecil. "What? It's a good book."

I did know what the Kama Sutra was thanks to Fitz's crazy Aunt Marble. I received a copy from her as an eighteenth birthday gift.

Scotty was the next to answer, "Are ya sayin'...Fitz gave ya porn?"

"It's a very old book...along the same lines as the Kama Sutra. The man who sold ya the book...was the man I escaped all those years ago. He's a dark little man...and dirty," she made a face of disgust.

"That's why he asked about ya...and why he picked out that book for ya!" Fitz said.

I went somewhere far darker than anything that book could have held. I was picturing the creepy Leprechaun and

Miss Elanor. I shook my drugged head to clear the unwanted vision.

She continued, "What happened at the Willow was a protection spell," Miss Elanor explained. "That man found a way back to me, through you! I put the pictures of the people who needed protection, on her limbs."

"So why were Janie and I on the other side from the men?" Fitz wondered out loud.

"That only had to do with North, South, East and West. It's my family's way. There was no curse!"

"So...you didn't curse the women who dated Martin, either?" I asked.

"What the...of course not!" Miss Elanor shook her head.

"But, the hives and the fairy ring?" I put my hands up to address where I was.

"I can answer those," said Martin stepping forward. All eyes bounced to him. "See the lady with the hives, we found out later, was allergic to our strawberry hand soap. Every time she washed her hands, she'd break out horribly. We could have accommodated her reaction, switched soaps. But the truth was she had little interest in me. When she found out what the problem was, I guess she just decided that the hives weren't our real problem. We just weren't compatible."

Everyone nodded as a way of understanding.

"And the lady who passed out in the fairy ring," Martin continued, "Well, she was fond of our whiskey. Very fond," Martin added. "I didn't want her around the boys, so we stopped seeing each other. She didn't take it well though. We were broken up, and in a drunken stupor, she showed up and passed out in this very ring. The old stable hand found her while exercising the horses. Miss Elanor walked down to the ring and told her not to come back. In her own drink addled mind she thought Elanor was a spirit." He laughed, "I drove her home.

She was so convinced of what she thought she saw, I never saw her again," he winked at Miss Elanor, who smiled at a memory they shared.

"And the lady with the cut break line?" I asked, timidly.

"Ah," Martin nodded. "She had been seein' a man before me who was crazy jealous. He cut her brakes as a way of telling her how much he loved her. Like a 'If yer not with me, you'll be with no one', kind of thing," he shook his head. "She actually took it as a great show of love. I decided, anyone lumberin' around that kind of crazy, was best to give her my blessin' and back clean off."

"Okay," Fitz nodded. "I know why you were so mean to me. And I guess...I get it! But, why were ya so mean to Janie? She doesn't even date Cecil."

This one seemed harder for her to say out loud. I was staring at her and watched her gulp hard before saying, "I thought...she was interested in Martin."

My eyes rounded, but I had no idea what to say about this.

Fitz put it all together in her head, and looked from me to Elanor, and nodded, "Ahhhh!" I was still a heartbeat or two behind, but I blame the drugs.

"I understand how protective ya are, Elanor," Martin turned to her, "But..."

Elanor's eyes filled with tears. They stared at each other for a long moment before Martin asked with great surprise, "Do ya feel...for me?" he questioned.

Elanor dropped her eyes, and nodded slowly.

I was starting to get it. This wasn't about me and Cecil, or me and Martin. This was about Martin and her.

Martin put his hand to her cheek and searched her eyes.

The whole staff smiled as Elanor began to sob.

"Why didn't ya tell me?" Martin asked.

"She was my best friend."

"And my love," he said. "Do you really think, she would have chosen anyone else fer me?"

They hugged and I got to see a real smile on Miss Elanor's face. I'll be damned, there was beauty there. It was just well hidden behind years of denying and hardening her own heart. The whole staff looked elated. Mary and Carrie were holding back sobs behind their hands. Even Fitz gave Miss Elanor and Martin a heartfelt nod. Now that everything had been explained, everyone was nodding and turning to walk away, I said loudly, "Um, hello!"

"Oh Janie, yes I'm sorry. Was there somethin' else ya wanted to ask?" Martin queried, holding Miss Elanor's hand in his.

"So," I looked at Miss Elanor, "You were mean to me because you thought I was after Martin? Is that why you're mean to Alex, too? Because Cecil's in love with her?"

Cecil's eyes rounded, "What?" He turned to Alex, then back to me. "Why would ya ever think that?"

Alex shot me a look of pure loathing that I was quite used to by now.

I decided to come clean, "Fitz and I overheard you talking to Hanna at the pub that day. I heard you say it was against your better judgment and given your history, this was hard for you...and..."

"Yeah," he smiled and took a step forward. "It IS against my better judgment," he nodded his head, "To be in love again. But...I'm not in love with Alex."

He stepped over the fairy ring and lifted me to my feet. "Oh," I said, smiling from ear to ear. We embraced and tears welled up in my eyes. I felt like I took a breath for the first time in weeks. It was the kind of breathing you do when you're relieved, and grateful, and hopeful. Then it dawned on me. "I still have one question," he looked deep into my eyes, "Yes?"

"Who the hell braided my hair?"

Everyone shook their heads as I looked from face to face. "Don't look at me," Alex said, raising her hands when I looked at her.

"No one? Really?" I asked.

"Well, ya are in the ring of stones," Martin pointed out.

I turned a shocked look to Cecil, "Get me out, out now!"

Scotty turned to all of us and said, "Wait! As long as yer all here, all the people I love...I can't think of a better time." He got down on one knee, and took Fitz's hand. He was reaching into his pocket...

Fitz looked down at her sweaty, mud covered self and touched her wrecked hair-don't, her eyes bugging out. "No!" she yelled and took off running up the hill.

Scotty looked dumbfounded, as he watched her, knees to chest, back up the meadow. "What the hell?" he looked at me.

I had to laugh, "I think she planned on looking a bit more Fitzy when this happened."

Scotty took off after her, "Fitz! Wait! Ya look beautiful! Come back!"

27

AND THE BAND PLAYED ON

Back up at the Castle, Fitz changed, and Miss Elanor and Martin helped unbraid my hair. Martin pulled something from one of my braids, and showed it to Elanor.

"It couldn't be!" she gasped and put her hands over her heart.

"What, what's wrong?" I asked.

"This is the coin we left for the fairies," Martin smiled.

"I swear to God I didn't take it!" I put my palms up.

"Ya couldn't have," Elanor said. "We left it there after we sprinkled Margaret's ashes under the Willow. Years ago," she added.

I felt a prickling of my flesh as they smiled at each other. It was a sign for them. I was just the bringer of said sign.

Back at the festival, an announcement was being made by Big Dave. He smiled broadly as he addressed the crowd. Cecil had been voted in to take over the Distillery. Everyone applauded, except me. Martin took the microphone and explained how stressful the last few months had been. But he was ready to retire and hand over the company to both of his sons. Cecil would run in his father's place in Ireland, and Scotty in America.

I looked at Cecil, wide eyed. "This is what had Scotty and your dad so...not right?"

Cecil nodded, "Aye. There was a good chance that the workers and the board wouldn't want me to sit at the head of the table. There's some history there. Some still had their own opinions. That's what all the meetins' were about."

I nodded in understanding.

"Scotty doesn't want to be away from Fitz. And I owe him this, for all the years I've lived like a selfish boy while he worked his ass off. If only I had met ya sooner."

I could feel it when he said this. He meant it. "So you're staying in Ireland," I said. I was trying to blink back burning tears.

"It's the only way. Dad deserves to retire," he said looking at his father and Elanor. "Looks like a whole new chapter for him. For them, he smiled."

I watched Martin kiss her hand, making Elanor smile from ear to ear.

"And Scotty...he deserves this too," Cecil raised his glass to his big brother.

Scotty raised his glass in return to Cecil and nodded, before he took the microphone and pulled Fitz on to the stage. There, he got down on one knee as she beamed. Perfect hair and make-up, only set us back half of an hour. But a girl's fairytale come true, is worth however long it takes. She accepted the three carat family heirloom and became engaged to the man of her dreams, as I cried tears of great joy for my best friend.

In the midst of all the dancing and celebrating, Cecil and I walked to the stables.

I wanted to get in a goodbye to Babygirl before my morning

flight. I kissed her brow and quietly told her that I would see her again.

Cecil and I didn't speak as we walked hand in hand to the Willow. It had been a long month and I was just now fully absorbing and understanding everything that had happened. Under the Willow's branches, we sat. I was starting to feel like me again. I was breathing again.

Finally, Cecil said, "Ya know, I just wonder sometimes."

"What do you wonder?" I looked at him.

"I wonder what would happen...if I just kissed ya?"

I too had wondered this. In light of all the changes that had been presented, I didn't know if this was a good idea. I knew now what he meant to me. I knew that I had no choice but to miss him, and that I would. Would I do this to his heart? To my own? I had been quiet too long and I could tell he was recoiling from his words, when I finally said, "There's only one way to find out."

There, under the Willows branches, I leaned in and brought my lips to his. We kissed...and kissed, and kissed again until the sun rose. It was a lot more PG13 than anyone would have imagined, given the tension between us. But I was still that girl the one who needed the promise of something more. Feeling him close to me, kissing me, holding me...I wouldn't have traded that night for anything.

At the plane, Elanor, Martin and Cecil, said their goodbyes to Scotty, Fitz and me. Elanor hugged us and thanked us as she smiled at Martin. He put a kiss on our cheeks and bid us a safe journey, and to come back soon.

Cecil took me aside and handed me an envelope. It wasn't from him though. "This came yesterday for ya." I looked at the return address: NYPD. I opened it, and my Rune practically jumped into my hand. I smiled and laughed before wrapping my arms around his neck.

"I'll miss you," I said, staring up into the bluest eyes I would ever see.

"Not for long," he answered, and kissed me again to the hoots and hollers of the whole family.

I made it inside the plane and put the Rune in my pocket. Patting it, I told it, "Welcome home." I chose a window seat, so I could wave goodbye to Cecil. I no longer cared about my fear of flying. As he became too small to see tears started to fall.

Fitzy came and wrapped her arms around my neck, putting her head on my shoulder, "Don't be sad Janie girl. Everything will work out. I promise," she kissed my cheek.

I nodded and sniffled back sobs.

The attendant stepped forward, "We will be stopping in New York just long enough to refuel. Is there anything you'd like me to order for ya Miss?" he asked, handing me a tissue.

Fitz answered for me, "We're gonna need some shitty champagne and a Black Forest Cake."

THE END

Don't miss JANIE ON BOARD
Available Now

The third entry in the heartfelt, madcap* Janie Chronicles *has Janie O'Connelly wishing she missed the boat.

When Benny proposes to kooky Aunt Marble, it's required that Janie, her newly designated Spirit Daughter, be in attendance. Janie is honored (kind of) to be included, until she learns the wedding is taking place off the coast of Mexico... on a ship.

Adding to Janie's boat and ocean phobias is the revelation of Barry's feelings for her. Through choppy waters, Janie must examine her growing feelings for heartthrob Cecil while imagining the possibilities offered by Barry (who just happens to be her lifelong crush).

The heart wants what the heart wants... But who will that be?

Turn the page for an excerpt from *Janie on Board*.

1

JANIE ON BOARD

"So then what are you going to do to me?" I asked, biting my lower lip.

"I'm goin' to kiss ya…starting at yer beautiful lips…moving down to yer sexy neck…"

I let out a little moan of approval.

"…all the way down to yer toes," Cecil said.

My face crinkled up, "Could we avoid the feet?" I asked.

"Why, what's wrong with yer feet?" he asked.

"Nothing! I just walk barefoot a lot," I answered. "I know where they've been."

"So what if I had a foot fetish?" Cecil inquired.

I rolled this thought around in my head and was happy he couldn't see my face through the phone. Finally I asked, "Do you?" trying not to sound judgy.

Cecil laughed, "No. It was just my way of sayin' *every inch of ya.*"

I smiled from ear to ear and got comfortable, "Well, okay then…go on…"

I had been home from Ireland for two weeks and still had

not adjusted to the changes around me. Between my mother and my *Southern Belle* landlady, Betty, my house had gone through some transformations of its own.

I had been told that my house was to be painted and had expected this. I had not expected the flower boxes on my windows, the used brick pathway that led to my new front porch and wrought iron screen door.

When my cab pulled up out front, I did a double take. Then I stepped inside…all new wood flooring that led to my completely redone kitchen; new stainless steel appliances, new cupboards and sink and a huge wrought iron cart that held my top of the line espresso maker that Fitz had finagled for me when a 'Home Store' employee attacked me in aisle two. I had no idea where my coffee cups were, and more importantly, where my wine corkscrew was. (I could drink wine out of the bottle if I could open the damned thing) My whole kitchen was like a great adult scavenger hunt. I had been adjusting and had to admit, it was beautiful, so thank you Betty and mom.

The biggest adjustment I had to make wasn't the new house, or mom and Betty's newfound friendship (which was the epitome of opposites attract), it was missing Cecil. During our time in Ireland, Fitz, short for Sarra Fitzpartick (my best friend since naptime was still *a thing* in class), had been working for and staying with the Callaghan's. Callaghan's turned out to be a manor. Well, more of a castle. In fact it was a 300 year old castle. And the family business you ask? Whiskey! The family not only owned the castle, but the Callaghan distillery.

Fitz had been dating the eldest Callaghan son, Scotty, when his brother Cecil and his dad, Martin, made their way to the US to handle distribution deals that would bring their whiskey to the States.

I had met Cecil on that fateful trip and was immediately attracted to him. Okay, parts of me were. He had a reputation as a bad boy and possible man-whore, and *that* was never my thing. Their father Martin had seen my work, and hired me to do two paintings for him; one of the Castle and the other of the Distillery.

Fitz, with her flaming red hair, green eyes and skin that looked like fresh milk, was the perfect Irish lass to be the new spokesmodel for the Callaghan product. So off to Ireland we went. Our stay was one of great mishaps and misunderstandings, but what I did find out was Cecil wasn't really a bad boy and I really cared for him. We also found out that Cecil would be taking over his dad's company in Ireland, and Scotty would be handling the newly found Callaghan distribution in America. This was great for Fitz, who had become engaged to Scotty on that trip. It was not as good for me as Cecil and I had admitted we had feelings for each other right before I headed home. And home is where I'm at…missing him, all day, every day.

We have been calling and texting as much as possible, but with the time difference, we were always on a different page. My day was just beginning as his was ending, and vice versa.

Truth was, I hadn't left the house much during the last two weeks. I had made every excuse in the book not to go to Fitzpatrick's Pub or even Sunday night dinner at my parent's house. If I didn't know better (and I'm not sure I did, having never felt this way before), I'd think I had let a little depression creep in. But tonight, I'd have no choice. Tonight was Fitz's engagement party and the maid of honor/best friend's attendance was not only expected, it was required.

I unglued my ass from my couch and hit the shower. While I soaped up, I heard my phone ringing. I took off like a bolt, grabbing a towel as I ran. I slid across my new wood floors and came to a halt right in front of my phone. But it was too late. One missed call from Cecil was flashing on my cell. I called right back, but it went straight to voicemail.

I never knew what to say to voicemail. It always seemed like a third party was listening, or the recorded message was somehow judging mine. I went for the standard, "Sorry I missed your call. I was in the shower. I miss you." All the way back to the shower, I questioned why I said I was in the shower, like he needed that piece of knowledge.

After my shower, I reached for my 501's and then worried that maybe I should dress up a bit. I mean, it was my BFF's engagement party. Should I really show up the frumpy mess I was on the couch, only washed? I put on a sundress and pretended to do my hair, which actually meant throwing the long blonde mess into a bun. Mascara was applied and some lip gloss was how I finished my attempt at make-up.

I grabbed my purse and sandals and headed south for the eight blocks that separated me from Fitzpatrick's Pub.

I had asked ahead of time if there was anything I could do, seeing as how I would be the maid-of-honor. Fitz's reply was, "Just get your ass here by 7pm." At 6:50pm, I entered the pub. I wasn't surprised to see that we had a fill-in bartender. After all, the Fitzpatrick family, who usually manned the bar, would be sharing in tonight's festivities.

Fitz saw me enter and made a B-line my way. She was clad in a cream colored, body hugging satin dress that went to the floor and boasted a plunging neckline with diamond collar. Her long red hair was swept up and clipped with a diamond barrette. Long ringlets fell around her perfectly painted face. As always, she was stunning.

"I have to talk to ya," Fitz said, grabbing my arm and leading me to the closed restaurant on the other side on the building.

"What's up," I asked when she closed the door behind us.

"Somethin' horrible has happened," she started.

Panic entered, was it mom, dad, Cecil, "What? What's wrong?"

"My best friend has been M.I.A. for nearly two weeks. I'm scared she's gone fer good," she gave me a hurt look.

"I know, I've been kind of…wonky," I said.

"I get it. I do. But this is to be the best night of my life so far, and I need ya HERE."

I nodded, "I know and I get it. I'm so sorry. I will be HERE," I said. "I'm really happy for you, Fitzy," I hugged her.

"I know. It just needed to be said," she hugged me back.

"You look amazing, by the way," I added.

"Good start on that best friend comeback," Fitz laughed. "Now let's go find some cocktails."

Back at the bar, I ordered a Black & Tan and a shot of Bushmills. People were everywhere. Our high school friends were woven in with family. I said "*hello*" to the two Fitzpatrick boys I could see, Danny, Andy and their wives. Coming through the crowd to join us was Pauly and his wife Mona. I had to quickly paint on a smile. Mona had a deep resentment for me that she didn't bother to hide. I wasn't sure what I had done to warrant such open disdain from her.

"Oh Janie," Mona began, "I wasn't sure if that was you, or if one of Fitz's old school chums took up cross-dressing."

"Yep, I'm a tall one," I shook my head at her ridiculousness.

"Oh, that's not what I was referring to," her smile getting sticky. "I was just referring to your…" she looked me up and down, "less than feminine ways."

I took a deep breath and was planning my exit route when Pauly piped up, "Stop it Mona," he told his wife through a tightened jaw.

"What?" she asked innocently. "I was just saying…"

Pauly cut her off, "Yes I know what yer sayin'. I'm tired of ya attackin' Janie. Sick of your pettiness," he put his hands up. "Yes, I had a crush on her when we were young. Yes, I know now how wrong it was to tell ya. But that was a hundred years, a marriage and two kids ago. Fer God sakes, let it go, woman!" his Irish accent thick with anger.

I stood there uncomfortable and dumbfounded while the other wives laughed behind their hands. I never had any idea that Pauly had a crush on me. And finding out this way was more embarrassing than flattering.

Mona stormed off, barreling through the crowd. Pauly apologized before he took off after her.

"Well," Danny raised his glass, "guess we finally know why she's such a bitch to ya, huh?"

Andy laughed, "It wasn't a big deal. We were playin' a stupid game, and it was like five years ago. It was Pauly, Mona, my wife and me. Pauly had to admit to a crush he had, but had never revealed. He said you," he pointed to me. "And he also said it was when we were kids and it lasted fer like two minutes, but Mona just couldn't let it go," he shook his head.

I nodded, at least now I had some understanding of her dislike of me, even if it was ridiculous.

Fitz saw the scene from across the bar and came to find out what was going on. As Danny filled her in, she nodded, "Well there ya go, that's why she's such a bitch to ya, and why she hit on Cecil."

The brothers both raised their eyebrows, "She hit on Cecil?" Andy asked.

I tried to play it down, but Fitz kept the ball rolling, "She sure did! She was sittin' in his lap, and said she was *keepin' him warm* for Janie!"

"Tis true?" Danny asked me.

"Well, um, it wasn't really…" I started, but Fitz cut me off.

"She sure did! Heard it with my own ears, saw it with my own eyes!" she nodded.

The brother's raised their brows to each other again and nodded.

"What? What's happenin'," her eyes darted between her brothers. You two are havin' one of those *mental conversations* that's meant to keep me out!" Fitz gave one eyebrow a raise. She was learning how to do the Mom look. Or in her family, the Mum look. I had to admit, she was getting pretty good at it.

It took a moment, but Andy finally nodded to Danny, "They've been on the rocks fer quite some time now. Pauly has even mentioned the '*D word*.'"

I was busy guessing that their '*D word*', wasn't the same as mine.

"No," Fitz brought her hand to her mouth, "Divorce?"

See, not the same, I thought to myself.

The brothers nodded in unison.

"So, is she blaming Janie fer this?" Fitz asked.

"What?" I finally piped up. "How? We never dated, or even kissed. How the hell could I be blamed for this?"

"Well think about it? If she's batshit enough to torture ya for a crush ya didn't even know about, I'm guessin' she's crazy nuts. Crazy nuts people need to blame someone," Fitz added like it made perfect sense.

My fear was that in Mona's mind, it did make sense.

"Don't ya worry luv," Danny patted my arm. I'm sure it'll be fine. Once she's sober," he added.

"And if not," Andy interjected, "my money is on you," he smiled.

I faked a smile and looked at Fitz, "BAR!"

2

DRAMA, DRAMA, DRAMA

Cocktails were needed for this kind of drama, I thought as I ordered two Bushmills and another beer. When the Bushmills came, Fitz grabbed one and we shot them down.

"Wow, it's so strange to finally find out why she's been so awful to ya, all these years." Fitz said.

"It's just crazy though. It was when we were kids. I mean, who cares about a child's crush?"

Fitz made a face at me. It was old information for me, but newly acquired by Fitz, that I had had a secret crush on the youngest of the Fitzpatrick boys, Barry, since we were kids. That lifelong crush had slowly faded away when he met the woman of his dreams in Ireland and announced their engagement. Then, I met Cecil. My feelings for him, as new as they were in comparison, made any crush on anyone else *null* and *void*. I was deeply in…*like* with Cecil, I assessed. But I had to admit, once upon a time the feelings I had for Barry were very real to me. Maybe Mona's *crazy* was just as real to her.

"Speak of the devil," Fitz grinned as her brother Barry approached.

"There ya are Fitzy," Barry said pulling her off her stool via bear hug. He swung her around, "I'm so happy for ya, sis," he kissed her cheek before putting her right on her feet. He turned to me and nodded, "Janie."

"That's all I get?" I laughed. "Usually I get a hug, too. You don't have to spin me though."

Awkwardly, he hugged me; one where he wasn't sure where to put his hands or how long to hold on. As he pulled away, Fitz gave him a crooked grin, "Are ya blushin'?"

"No," he answered quickly. "I'm fine. Can I get a Black & Tan?" he asked the barmaid as she passed by. "So I saw Mona and Pauly havin' it out in the parkin' lot. What's goin' on?"

"Oh that," Fitz began. "Apparently Pauly called Mona on her treatment of Janie, told her to knock it off."

Barry nodded, "Yeah, I've never understood her problem with ya," he nodded to me.

"Well I think it's been made crystal clear now. Turns out, Pauly had a crush on Janie and Mona knew about it," Fitz explained.

Barry looked from me to his sister, to me again, "He has a crush on ya?"

"No, no," I shook my head, "he HAD a crush on me when we were kids, that's all."

"And he just blurted this out?" Barry asked. "Just, *I have a crush on ya, Janie*?"

I stammered, " Um no, it was more like, *'I said I had a two minute crush on you when we were kids and Mona can't let it go*, type of thing," I explained.

Just then, Fitz's mom (Mum as we called her), and her crazy Aunt Marble came up and took me into an embrace.

"Oh dear girl, we just heard through the grapevine, that Pauly is in love with ya," Aunt Marble said. I looked around frantically, who was the misinformed *grape-viner*?

Mum chimed in as my head began to shake 'NO' furiously, "I feel like a bad person, especially since that woman has given birth to two of my grandbabies, but oh, how I wish it had been you!"

"Oh me too," Aunt Marble nodded to Mum. "Can ya imagine what a great mother Janie would have been?"

"You have the wrong idea," I practically plead.

"Ya don't like Pauly," Mum asked, with visible heartbreak.

"I do, I love him…but as a brother, Mum. He's like a brother to me. Nothing more," I added.

I was trying not to hyperventilate, what the hell was happening? Barry looked upset as he stood and walked toward the front door.

"Mum," I had to say to pull her attention out of her own thoughts, "Pauly's not in love with me. Not at all," my head shook. "He just had a small, fleeting crush on me as a kid, that's it," I put my hands up.

Mum and Aunt Marble rolled this around in their heads then looked to Fitz for validation. She nodded, letting them know that the *grapevine* had been mistaken.

Mum looked back at me, "But then…why are they gettin' divorced?"

I don't know that they are," I stammered. "I really don't KNOW anything."

"Oh," Mum said, looking very confused.

"We really don't know what's happenin', Mum," Fitz added.

"Well okay then, dear," Mum said to me and kissed my cheek. "My mistake," she and Aunt Marble left in search of the *grapeviner* to clear-up the misinformation.

I turned to Fitz, "That was weird," I said.

Fitz's attention was elsewhere though "Barry just took off. It's my engagement party, and he just left?"

"Maybe he went to find Pauly and check on him. After all, Mona is kind of relentless," I added.

Fitz nodded, but looked upset. Barry wasn't just my favorite of the brothers. Fitz and Barry were the closest in age. She loved them all well, but had a soft spot for Barry.

The party raged on and at stroke of midnight, Fitz's finance, Scotty, took the microphone and addressed all gathered for their engagement celebration.

"I'd like to thank everyone...not only fer bein' here for this amazing night, but makin' me feel so welcome." His Irish accent, I noted, had been well pickled. He raised his glass to his new in-laws, "Ya raised a fine woman and I am so proud to call her mine. And Fitzy," he took her hand, "I'll move Heaven and Earth if need be, to make ya the happiest woman in the world."

Fitz replied, "I'll never need the world, my love. You will always be more than enough for me!" they kissed.

People hooted and hollered, while a few women dabbed tears from the corner of their eyes. It was beautiful. Just then two women in baker's uniforms carried out a three tiered platter of silver and gold topped cupcakes and presented them to the couple.

Fitz said into the mic, "These are to be the colors for our weddin', silver and gold. To twenty-five years, then twenty-five more," she raised a champagne glass to her husband.

Taking a silver iced cupcake from the top tier, she fed it to Scotty. Again the crowd roared their approval.

I was so overjoyed for her but somewhere inside, I was missing Cecil and couldn't help but wish he was here with me. Just then, over the microphone I heard, "There you are, you bitch!"

Heads turned and everyone's eyes searched the crowd. Mona was standing in the middle of the pub looking a bit drunk, and a lot pissed. People moved as she made her way through the party.

Fitz's brow furrowed, trying to assess just to whom Mona was referring. I, on the other hand, had no doubt as her eyes burned into mine.

"Look at you," Mona slurred, "just standing there without a care in the world. No thought at all given to the home you've wrecked. YOU HOME WRECKING WHORE!" she screamed.

I had to admit, I was somewhat used to being called a bitch, but whore wasn't a word usually thrown my way. I started shaking my head as Mona drew near.

Fitz lunged but was restrained by her brother Danny, "Yer not fightin' at yer engagement party," he informed her. What he said next, made me wince, "Janie can handle this."

Fitz was still struggling against Danny when he said, "Fer God's sakes woman, think of the dress!" Fitz looked down at her beautiful handmade and perfectly tailored gown, and nodded to her brother.

Out in the crowd family and friends began whispering to each other behind their hands. Great, I was going to be the talk of the town.

"That's right, Red. Back off!" Mona slurred to Fitz. "This has been coming for some time and it's between Janie and me," she said turning her attention my way.

I put up my hands in a submissive pose, "Look, Mona, I'm a little confused about whatever's happening here. Maybe you and I should talk. Ya know, clear the air."

"Clear this, bitch," Mona said, as she grabbed her crotch.

I wasn't 100% certain, but I think she just told me to suck her 'D'. I couldn't help making the face of confusion wrapped with revulsion.

"Look," I said, "I really don't know what you're thinking, here. I mean, if it's about that ridiculous crush thing, from childhood," I added, "it's no big deal. It means nothing!"

"No," Mona breathed, "It means nothing to you!" she

hissed, jutting out her chin as she drew nearer. "That's the problem, little Janie, it means nothing to you," she shook her head. "My heartbreak: nothing! My discomfort of having to see you at every holiday, every birthday, every fucking occasion: Nothing to you! Because apparently, this family, treats you like you ARE family," she teetered on.

"Thicker than blood," Fitz said, needing to be restrained again.

"Oh, that's right, Fitzy. Always there to fight her battles! Just once, I'd like to see this mess of femininity, stand her own ground," Mona said.

"Crap," I whispered under my breath. This was not the night I had planned for. Mona kept walking. She was within charging distance now, as the crowd spread like the *parting of the Red Sea.*

"Mona, I didn't even know…about anything…until this evening," I explained. "You're the one who's been hating me, torturing me, for something I didn't even know about. If just once, you had talked to me, we could have put this to rest a long time ago."

"Oh that's right," she stumbled closer, her eyes filled with hate and voice filled with cheap wine. "My Pauly isn't good enough for you, is he? No, not little Janie. No one's good enough for her!" she screamed.

Now I was really confused. Mona had spent years telling me how worthless I was. How I couldn't keep a man. How I was too tall, and awkward. And now she thinks that I think…I'm too good for someone? Where the hell was she going with this? That's what was going through my mind when she put her head down and charged me.

Running at me, all of her five-foot-nothing frame coming fast, I just had time to try and brace myself. Sneering like an animal in attack mode, her arm was coming up from her side and I was sure it was going to be a right hook. But then just before she got to me, I saw it. A gold blur caught my eye. I cocked my head at the sight as if paralyzed by its shimmer. It was coming directly at my face. It connected with my nose and made a smooshing sound. Gold cupcake blurred my sight as I stood in shock trying to understand what had just happened.

Mona backed away from me, eyes still glittering with hate, "Now you know what it feels like to look stupid in front of the people you love. Just like your very existence has done to me for the last five years."

Fitz, who had been struggling against her captor during Mona's run at me, dropped her jaw in stunned silence. The whole bar went deathly quiet. Women covered their mouths with their hands, eyes rounded as they waited for my retaliation to spring into action.

Wiping cupcake and gold frosting from my eyes, I began to laugh. My hair sparkled with golden highlights, as I licked the frosting from my fingers. That's it? After five years of so called torture that I unknowingly put her through, no less, this is what it had boiled down to? I got cup-caked? I guess I figured that this made us even somehow.

"So is this over now?" I asked, more than willing to take one for Pauly and put an end the nonsense Mona had let brew in her head.

"Over?" she asked, eyes wild and more batshit than I remember, "It'll never be over. Every time you turn around, I'll be there. Every bad thing that happens to you, my hand will be involved. Every little bit of bad luck that touches you, it will have been sent by me," she made a strange sign with her hands, (one I didn't know) then turned her back and marched out.

Danny released Fitz as the door closed behind Mona. She ran to my side and started cleaning my face with a napkin, "Damn Janie, ya shoulda clocked her!"

I was still staring at the closed door Mona had just stomped out of, "She really thinks that I want Pauly, or he wants me? This is so…ridiculous."

People started to form groups and soon enough conversations went to other things.

"Well, I'd be careful if I was you. She's a snakey bitch, that one" Fitz warned.

"I just can't see how any of this makes any sense to her," I shook my head.

"I'm not sure in her mind, it has to. Obviously she's a little off her rocker to threaten ya that way."

"Threaten me?" I asked. I guess I had heard what she said, but didn't really think I had anything to worry about.

Mum and Aunt Marble came to my side and were visibly concerned.

"I still can't believe she cursed ya, and all. And in a room full of people, no less," Aunt Marble gave a head nod.

"Cursed?" I asked, wondering if this was more lore I didn't understand.

"Definitely," Mum nodded to me. "Did ya see what she did with her hands?"

I had, and was under the impression it was vaginal symbol. "I did. I have no idea what it means, though," I confessed. I didn't want to throw my *vagina symbol* suspicions out there.

"Oh my dear," Mum continued, "It was the symbol of the *Watchful Eye*." Mum made the symbol with her own hands. "Tis huge in the craft! There's one for protection, and…"

Aunt Marble finished Mum's thought, "And one for the destruction of yer enemies."

I stood there, blank faced for a moment or two. It still looked like a vagina to me. I was under the impression she was calling me a pussy, and a quite large one, at that. "Are you saying…Mona is a dark…," I couldn't find the word or even embrace the notion, "something?" I concluded.

"I've always had my suspicions of that one," Aunt Marble nodded to Mum.

"Aye," Mum nodded in agreement.

I was trying not to laugh, but Fitz was mulling something over.

As most of the frosting was removed, it left a golden glow on my face that put me in mind of C3PO, but I was no worse for the wear. Back to drinking and mingling, I went.

It was just about 1:00am, when a happily plastered Benny took the microphone and called out to bring our attention his way. It was the first time I had seen him in long pants, but I knew that underneath them were the knobby knees with black calf high socks he usually wore with his white Velcro shoes.

"I'm sure as most of ya know," Benny began in his New York accent, "I have been dating Marble for a few months now," he raised his glass to her. "She and her wonderful family have made me feel so welcome." The crowd cheered and raised their glasses to the Fitzpatrick brood. "That's why, Marble," he said, "we're not getting any younger, my dear." Crouching down on one knobby knee, he said, "Say you'll be my bride and we can spend the rest of our lives together."

Mum looked happily shocked, I smiled from ear to ear, Aunt Marble's overly magnified eyes rounded behind her coke bottle glasses as she covered her mouth and nodded 'YES' furiously. The crown cheered, but Fitz's eyes narrowed into slits.

Benny and Marble embraced. Still searching for his balance on one knobby knee, he put a huge diamond on her finger. Everyone was applauding and cheering, cheering again. Everyone but Fitz, that is.

"What's wrong with you?" I asked her. "Don't you like Benny?"

"Course I do! He's a wonderful man," she added, but the look on her face didn't change.

"Okay. So what's the problem?" I asked.

"They're gonna steal our thunder!"

I shook my head, "Whose thunder?"

"Mine. Mine and Scotty's! They're gonna steal our weddin' thunder!"

"I don't think that's gonna happen Fitz. I mean, I can't imagine that they're planning the kind of lavish wedding you and Scotty have in mind," I said.

"He's already proposed to her, at MY engagement party. That's piggy-backin'!" Fitz exclaimed.

"Like I said, I wouldn't worry about it. I mean, he was probably just overcome by all the family and the…" (I was reluctant to say 'moved by the moment', as the engagement party had already seen some not-so-festive action) "…how beautiful you look." I finished, hoping this would make her happy.

Fitz smiled and said, "Maybe yer right. We should go congratulate them." She grabbed my hand and pulled me through the crowd. As we approached though, Aunt Marble's words stopped Fitzy dead in her tracks.

"I love the idea of silver and gold as well. Those should be out colors, too," she said to Benny.

"Anything ya want. Sky's the limit, baby!" Benny told her and kissed her hard on the mouth.

Fitz spun wild eyes my way, "Ya see! I told ya! And there's no way they're makin' it to their 50th!"

I leaned in closer so no one else would hear, "Oh come on! You know Aunt Marble! She's probably gonna put him in a silver shorty-pants tuxedo and wear a gold muumuu.

Fitz rolled the image around in her brain and grinned, "Yer right," she said. "I'm being ridiculous."

"Little bit," I offered. "Now let's congratulate them."

As we turned to Aunt Marble, she said, "Oh Fitzy, maybe we should have a double weddin'?"

Fitz's horror filled eyes turned to me again.

I nodded, showing her that I did see the crazy, then pushed her into an embrace with her batshit crazy Aunt.

ABOUT THE AUTHOR

Edith Scheffer is a SoCal native, now blissfully transplanted to the Pacific Northwest. A gypsy at heart with the soul of a witch, Edith has wandered but never been lost. She loves sleeping under the stars and moon, walking in her bare feet, dancing to an eclectic playlist of favorite songs, and proudly parenting her exceptionally fierce and fabulous daughter, Brenna. Edith can mix the perfect drink (bartender by trade), massage your aches away (licensed massage therapist), and entertain you with her many novels (yes, she writes, too!). Her works include The Janie Chronicles, *Winged*, and *Fallen Gracefully*. You can discover more at edithscheffer.net.

facebook.com/AuthorEdithScheffer

goodreads.com/edithscheffer

www.ingramcontent.com/pod-product-compliance
Lightning Source LLC
Chambersburg PA
CBHW051200190726
48288CB00006B/1738

* 9 7 8 1 9 5 4 1 7 4 0 3 0 *